THE LOCATION APPEARED TO BE NOTHING MORE THAN DENSE BRUSH WHERE THE ROAD ENDED

The crystal-clear picture on the screen changed to a swirling mesh of colors based on radiant heat. On the screen the figures beneath camouflage netting showed up immediately. Roughly two dozen individuals moved about, spread over an area the size of a soccer field.

Several bright spots indicated where industrial furnaces were active, and in one section of the field several large vehicles sat clustered in parallel rows. Cool rectangular blobs revealed Quonset huts and long, narrow buildings of concrete and wood.

The tension in the room grew as they waited for the field teams to strike. Barbara Price leaned forward and grabbed the backrest on an office chair. She squeezed it hard until her knuckles shone white from her grip.

Then, on the screen, all hell broke loose.

DON PENDLETON'S

STONY

AMERICA'S ULTRA-COVERT INTELLIGENCE AGENCY

MAN®

Critical Intelligence

A GOLD EAGLE BOOK FROM

WORLDWIDE®

TORONTO • NEW YORK • LONDON
AMSTERDAM • PARIS • SYDNEY • HAMBURG
STOCKHOLM • ATHENS • TOKYO • MILAN
MADRID • WARSAW • BUDAPEST • AUCKLAND

First edition February 2011

ISBN-13: 978-0-373-61995-5

CRITICAL INTELLIGENCE

Special thanks and acknowledgment to
Nathan Meyer for his contribution to this work.

Printed in U.S.A.

Critical Intelligence

PROLOGUE

The CV-22B Osprey hung over the South American landscape like a nocturnal bird of prey.

The CV-22B was the Air Force version of the more famous Marine Corps Vertical Take Off Landing troop transport. Outfitted with extended-capacity fuel tanks, the CV was designed for long-range reconnaissance work or deep-penetration raids.

Jack Grimaldi and Charlie Mott worked the controls of the aircraft, navigating it across the jungle at the upper range of its flight ceiling. In the cargo area were the men of Phoenix Force and Able Team, elite commandos from Stony Man Farm, the ultrasecret extrax legal agency based in Virginia.

The Stony Man warriors were outfitted with military free-fall parachutes. They would be the advance force for phase one of the assault operation.

Grimaldi's voice came over the intercom. "Boys, we're rolling hot over the LZ. Commence final prejump checks."

Both tactical teams rose from their sling seats and began, for the third time, to check the harness and fittings of their jump buddy's parachute.

Once his check of Gary Manning was done, David McCarter looked to Carl Lyons, who gave him a thumbs-up. Around them the air was rich with the smell of engine heat and the noxious scent of aviation fuel.

"We're up and ready, Jack," McCarter said into his throat mike.

"Copy," Grimaldi replied. "Line up. Charlie's dropping the ramp now."

Gary Manning finished off a chocolate bar in two bites and fell in behind McCarter as Calvin James and T. J. Hawkins lined up after him. Able Team took point position next to the exit, where a Stony Man jumpmaster stood ready.

Outside, the night sky, a cloudless color of indigo, stretched away into the horizon. Above the jumpers and to their right an indicator light blinked from amber to green.

The jumpmaster's hand came down on Carl Lyons's shoulder, slapping it hard enough to make a pop over the drone of the Osprey's engines. Like a sprinter out of the blocks the ex-LAPD detective surged forward.

In a modified waddle against the bulk and weight of his parachute, rucksack and weaponry Lyons hit the ramp fast, rushed to the edge and plunged off without hesitation. Behind him in a line resembling lethal penguins the night fighters of Able Team and Phoenix Force followed.

The updraft struck Lyons hard enough to push his goggles against his face. He went into a spread-eagle position and carefully spun around so that he could get a visual on the circling Osprey. The Stony Man commandos shot out of the back, one after the other like Olympic cliff divers going for gold.

The jump was a down-and-dirty and within seconds the Cypress II electronic automatic activation devices began deploying the parachutes. Lyons grunted softly as his harness jerked up tight into his body under the brake of the opening chute. His feet swung out wide and he let his rucksack fall to the end of its tether.

Below him he quickly identified the lights of their initial target.

"Ironman to team," Lyons said into his throat mike, using his nickname. "I have eyes on objective Alpha to southwest," he finished.

"Copy," each man answered in reply.

McCarter fell through the quiet with only the rush of wind and the rustle of silk to break the silence. On his wrist altimeter the meters dropped off at the speed of gravity. He felt like a meteorologist in the deceptively peaceful eye of a tornado.

At the one-thousand-foot mark the details of the objective resolved into sharper relief. The landing strip was suitable for small planes and had been carved with a powerful bulldozer out of the jungle.

Utilized by narcoterror cells operating out of the coca fields of South America, the runway had a prefabricated home at one end and a 4x4 Nissan pickup outfitted with a roll bar of lights at the other end.

All a pilot had to do to land an illicit load was to put his plane down between the two illuminated spots. The runway itself was guarded by narcoguerrillas affiliated with FARC commanders.

And, unbeknownst to themselves and Stony Man, the global network known simply as Seven.

McCarter eyed his altimeter. At the appropriate height he initiated the command. "Phoenix, we are at mike mark. Execute!"

"Copy." The team reply sounded off simultaneously.

Instantly, the other four members of Phoenix Force pivoted hard and pulled their risers against the drag of their parachutes.

The four-man detachment split off from Able Team and turned toward the lights of the mobile home on the covert runway below.

They descended, death from above.

Carl Lyons craned his neck above and checked the position of Rosario Blancanales and Hermann Schwarz. Both men were strung out in a loose half circle from him, deftly maneuvering their canopies toward the landing zone.

Lyons looked back down after checking the GPS readout next to his altimeter. The ground beneath his dangling feet rushed up toward him. The landing zone was a table-flat stretch of dirt road behind a knife edge of hills half a mile to the east of the runway.

An NRO satellite image series from a month before showed a lightning-strike brush fire had ripped through the area, clearing the light foliage cover and further opening the spot up to an airborne insertion.

Lyons, Blancanales and Schwarz landed in sequence, rolling feet, thighs, shoulder and absorbing the impact in a smooth roll that brought them up to their feet. They functioned quickly, without words, going through a choreographed routine each man knew intimately.

"Ready?" Lyons asked.

"What did Mr. Spock find in the toilet?" Schwarz asked, clicking his safety off.

"Swear to God," Lyons hissed. "Not another poop joke."

"The captain's log," Schwarz finished. "And don't trample on my First Amendment rights."

Blancanales put a restraining hand on Lyons's arm. "Don't," he said. "That crazy son of a bitch has all the explosives on him. If you punch him, he might explode."

"Let's just move out, *please,*" the ex-cop growled.

PHOENIX FORCE crouched in the ditch.

Across the dirt road, light blazed from the trailer's windows. Occasional shadowed silhouettes passed before the windows. In the front yard two light pickups were parked in a loose L formation in front of the doorway.

A single sentry smoked a cigarette, AKM slung casually over one shoulder.

In the gully, Hawkins laid his crosshairs on the man.

Looking through a pair of light-enhancing binoculars, David McCarter, the Phoenix Force leader, scrutinized the far end of the field where Able Team was slated to remove the vehicle-based sentries. Targets moved in his optics but he caught no sign of Able Team, which was good.

"You good, Hawk?" McCarter whispered.

"Five by five," the Texan drawled. "Give the word and this ass clown goes down."

"Phoenix to Able," McCarter said into his throat mike. "We are in position and prepared to execute."

There was a moment of silence, then Able Team's leader responded.

"Copy that, Phoenix. We're in position. I count three bad guys out here about to go to sleep," Lyons said.

"Common?"

"I have eyes on one sat phone. That appears to be all, unless they have more equipment inside the vehicles."

"Roger," McCarter acknowledged. "Target at will. Phoenix commencing."

"Able out." Lyons signed off.

"YOU GOT A CLEAN SHOT on all of them?" Lyons asked in double-check.

The three men lay belly-down on the ground sixty yards out from the terrorist sentry post. Ahead of them the unconcerned trio lounged with a casual sense of security that belied their deadly trade.

"Dead-on," Blancanales confirmed.

"Ready when you are," Schwarz said, voice cool as a kitten purring.

Lyons drew himself up to his hands and knees. "Let's do it," he grunted.

The deadly three-man squad leaped to their feet and began moving forward. Their M-4 carbines were up and tucked tightly into their shoulders as they stalked ahead, moving heel to toe.

Ahead of them one of the narcoterrorists leaped forward, waving his hand in the air and loudly braying like a donkey. The man thrust his hips forward in a piston action and brought his swinging hand down in a spanking motion.

The other three South Americans began laughing uproariously at the theatrical antics of their comrade in arms. One of them turned sideways, folding over at the waist, and began slapping the hood of his truck.

Lyons filled his sight with the wildly undulating comedian.

His finger took up the slack on his carbine and from thirty yards out the 5.56 mm round cracked as he fired. The back of the man's head exploded, spraying bits of blood, brain and bone into the air.

The man crumpled forward like a rag doll into the dirt between the vehicles.

Beside Lyons, in a loose flying-wedge formation, both Blancanales and Schwarz triggered their weapons. The rifles cracked in unison and the flanking guerrilla sentries were thrown backward, 3-round bursts slinging loops of blood into the air.

The terrorist who'd been convulsing in laughter on the hood of his truck looked up in surprise at the weapons discharging.

The Able Team warriors sprinted forward, long strides eating up ground at a furious pace. The terrorist cast around him in bewilderment, his expression wavering between terrified and incredulous.

He fumbled for the AKM on a shoulder strap, the weapon shaking in his frightened grasp. Some sense of impending danger alerted the FARC death merchant and he looked up. His eyes grew wide as he saw the three blacked-out commandos charging toward him.

"Dios mio," he whispered, rifle forgotten.

Three M-4 carbines fired as one from a distance of less than fifteen yards.

"Take him," McCarter instructed.

Hawkins fired before the Briton finished his sentence. His

silenced M-4 chuffed once. A single smoking 5.56 mm casing popped out of the weapon's breech and arced through the air.

The sentry staggered backward as if he had just been punched in the chest. The man looked down, shock on his face, and his cigarette tumbled from his lips.

The man toppled over backward and disappeared from view behind one of the trucks. Hawkins's spent shell casing hit the ground of the drainage ditch and came to rest.

"Go! Go! Go!" McCarter barked. The ex-SAS veteran jumped up, carbine at the ready, and charged toward the trailer. Behind him the remaining three members of Phoenix Force instantly followed.

Fifty yards back, Rafael Encizo covered their rear security.

As they sprinted forward the unit automatically split off into two teams of two. McCarter and Hawkins ran for the front door, while Calvin James and Gary Manning peeled off to target the rear door of the structure. As they ran closer they could make out the faded white paint and black lettering reading Doctors Without Borders.

In a bitter twist of irony the mobile home was the stolen remnant of some forgotten humanitarian mission.

McCarter hugged the front of the trailer as he ran, weapon up and sighted in on the front door. Behind him Hawkins jogged with his weapon at a higher angle, covering the windows.

From down the runway the sounds of Able Team firing could be clearly heard.

McCarter ran up to the metal steps suspended below the front door of the trailer and spun around them. He kept the light carbine up and ready with the muzzle covering the entrance as his left hand went to the suspender of his H-harness web gear and jerked an M-67 fragmentation grenade free.

Hawkins put his back against the trailer, muzzle of his own M-4 pointed upward as he reached out with his left hand and put it on the doorknob. He met McCarter's eyes. The fox-faced Briton nodded once.

Hooking the ring of the safety clip to the thumb of his trigger hand, McCarter pulled hard and threw the pin into the dirt. He opened his fingers and let the spoon fly free, igniting the fuse.

Hawkins nodded back. His fingers twisted the handle all the way back and he yanked the flimsy door open. McCarter leaned forward and tossed the grenade through the opening at ankle level.

The OD-green metal sphere flew inside the door and bounced.

McCarter and Hawkins both turned away from the opening, throwing shoulders up against the coming blast.

Manning and James cut around the end of the trailer and ran up to the back door. Like the front, this rear entrance was serviced by three metal stairs inside runner struts welded to the bottom of the trailer frame.

Windows broke the surface of the mobile home, spilling bars of light out into the desert night. From this close to the structure it was easy to discern the hum of the generator placed next to the back door.

James cut wide around the generator housing and took a knee at an angle to the back door, weapon up as he provided security.

He and Manning saw the terrorist at the same time. The Hispanic man was adorned with a shapeless black beret and a full black beard that obscured most of his face in a tangle of knotted hair.

He stood over a kitchen sink and casually looked outside as he washed his hands. Manning drew a tight sight bead directly between the man's eyes at the center of his beetled brow.

Both Phoenix Force commandos paused for a moment. Suddenly, the man's eyes jerked wide in surprise and James tightened his finger on his trigger.

The grenade explosion filled the space behind the man. Suddenly a thin red syrup splashed the windowpane just as the glass burst outward from the concussive force, spraying shrapnel out in a deadly arc.

Manning and James automatically shifted the muzzles of their weapons and let loose with a long series of 3-round bursts, tearing the rear door to shreds and throwing a wall of lead into the trailer to cut off retreat for the terrorists trapped inside.

From the other side of the trailer came the distinctive sounds of M-4 carbines firing as McCarter and Hawkins moved in to mop up.

Smoke rolled out of shattered windows as the firing stopped.

"Clear!" McCarter barked.

"Clear!" James shouted.

"Phoenix has seized objective," McCarter announced.

"Able is clear," Lyons confirmed through the com link.

"I copy." Jack Grimaldi's voice broke in from where he circled the Osprey CV-22B overhead. "Airfield secured. We're coming in."

CHAPTER ONE

Barbara Price opened her eyes.

She awoke clearheaded and alert, knowing exactly where she was and what she needed to do.

There was a war being fought in the shadows and as the Stony Man mission controller, she was at its epicenter. Her eyes went to the window of her bedroom. It was dark outside. She looked over to her bedside table and read the time on the glowing red numerals of her digital clock.

She had been asleep for a little over four hours. She sat up and pushed a slender hand through her honey-blond hair. She felt revitalized after her power nap, and with a single cup of Aaron "Bear" Kurtzman's coffee, she knew she'd be ready to face another day.

She got up and smoothed her clothes before picking up the copy of the *Washington Post* she had placed by the bed. Before stepping out into the upstairs hallway of the Stony Man Farm main house, she reread the headline that had jumped out at her.

Government Accounting Office Finds Fraud
    A GAO investigation led by Deputy Director Hammond Carter has led to a senate investigation of funding for several "black op" Pentagon units…

Disgusted, Price stopped reading. The mission controller had too much on her mind at the moment to worry about politics as usual in Washington, D.C.

She frowned. The name "Hammond Carter" was unfamiliar.

If there was a new player trampling through intelligence and special operations playgrounds, then she needed to be on top of it. She resolved to have her computer wizard Akira Tokaido see if Stony Man had any files on the man.

As she walked down the hall and then the stairs to the main floor of the farmhouse she began mentally clicking through options and categorizing her tasks. She had men in the field, preparing to go into danger and, like the conductor of a symphony, it was her responsibility to coordinate all the disparate parts into a seamless whole.

She was in the basement and headed for the rail system to the Annex when the cell phone on her belt began to vibrate. She plucked it free and used the red push-talk button to initiate the walkie-talkie mode on the encrypted device.

"This is Price," she said, voice cool.

"Barb," Carmen Delahunt began, "the teams are in jump-off mode."

"Thanks, Carmen," Price told the ex-FBI agent. "I'm in the tunnel and coming toward the Annex now."

"See you in a minute." Delahunt signed off.

Price put her phone away and got into the light electric rail car. The little engine began to hum and she quickly picked up speed as she shot down the one thousand-foot tunnel sunk fifteen feet below the ground of Virginia's Blue Ridge Mountains.

Things were starting to come together, and Price could sense the tingle she had first felt as a mission controller for long-range operations conducted by the National Security Agency. It was there she had made her bones in the intelligence business before being recruited by Hal Brognola to run logistics and support at the top secret Stony Man Farm.

It had been quite a promotion, she reflected as the rail car raced down the subterranean tunnel past conduit pipes and thick power cables toward the Farm's Annex, camouflaged underneath a commercial wood-chipping facility.

Stony Man had operated as a clandestine antiterrorist operation since long before the infamous attacks of September 11 had put all of America's military, intelligence and law-enforcement efforts on the same page. Stony Man operated as it always had—under the direct control of the White House and separate from both the Joint Special Operations Command and the Directorate of National Intelligence.

Stony Man had been given carte blanche to operate at peak efficiency, eliminating oversights and legalities in the name of pragmatic results. It also, perhaps most importantly, offered the U.S. government the ability to disavow any knowledge of operations that went badly. Sometimes the big picture could be a very cold and unforgiving snapshot.

This left Stony Man and its operators particularly vulnerable to certain types of exposure. One hint of their existence in a place like MSNBC or the *New York Times* could lead to horrific outcomes.

The electric engine beneath her seat began to power down, and the rail car slowed to a halt. She pushed the morose reflections from her mind as it entered the Annex building.

Things were ready to roll hot; she could not afford to be distracted now. She stood and stepped out of the car. Fluorescent lights gleamed off linoleum floors and a sign on the whitewashed wall read Authorized Personnel Only. Beside the sign a member of the Farm's security staff nodded to her and reached over to the keypad that controlled the door to the tunnel. The fit, broad-shouldered man wore a black uniform and carried a 9 mm H&K MP-5 submachine gun.

Coming through the door, she was met by the wheelchair-bound Aaron Kurtzman. The big man reached out a hand the size of a paw and gave her a steaming mug of coffee. She eyed the ink-colored liquid dubiously.

"Thanks, Bear. That's just what I've been missing—something that can put hair on my chest."

The pair of them had exchanged that exact same greeting so

many times it was like a *Groundhog Day* moment. Both took comfort in the repetition.

Kurtzman turned the wheelchair and began to keep pace with the female mission controller as they made for the Communications Center.

The former Big Ten college wrestler lifted a massive arm across a barrel chest and pushed his glasses up on his nose beneath a high forehead with a deep horizontal crease. Price had once teased him that the worry line was severe enough for him to be awarded a Purple Heart.

After he'd earned his Ph.D. from the University of Minnesota, Kurtzman had been a computer programmer in one form or another. He was a Stony Man veteran who had been with the Farm since the beginning, and his wheelchair was a constant testament to his dedication.

"McCarter just called for Phoenix," he said, his voice a low rumble. "They're set up with Grimaldi at the secure helipad. Lyons did the same for Able Team. They're in place and ready to execute."

"Good," Barb said. She took a drink of the extrastrong coffee and pulled a face. "I'll alert Hal, then. All we need is the go-ahead from the President."

The pair entered the massive Communications Center and into a maelstrom of activity. Price paused at the door like a commander surveying her troops. She liked what she saw.

Kurtzman glided over to his work area, where it looked as if a bomb had gone off. His desk was covered in faxes, paperwork and the exposed wiring of a half dozen devices. Behind his desk a coffeepot, stained as black as the mud that filled it, bubbled like a tar pit.

Next to Kurtzman's desk, fingers flying across a laptop while monitoring a sat link, Akira Tokaido bobbed his head in time to the music coming from a single earbud. The lean, compact hacker was the youngest member of Stony Man's cybernetics team and the heir apparent to Kurtzman himself. The Japanese

American cyber wizard had at times worked virtual magic when Price had needed him to.

Across the room from Tokaido sat his polar opposite.

Professor Huntington Wethers had come to the Stony Man operation from his position on the faculty of UCLA. The tall, distinguished black man sported gray hair at his temples and an unflappable manner. He currently worked two laptop screens as a translation program fed him information from monitored radio traffic coming out of France.

Carmen Delahunt walked through the door between the Computer Room and the Communications Center. The red-headed ex-FBI agent made a beeline for Barbara Price when she saw her boss. The only female on the Farm's cyberteam, she served as a pivotal balance between Tokaido's hotshot hacking magic and Wethers's more restrained, academic style.

She finished her conversation and snapped her cell phone shut as she walked up to Barb. She pointed toward the newspaper in the mission controller's hand.

"You see that about GAO investigations?" she asked. "I started running an analytical of our financial allotments and expenditures, just to double-check none of our money originated in accounts tainted by the investigations."

Price smiled. "You read my mind, Carmen," she said. "Once we have Phoenix and Able taken care of, why don't you send me a summary in case anything comes of it."

"Will do." Delahunt nodded. "I have to double-check the South American arrangements we made for the team's extraction with the 'package'—if it comes to that. It's nice to be able to tap the resources of larger groups like the Pentagon's Joint Special Operations Command, but coordination is a nightmare."

"Let me know if anything goes wrong," Price said.

Delahunt nodded, then turned and began walking back across the floor toward the connecting door to the Annex's

Computer Room, her fingers punching out a number on her encrypted cell phone.

Barbara Price smiled.

She could feel the energy, the sense of purpose that permeated the room flow into her. Out there in the cold eight men on two teams were about to enter into danger for the sake of their country. If they got into trouble, if they needed anything, they would turn to her and her people.

She did not intend to let them down.

She made her way to her desk, where a light flashing on her desktop phone let her know a call was holding. She looked over at Kurtzman and saw the man returning a telephone handset to its cradle. He pointed toward her.

"It's Hal on line one," he said.

"Thanks, Bear," she answered.

She set her coffee down and picked up the handset as she sank into her chair. She put the phone to her ear and tapped a key on her computer, knocking the screen off standby mode.

"Hal, it's Barb," she said.

"I'm outside the Oval Office right now," Brognola said. "Are the boys up and rolling?"

"As we speak," Price answered. "Tell him operations are prepped to launch at his word."

"All right. Let's hope this one goes by the numbers," the gruff federal agent said.

"As always," she agreed, and hung up.

"All right, people," she announced to the room. "Let's get ready to roll."

CHAPTER TWO

Bogotá, Colombia

Lieutenant Colonel Sim Sin-Bok lit his cigar.

The North Korean intelligence officer narrowed his eyes in pleasure as he inhaled the thick, strong smoke of the *Corona Grande*. The rich nicotine entered his bloodstream and he immediately felt the euphoric rush. He relaxed into the plush leather seats of the BMW X3 and released the tobacco smoke through his nose in a sigh.

"Nothing but the best, eh, my friend?" Jimenez Naranjo purred.

The FARC commander was seated directly across from the covert representative of North Korea. The two men rode in comfort as the sleek, black BMW SUV flew down a jungle road leading deeper into mountains.

"I must admit," Sin-Bok said in accented Spanish, "I have come to enjoy our little liaisons."

"Your boss, he enjoys our money, too. No?" Naranjo winked, flashing white teeth.

"As much as yours enjoys our armaments," Sin-Bok countered.

The intelligence officer had been all over the Pacific Rim and Middle East in his years of service with the most glorious leaders. He had come to have a grudging respect for the FARC commander Naranjo in the course of their dealings, but weapons sales to violent groups always left him feeling nonplussed at best.

The SUV raced along the jungle road, cutting deeper into the mountain stronghold of the last nebulous Communist insurgency left on the planet. More than any ideological revelations, it had been the extortion of Colombian drug barons by the FARC guerrillas that had propelled them down a road toward the sort of capitalism they claimed to despise so much. They claimed their actions were about the rights of the peasant farmers to grow a crop that turned them profits and improved their lives.

For all Sin-Bok knew, the FARC leaders believed that. But he also knew that the influx of cocaine money had made things like up-armored diplomat-model BMW SUVs available to what had once been a rabble force dressed in rags. They were also able to purchase guidance systems such as the ones he carried on a flash drive in his briefcase. Guidance systems that could turn shoot-and-forget munitions such as old Soviet S-7 grail rocket launchers into weapons of pinpoint accuracy, capable of disabling a tank or knocking even American combat helicopters out of the sky.

Naranjo moved his hand down and hit a lever button on his seat rest. Behind him the vehicle's glass partition powered smoothly up, the engine making a subdued whine as it closed.

Sin-Bok kept his face inscrutable. He had dealt with Chinese Tongs based in Hong Kong, with representatives of Hamas and the Syrian government. He had sold or bought illicit goods from them all. He did not rattle easily and best of all, his ability to eat outside of the famine pit that was North Korea had left him with a bit of a pot belly. Such a belly was an indication of power in his nation. Men noticed and feared those grown so powerful they could be fat. Women took note and were appropriately impressed.

Sin-Bok cocked an eyebrow toward Naranjo.

When the FARC leader spoke he carefully enunciated each

word so that there could be no misunderstanding. And he spoke in English.

"Two plus five equals seven," he said.

Sin-Bok felt a cold squirt of adrenaline hit his stomach. He felt his throat swell up from the reaction and he forced himself not to swallow and thus reveal his surprise and nervousness.

By the dragon's luck, he thought wildly, *this cannot be.* Then he thought, *Their servants truly are everywhere.*

On his lap his hands tightened momentarily around his attaché case. Then relaxed. He met Naranjo's eye and nodded once, sharply.

"Three plus four equals seven," Sin-Bok replied, also in English, completing the code parole and establishing his rank as one higher than his contact.

The two agents of the shadowy organization stared at each other for a long moment. Naranjo opened a lid set between his rear-facing seats and pulled out two cut-crystal tumblers and a bottle of expensive rum.

He poured Sin-Bok a glass and handed it over. The North Korean espionage agent took it without a word. The enhanced suspension on the BMW made their vehicle ride like it was on rails. He sipped the sugar-cane liquor, enjoying the sharp alcohol.

He carefully set his tumbler on top of his leather attaché case and picked up his cigar from the ashtray. He drew in a lungful of smoke as the FARC narcoterrorist and field agent poured himself a drink.

After Naranjo had put the bottle away, Sin-Bok spoke again.

"I take it these guidance systems aren't just headed for your jungle camps," he observed.

"Ah, no," Naranjo admitted, switching back to Spanish. "I, like you, am a link."

With a rueful look Sin-Bok held up his glass. "Here's to Seven," he said, voice rueful.

White House, Washington, D.C.

HAL BROGNOLA LOOKED OUT the east door of the Oval Office and into the Rose Garden. Beside him in a comfortable chair sat the special envoy to North Korea. They faced the President of the United States in his traditional seat behind the desk made from the timbers of the HMS *Resolute*.

Behind them in the northeast corner a grandfather clock built by John and Thomas Seymour ticked out the passing of time. Waiting for the President to finish reading the report, Brognola looked down at the carpet on the floor, noting the presidential seal. He'd been in this office a good many times over the years, seen more than one man pass through the job, seen the job age them all.

The President sighed. He tossed the national intelligence estimate addendum down on the desk and leaned back. He folded his hands in a pensive motion and cocked an eyebrow at Brognola.

"You're sure, then?" The question was perfunctory.

Brognola nodded once. "Yes, sir."

The President frowned and twisted slightly in his seat. "Let's get 'em on the line," he told the envoy.

The special envoy leaned forward and tapped a few numbers out on the handset located on the desktop. He activated the speakerphone function and leaned back while the number dialed. After two digital ring tones a smooth feminine voice answered, Korean.

The envoy answered in Korean, then stated, "With your permission, Mr. Ambassador, I would like to switch to English."

There was a brief pause, then a sharp, almost shrill man's voice spoke in quick, truncated syllables. The North Korean regime did not maintain a diplomatic presence in the United States, and the men in the Oval Office were speaking to the leader of the U.N. delegation in New York.

"Yes, English is fine," the ambassador said. "But whatever

language we choose to continue wasting our time in, the fact still remains constant. The Democratic People's Republic of Korea has no knowledge of the activities of which you speak. We consider such activities as a personal insult on the character of our most beloved leader, the eternal president, Kim Jong-il. Frankly a continuation of this so-called investigation will be construed as a hostile act."

Brognola shifted his gaze away from the conference call toward the President's face. It remained impassive except for the slight tightening of muscles along the jaw, indicating that he was grinding his teeth.

"Mr. Ambassador," the envoy began, "we consider the arming and training of known terrorist groups such as FARC to be hostile acts."

"Fortunately for the United States, Korea has not undertaken any of these activities."

"Why is that 'fortunate' for us?" Brognola interjected.

"Because," the voice continued, "if such an error in perception was to occur, the United States might be tempted to do something rash in response."

"I trust you've read the dossier I sent you earlier," the envoy prompted.

At his desk the President made a steeple of his long, slender fingers and leaned slightly forward in his chair. He was due to a staff meeting to discuss implementation of public health care options in twelve minutes. Brognola could see the President growing more annoyed with the futile game they were now playing with the North Koreans.

"I have seen the dossier," the ambassador admitted. "I saw nothing compelling in those documents. The idea that a member of our security services would be working as a trainer and liaison for a FARC cell in Colombia is obviously impossible. That leaves only two explanations for your report that I can see."

The envoy let out a sigh and leaned back in his chair. "And those explanations would be…?"

"Either your much vaunted intelligence services are mistaken or, second and more likely, you are attempt to fabricate this evidence to justify a preemptive strike on our homeland." The ambassador paused, then began speaking in a much louder, much shriller voice. "This is inexcusable! We will not be the victim of your imperialist plots! We will defend our home by any means necessary from your Western aggression!"

The President looked over at Brognola. He silently mouthed the word *imperialist* to the big federal agent. Brognola shrugged, then murmured under his breath, "They're a little like Cuba," he explained. "Forty or fifty years behind. They probably just got a copy of *Dr. Strangelove* in Pyongyang last month."

The President made a sour face as the ambassador continued to bark his outrage over the conference link. He made a chopping motion with one hand toward the phone, then nodded at the envoy.

"Mr. Ambassador," the envoy interrupted, "your protests have been noted. We will not be speaking of this matter again. Good day." He cut the connection.

"Okay," the President said. "I gave it one last try. We don't know what kind of brinksmanship they're trying to pull off this time, but they can go to hell." He spun around in his chair and looked out at the Rose Garden. "Your boys in position to execute our contingency plan?"

"It seems our contingency just upgraded to primary," Brognola said. "And yes, my crews are in place and ready to roll."

"Then proceed," the President said.

Once they left the office Brognola and the special envoy went in separate directions, each man pulling out a NSA-encrypted cell phone. The director of the Justice Department's Sensitive Operations Group hit the number 1 on his speed dial option. Two rings later Barbara Price answered.

"I just got out of my meeting with the Man," he informed her. "We are ready to execute."

Stony Man Farm

BARBARA PRICE STOOD in the hallway in front of the door leading to the Communications Room. She said goodbye to Brognola and cut the connection on her phone before opening the door.

Price entered the room like a gust of wind. The attractive mission controller wore a headset communications link and carried a matte-black cell phone PDA with NSA security upgrades.

She walked across the room, nodding to where Akira Tokaido and Carmen Delahunt sat at workstations. A giant flat screen was fixed to the wall above their heads. The monitor was silent and still, for the moment showing only the screen saver: an image of the movie poster for *The Magnificent Seven* with the quote from the script, "We deal in lead, friend."

"Time?" Price asked.

"M-Minute minus twenty seconds," Kurtzman replied.

From the other side of the room he used a blunt, square-tipped finger to toggle his wheelchair away from his workstation. The electric engine of the power chair ramped up as the leader of the Stony Man cybernetics team pulled even with Stony Man's mission controller.

"Okay," Price said. "Bring central synchronistic communications online."

At her station, Carmen Delahunt typed a command on her keyboard. Inside Price's headset earjack, the receiver popped and the ex-NSA operational manager nodded once to Delahunt.

"Stony Base to Stony Eagle," she said. "Radio check, over."

Instantly the voice of Stony Man pilot Jack Grimaldi answered, coming over the digital link with crystal clarity. "Base, this is Bird," he replied. "I have good copy."

Price gave a curt nod to herself and turned toward the communal HD screen and pointed a finger.

Kurtzman tapped a command on an interface board built into his power chair and the screen switched to a satellite image of the Earth. The observation platform was a Keyhole satellite in near-Earth geosynchronous orbit completely dedicated to the needs of Stony Man operational taskings.

"Stony Base to Stony Hawk," she continued.

"Stony Hawk, good copy," Able Team leader Carl Lyons answered in clipped syllables.

On the screen the sat image rotated until the HD monitor showed the Western Hemisphere. Kurtzman tapped out a few clicks on his keypad, centering the screen over Central America, and then began to tighten its resolution as it slid down toward the southern continent. Kurtzman hit another command key and a political map was overlaid on the topographical features.

"Do you have eyes on target?" Price asked.

"Affirmative," Lyons responded.

"Eagle, give us your position," Price told Grimaldi.

"I'm in a holding pattern behind Hill 372, about three klicks out," Grimaldi said.

On the overhead monitor the political map showed Colombia. The spy camera tightened its resolution even further and suddenly the POV began descending at a rapid rate.

To the onlookers it seemed as if they were in the nose of a plane as it dive-bombed through wispy patches of clouds toward the earth below.

"Hawk and Eagle, we are green light go," Price said. "I repeat, we are green light go."

"Copy," Grimaldi answered.

"Copy," Lyons said.

Price looked to the wall. On one side of the image, scrolling vertically were GPS coordinates blinking rapidly next to numerical sets of longitude and latitude readings.

Patches of green and brown, at first unidentifiable, formed

into a jungle canopy over a series of rolling hills. On the south-east side of the screen a broad, fast-moving river cut through the trees. Up the sheer plateau from the water, a brown dirt road cut out of the rugged geography.

From his position at his workstation Akira Tokaido manipulated the sat image. The camera view settled on a flat area of the map. At first the location appeared to be nothing more than dense brush where the road ended.

"Toggling to IR," Tokaido informed the room.

His thumb struck the appropriate key and instantly the crystal-clear picture on the screen changed to a swirling mesh of colors based on radiant heat that made the monitor appear like a watercolor canvas.

On the screen the figures beneath camouflage netting showed up immediately. Roughly two dozen individuals moved around, spread over an area the size of a soccer field.

Several bright spots indicated where industrial furnaces were active and in one section of the field several large vehicles sat clustered in parallel rows. Cool rectangular blobs revealed Quonset huts and long, narrow buildings of concrete and wood.

The tension in the room grew as they waited for the field teams to strike. Barbara Price leaned forward and grabbed the backrest on an office chair. She squeezed it hard until her knuckles shone white from her grip.

Then, on the screen, all hell broke loose.

CHAPTER THREE

Colombia

Carl Lyons lifted his Bushnell binoculars and scanned the FARC camp below. Able Team's position was located right above the only road leading into the terrorist outpost. This was a hammer-and-anvil operation, with Able Team serving as the anvil.

The readout on the range finder built into the optics showed 204 meters. Sweat trickled down Lyons's body, sliding over his feverish skin to collect at his armpits, navel and groin. He was a big man and heavily muscled, which made the heat a burden to him. He was growing crankier by the second.

Behind him in the brush Hermann "Gadgets" Schwarz slapped a mosquito. The Able Team electronics genius was crouched next to a 80 mm mortar. Lined up in front of the squat weapon's base plate were six rounds: two high explosive, two antipersonnel, two white phosphorous. He lowered a compass and quickly adjusted the angle of the tube based on his reading.

On the ground a tripod-mounted electronic device hummed softly. The size of a PowerBook it had an antenna dish set in the top that slowly rotated. On loan from the Pentagon through the DARPA—Defense Advance Research and Projects Agency—program, the XM-12 was a field-portable scrambler unit capable of disrupting digital signals in addition to radio waves.

Out in front of Schwarz and Lyons the third member of Able Team lay belly-down on the soggy ground. Ex-Special Forces sergeant Rosario Blancanales had his right eye suctioned up close against the rubber cup of his sniper scope.

"You heard the lady," he growled. "Let's do this thing."

"Phoenix inbound," Grimaldi informed them over the com link.

"*Adios,* assholes," Blancanales muttered to the narcoterrorists. Behind him Schwarz picked up the first HE round.

In the reticule of his scope the Puerto Rican's crosshairs were settled on a bearded FARC soldier manning the machine gun position at the entrance to the camp.

The man wore dark khaki fatigues stained with sweat. His tangle of long, greasy black hair was kept back by a shapeless black beret, and he wore a 9 mm Browning Hi-Power in a belt holster opposite the sheath for a wicked-looking machete.

He laughed, and blunt, very white teeth stood out like neon against his walnut-brown complexion. On his web gear he carried a sat phone, which had first alerted Blancanales that this was a leader. Two other soldiers, much younger and beardless, stood around listening to the older man talk, M-16 A-2 assault rifles in their hands.

Blancanales slowly released his breath and felt his world narrow to the crosshairs of his scope. The FARC leader's fatigue shirt was open to the belly, revealing an expanse of curly black hair across his lean chest. A gold chain hung down between the man's pectoral muscles. Blancanales's crosshairs centered there.

From the valley there was the sudden sound of an approaching helicopter. The man snapped his head around at the noise. The M-21 sniper rifle with folding paratrooper stock coughed once as Blancanales squeezed the trigger in a slow, controlled movement.

Across two hundred yards he saw the FARC leader jerk as the 7.62 mm NATO round struck him. In the sniper optic Blancanales saw blood halo out behind the man in a fine mist.

The target half spun, crumpled to his knees, then fell forward on his face.

The two sentries standing next to the dead man swept up their weapons. They turned toward the sound of the helicopter, spun back toward the road from where Blancanales's round had come. They brought their M-16s to their shoulders and started shouting in Spanish.

Lyons opened up with his cut-down M-60E.

He had the machine gun supported on a fallen log and fed from a green plastic, 200-round drum magazine. The weapon roared to life with a stuttering thunder as hot shell casings arced out of the receiver and spun to the forest floor.

The earth in front of the FARC sentries erupted in a series of geyser spouts as he walked his fire in on them. Behind him Schwarz released his hold on the mortar round, dropping it smoothly into the tube. It went off with a throaty *bloop*. Lyons's rounds struck the two men.

The heavy-caliber bullets buzzed into the FARC sentries, hacking them up like spinning axes. They spun and jiggled like marionettes dancing for a puppeteer. They staggered, dropping their weapons, then flopped to the ground still quivering.

Schwarz's 80 mm HE mortar round struck the camp dead center of the FARC motor pool. A black Ford Excursion with its roof cut off and massively oversize tires exploded. A ball of black smoke and orange flame mushroomed out. The vehicle was picked up off the ground and spun end-over-end, crumpling an old school bus repainted OD-green. Two five-ton Oso-12 trucks had their windows blown out, and a FARC soldier walking past was picked up and thrown like a rag doll.

Blancanales drew down on a running soldier and pulled his trigger. The man fell in a tangled heap.

Lyons eased up on his machine gun and activated his throat mike.

"Eagle, this is Hawk," he said. "The front door is sealed. Deploy."

"Copy," the British-accented voice of David McCarter replied.

"Drop the WP right on the road in case anyone tries to drive out," Lyons told Schwarz.

Schwarz nodded, then twisted the elevation knob on the mortar down several clicks. He lifted a white phosphorous round and dropped it in. The mortar went off and the round lobbed outward in a tight arc. The WP bomb struck the earth at the sentry post and detonated. Instantly the corpses at the impact site burst into flame.

Satisfied, Schwarz dropped his second round on the same angle and turned the entrance to the FARC camp into a raging conflagration.

"Keep an eye out for our Korean guest," Lyons told Blancanales.

The ex-Green Beret nodded and continued sweeping his scope across the camp below them, hunting for targets of opportunity. Lyons opened up with his M-60E and directed suppressive fire on the FARC compound.

JACK GRIMALDI lifted the Blackhawk straight up out of the shallow jungle valley and bunny-hopped the bird over the hilltop. He put the nose of the helicopter down and raced forward, flying at treetop level. Two hundred yards out, his thumb flicked up the red safety cover to his rocket pod.

The FARC compound had two 20 mm antiaircraft emplacements providing security and they were Grimaldi's first priority. He banked the bird hard, brought it on line with the narrow, fast-moving creek below and gunned the Blackhawk hard toward the camp.

His thumb depressed the button.

Instantly twin seven-inch rockets from pods under his weapons platform launched toward the camp. The projectiles whistled out, leaving contrails of white smoke behind them as they flew.

They both hit the sandbag walls encircling one of the 20 mm AA cannons and exploded. Gunny sacks, body parts and pieces of the guns went flying. Grimaldi worked his foot pedals and maneuvered the yoke. The Blackhawk banked hard, then spun around on its axis until the nose was orientated 120-degrees on a separate plane.

Through the windshield Grimaldi could see the antiaircraft crew scrambling to bring the 20 mm cannon to bear. Men's faces twisted in fear and anger as they swarmed like ants around the gun placement. The helicopter remained level under Grimaldi's hand. Again his thumb found the activation toggle.

Two more rockets leaped from their pods and swept forward, spiraling inward on synchronous flight paths. FARC gunners threw themselves out of the artillery pit in a desperate attempt to avoid the blast, but the twin explosions caught them in a concussive wave of lethal force.

"Here we go!" Grimaldi yelled into his throat mike.

The Blackhawk yawed hard, then settled into a hover fifty yards off the broken, uneven ground. Camouflage netting across the compound was ripped off and tossed into twisted heaps around the aluminum pole frame work, revealing men, sheds and tin-roofed buildings. A cloud of dust sprang up like fog as the topsoil was ripped from the ground by the force of rotor wash.

A thick hemp rope was kicked out of the cargo bay door. An instant later T. J. Hawkins, ex-Delta Force operator, appeared in the doorway. He wore a black sporting helmet and clear visors over his eyes. His hands were covered by thick welder's gloves.

"Go! Go! Go!" David McCarter shouted.

Instantly, Hawkins stepped off the helicopter and onto the rope, sliding down the hemp weave like a firefighter on a pole. He was halfway down when the second man appeared in the door, then grasped the rope. Rafael Encizo, veteran anti-Castro guerrilla commando and combat diver, stepped off and dropped like a stone.

On the ground Hawkins shuffled forward a few places and took a knee, weapon coming up. Encizo dismounted the rope and took up a position to Hawkins's left, his own weapon up as Calvin James, former Navy SEAL and trained medic, hit the rope.

Hawkins saw two men in Russian military fatigues run out of an outbuilding, weapons up. He drew down on them and used his M-4 carbine to cut them down.

Beside him Encizo unleashed his own firepower, an M-249 Squad Automatic Weapon, in stuttering bursts.

James hit the ground, bending at the knees to absorb the force of the impact, and a second later Gary Manning, former Canadian Special Forces soldier and explosives expert, also landed. The Canadian put his own M-60E in the pocket of his shoulder and fired over the heads of his teammates as he shuffled forward.

James peeled off to Encizo's left, forming the anchor point on one end of their wedge formation as Manning shuffled into position on the opposite side. Behind them McCarter was on the ground, his M-4/M-203 combination carbine grenade launcher up and tracking for targets.

"Clear!" McCarter shouted.

The ex-SAS trooper walked smoothly forward, weapon up and finger on the trigger. Behind him the assault rope was disengaged by the helicopter loadmaster and door gunner, a sergeant from the 75th Ranger Division on loan to Stony Man's blacksuit security detail.

"Copy!" Grimaldi responded.

The helicopter's turbine engines screamed as the pilot climbed the bird up to a better altitude. The loadmaster/door gunner slid over behind an M-134 Gatling gun and rotated the barrel cluster around to bear on the compound.

"Advance," McCarter directed.

Instantly the unit began shuffling forward, firing their weapons as they moved. Above them the Blackhawk drifted along, the 7.62 mm minigun firing ahead of them. The weapon's massive rate of fire had twinkling, smoking hot shell casings dropping down on them like metal raindrops.

In front of them FARC soldiers tried desperately to mount a defense, but the triple impact of speed of attack, aggression of action and firepower coupled with surprise was proving more than they could deal with. FARC guerrillas soaked up bullets like sponges, were scythed in two or battered into submission.

Hawkins walked his muzzle in measured angles from left to right, dropping running, screaming targets with each squeeze of his trigger. Encizo used his SAW from the hip, triggering one short burst after the other. He saw a door to a long, low barracks-style building swing open and he took it under fire immediately. Red tracer fire arced through the opening and dropped a knot of FARC guerrillas.

"Able, do we have eyes on?" McCarter demanded through his com set. Beside him Manning used his M-60E to blast into an armored sedan being used as cover by a handful of enemy combatants.

"Negative," Lyons replied. "To your five o'clock I have the command bunker."

McCarter looked in the direction Lyons had indicated and, as if to punctuate the ex-cop's directions, Schwarz put an 80 mm mortar round down on top of a jet-black armored BMW SUV parked near a concrete structure. The luxury sport vehicle went up like a Roman candle. A moment later another mortar went off.

"I have eyes on bunker," McCarter answered. Beside him Gary Manning mowed down three FARC soldiers attempting to set up an RPK machine gun.

"Good," Lyons replied. "Blancanales said he scoped our target entering the bunker twenty minutes ago."

"En route," McCarter confirmed.

Machine-gun fire erupted from just ahead and to the left of them. Bullets cut toward the assault force in a lethal wave. The concussive force of the heavy-caliber rounds cutting through the air next to their bodies buffeted Phoenix Force and they all went down in defensive sprawls.

"Machine gun, left!" Encizo called out.

The team looked toward the position and saw a reinforced foxhole with a sandbag roof. A .30-caliber machine gun burped out another burst as the gunner tried to find his range.

Manning, armed with his own machine gun, cut loose, trying to suppress the other gunner's fire. His bullets gouged up furrows of earth just in front of the position and slapped into the dirt-filled sandbags, causing the FARC machine gunner to flinch.

Encizo lifted the barrel of his SAW and added to the maelstrom of fire.

McCarter used the barrage as cover enough to risk popping up to one knee. He tucked the butt of his M-4 into his shoulder and triggered his M-203 attachment. A 40 mm fléchette round shot from the barrel and arched like football into the enemy position.

A heavy bang sounded and smoke began roiling. Razor-sharp fléchette darts scissored into the machine gunner and his assistant, cutting the men to bloody ribbons.

Phoenix rose as one unit, weapons up. Manning stepped forward and unleashed the M-60E in a wide arc in front of them, spraying the camp in a crescent-moon pattern designed to keep other defenders from gaining momentum.

"Bunker!" McCarter yelled. "Gary and Rafe, cover!"

The two machine gunners ran forward and threw themselves down to give themselves overlapping fields of fire. Behind them the other three members of Phoenix Force prepared to storm the bunker.

CHAPTER FOUR

Inside the FARC command bunker Lieutenant Colonel Sin-Bok could hear the men outside screaming as they died. He was out of the way, in a corner, holding tightly to his attaché case and a .45-caliber M-1911 pistol Naranjo had provided him once the attack started.

Outside, bullets struck the bunker and everyone heard them bounce off the concrete. All eyes kept glancing toward the barred and reinforced door at the front of the structure. It was the only way out or in.

If the North Korean was going to make an escape, his only option was out through that door. When the raiders outside came, it would be in through that same door. Sin-Bok's entire world had shrunk to a four-foot-by-three-foot piece of steel hung on reinforced storm hinges.

Across the room Naranjo cursed loudly and threw his sat phone to the ground. It burst apart on the hard-packed floor, plastic pieces spraying out like shrapnel. The other group of people trapped in the bunker cringed at his outburst.

"I can't get a signal out!" Naranjo shouted. "They're fucking blocking communications."

"Who?" Sin-Bok demanded. It made a very real difference who *they* were. "Is it your government?"

Realizing immediately what Sin-Bok feared, Naranjo scowled and shook his head. "No," he said. "All we've seen are norteamericanos, maybe Europeans. I do not think these are Colombian Jaguars," he finished, referencing the Colombian military's elite unit.

"Then the flash drive has to make it out," Sin-Bok said.

Naranjo opened his hands and looked around in question.

Salvation didn't appear to be within reach. Sin-Bok quickly looked around the bunker again. He saw a fourteen-year-old girl in oversize fatigues and holding a ridiculously outsize M-16. Her brown eyes were almost comically big.

FARC, like most Third World insurgencies, recruited heavily from younger members of their impoverished society. Sin-Bok, who had been raised and conditioned since birth to put nation before self, understood this. He also understood how abhorrent the concept of child soldiers were to the Western powers.

"You," he barked. "Come here!"

The girl started when she realized he was pointing toward her. She cut her gaze to Naranjo, who, confused, nodded. As the girl began crossing the room, a burst of gunfire slammed into the bunker door.

"They're coming!" Sin-Bok snapped. "Hurry! Now, someone give me a condom."

Naranjo looked as if he'd been slapped. "This is hardly the time for—"

"Shut up, you fool," Sin-Bok snarled. "The flash drive must get out. I need a condom."

Despite being born to a heavily Catholic country, many of the FARC soldiers, heavily influenced by secular Marxist ideals, had a prophylactic on their person. Rubbers were as ubiquitous as cigarettes among soldiers.

Working quickly, Sin-Bok tore open the wrapping and pulled the lubricated sleeve free.

He dropped the flash drive inside the condom and quickly tied a knot in the end. He handed it back to the girl. She held it out in her hand as if it was a snake. She looked back at the North Korean.

Sin-Bok waved his hand at her. "Hurry, hurry."

Shrugging, the girl leaned her M-16 against a table and began pulling at her belt buckle to loosen her pants.

"No, no, no!" Sin-Bok yelled. "Swallow it, you idiot!"

The girl made a face but quickly slid the material into her mouth and swallowed hard. She gagged once and coughed, then was done. Satisfied, Sin-Bok stepped up close and grabbed her by her thin arms.

Pulling her close, the North Korean locked eyes with the frightened girl. "Listen close," he instructed. He spoke an address in Bogotá to the girl, made her repeat it. "Now get naked. Go to the corner and do not fight. If the Americans make it through and we lose, pretend you were kidnapped. Then, later, you get that flash drive to the address I just gave you."

"Seven must prevail," Naranjo muttered from over the Korean's shoulder.

"Seven must prevail," Sin-Bok agreed.

OUTSIDE THE BUNKER DOOR the Phoenix Force entry team prepared for the final assault.

Manning and Encizo formed anchor points on opposite sides of their skirmish line. Up on the hill Able Team provide a second level of security overwatch. The battlefield was spread out below them like a chessboard. Jack Grimaldi, from a stand-off position, continued to use his missiles and machine gun to devastating effect along the periphery of the compound.

Calvin James let his main weapon hang loose from its strap as he manipulated an industrial caulking gun. Beside him Hawkins presented timing pencils with preset timers.

McCarter surveyed the iron door as James and Hawkins prepped the demolition charges, a grenade in one hand. "Quarter-inch internal hinges, likely with reinforcement points at the latch and corners," he said.

James nodded. "I brought a big hammer just in case," he said.

The foam shape charge squirted out of the caulking gun like icing from a chef's pastry applicator. With expert dabs and straight lines the ex-SEAL wasted no time in positioning his charge at the most precise locations. Finished, he stepped back and tossed the caulker aside.

"'That'll do, Pig. That'll do,'" he quoted.

Hawkins snorted as he quickly placed the timers and started the countdown. "Fire in the hole, people," he warned.

The entrance into the bunker was a short set of steps leading four feet down into the ground with sandbag walls built up on the side. Moving quickly and under covering fire from the support units, they peeled back from the doorway.

The charges went off with a loud, flat bang, and black smoke rolled out. Immediately automatic weapons fire burned out of the opening from inside the bunker.

"Hawk!" McCarter ordered.

The lanky Texan rushed down the steps, slid into a corner of the doorway and produced an awkward-looking assault rifle from a sling carry on his torso.

The CornerShot Assault Pistol Rifle boasted a steel hinge that allowed the weapon to be folded into an L-shape and fired around corners. The version used by Hawkins now had a digital folding heads-up-display screen and handgun at the end of the weapon capable of firing 5.56 mm ammunition.

Coolly, Hawkins swung the weapon around the corner into the teeming confusion inside the bunker. A shape loomed up, filling the screen. Hawkins pulled his trigger three times and the shape went down.

"Do you have eyes on?" McCarter demanded.

"Negative," Hawkins replied. He snapped the weapon back around in the other direction. "Hold on!" he said. "There! I have eyes on Target Pusan Kim chi. He's at position fourteen-thirty."

"Fourteen-thirty," the team repeated out loud, using the twenty-four-hour indicator for two-thirty on a clock.

McCarter, grenade primed, chucked the little hand bomb in a slap-shot maneuver around the corner as Hawkins folded back out and switched out weapons.

There were curses in Spanish and a cry of terror, then the stun device went off with a brilliant flash and a deafening bang.

"Go! Go! Go!" McCarter barked.

Hawkins charged down the steps into the smoke, weapon up, visor in place. He stepped across the threshold and button-hooked to the left. Two steps behind him Calvin James rushed into the room, twisting to the right. McCarter tapped Rafael Encizo on the shoulder, then charged in after Hawkins and James.

Encizo rushed down the steps into the hellbox.

Behind them Manning held their direct six while the guns of Able Team provided overwatch support fire.

Already pockets of resistance on the compound had begun to fade. Vehicles burned, FARC corpses lay like trash on the ground and Grimaldi's Blackhawk hovered over the scene, miniguns blazing in sporadic bursts.

Inside the bunker Hawkins rushed forward.

Disorganized and wounded FARC guerrillas stumbled past him. He shot two, skipped over their falling bodies and reached the huddled form of Sin-Bok. The North Korean operative looked up and Hawkins dropped a haymaker on his face two inches up from the point of the man's chin.

The target dropped, and James rushed forward, spinning around to cover the rest of the room as Hawkins slapped plastic riot cuffs and a dark hood on the Korean. Out of the smoke and dark a screaming FARC officer appeared, a .45 ACP filling his hand.

The pistol roared, the muzzle-flash illuminating the gloomy bunker like lightning. Two heavy slugs slapped into the concrete above the Korean's head, and James realized the man had been trying to silence the foreign agent. He shot the FARC officer twice, once low in the stomach and once through the face as he folded.

"Let's go!" Hawkins grunted.

Across the room Encizo and McCarter were clearing the rest of the bunker with ruthless, mechanically murderous proficiency.

James helped haul the groggy Korean to his feet. He turned away from the man, hand on the pistol grip of his weapon. His eyes scanned the room as they began moving forward, looking for any last-second piece of intelligence or overlooked threat.

"Damn, hold on!" he shouted.

Hawkins turned, pushing the Korean down and bringing up his weapon. He jerked around, looking for the threat, but didn't see anything moving. He looked down and saw what James was looking at.

The girl was in her underwear and huddled against the wall. A dead FARC soldier lay bleeding in front of her. She looked up at the masked and heavily armed commandos with stark fear.

"Hey, boss," Hawkins called to McCarter.

"Who are you? How did you get here?" James asked the girl in Spanish.

"What?" McCarter demanded. He looked over. "Shit," he said simply.

"My name is Maria," the girl said. "I'm from the village of San Sebastian. I want to go home, please."

"This is mission creep." McCarter spit.

"We put her on the Blackhawk," James said, "turn her over to our South American liaison. *They* contact a relief agency. No fuss, no muss. Just a chopper ride."

McCarter hesitated, even though everyone there knew there was no way they were leaving a helpless teenage girl behind them.

"Fine," the ex-SAS trooper said. "But she's your baby till we hand her over to our Agency contact."

"No problem," James answered.

McCarter spoke into his throat mike. "Phoenix, we are leaving."

THE COMPOUND WAS DOTTED with fires. Corpses, broken weapons, body parts and the cinder hulks of destroyed vehicles specked the ground.

Keeping their security level high, Phoenix Force approached a flat stretch of ground as Jack Grimaldi brought the Blackhawk in for a landing. From the opposite side of the clearing Able Team broke cover and began their approach to the helicopter.

As the teams crammed into the troop transport bay under the watchful minigun, Carl Lyons looked over to where the girl sat quietly. James's black fatigue shirt was hanging off her.

"What the fuck?" Lyons demanded. "You can't go anywhere without finding strays?"

James laughed from behind his balaclava. "That's why I signed up, man, to meet new people and make friends."

Lyons turned and looked at the carnage the Stony Man teams were leaving behind as the helicopter lifted off.

"Oh, man." The ex-cop chuckled. "We made plenty of friends today."

"Yeah," McCarter agreed. "But we just don't seem to play well with others."

Kiev, Ukraine

KLEGG SIPPED HIS DRINK and watched the clubgoers through slitted eyes.

The vodka was expensive and ice-cold so it went down with little more bite than frigid water. The dance beat, a hypno-industrial blend of tribal-styled rhythms, was two years past hip in New York and three in Europe. Despite this the meat-packing plant turned trendy nightclub was crowded with young, inebriated and apparently sexually frenzied young people fueled with chemical cocktails and copious amounts of hard alcohol.

Next to him Svetlana scanned the crowd with the bored indifference of the nouveau riche. She was fashionably anorexic with thighs thinner than her knees and bare buds for breasts.

She was draped in a Pierre Cardin silk number with all the ridiculously expensive space-age, unisex, avant-garde styling that implied. She let a hand drift to the flat plane of her stomach, her eyes as large as a character's in a Japanese manga above the drawn, stark lines of her cheekbones.

Klegg had known her for three days and in that time he'd never seen her eat anything but the olive from her vodka martini. Her energy, both in bed and out, seem entirely fueled by Stolichnaya Gold vodka and cocaine. She performed the most depraved of sexual acrobatics with the same robotic expression and untouchable eyes she used now to survey the club.

Glassy-eyed women in heavy makeup and tight, revealing clothing made their way past them to the concrete dance floor. Stalking them like wolves, strung-out male Russian urbanites, or the occasional steroid monster, followed in close pursuit.

Svetlana nodded to innumerable numbers of the club crowd. Her true value lay not in her penchant for kinky sex but in her vast, tangled social connections.

The youngest daughter of an extremely powerful and corrupt Moscow oligarch, she was more courtesan than prostitute. Klegg had flown halfway around the world and paid her in Colombian emeralds to secure an important introduction.

Upon accepting his request and payment for her services as social purveyor, she seemed to have slept with him out of habitual reflex rather than any sense of obligation.

Klegg himself had gone along with it because while vapid, she was still beautiful and because he had promised himself, upon passing the New York bar exam, that he would sleep with a woman from every continent.

After that challenge he had further redefined his goal to include economic regions and geographical features. It had only cost him one marriage and a stubborn case of herpes to meet his goal.

Klegg always achieved his goals, no matter what the price.

Kiev, he decided, really wanted to be Moscow and Moscow, he knew, really wanted to be Los Angeles.

His eyes scanned the crowd in a slow sweep like a radar dish. The images came back to him in jumbles: two girls in a booth making out while a crowd of onlookers gathered around. Stoned women on the dance floor slinging chem-lights around on strings while their dresses crept up their anorexic thighs. A long, greasy-haired kid in a thousand-dollar jacket dealing Ecstasy in front of the restrooms under the watchful eye of two hired thugs with bodies by Dianabol and eyes like polished steel mirrors.

The place smelled like sweat and cigarettes and liquor and sex. The din of the DJ's stereo system was enough to qualify as a sonic weapon. Klegg could literally feel the 2-4 backbeat of the bass shake him with tactile force as it pumped out of the massive speakers.

He wasn't here to have a good time.

He spoke Russian, among four other languages, and he was young enough not to stand out too terribly in the club during the initial surveillance. His cover was simple and straightforward because it was, in fact, his profession. He was a procurement specialist for a private contractor specializing in large-corporation inventory.

He made deals for engines in Peru, he acquired stockpiles of diamonds in South Africa, he secured binary processors in India, he obtained cooling systems for French Mirage jets and sold them to African dictators.

All the while he built his networks of shady lawyers, street contacts, intelligence agents, criminal syndicates, ship captains and bush pilots. Today he was going to expand that network into the field of soldiers for hire, and Svetlana was going to help him.

"There," the woman said.

Across the dance floor near where a phalanx of bouncers guarded the club's entrance he saw Milosevic. The Russian lawyer came in like a visiting emperor, his entourage part Praetorian guard, part sycophantic toadies and part pleasure slaves.

Klegg reached down to where his attaché case rested against his leg. He took the not unsubstantial weight of the thing in his hand and stepped away from the bar. Across the room Milosevic was shown to a private area at the top of a short flight of stairs leading to a balcony over the dance floor.

A massive, impassive-faced thug with the body of a professional wrestler and an Armani suit stood sentry before the red-velvet rope dividing the stair and viewing lounge from the common dancers and general population.

As they approached, the man's head turned on a bull neck like a 20 mm cannon on an APC gun turret. His eyes were cold chips of blue. Klegg felt an instant rising of his own hackles as he drew closer. It was an instinctual reaction to so much rival testosterone. The potential for conflict was intense. It wouldn't pay to lose his head, and this was what Svetlana was earning her percentage for.

He let a small smile play across his face as the bodyguard's eyes were drawn away from him, a man with a briefcase in a Ukrainian nightclub, to the slinky form of the icy blonde. The guy might be tough, Klegg mused, but he wasn't a pro.

Behind the guard up the stairs Milosevic was opening a bottle of champagne. He said something and everyone in the group laughed like marionettes. A flamboyantly gay man with purple spiky hair and tight leather pants shrieked his giggles like a siren and dumped a copious amount of white powder down directly on the glass top of the low table set between the party's couches.

"Dmitri," Svetlana pouted. Her hand went to the mile-wide expanse of his chest. "You act like you don't remember me." Her chin came down, and her eyes looked up as she made coy into a seduction power play.

She was like a big-league power hitter, Klegg realized. Her

technique wasn't subtle; she'd either strike out completely or knock the ball out of the park. And like a high-paid baseball home-run specialist she'd knock more out of the park than she'd lose…until age and the drugs caught up with her.

Dmitri broke into an easy grin, his eyes trailing down her body like the laser guidance system of a jet fighter locking on to target. He replied in guttural, bass Russian, his chest rumbling like the engine of a Harley Davidson motorcycle.

"I remember you, Svetlana. That time in Moscow—" he began.

"We stayed up *all* night," she answered, and they laughed together.

Dmitri caught sight of Klegg standing behind her and his smile hardened. Catching the shift in him Svetlana put her hand on his chest again, drawing his attention back to her the way a tiger's eyes will follow a piece of raw meat in the hands of a circus trainer.

"How is he?" she asked. "Does he ever talk about me?" She sounded so sincere Klegg, who had planned the ruse with her, was almost fooled despite himself. Dmitri grinned knowingly and Klegg could see he had bought into the act completely.

"Of course, baby," the bodyguard purred. "Like anyone could ever forget you." He shrugged his shoulders and the effect was like seeing tectonic plates shift. "But you know how he is. Everything, all the time—it's hard to look back. Hard to keep track."

"Let me talk to him," she purred.

He started to shake his head no and she slid two crisp folded American hundred-dollar bills into his hand before he could speak. He made the money disappear and reached for the hook to the red rope strung between the stanchions in front of the short flight of stairs.

"Okay, 'Lana," he growled. "But just you. I don't know your boyfriend, and Milosevic doesn't want to make any new buddies."

He stared at Klegg as if daring him to argue.

Klegg said nothing. Everything was going according to plan. Svetlana reached up and kissed Dmitri quickly, leaving a lipstick mark so red on his pale skin it looked like a wound. Then she was up the stairs and being greeted like an old friend.

Klegg waited patiently, ignoring Dmitri's hard stare. He waited while Svetlana passed kisses of greetings all around and hugged Milosevic. She laughed at something he said, then helped herself to a line of the coke and a glass of the expensive champagne. Milosevic seemed generally happy to see her and, having spent time with the lady himself, Klegg could understand why.

After a few moments, once she was comfortably ensconced next to the Russian syndicate lawyer, he saw her lean in close, hand on Milosevic's thigh, and begin whispering in his ear.

Klegg, long attuned to these things, watched Milosevic's body language change. The smile, a social mask, stayed in place, but when his eyes cut away from Svetlana and down the stairs to Klegg they glittered like a snake's, sizing him up.

Klegg smiled slightly back in acknowledgment.

It was time to make his play. He was a six plus one.

CHAPTER FIVE

Stony Man Farm

The Bronco pulled out of the dirt road emerging from the orchard and came to a stop at the foot of the hill. Doors were kicked open and the five members of Phoenix Force emerged from the vehicle. Gary Manning unwrapped a protein bar and began eating it.

"Good God, Manning," Calvin James said. "Are you *always* eating?"

Still chewing, the massively muscled Manning looked at him and shrugged. "I'm in a bulking phase. I want to see how much weight I can put on and still keep my two-mile-run time under eleven and a half minutes."

"Christ," Rafael Encizo groused. "If you get any goddamn bigger we'll never get the helicopter off the ground."

"Then I'll just leap to the target in a single bound," Manning shot back.

Moments later a second SUV pulled up, this one containing Able Team and driven by John "Cowboy" Kissinger.

Kissinger had done time as a DEA agent before coming to work as armorer for the Stony Man operation. When it came to tactical equipment, firearms and explosives, he combined the creative insight of Akira Tokaido and the intense analytical skills of Professor Wethers.

McCarter took a sip of his coffee out of a cardboard cup and looked over at the armorer. Kissinger was laughing in response to something Hermann Schwarz was saying.

"Oh, Christ," the Briton muttered as Manning strolled up beside him. "Schwarz is telling jokes again."

The Canadian moaned in response as the two field teams converged. Schwarz kept right on talking, his eyes fairly dancing with delight as Carl Lyons, his favorite target for off-color humor, studiously ignored him.

"You think that's bad, Cowboy?" Schwarz asked Kissinger. "One time after we got our operational bonuses we went in on a cattle ranch."

"Oh, man," Calvin James muttered to T. J. Hawkins, "this is going to be awful."

"Usually," Hawkins agreed. Then, momentarily taken back by the outlandishness, he turned toward James. "Wait, *did* they invest in property?"

"The only property Lyons ever invested in was the stripper pole he put up in his condo," James replied.

"So we decide to buy this bull," Schwarz continued. "You know, to increase our stock."

"Please shut up," Lyons said, his voice dull with hopelessness. "Can't we just train?"

Schwarz continued as if he hadn't heard. "So I go over there and Carl is all down, really bummed, says the bull just eats grass all day and won't even look at the cows." Schwarz stopped talking long enough to cut his eyes over to the burly ex-LAPD detective. The man looked resigned and Schwarz's grin grew. "So I tell him to get a vet out quick to fix the problem. Two weeks later we get scrambled by Barb for a deployment."

"Where I wished you'd suffered a horrific wound to your mouth," Lyons added.

"And I ask Carl how things are going and he's happy as hell! 'The bull has taken care of all my cows, broke through the fence and has even serviced all the neighbor's cows!' I'm all like wow!" Schwarz laughed. "What the hell did the vet do to that bull? 'Just gave him some pills,' said Carl. So I'm like, what kind of pills? And Carl looks me straight in the eye—this is no bullshit—and says 'I don't know, but they sort of taste like peppermint.'"

Schwarz immediately began laughing at his own joke, folding almost in two with mirth as he guffawed. He looked up and saw the rest of the men from Stony looking at him with flat affects. "What?" he demanded. "He said 'they taste like peppermint!' See, he was *eating* the horny pills." Out in the long grass, crickets chirped. Schwarz frowned. "These are the jokes, people."

Rafael Encizo shook his head in pain. "You've got a real gift, man."

"Yeah, he's got a gift," Blancanales replied. "He's got such a gift Hal had to go to the freakin Oval Office to keep the CIA from stealing his jokes to use on the prisoners in Gitmo."

"Oh, man." McCarter shook his head. "If the ACLU thought sleep deprivation was torture they would have lost their minds if they'd ever heard Schwarz telling detainees jokes."

Schwarz stood, his face holding a shocked expression. "You know Jesus said a prophet is never revered in his own land. Now I know what he meant."

Kissinger burst out laughing in incredulous mirth. "Yeah, Hermann, whenever I think of Jesus I think of you, man." The armorer stepped forward, shaking his head. "How 'bout I show you guys why I brought you out here before Carl picks up Blancanales and beats you to death with him?"

"Sure." Schwarz shrugged. "I like new toys as much as the next electronics genius."

"You can see," Lyons observed, "he's as modest as he is funny."

"Please tell us what you brought," Manning begged Kissinger.

"Let me introduce you boys to a little bit of gear I appropriated from DARPA by way of our good friends at Lockheed Martin."

"Jet pack?" McCarter, a pilot, asked, only half joking.

"Close." Kissinger nodded and led the teams around to the rear of his SUV where he lowered the back hatch. "Exoskeletons."

"Exoskeletons?" Encizo asked.

Kissinger nodded. "Yep. Called HULC." He began handing out surprisingly compact packages. "We do the first trial out here on a few hill runs, then I had Hal go through Justice and get us some time at the Marine Corps obstacle course down in Quantico. We're going to put these mothers through a workout, then see if they'd be any use to you shooters out in the field."

Hawkins looked at his package. "They call it the Hulk?" he asked.

"No," Kissinger replied. "Not the Hulk, but HULC, or Human Universal Load Carrier. Just stretch out the legs, then step into the open foot pads. Secure the straps at thighs, waist and shoulders. Supposedly they've got it spec'ed out for two hundred pounds at a top speed of ten miles per hour. But you're supposed to be able to crawl, jump, kneel, squat in it."

"How does it work?" Schwarz asked, all humor gone as the prospect of new tech was put in front of him.

"Four lithium-ion batteries go into that pouch at the small of your back. They power sensors in the footpads, the microprocessors that read them and move the hydraulic system."

Lyons frowned while the others began putting on their units. "How quick can we unass 'em if we need to?"

"Once you get the hang of it, the contractor told me under thirty seconds," Kissinger replied.

"Oh, that's good," Schwarz said. He began doing deep knee bends in his combat apparatus. "You see, since he took that medicine I told you about, Ironman's been real, real concerned with getting his clothes off in a hurry."

"You got one of these things with a dog muzzle?" Lyons asked. "That could help me out."

"I'll see what the boys at DARPA have to say." Kissinger nodded.

The Stony Man tactical teams secured themselves into the exoskeletons and began warming up the gear. First they paired up and ran a series of sprints up the hill. There was no improved performance, but the HULC tactical system provided surprisingly little hindrance to their speeds.

"What's DARPA tell you so far, Cowboy?" Manning asked. "It look like Lockheed is going to get the contract?"

Kissinger nodded. "Yep, the boys at JSOC loved 'em. They're talking that if the test results hold up, they'll go beyond Rangers and maybe deploy them to general infantry units in the Marines and Army."

Kissinger lowered the rear gate of the SUV where he had loaded a pallet with training weapons and prepacked rucksacks filled with sandbags. "Let's start loading you supermen up and see what these bad boys can really do."

Farmhouse

BARBARA PRICE SAT in the kitchen of the old farmhouse and slowly drank a cup of coffee. In front of her she had a stack of satellite images, an encrypted Kindle DX and a PowerBook logged into A-Space.

A-Space, or Analytic Space, was a social networking and common collaborative workspace for all the members of the USIC, or United States Intelligence Community.

The Stony Man mission controller was using the site to search through the Library of National Intelligence for seemingly unrelated links that formed a pattern.

As a dedicated part of her counterintelligence security measures, Kurtzman's cybernetic team had been tasked with searching the browser on a rotating basis, making sure no evidence, concrete or oblique, about Stony Man Farm made it onto the site.

Once upon a time in America, great firewalls of competition and compartmentalization mindsets had kept the disparate fiefdoms of the USIC separate from each other. In those days Stony Man Farm had been the main off-the-books weapon of choice by the Executive Branch looking to battle terrorism.

Post 9/11 many things had changed in America. Compartmentalization had gone out of vogue with a vengeance. Other "tip of the spear" organizations like the Joint Special Operations Command and the CIA's Special Activities Division had seen themselves refocused into areas traditionally deemed off the books and thus the province of Stony Man.

Also intelligence activity oversight committees in the House and Senate had started looking into corners and under rocks that before had remained unmolested. Several high-profile scandals had already rocked the espionage and military communities.

All of those would seem like the high jinks of a naughty PTA president in comparison if the full scope of Stony Man's operation ever came to light.

The list was endless: extrajudicial killings of foreign nationals and American citizens; violations of federal, state and local laws and statues by the truckload; operations conceived, designed and executed in full and complete violation of the Posse Commitatus Act; war crimes as defined by the Geneva Convention and Uniformed Code of Military Justice. The list stretched out and led up the chain of command all the way to the Oval Office.

Theoretically at least, in several ways the Stony Man operation was many a U.S. lawmaker's and citizen's ultimate big brother nightmare. In practicality it was the best defense the nation had ever instituted.

In theory, Price thought wryly of the old axiom, theory and practice were the same. In practice they never are.

She dialed down the Kindle DX screen, scrolling through the digital display of the after-action report CIA interrogators at a black site camp on the island of Diego Garcia had sent back. It continued the results of the interrogation of the North Korean, Sin-Bok.

Most of the information was unspectacular. The agent hadn't been taken as an investigation tool but rather as a behind-the-scenes warning to Kim Jong-il to not play his brand of lunatic hardball in the Western Hemisphere.

However, something odd had caught Price's eye. While under a modest dose of sodium thiopenal and slight measures of the euphoric agent lysergic acid diethylamide, the North Korean had babbled merrily on but his answers had been incoherent, often shifting from language to language and even into the random, including rattling off simple mathematical problems.

"'Three plus four. I'm three plus four,'" Price quoted to herself.

It was abnormal even for a person tripping on LSD. She leaned back in her chair and smelled the fresh air of the Blue Ridge Mountains. She picked up her Montblanc pen, a gift from Hal Brognola, and tapped her chin in a reflexive motion.

On a whim she typed "three plus four" into the search option on A-Space. Found nothing. She shrugged. It had been a wild shot anyway. Perhaps Hunt or Akira could...

"Stupid!" She laughed suddenly.

Leaning forward, she put her pen down with a click next to her ceramic mug of coffee. The keys on the PowerBook tapped rapidly as she typed in the word and hit Enter: "Seven."

CHAPTER SIX

Kiev, Ukraine

Klegg sat. He didn't offer to shake hands. Milosevic regarded him with a reptile stare, eyes bloodshot. He watched as the American set the attaché case carefully between them.

Milosevic cocked an eyebrow in question. Klegg smiled slightly and held his hands out in a welcoming gesture. Beside him on the couch Svetlana was completely ignoring him now that her job was done.

She giggled madly as another girl in a brilliant couture dress pulled out a water bong of thin-cut crystal and splashed vodka from a bottle out of an ice bucket into the main chamber. The entourage around them chattered in Russian under the watchful eyes of Milosevic's bodyguards.

Kiev made Klegg think of what Dodge City had been like during the cattle days or San Francisco during the gold rush; a wide-open frontier town where the law didn't apply to anyone with money.

Beside him another loose pile of cocaine was casually split across the table as a laughing twentysomething with dragon tattoos on his scrawny arms and a diamond stud in his nose opened a velvet drawstring pouch and dropped buds of deep green colored marijuana into the mix.

"I'm supposed to ask what you want, I know," Milosevic said in English. "But I don't like playing twenty questions."

"Twenty-two pounds," Klegg supplied for him.

"Twenty-two pounds?"

"Twenty-two pounds," Klegg confirmed.

"For what?"

"Call it earnest money, for a conversation."

"Which conversation?"

"The one we're about to have."

"Why would you bring me twenty-two pounds to have a conversation? This conversation—" Milosevic leaned forward "—which is starting to become ludicrous."

Twenty-two pounds was the exact weight of one million dollars in one-hundred-dollar bills.

Beside Klegg, Svetlana had taken a fat, sticky bud and coated it liberally with powdered cocaine and then thumbed it into the bowl of the vodka-filled bong. The giggling mad man with the nose diamond provided a pocket lighter that seemed closer to a butane torch, and the coven huddled around the implement.

"There's nothing ludicrous here," Klegg assured him, not without a sense of irony. "I'm giving you that money to listen to my proposal. To consider it seriously. If you say no to what I'm suggesting, fine—you take the money and we part on good terms. But I'm not here to talk real estate or banking or oil futures out of Chechnya."

Milosevic snapped his fingers and settled back in his lounge chair. The music in the club was deafening but the ballistic plastic surrounding the deck landing muted the sound to a tolerable level.

A muscle-heavy thug with a crew cut and fifty-five-inch chest bent down and picked up Klegg's briefcase. Beside him Svetlana coughed and a cloud of cocaine-laced marijuana smoke rolled out like smog from a chimney. Immediately, Klegg felt light-headed and he instantly wondered if that wasn't part of Milosevic's plan.

"Talk," the ex-KGB operative said. "You have purchased five minutes in which to interest me." He lit a cigar. "Frankly, I don't expect you to succeed."

"I came here on certain assumptions."

"Dangerous."

"It can be," Klegg conceded. "But risk preempts reward. For example…six plus one equals seven."

The Russian made a face. If he was surprised he didn't show it. "Just as five plus two equals seven," he replied.

"Even my assumptions are grounded in certain…continuities," Klegg smiled.

Milosevic waved his free hand in a "come on" gesture. Svetlana passed the bong to the girl in the red couture dress.

"The first assumption," Klegg continued, "is that you retained your contacts from your time in a KGB station house in eastern Africa. That you could, if properly motivated, reach out and reactivate stringers, cells and networks across the region."

"You must have these kinds of contacts among your own community," Milosevic countered. "Why come to Ukraine to get what you could get in London or New York?"

On the couches the entourage exploded into laughter and applause as Svetlana and the girl in the red dress began making out.

"Because," Klegg said slowly, "I need contractors and operatives who don't mind pulling down on Westerners. I want businessmen, not ideology. For that, it was come here or go to Palermo."

"Rio, Caracas," the Russian offered. "Even Uruguay."

"I go to the cartels, I might as well go to the fucking monkey house at the zoo." Klegg paused. "Though for what I have in mind, an outer circle of cannon fodder might be appropriate, given an inner cadre capable of dealing with them afterward."

"A fixer who exercises total unit closure on his field talent tends to have an abbreviated career," Milosevic countered.

"You'll land on your feet, I'm sure."

Milosevic released cigar smoke in a huge plume and settled back comfortably in his chair. His eyes cut over to where

Svetlana was making out with the girl from his entourage. The Russian oligarch looked back at Klegg.

"You start tying up loose ends, it can sometimes be hard to know when to stop."

Now it was Klegg's turn to shrug. "Tie up the knots that can't tie you back. Call it acceptable."

Like a scene out of *Faust,* Milosevic leaned forward and extended his hand.

IT WAS COLD in the alley outside the Kiev nightclub.

Klegg's and Svetlana's breath plumed up between them as they kissed furiously. The American plunged his hands inside the woman's ankle-length fur coat. Her eyes were glassy marbles as they kissed. He ran his hands over her body underneath her coat, stroking her up to a fever pitch of excitement.

She moaned as his fingers worked at her.

The back door to the nightclub was just a few yards away and the muted sound of the dance beat music rattled the blacked-out windows in their frames. The alley smelled strongly of the urine of drunk and stoned patrons. Garbage overflowed out of battered old cans and three giant green bins.

Rats, braving the frigid chill to get the remnants of greasy food, swarmed across the refuse and watched the humans with glittering eyes.

Though thousands of citizens of Kiev went about their lives within little distance of couple, it was as if they were alone in a vast, urban wasteland of empty windows, rubbish and deep shadows. It called to Klegg's mind the poem *The Waste Land* by T. S. Eliot.

"I'll show you fear in a handful of dust," the lawyer thought idly. It made no sense but his mind was starting to click with adrenaline.

"Now," Svetlana whispered in his ears. "I want it now."

"Now?" Klegg asked, his heart starting to beat even faster.

"Yes, yes," she breathed.

"Okay." He laughed. "But remember, you asked for it."

The American psychopath stepped back from the Russian woman, leaving her gasping. Her glassy, red-veined eyes opened in confusion.

Klegg grinned like a maniacal clown.

His hands went to the small of his back underneath his coat. He emerged with a pair of nunchaku.

The martial-arts weapon was designed from the width of a single, slightly thicker than average handle cut smoothly down the middle, allowing for more compact and thus easier surreptitious carrying. The handles on the thicker edges were octagonal, presenting a variety of sharp edges for contact when swung.

"My favorite movie when I was growing up was *Enter the Dragon*," Klegg explained, speaking fast as his breath continued coming harder and faster. "Nylon cord and teak wood. I walked right through airport security with this."

He assumed the rear defense stance. Dramatic, almost cinematic in nature, with most of his weight resting on his outstretched forward leg while his torso was held back, arms up, nunchaku held along the outside of his right arm.

"W-what?" Confusion. The beginnings of fear.

"I'm not going to lie," Klegg snorted. "I like this weapon 'cause it's so fancy. Does a lot for my self-esteem."

He exploded into motion, whipping the segmented clubs around through an intricate pattern of moves: reverse shoulder swing into a figure-eight swing, down into an underarm grip.

He was grinning so wildly now his smile threatened to split his face. He forcefully exhaled and performed a cross-back swing too fast for the eye to follow, and Svetlana, at last understanding what was about to happen, opened her mouth to scream.

The end of the nunchaku whipped around and slapped the woman across the jaw. Her head snapped to the side and her scream was cut short by the impact. Blood painted the dirty snow in stripes of scarlet. She stumbled back, long heels sliding on the icy ground, only the alley wall keeping her up.

Klegg, eyes burning, moved in, the nunchaku cycloning through its figure-eight pattern. He struck her again, then caught the stick under his arm on the rebound. Her head snapped back and this time teeth flew like tumbling dice.

She sagged to her knees and her ruined face poured blood out in a hot, sticky puddle beneath her.

Klegg lashed out again and again. His skill was not simply that of a choreographed dancer; he could swing the arcane weapon with deadly force. The teakwood handle made sickening crunching sounds like cracking ice as it slapped into Svetlana's skull and jaws over and over.

Blood splatter painted the walls, painted the ground, soaked the woman until her face was a mask of it. She couldn't find the strength to scream, couldn't drag in enough air to cry out before she was struck again.

She could only whimper.

Klegg's smile was a horrible rictus on his gleaming face. His breath came in short, hard pants like a man having sex. The concussive shock of each blow traveled back up his arm with each strike.

Finally one of the octagonal edges of the striking club caught the ravaged woman a glancing blow along her temple and she was knocked unconscious. She sagged face-first to the ground, still as a slaughtered carcass. Klegg struck the back of her head two hard snaps and more blood matted her once silky hair.

Gasping for breath, he moved around behind her and took each side of the nunchaku in an underhand grip. He bent and looped the nylon cord under her chin then twisted. He twisted until he felt her larynx crumple like an empty soda can under his heel and he rose, dropping the weapon to lie beside Svetlana's rapidly cooling corpse.

He took off his gloves and ran a hand through his hair. He

straightened and smoothed his overcoat. He reached down and adjusted his still prominent erection in his slacks.

Without hurry he lit a cigarette and blew smoke out in twin streams from his nostrils. Slowly his heart slowed and his breathing calmed. His erection began to fade.

He smoked half the cigarette down, then dropped it to the ground. It landed in a sludgy pool of snow and blood, instantly extinguished.

He turned and walked calmly from the alley to hail a taxicab. He had no fear of the police. Kiev was a wide-open, dirty city and he was under the protection of Milosevic, the biggest villain of them all.

Things were working out just right, he decided.

Stony Man Farm

BARBARA PRICE sat at her desk in the Annex.

She had three computer screens open in front of her, each with a spreadsheet showing expenditures for separate areas of the Stony Man operation. She had itemized ledgers for the armory, for Transportation and for Buck Greene's security projects. Requisition forms for jet fuel alone were enough to make clerks from the Governmental Accountability Office gray with shock.

Price looked at the tally and shook her head as she typed in her authorization code.

The public was always in some outcry about thousand-dollar hammers or eight-hundred-dollar toilet seats. The truth was the number crunchers at the GAO would never have made such oversights. Those inflated purchase orders were designed to hide covert-action expenditures for clandestine units and projects just like Stony Man.

There was a knock on the office door and she looked up. Carmen Delahunt stood in the entrance, a tired look on her face and a manila file folder in her hand.

"Got a second?" the redhead asked.

Price pushed herself back from her desk. "Sure," she said. "What've you got?"

"Multiples of Seven."

"Really?" Price arced an eyebrow.

Delahunt entered the room and took a seat across from Price at the desk. She laid out her folder showing several computer printings and a couple of glossy jpg enlargements.

Delahunt began leafing through them, talking fast, the way she always did when she was onto something.

"I started cross indexing intelligence estimates and after-action reports like you'd asked," she explained. "Looking to see if anything relating to Seven came up."

"You found something?"

"I found a motherlode, Barb. I've got Seven cross-indexing things going back *decades*. Some of it can't be related—the search is too broad, but you've tapped into some kind of thread here. Pieces from a thousand different puzzles that nobody realized they were even supposed to be looking at."

Price leaned forward, caught up in her enthusiasm. She reached across the desk and pulled a codex Delahunt had printed up. Her vision swam as she saw some of the events and people highlighted.

Kabul urban police. Princess Diana. Baghdad Green Zone. Kiev. Israel, 1968. CERN. The Vatican. Charles Lindberg. Hangar 21. White Sands, New Mexico. Ho Chi Minh City. Aldrich Ames. There was such a collage of information it was impossible to make sense of.

The list went on.

"As interesting as these initial surveys are, they're basically cold cases," Delahunt continued. "Some much less cold than others, but for now, cold cases." She paused. "Except for this."

Price looked up from the codex. "What?"

"Canada." Delahunt slid a paper-clipped report to Price. "Toronto."

"Give me the through line."

"Our Department of Energy runs a contract research facility there. Ostensibly to study alternative fuels. Green tech, stuff like that. From what I've gathered, though, much of the science is a little more experimental. A little more theoretical."

"And?"

"And the DOE put in a request to the FBI last week to conduct a counterintelligence operation on the facility as internal security had started reporting recruitment approaches being made on their employees by unknown operatives looking to do pay-for-play deals. Also, electronic countermeasures had been tripped in the last forty-eight hours indicating someone was doing a hostile analysis of their hard site security."

"Standard Bureau stuff." Price nodded. "Could be anyone looking to see what goodies are being cooked up. Hell, it could be industrial even, not political."

Delahunt nodded. "Still could be. Nothing's been proven. However the FBI team they sent to Toronto managed to catch a glimpse of someone seen surveying the employee entrance."

"Custody?"

"No." Delahunt shook her head. "This wasn't a joint op with the Canadians. They took his photo and requested RCMP help with digital analog forensics."

"They ID the guy?"

"Sure. Man named Jen Duh sh Tyen Tsai."

"If Schwarz were here you'd know he'd say—"

"Gesundheit," Delahunt agreed. "He's a funny man that Hermann."

"Yeah, but looks aren't everything."

"You got that from him, didn't you?"

Price took a sip of coffee and shrugged. "Sometimes he's funny. Mostly he's just funny 'cause he's trying to be funny and fails." She set the mug of coffee down. "But surely Mr. What's-his-name doesn't go by that handle."

"Mostly just Jen."

"What do we know about him?"

"We know he's in Toronto. We know he's a sort of free agent between Chinese Tong running underworld activities there. Part courier, part outside hit man, part information broker."

"So a criminal mercenary with connections to Chinese syndicates is running a surveillance operation on a DOE private contractor facility. And you tied him in to Seven how?"

"Look at his sleeve." Delahunt gestured toward a RCMP file photo. "His left arm, inside, above the elbow."

A "sleeve" was a slang term used by tattoo enthusiasts to indicate an arm that was entirely covered by ink designs from deltoid to wrist. Jen Tsai's was covered in swirling images of Chinese characters, mythological demons and iconography in bold reds, blues, yellows and black.

"Where? I don't see…" Price trailed off as she scrutinized the photo. "Ah."

Just above Jen Tsai's elbow was a horned demon skull, screaming mouth lined with fangs. Flames swirled inside the gaping jaws, and in the center of the flames were the numerals 1+6=7.

"Yeah," Delahunt agreed. "Little odd for a hardcore Chinese gangster to be sporting primary arithmetic in his colors, no?"

"Oh, yes," Price answered.

"We have his probable twenty?"

"We most certainly do."

Price picked up her coffee mug. "Good. I'll call Hal have him pull the Bureau boys off surveillance. Then I'll send Able Team around to knock on some doors."

"Knowing Ironman, it'll be heads that get knocked more than doors."

Price shrugged. "Whatever…"

CHAPTER SEVEN

Toronto, Canada

Regent Park, 3:00 a.m., the streets were quiet.

From behind the wheel of the black Excursion SUV, Carl Lyons surveyed the neighborhood. The vehicle had been waiting for them at the airport.

Lyons watched the streets with the cynical, jaundiced eye of a veteran cop.

Regent Park's reputation preceded it. Fifty percent of the people living in the urban area were teenagers and sixty-eight percent of all the people there were settled in well below the national poverty rate for the rest of Canada.

With poverty, the lack of aspiration, and the loss of hope came crime and most often violent crime. Regent Park was a tough neighborhood not unlike any other bad neighborhood in any other First World country. It wasn't Islamabad or Caracas, but it could still kill you.

"Keep an eye out for gangbangers working as sentries for drug dealers," Lyons muttered.

"This isn't my first rodeo, *Hefei,*" Blancanales reminded him.

Lyons grunted and turned down Queen Street East. In the back Schwarz was using his CPDA to run a more sophisticated GPS unit than the one that had come with the big Excursion. The CPDA he had begun using was a SME PED, or Secure Mobile Environment Portable Electronic Device.

Barbara Price had managed to secure a crate of the high-end

encrypted devices from her old bosses in the Puzzle Palace, the National Security Agency.

"You notice some bastards have torn down all the street markers?" Schwarz observed.

"So police have a hard time responding to incidents or giving their location for backup," Lyons said.

"Hey," Schwarz replied in his best faux-Hispanic accent, "this ain't my first rodeo, *Hefei*."

"You guys are assholes."

Schwarz leaned forward and nudged Blancanales on his shoulder. When the ex-Green Beret turned he saw Schwarz grinning madly, hand up to his ear as he mimicked holding a phone.

"Bring-bring." Schwarz giggled, then made his voice deep. "Kettle? Yes, this is Pot, um, you're black."

"I'm an asshole?" Lyons snapped. "*I'm* an asshole? On what grounds?"

"On the account of your warm and overly gregarious people skills." Blancanales laughed.

"Hey," Lyons snarled. "Some people are like Slinkies, not really good for anything…but they still bring a smile to your face when you push them down a flight of stairs."

Outside the vehicle rows of dingy brick buildings from the Toronto Community Housing Corporation slid by in uniform ranks.

The city planners had originally visualized Regent Park as a transitional community, and it was Canada's largest experiment with a social housing project where people on social assistance could find affordable housing until their circumstances improved.

That had turned out to be very few and the population had stagnated, then grown. Eventually it had also become an immigrant community neighborhood. Into this melting pot of urban squalor Jen Tsai had moved, establishing links with local street gangs and building a safe haven for himself.

Lyons turned onto Parliament Street and began driving north in the general direction of the more upscale, historical Cabbagetown.

"There," he said. "On the right is Regent Park—that's our primary landmark. See what the GPS is saying."

"Already on it," Schwarz acknowledged.

"Circle the tenement when we get there," Blancanales said. "We'll finish the three-sixty survey then I, not being so *muy blanco,* can hop out and cover the back door."

"Hey," Lyons said, "this isn't my first rodeo."

"Everyone's a comedian in this crew." Schwarz spoke up. Then he said, "There. On the right, facing the park, that's our building."

"Let me swing around back," Lyons said. "You got anything on the police scanner?"

"Negative," Schwarz replied. "I got one domestic-disturbance call as we rolled in but after that nothing."

"There we go," Blancanales said.

The Able Team warrior looked out their windows and into Regent Park.

A group of African-Canadian youths stood beside a children's playground. They were dressed in typical hip-hop regalia and with openly hostile looks watched the SUV as it cruised slowly past.

The clique that ran Regent Park, and the one with whom Jen Tsai now made his deals, according to RCMP records, was the PBS, or the Point Blank Souljahs, the remnants of a much more powerful organization called the Regent Park Crew that had controlled cocaine traffic in the 1980s and '90s and was now defunct.

"Good thing our windows are blacked out," Schwarz said. "Or those Souljahs would think we were cops."

"As it is now," Blancanales pointed out drily, "they might decide we're an enemy crew on a drive-by mission."

"Then they wouldn't be far wrong, would they?" Lyons grunted.

"Not really," Blancanales agreed. "You want me to contact Wethers now?"

"Yeah, bring him up." Lyons nodded. "Schwarz, you got the shotgun mike ready?"

"I'm on it like Blue Bonnet."

Lyons nodded to Blancanales, who spoke into his own SME PED. "Able to Stony Bird," he said, initiating contact.

"Copy," Wethers answered immediately. "I have you up on my video display. I see your twenty."

The camera feed to the video display Professor Wethers referred to was mounted into the nose of an RQ-7 Shadow, a light, compact tactical Unmanned Aerial Vehicle. Only thirty-six feet long and boasting a fourteen-foot wingspan with a weight of 375 pounds, the UAV was much smaller than its larger cousins, the MQ-9 and MQ-1 Reapers.

Able Team had launched the vehicle from a portable launcher they'd mounted on the roof of their SUV from the top of a deserted commercial parking garage. With a flight endurance of six hours, a sixty-eight-mile range and service ceiling of fifteen thousand feet, it was exactly the kind of tool they needed for the low-profile urban operation.

"Go ahead and give our boy Jen a call," Schwarz said. "I'm up."

Lyons and Schwarz cued up their headsets while Blancanales used his SME PED to dial Stony Man Farm. Waiting at a com station just outside the remote pilot setup Wethers ran the RQ-7 from, Kurtzman took the incoming call and shuffled it through his system to make it anonymous before routing it back to Toronto.

After three rings Jen Tsai answered. "Hello?" he said in English.

Blancanales lifted his arm and gave Schwarz a thumbs-up.

Lyons subvocalized into his throat mike to Wethers. "We're

on. Start triangulation." Behind them Schwarz powered down the back window and pointed a compact directional mike at the building housing the Chinese gangster.

"Hello?" Tsai repeated, this time sounding pissed off.

"You fucked up the job on the lab," Blancanales said. At Stony Man, Kurtzman was feeding his voice through a distorter so that it came out deep and gravelly. "You got made by Mounties." He paused then added, "Seven is not pleased."

"It's not over yet!" Tsai shouted into the phone. "I can handle the cops here. I'm still going to get an in."

"No denial, right to defensive begging, nice," Lyons murmured into his throat mike.

"We're getting everything," Kurtzman assured him.

"Excuses don't cut it," Blancanales said.

Behind him Schwarz looked down at the scrolling screen of his SME PED.

The signal from Jen Tsai's phone was shown against a 3-D structural blueprint of the public housing building as it was triangulated between Schwarz's parabolic mike and the sensory instruments in the nose of the RQ-7 Shadow controlled by Wethers.

There was a pause after Blancanales's admonishment.

For several tense seconds the conversation was still. Lyons looked in his side mirror and immediately sat up. Approaching the idling SUV were four of the gang members they'd passed earlier. The gangsters' hands were stuffed deep into the pockets of their hooded pullover sweatshirts.

Lyons swore softly; he knew what was happening immediately. The Point Blank Souljahs crew had noticed an unidentified SUV with blacked-out windows rolling slowly through disputed drug territory then parking in front of their housing unit.

They were coming to kill trespassers and once they got a good look at Able Team the lead would start flying all the sooner.

On the phone Tsai suddenly spoke again, voice rich with suspicion. "One plus six."

Blancanales turned and looked at Lyons, then back over his shoulder at Schwarz, hand up and face questioning. "What do I say?" he mouthed silently.

Lyons cut his eyes back to the approaching gangsters. He saw the leader produce a TEC-9 machine pistol. He turned back toward Blancanales and pulled out his silenced Beretta 92 with extended magazine.

"One plus six!" Tsai barked into the phone.

"Fuck it!" Lyons snarled. "Hang up, we'll roll hot. I'm tired of all this goddamn sneaking around anyway."

"We just got here!" Schwarz protested.

"Hurry up," Blancanales answered him. He caught sight of the approaching gangsters in the rearview mirror and snapped his cell phone shut, cutting off the angry Tsai. "If you don't move fast, Schwarz, then Ironman is going to kill all the good ones."

Stony Man Farm

BARBARA PRICE, hair still damp from her shower, finished dressing.

She was in the bedroom of the farmhouse where she kept toiletries and clothing for the times she spent overnight at Stony Man. Most weeks she spent more time sleeping here than she did at her D.C. town house.

The shower in the room's bathroom was running as Mack Bolan rinsed off. He'd just returned from somewhere, doing something—Price had no idea what.

He'd smelled like gunpowder and had blood under his nails. The past half hour had been stolen moments, but stolen moments were the only moments the casual couple got.

She thought idly about perhaps stripping down again and

joining him in the shower. What was another fifteen minutes if she was in a stealing mood?

The push-talk application on her SME PED broke squelch and she heard Kurtzman's gruff voice call out to her from across the Farm in the Annex.

"You on, Barb?" the leader of the cyberteam asked.

Price sighed and rose off the rumpled bed. She felt a pang at the missed opportunity but by the time she reached the phone the feeling was gone. With practiced self-discipline she slammed her shields down, brought her discipline up and become once again mission controller.

"Go ahead, Bear."

"Barb, Carmen has pulled something out possibly relating to Seven. I think you should take a look."

"Copy. I'm en route to your twenty now."

"I'll have the coffee ready."

"Don't threaten me, Bear."

Price turned to look in the mirror over the dresser and pushed a stray strand of her blond hair behind an ear. Pieces of the puzzle were starting to come together. Whoever this Seven was, Price could tell she was starting to get their scent in her nose now.

It's only a matter of time, she thought. She left the room, mind completely absorbed in the problem now.

Bolan would figure out something had come up easily enough.

CHAPTER EIGHT

"What did you find?" Price asked.

The Annex was a flurry of activity. Akira Tokaido's desk area looked as if a bomb had gone off. Red Bull cans and Snickers candy bar wrappers lay cast around like spillover from a landfill. His fingers hammered his keyboards while the Smiths cranked out of the earbuds of his iPod.

"I found more cases of Seven," Delahunt said. "Bear is setting up the display right now."

Across the room Kurtzman was plugging a flash drive into a media presentation station connected to a large flat-screen monitor set on the wall. The screen saver showed the actor Mel Gibson in his costume from the *Road Warrior.*

"How recent?" Price asked.

"I found some interesting links to both our old MERGE and TRIO operations, but that's old, though it does raise all sorts of questions."

MERGE had been a criminal network consisting of elements from the Mexican mafia, Corsican crime families and Colombian cartels. TRIO had proved to be an Asian counterpart to MERGE, formed by Chinese, Japanese and Mongolian organizations.

"Seven was behind both those unifications?" Price sounded incredulous. "That kind of global influence is insane."

"It's not definitive," Delahunt admitted. "But now that I know what to look for, I'm linking things together that have no business being connected. It's like a conspiracy theorist's wet dream."

"Ready," Kurtzman announced.

The women turned toward the display screen.

A line of bodies lay in sequence on a green tarp. The corpses were bullet riddled and all black male adults. Standing around them were five Caucasian men in desert camouflage stripped of rank and identification, all holding American weapons.

Price didn't recognize the men but she saw one was holding a Stoner M-63 light machine gun. "SEALs?" she asked.

"Yep, DevGru," Kurtzman replied, using the shorthand for the unit that had replaced the legendary SEAL Team 6. "In Somalia, last year. Tag-and-bag mission of al Qaeda in Africa. Major communication node and his team of bodyguards."

"What am I looking for?"

"There," Delahunt said. "On the one with gray hair, the leader. Bear, blow up his left clavicle."

Kurtzman grunted and worked the control pad on his automated wheelchair. A mouse drew a box around the indicated area, then blew up the resolution. A series of stars about the size of a dime were tattooed in blue ink.

"You said these guys are AQ in A?" Price frowned. "I thought Muslims weren't big on tattoos."

"Exactly," Delahunt agreed. "Bear, go ahead and rotate the picture, if you'd be so kind."

Kurtzman muttered something about "being the boss" and used his mouse to rotate the image.

"Oh," Price said. Her voice had a toneless finality about it. "Scramble David's boys. Tell 'em they're getting an all-expense-paid vacation to sunny, tropical Africa, courtesy of Aunt Barb and Uncle Sam."

The star tattoos formed a distinct icon: 7

DAVID MCCARTER EASED the yoke of the Cessna down and leveled the plane out. He began running down his checklist of readings before recalculating his flight plan and finally setting the autopilot.

Out through the windows of the twin-engine prop the Atlantic was a deeper blue reflection of the crystal-clear night sky. Behind the plane Martha's Vineyard fell away and McCarter had the nose of the plane pointed on a direct azimuth to the lights of Atlantic City, an easy hop.

"The view is beautiful," Lisa said.

McCarter turned and looked at the chief aide to the current congressional whip. She was a stunning redhead with wide, clear blue eyes. She was dressed in pearls and a little black dress that showed her assets at their most advantageous.

"Yes, it is," McCarter agreed.

She looked over and saw him staring at her. She laughed unselfconsciously at the old line. Timing was often more important than originality.

"You're bad," she teased, comfortable with the game they were playing.

They had just come from dinner at the exclusive Thorncroft Inn on the Vineyard and were on their way to a penthouse suite and night of gambling at the Trump Taj Mahal.

McCarter smiled wickedly.

His eyes traveled to the deep line of her cleavage. For about the millionth time he thanked God for his British accent. He eased back in his pilot seat and lifted his hands off the controls.

"Look," he said. "It flies itself, no hands."

"Very impressive." Lisa's eyes sparkled mischievously. "Let's see what I can do without hands."

"Oh, yes, let's." McCarter nodded.

Just as the sultry redhead leaned over to kiss him, his phone rang.

"No," he moaned.

His phone was off. There was only one signal capable of turning it on. It was the Farm.

Lisa looked at him as he grabbed the phone. "You're not going to take that, are you?" she snapped, clearly offended.

"Sorry, luv." He grinned weakly. "Saying no is not an option."

"It is for me," she replied.

RAFAEL ENCIZO SPOKE LOUDLY into his headset.

"Taste it! How does it taste? Taste it!"

On the wall-mounted big screen his Madden '11 avatar of Tony Romo released a long perfect spiral half a second before a Denver Broncos defensive back smashed into him like a runaway freight train.

Encizo was up off the couch cushions as the game's POV camera shifted smoothly, focusing in on the tightly spiraling football. Deftly, Encizo clicked onto his pass receiver and manipulated his POV to catch the ball.

Two Bronco cornerbacks converged on his receiver. Adrenaline flooded his system and his focus narrowed as he stayed in the pocket. He was going to get hit but he was going to catch the ball.

The SME PED in his shirt pocket shrieked to life.

"No!" Encizo roared.

His arms jerked in surprise and he jumped up, knocking his Boston lager beer bottle and a plate of nachos over onto the hardwood of his houseboat's floor. His thumb jerked and on the screen his receiver fumbled the pass. The player was hit by a cornerback and sent spinning. The ball was up and tumbling in the air.

The SME PED rang again.

Maria, his neighbor down the dock and sometime paramour, came rushing into the room still wet from the shower. He had taken her diving today, introducing her to the use of all the scuba equipment now piled in the corner. He'd held rather high hopes about how she was going to return the favor.

On the screen the Bronco defender snatched the loose ball and began running.

"Jesus Christ," Encizo moaned, and ripped the plug on his internet connection. He couldn't bear to watch.

The secured cell phone rang a third time and he waved Maria back as he answered.

"Go for Encizo." He sighed.

THOMAS JEFFERSON HAWKINS sat in his apartment.

The wide-open loft had the feel of a training hall. A weight set with a bench sat in one corner across the floor from his fifty-four-inch TV. Next to the weights he had hung a heavy bag.

Ignoring the show on the big screen, he hopped up and began pacing back and forth. He glanced at the silent SME PED sitting in the center of his coffee table.

He walked over to the heavy bag and slapped out a series of Thai kickboxing-style low kicks for a three-minute sprint round, then settled under the 225 pounds on the bench press and cranked out an easy fifteen reps.

He hopped up and looked at his phone. It hadn't moved.

He sighed, then walked toward where he'd set up his kitchen on the open floor plan. Opening the refrigerator, he pulled out a half-gallon carton of milk and drank it down. He tossed the carton in the trash and walked over to his kitchen table.

There was an M-1911 A1 sitting next to a *Maxim* magazine with Megan Fox on the cover. Lost in thought, he quickly disassembled then reassembled the pistol by touch while he read a tech article on how to wire his stereo system for surround sound.

He looked at the encrypted phone.

He hit the bag for another three-minute session, then cleaned up and overhead pressed the weight on his bench press barbell for five easy reps. He cocked an eye at the phone. It sat like the Sphinx.

"Screw it," he said.

He grabbed a bottle of Longhorn beer and knocked the cap

off. Taking a long swig, he wandered over and flopped down on the black leather couch. He took a long pull off the beer and reached for the television remote.

The phone rang.

"Works every time." He grinned.

GARY MANNING DRUMMED his fingers on the table with one hand. With the other he ate a banana.

Behind him floor-to-ceiling windows showed the skyline of Washington, D.C. The conference room was nearly empty. Other than the beautiful blonde sitting next to him, they were alone.

She turned, saw him eating and smiled before shaking her head. "You just ate!" she mouthed silently. Manning shrugged and threw the peel in a wastepaper basket.

A video monitor on the wall in front of them had been divided into six separate screens, each one showing the active vice-president of each of the major divisions of North American Plastics, for whom Manning was a security consultant. Frequent and persistent attempts to steal technology or sabotage international facilities were an occupational hazard, and Manning's expertise was highly valued.

"There has been a sustained campaign to discredit our international image," one of the VPs stated.

Manning glanced over at the woman sitting next to him. Her name was Rachael Sinclair and she was a recent arrival at the corporation.

She peered over her fashionable glasses at the information on the table in front of her. She looked up, caught Manning's gaze and shook her head. She reached out and gently wiped the side of his mouth.

She looked back down, circling an errant number with a red pen as the VP talked on. Manning suddenly felt as if he'd just stepped out of the door of an aircraft at thirty-thousand feet.

His heart hammered as adrenaline flooded his system and his neck grew red under the collar of his button-down shirt.

Just like that, he decided. He was going to do it. Tonight, as soon as the VPs were done with their security updates.

Inside the pocket of his tailored slacks he felt his SME PED vibrate.

He closed his eyes. Of course, he thought.

CALVIN JAMES STOOD NEXT TO the coroner in the examination room at Bethesda Medical Hospital. On the table in front of him, under the harsh illumination of overhead fluorescents, lay a cadaver.

"Are you even sure that's a person?" Hal Brognola asked.

"Female for certain," James replied. "Age remains undetermined at present."

The corpse recovered from Victory Lake, Fort Benning, Georgia, had been submerged for at least seventy-two hours. The decomposition was advanced.

"I appreciate you coming in to help, Cal," Brognola said. "The Pentagon doesn't request Justice put many people in the Witness Protection Program, and if this is one of them then we've got to keep it close to our vest until we can figure out what's going on."

"Not a problem," James nodded. "What more can you tell me?"

"I had Carmen Delahunt go over the recent reports," Brognola said. "There was a missing-person report filed forty-eight hours ago for Sabrina Caust, or as she used to be known before defecting, Katharina Smolosvitch. The Marshal Service had put her in Atlanta almost a decade ago. She married a drill sergeant last summer and moved to on-base housing."

"Has he been notified?"

"He's on his way now," Brognola acknowledged. "He's bringing a hairbrush and razor for the DNA sample cross-comparison."

The door to the exam room opened and a representative of the provost-marshal came in. He nodded his greeting, then looked down at the cut-open body and blanched.

"She's like a big sponge!" the man stammered.

"The process is sometime referred to as superhydration," James replied. "If you keep your hands submerged for a long time the thick skin on your palms and fingers swell up, but since it's connected to another layer of skin underneath that doesn't expand, the surface flesh buckles or prunes. This body has been underwater for days. Everything is swollen and distorted from being saturated with water."

The provost rep tugged at his collar, "I, uh, I see." He looked around. "I was sent over with the lab results."

"Thank you, just a second," James said.

The coroner opened the throat of the woman's body, expanding the cavity he'd made after cutting a section of her rib cage free.

"She drown?" Brognola asked.

"Her sinus cavities, air passages, lungs and even down to her stomach are all holding water." The coroner looked down at the body and frowned, as if questioning his observation. "We'll see what comes back on my toxicology scan, body and water, just to get a clearer picture of what happened to her."

"Got drunk and went swimming?" Brognola suggested.

James shrugged. "There's hemorrhaging in lungs and sinus. That's a clear indication she was alive when she went into the water."

"I've got the report," the provost rep repeated. He looked green as the coroner removed and weighed the woman's lungs.

"Tell me what the analysis of the water in her lungs says," James said.

"Here it is. Says normal levels of fluoride and iron. Same with calcium, magnesium and then trace amounts of other chemicals and elements." He held up a clear plastic evidence bag. "The tag says they filtered the water in the lungs and this is what they got."

James looked up and saw the man holding the bag. It appeared to contain numerous small particles. He took the package and then examined his sample under the dual plate comparison microscope. He frowned at the results, deep in contemplation.

"Hair," he stated. "Small segments one-eighth inch or smaller."

"Hers?" Brognola asked.

James shook his head. "No. She's white-blond and these are very dark, black."

Just then the phone rang. The provost scrambled to answer it. He hit the conference call button. "Go ahead."

"We've got the husband here with the hairbrush you requested for DNA sampling."

"Let me guess." James held up a hand. "He's got black hair and he's clean shaven."

There was a pause as the desk sergeant absorbed the information. "Yeah," he confirmed.

"Thank you," James said. He indicated for the provost to hang up the phone. He turned toward Brognola. "In my opinion I think we have enough to take him into custody. I think we're dealing with a domestic dispute and not anything to do with her espionage connections."

Brognola raised his bushy eyebrows in surprise. "You sure?" he asked.

James pointed to the computer spectrum analysis sheets. "I'm pretty convinced the base commander hasn't started putting fluoride in Victory Lake. Fluoride was in the water we drained from her lungs—that matches tap water. Also these flecks are beard stubble. I'm willing to bet the ass clown outside shaves in the shower."

Brognola immediately put it together. "He drowned her in

the bathtub then dumped her body in the lake to cover his tracks."

"I'm on it!" the provost said, and left the room.

"Not bad, Cal." Brognola smiled.

James shrugged then quipped, "Elementary."

Over on the coroner's desk his SME PED rang.

CHAPTER NINE

Stony Man Farm

Barbara Price burst through the door of the Annex.

Her mouth was set in a straight, hard line as she looked toward the monitor showing the live feed from the UAV piloted in Toronto by Hunt Wethers. Kurtzman sat behind Tokaido, who was serving as deployment manager for this operation.

On the screen the SUV driven by Able Team was clearly visible. In the IR the four figures approaching the vehicle glowed like ghosts.

"Christ," Price snarled. "Those gangbangers?"

Kurtzman turned in his seat and nodded. "We knew going in that this neighborhood is an armed camp."

Price snatched up her headset from the desk and slipped it into place. "Still a little early to be shooting people, don't you think?"

"Target is on site. We have confirmation," Tokaido said.

"Ironman," Price said, "is confrontation necessary?"

"I don't see any way around this," Lyons replied. "They're armed, they're angry, they're in our way. You want to loose Tsai?"

Price frowned, paused, then replied, "No. But I don't think shooting up Canadian citizens is the kind of op we're trying to run."

"Narcoterrorists are narcoterrorists in Caracas, Mogadishu or Regent Park," Lyons attested. "Besides," he added, "we've fucked up gangbangers before. Catalina and Los Angeles to name a few."

Even though Lyons was referencing actions that had occurred before her tenure as mission controller she was well versed in the history of Able Team's actions on those missions. They had been blood baths, by necessity.

"Your call," she said simply.

"We're rolling hot," Lyons informed her. "Wethers, give me a communications blackout of the three-block area."

"Understood," Wethers replied.

He activated the electronic jamming gear in the nose of his UAV, killing cellular traffic and activating the interdiction device placed earlier by Hermann Schwarz in the landline switchboard for Regent Park.

"Able up!" Lyons signed out.

Regent Park

IN THE BACKSEAT of the SUV, Hermann Schwarz uncoiled into motion.

He tossed the SME PED and parabolic shotgun mike onto the seat next to him as both Carl Lyons and Rosario Blancanales cleared leather on Glock Model 20 10 mm pistols.

In the backseat Schwarz pulled a silenced M-4 Commando from the floor. The M-4 carbine, most commonly in use by the U.S. military, had a 14.5-inch barrel while the M-4 Commando utilized an 11.5-inch barrel in combination with telescoping buttstocks.

Schwarz outfitted his weapon with a 200-round drum magazine and an eight-inch sound/flash suppresser upgraded by Stony Man armorer, John "Cowboy" Kissinger. The electronics genius shoved open his door and button-hooked out onto the street.

The body of the diplomat-grade SUV was between him and the approaching gangsters. Throwing the buttstock into his shoulder the Army special operations veteran executed a "slicing the pie" maneuver and angled around the rear bumper to engage the enemy combatants.

Four Regent Park Souljahs stopped cold.

Dressed in bulky, loose-fitting clothes each of them held a TEC-9 machine pistol and wore a stocking cap. Blancanales emerged from the passenger door and scrambled to cover them across the hood of the SUV as Lyons followed him across the front seat and out.

"Freeze!" Schwarz snarled.

He picked a target at random and touched his finger to the smooth metal curve of his weapon. An Aimpoint laser sight blinked on and a red dot appeared on the chest of the startled man.

"Shit!" the youth shouted in surprise.

The three other members of the gangster's crew lifted their TEC-9s in terrorized shock. Blancanales slammed his arms down hard on the SUV's hood, his Glock M-20 level.

"Don't you fucking do it!" he barked.

Coming out the passenger door, Lyons turned and skipped in a sideways motion around behind Blancanales, adding his pistol to the standoff.

For a long, tense moment the two groups stared at each other.

"Cops!" One of the gangsters spit.

The one in Schwarz's sights looked down at the red dot seemingly glued to his chest. "It's cool, man," he muttered. His hands were up, which would have been fine if he wasn't holding a machine pistol. "Be cool," he repeated.

But the crew member on his right, eyes bloody red from drug use, was shaking his head like an autistic child in a fugue state. "Oh, man," he muttered in a disjointed mantra. "Oh, man. Oh, man, I ain't going back to jail. Oh, man, I tole you fuckers I wasn't going back if it came to it, oh, man."

"Easy," Lyons growled. "You set those piece-of-shit guns down. We don't have to do this the hard way."

Down the vehicle from him, Schwarz used his thumb to click his fire-selector switch off single shot and onto 3-round burst.

A breeze stirred the trees in the park, rustling the leaves. Several streets over a car alarm went off then went silent. A jet flew by overhead.

"Oh, man," the stoned gangster repeated.

"Easy, Bone," the man in Schwarz's crosshairs warned. It sounded more like a plea as he crossed his eyes to keep focus on the laser dot.

When the action happened it came from neither Bone nor the terrified gangster in Schwarz's sight. The gangster on the far right suddenly twisted and took off like a sprinter from the starting blocks.

Schwarz snapped his muzzle onto the man. The gangster's arm came up, holding the TEC-9 in the thug-style sideways pose made popular by hip-hop videos and a complete misunderstanding of basic marksmanship fundamentals.

The TEC-9 burped and 9 mm slugs dented the body of Able Team's SUV. Schwarz squeezed the trigger on his M-4 Commando. The receiver cycled through a 3-round burst and the spent shell casing tumbled into his brass catcher.

Teflon-coated 5.56 mm slugs slapped into the thug's head from under fifty yards. His cranium caved in and his face exploded outward. The gangster rolled with the high-velocity impact, tumbling forward in a loose somersault and spilling off the sidewalk into the grass of Regent Park.

The Souljah named Bone screamed in wild, bloody red rage, part desperation, part drug intoxication.

His face twisted into a mask of insane intensity. The TEC-9 machine pistol cradled loosely in his grip snapped up. Lyons and Blancanales fired simultaneously, the unmuffled 10 mm pistols banging loudly.

The Souljah went down, leaving blood hanging in the air above him like scarlet rain in the light of the streetlamp. Schwarz stepped around the corner of the SUV and gunned the other two down.

"Fucking typical!" Lyons snarled. "Surprise is gone, let's just get the son of a bitch Tsai before he bolts."

"Oh, man," Schwarz moaned. "It's Caracas all over again."

"No time to piss and cry," Blancanales said. "Let's just go jerk Tsai out and then get."

The Puerto Rican slammed the door to the SUV closed and Lyons hit the control on his key chain, buttoning it up tight.

Able Team turned and sprinted across the street toward the housing complex, eyes sharp for further armed drug soldiers. They spilled around a long, late-model car painted primer gray and came up on the sidewalk.

Schwarz moved with his M-4 Commando tucked in the curve of his shoulder, muzzle up and tracking for threats. Both Lyons and Blancanales ran forward with their pistols held up beside their faces, fingers on triggers.

Lyons sprinted up the stairs of the stoop and kicked in the door. It exploded off its hinges with a sharp crack and fell. He jumped inside and swung the muzzle of the 10 mm around as Blancanales and Schwarz followed him inside.

Lyons yanked open the inner door of the building and charged through. He snapped his rifle muzzle around in pre-determined patterns to the right and then up a staircase.

Blancanales came in hard on Lyons's heels and took his sectors on the left.

A doorway down the hall just beyond the entrance way opened a crack, and Blancanales sprayed the gangster security element even as the blue steel barrel of the assault rifle emerged.

Lyons saw a figure in loose, dark clothes and black stocking cap with the logo of a Toronto sports team turn the corner of the staircase above him from off of the second-floor landing.

Lyons gunned him down, splashing the shooter's blood on the bare drywall directly behind him. The man dropped and his weapon fell, bouncing off the steps as it tumbled down the staircase.

Lyons ran forward and halfway up the stairs. He stopped, his weapon in a covering position, and Blancanales stormed past him to the top of the stair. The ex-Green Beret took a knee and swept his weapon back and forth as he knelt in the fresh blood beside the ambusher's corpse.

Schwarz was holding anchor with his M-4 Commando.

They were in a small building foyer with dim track lighting and a dirty linoleum floor. A staircase rose to their left, while a residential hallway ran straight in front of them. Across from the staircase stood a single elevator.

Gang graffiti had been spray painted on the control panel, declaring to all the world who controlled the building.

Schwarz found the stairs and covered them with his M-4 while Blancanales covered the first-floor hallway in case threats emerged from the apartment doors. Lyons took half a second to make his decision about how to direct his assault.

"I think we've still got the jump," he said, and moved toward the elevator.

"I'll cover the back stairs," Schwarz replied.

Lyons just nodded as he hit the button for Tsai's floor.

Splitting a unit and sending a teammate alone to man a vector of coverage wasn't a normal part of basic military, or even special operations, tactics. However, each man on Able Team had logged more trigger time than almost any other shooter for the U.S. government, either military or law enforcement. They operated at the extreme point of the spear, almost always alone, without backup and against superior numbers. The unspoken protocols developed under Lyons's leadership had proved effective on the harshest of stages.

Neither Able Team member thought twice about Hermann Schwarz going up those stairs by himself. Either man would have taken that assignment without a moment's consideration. The rear transition zone had to be covered; it was a task that needed to be done.

End of story.

The elevator bell rang as the dented metal doors slid open. Blancanales and Lyons were ready, covering the interior from overlapping positions. The elevator car was empty. Its walls were scrawled with gang graffiti and stank of urine, cigarette smoke and body odor.

Climbing inside was like crawling into a septic tank.

Lyons jabbed a blunt finger into the control panel as Blancanales took up position next to him. The bell rang again and the doors slid shut. Overhead the weak lights flickered as the protesting cables began hauling the car upward.

As the elevator rose Blancanales took out a firefighter key and gave it to Lyons. He inserted the key, overriding all control of the car. No one on a different floor would be able to call the elevator away and leave them stranded.

That finished, Lyons put his back against the left side of the filthy metal box while Blancanales mirrored his actions on the opposite side. They both sank to one knee and held their pistols out in two-handed grips.

The elevator shook on its moorings as it settled into place at the correct floor. Lyons twisted his head sharply to one side, cracking his neck. The doors slid open with a hydraulic hiss as the imperfect seal opened.

Their fingers tensed on triggers.

The hallway, six doors to each side, stretched out in front of them as empty and straight as a landing strip. Black garbage bags were shoved up against grimy walls and the stench was reminiscent of a landfill.

The filthy floor seemed to absorb the sickly yellow light of the overhead bulbs. Nothing moved. No sound could be heard. The hallway was as still as a mausoleum.

Cautious, Lyons shuffled forward, still in his crouch. Behind him Blancanales rose after ensuring with the firefighter key that the elevator doors would remain open. At the end of the corridor a metal fire door marked the staircase landing.

"Repeat target location," Lyons said into his throat mike. "Our orientation is from the elevator."

"From the elevator," Wethers replied instantly, "you need the last door on your left."

"Copy," Lyons acknowledged.

The big ex-cop readjusted his grip on his weapon, then rose out of his crouch into a modified Weaver stance.

"Ready when you are," Blancanales said.

Shuffling forward, Lyons nodded and the duo began their approach.

THE TWO Able Team fighters moved down the hallway, weapons up.

Cockroaches skittered underfoot and crawled across the bags of trash filling the hallway. Both men wrinkled their noses as they caught whiffs of baby diapers, rotted food and old ashtrays. They moved with an almost incautious haste as the clock ticked against them.

By the time they were halfway down the hall nothing further had happened. Blancanales moved in a sideways shuffle, keeping an eye to their rear as they advanced, but nothing stirred.

"This doesn't feel right," Lyons said. "Tsai should be ape shit after that phone call and us taking out his street soldiers."

"Not to mention that poor bastard pulling sentry on the first floor," Blancanales agreed.

As if on cue a door on the right at the end of the hall opened.

Lyons snapped his weapon toward the movement, finger poised on the trigger. His searching gaze met the dark brown eyes of a little girl. She looked to be about eleven and wore an old pink dress and no shoes. Her skin was the soft color of milk chocolate.

Lyons opened his mouth to order her back inside. She met his eyes squarely and screamed. The shriek was like an air raid siren, so shrill it echoed down the narrow hall with painful intensity.

"Jesus Christ!" Blancanales shouted in surprise. "She's an alarm system!"

Lyons had no time to answer. The little girl slammed her door shut and hell burst out of the walls around him.

CHAPTER TEN

From behind the apartment door to their right a main battlefield assault rifle roared to life on full auto. Heavy-caliber rounds clawed through the door and burned across the open space half a step in front of Lyons.

The rounds smashed into the far wall and punched straight on through. Lyons was on his belly in the next instant.

The floor was tacky with spilled liquid under his body. His elbow struck the black plastic of a garbage bag and a broken bottle edge cut him instantly.

He rolled up on his side and lifted his pistol. More assault rifle fire tore through the door. Behind him a gunman in a bulky parka and dreadlocks jumped out of a doorway, cut-down pump-action shotgun held in his fists.

Blancanales and Lyons opened fire.

Pistol jumping in his hands, Lyons pumped six rounds through the already shredded door, hoping to hit his assailant but mainly trying to suppress and harass, break the other man's momentum.

Blancanales pulled a smooth double tap and followed up in the same instant.

Two 10 mm slugs hit the shotgun-wielding gangster high on either side of his sternum, crushing ribs like kindling sticks and scrambling lungs. The third round cracked the man's skull high in his forehead, knocking him over.

The narcosoldier triggered his shotgun as he fell, dead before he hit the floor. The .12-gauge boomed like thunder in the hall, and a garbage bag next to Blancanales exploded under the impact. Buckshot pellets peppered the ex-Green Beret's right leg and arm, soaking his clothes with blood. Luckily the wounds were superficial.

Blancanales grunted under the impact but realized he'd been lucky. He snapped his smoking pistol muzzle back toward the door the shotgunner had emerged from then swung back around to cover the other doors.

Lyons pulled his trigger half a dozen more times.

He was ready with a fresh extended-rounds magazine as his bolt locked open and the last spent shell was kicked clear of the breech. His thumb tapped the release and dropped the spent magazine.

As it tumbled he seated the new clip into the butt and let the receiver snap forward, placing a new round. He started pulling the trigger again. Suddenly, Blancanales was standing over him and he heard the roar of the shotgun in the man's hands.

What was left of the door was blown inward off its hinges under twin blasts from the .12-gauge. Lyons used the cover to come up, spin around one posted hand and lunge forward into the doorway.

Down the hall the door identified as Tsai's swung open and two hard-eyed killers with military-grade H&K MP-5 submachine guns emerged wearing jet-black ballistic vests. Blancanales swung to meet them head-on, shotgun roaring in his hands.

On the floor Lyons landed on his stomach half across the threshold of the apartment door. He saw a skinny-looking teenager with bloody red eyes holding an FN FAL assault rifle. The kid looked stunned at Lyons's appearance and fumbled with the long battle rifle, trying to bring it to bear.

Lyons fired with his arms extended.

The Glock kicked in his hand as he rolled off his side and across his back. He fired again as he came up against the doorjamb and rose into a sitting position. He swung his pistol around out of the room and down the hall as the teenage gunner crumpled into a bloody mess behind him.

Blancanales fired the shotgun from the hip just before two 9 mm rounds struck the ex-Green Beret in the dead center of his own Second Chance vest, the kinetic energy sapped away by the titanium plate insert. Blancanales staggered back, stolen shotgun booming.

Lyons's handgun barked like a string of M-80 firecrackers going off. The submachine gunners stumbled backward, struck enough times to halt the momentum of their barrage.

Simultaneously both shifted fire. Lyons blew off the top of one man's head, and Blancanales used a .12-gauge round to remove the other's head at the neck.

Lyons came to his feet, Blancanales spun and dropped to a knee, covering the rear hallway. Bloody pools seeped out from the ripped and torn corpses, making a swamp of the spilled garbage in the hall.

"Tsai," Lyons said. "Let's get the bastard."

Blancanales grunted a response.

"You okay?" Lyons asked.

"Ribs," Blancanales explained. "I'll be fine."

"Schwarz, twenty?" Lyons demanded into his throat mike.

The third member of Able Team answered immediately. "I'm on your landing. Two perps guarding the stairs are down."

"Copy—hall secure. Come in and hold rear security."

The door at the end of the hallway opened in a moment and, holding his M-4 Commando, Schwarz slid into place. He made eye contact with Lyons, who nodded toward the door where Tsai was supposed to be.

Lyons moved quickly down the hall, pistol up and at the ready. Under cover from both Blancanales with his shotgun and Schwarz's M-4, he holstered his 10 mm and picked up one of the dead bodyguard's MP-5 submachine guns. He ejected the magazine, counted the rounds at 15 left and reinserted the clip.

He moved into place next to the open door of the apartment.

"Tsai!" he barked. "You make me come in there to get you and I'm going to be pissed."

A single gunshot ran out.

Lyons flinched backward but no round burned out his way. Instantly, he realized what could have happened.

"Shit!"

He went around the door in a tight button-hook maneuver, MP-5 up and ready. He entered the apartment much faster than he should have but he already knew what he was going to find.

Crossing the threshold into Tsai's apartment was like stepping into another world.

Squalor and poverty disappeared. The front door opened up on a living area filled with gaudy but high-end furniture. The walls were lined with multiple flat-screen televisions and movie posters in expensive frames.

On an end table made of black wrought-iron and cut crystal sat a collection of pornographic magazines, some loose cocaine and assorted drug paraphernalia.

On the couch behind the table sat Tsai.

Clinging to the wall behind the couch were most of Tsai's brains.

The criminal mercenary's corpse lay toppled over against the arm of the black leather couch and his blood covered it. A pistol hung loose in the slack fingers of his hand, and Lyons, long used to crime scenes, immediately noticed the powder burns and singed hair around the entrance wound at the man's temple.

Lyons shifted his muzzle around the room, looking for further bodyguards or any entourage Tsai might have kept.

"Target down—suicide," he announced into his microphone. "We'll toss the apartment for intel and head for home."

Whoever Seven was, Lyons realized, Tsai had feared them a lot more than he had Able Team.

Stony Man Farm

BARBARA PRICE WATCHED Jack Grimaldi pull the Sikorsky up off the landing pad and take off. She retrieved her cell phone and hit the speed-dial button.

"Brognola here," the big Fed answered immediately, voice gruff.

"Phoenix is away," she informed him. "All clear for Wright-Patterson?"

"Yes, I've arranged all the transfers for the international force. They'll spend an hour or so in Hangar 18, then be wheels up for Africa."

"Hangar 18?" Price laughed. "Don't you mean, Building 18?"

"Sure, but saying Hangar 18 is more fun."

"Because of the aliens?"

"Yes, because of the spooky aliens." Brognola laughed. "Cracks me up."

"You're getting as bad as Schwarz."

"I'll pretend I didn't hear that. How's Able?"

"Pissed off," Price replied. She turned and began walking toward the Farm House.

"I'll bet," Brognola agreed. "Couldn't be helped, though."

"Lyons is getting stitches and a tetanus shot. Blancanales had his wounds cleaned and bandaged. There's bruising to his ribs but he doesn't think there are any fractures."

"They got downtime?"

"Time down in place. They're in a Toronto safehouse until we're sure they're done up north. We need to go over the Power-Book and cell phone they sent back from Tsai's apartment.

Carmen thinks we'll have some juicy info for Justice, but we're not one hundred percent sure it's going lead us to Seven."

"We never know what we'll get until we get it."

"Most of the time," Price admitted. "I'll keep you informed."

INSIDE THE HOUSE Price found Carmen Delahunt waiting for her. Delahunt held her cell phone in one hand and an iPod in the other. The two devices were connected by a white electronic umbilical.

"You got something for me?" Price asked.

"I think so," Delahunt answered. She held up the two electronic devices. "I want you to hear something."

"Let's do it in the kitchen. I need a cup of coffee."

"You're in luck," Delahunt said. "Wethers baked a cake."

"Chocolate?"

"Always."

"This is a good day."

The members of Stony Man, whether the tactical teams or support personnel, did not live in states of suspended animation, coming alive only when some immediate threat appeared. They lived their lives between operations keeping the apparatus that was Stony Man functioning and to do so they gave up great parts of their lives in a manner of selfless dedication almost incomprehensible to the civilian populations they safeguarded.

As such they had formed a tight-knit community with its own rituals and patterns. Huntington Wethers's chocolate cake had become as much a pillar of that construction as Aaron Kurtzman's coffee.

Going down the hall, Price and Delahunt ran into Buck Greene, former Marine embassy security officer and current head of the Farm's elite sentinels, the blacksuits. He waved a clipboard at Price.

"Sorry to interrupt, Barb, but I need your signature."

"Spending money again?"

"I need to up our budgeted allowances on our fuel and ammunition expenditures. Aviation fuel has gone through the roof."

"Always," Price muttered, and signed off.

Each man on the blacksuits, rotating out of other special operations units, shot forty rounds of pistol ammo and twenty of rifle as part of their daily maintenance along with PT sessions, unarmed-combat defensive-tactics training and general subjects such as communications, first aid and land navigation on the property.

Greene had chosen the number of rounds fired by using a simple deduction. Forty pistol rounds was the number shot daily by the FBI's hostage rescue team and twenty that of a designated marksman on the USMC's FAST platoons.

Price and Delahunt entered the first-floor kitchen and poured coffee before sitting and cutting generous slices of cake free. They found Kurtzman had already beat them to the cake. He grinned guiltily as the women sat.

As the sugar and caffeine jumpstarted their cerebral synapses Price, as always, got down to business.

"What do you have, Carm?" Price asked, taking a bite of cake.

Delahunt pushed her connected cell phone and iPod across the table toward Barbara Price. The iPod would play the digital recording she'd burned, using the cell phone's speaker to broadcast the sound clearly.

"I cut out some snippets from the interrogation of Sin-Bok and then one of the phone conversations with Jen Tsai. I think it'll speak for itself."

There was a pause, then the drug-intoxicated voice of the North Korean could be heard clearly, speech slightly slurred.

"Three plus four, I'm three plus four," he repeated.

"One plus six," Tsai barked into the phone. "One plus six!"

Delahunt hit the rewind button and played the loop back again for Price.

"Three plus four, I'm three plus four."

"One plus six. One plus six!"

Price was nodding. "It's so simple it's perfect. Do we think there's any other levels to the use of the numbers, an alphabet substitution perhaps?"

"I have a theory," Delahunt admitted. "I think it might have to do with the rank of the people asking the questions."

"How so? Tsai was what?" Kurtzman looked down at his notes, "One plus six, while Sin-Bok is three plus four."

"Seems obvious that a North Korean intelligence officer would rate higher than a scut thug like Tsai," Price pointed out. "Not necessarily, but it makes sense."

"Exactly." Delahunt nodded. "One plus six versus three plus four. Three is higher than one, so takes less numbers to equal the sum of seven."

"So Tsai is a cutout. He's a level one," Delahunt continued. "Sin-Bok is more important. He brings more resources to the organization, so he's a three."

"So what we need," Price said, "is a six plus one."

"Let's hope Phoenix's target in Somalia doesn't off himself," Kurtzman muttered.

Indian Ocean

THE KROENIGER YACHT knifed through the waves.

The command bridge was blacked out, not unlike the con of a submarine. The ultraexpensive, cutting-edge technology of the vessel allowed navigation without visual clues of the environment. The controls provided the operator with all the information, and it was from dozens of these screens that the navigator proceeded.

Even the views of the exterior were processed through multi-angled POV cameras offering a 360-degree view of the vessel, all seen from HD screens strategically placed around the completely enclosed pilot chamber.

Klegg stood off to one side as Milosevic directed the officers on the bridge. The Russian intelligence agent had proved to be worth every penny of the considerable retainer he was getting.

Within hours he'd assembled a squad of ex-Spetsnaz to provide the nucleus of the operation. Then within two days he'd recruited a gang of Somalian irregulars to provide cannon fodder.

His connections and Klegg's money had purchased the Boston whalers, weapons and training equipment used by the pirate cohort. He'd used a corporate cutout to secure the Kroeniger yacht, and his connections with what had been the Eastern Bloc military-industrial complex had secured them the ultralight Raven UAV.

The Raven was aloft now, remote piloted by a Bosnian tech on the Kroeniger's flying bridge just above them. The UAV camera mount clearly showed the scene unfolding some three nautical miles away.

Klegg poured himself a vodka neat as he watched his plan unfold. He wore a double-breasted blazer of navy with gold buttons and piping over a white turtleneck and slacks. His feet were stuffed into spotless deck shoes. A Rolex Submariner rode his right wrist.

Compared to Milosevic in his gray khakis, the American looked like some Manhattan metrosexual playing sailor. Which, except for the cold-blooded psychopath part, he was.

On one screen a VLCC, or Very Large Cargo Container, ship plodded along at a sedate pace. It was so far out into the Indian Ocean that there wasn't even a hint of the African shoreline and Milosevic had seemingly correctly inferred this had given the VLCC captain and crew a false sense of security.

Three Boston whalers with powerful outboard motors now descended upon the vessel like hyenas running down a wounded elephant. The race between the powerful but ponderous VLCC and the quick, lithe whalers was so unevenly matched it was laughable.

Klegg sipped his vodka.

FEDOROVA YEFIMOVICH'S FAMILY had changed their name years ago.

Their true last name was Rasputin, and the association was too considerable to be borne. His grandfather had given up the name during the height of the Revolution after leaving the Soviet naval infantry to take post with an interior ministry prison guard unit.

Fedorova's father had followed tradition by going to work at a Siberian camp, rising through the ranks until he ran the largest prison in the Ukraine. Fedorova's path had been different but much the same. A stint with the MVD internal troops, working in Chechnya, then an ascension through the Vityaz, a counterinsurgency commando unit.

With the rise the criminal capitalism that had taken over his country after the fall of totalitarian communism, Fedorova had learned to adapt. The rest was an easy drift into mercenary work. First came work as a special purpose guardsman, then VIP protection in Iraq with private military companies, then into Africa for security details around oil and diamond industries.

Along the way he'd made his most lucrative contracts killing on order, drifting out of his mercenary role and into that of assassin. The hit today on the American VLCC ship was his best-paying gig yet.

He coldly eyed the Somalian pirates in the other Boston whaler.

Yes, even if he did have to work with scum this would still be his best paycheck to date. All he had to do was slaughter some American security personal. That was fine; he'd cut his teeth training to fight them anyway.

Ahead of them the side of the massive VLCC rose before them like a prehistoric cliff, towering above the assault force. Around him the men of his handpicked unit readied themselves.

CHAPTER ELEVEN

"Sniper," Fedorova ordered.

Instantly Sergeant Suracova nestled the legs of his bipod into position on the gunwales of the Boston whaler. Nestling into the buttstock of the SVD sniper rifle, Suracova flipped up the protective lens caps of his mounted IR scope.

Behind him three other burly ex-Spetsnaz soldiers prepped the boarding ropes attached to several crossbow units. The beam of the Jurassic vessel was over forty-three meters, hugely imposing.

"Making approach," Fedorova growled in Russian into his transmitter.

"Understood," Milosevic answered immediately from the command post on the yacht's bridge.

Overhead the UAV captured the unfolding scene in stark digital images. Through the sniper scope Suracova found his first target. A wide-shouldered man dressed in dark civilian clothes and a knit watch cap patrolled the stern of the ship, scope-mounted FN FAL main battle rifle cradled casually in his arms.

"Slow," Suracova said.

"Slow speed," Fedorova repeated to the coxswain.

Instantly, the man throttled down, smoothing out the movement on the boat over the water. Saltwater spray cooled Fedorova's face, filling his nostrils with the smell of ocean and slightly stinging his eyes.

He lifted a pair of Zeiss binoculars and brought the slow-moving VLCC into focus.

He zoomed in on the American. Milosevic's intel had identified the security detachment as a PMC recruiting heavily from former U.S. Marines and Navy special operations troops. Out of respect for their skills Fedorova was showing no mercy in this operation.

The vessel, the *Osaka Express,* was over 335 meters long with a deadweight capacity of 104,100 metric tons. The size of the thing was awe inspiring.

The SVD grunted slightly, the muffle system reducing the sharp high-velocity crack of the weapon to a suppressed cough. In Fedorova's binoculars the sentry stood on his toes and a halo of blood mist appeared behind his head.

Half a second later the man crumpled.

"Throttle!" Fedorova barked.

Instantly, the ex-Spetsnaz at the coxswain position gunned the massive twin outboard and the Boston whaler surged forward. The boats made their running approach from directly behind the VLCC, hammering through the choppy wake of the vessel's big corkscrew propellers hard enough to rattle teeth.

Once close they suddenly darted around the edge of the stern toward the vessel port, running close enough for Fedorova to reach out and slap the gray metal of the hull. Once fully parallel, the coxswain slowed the whaler to perfectly match the speed of the larger vessel.

"Grapnels!" Fedorova ordered.

The crossbow team settled into position and fired. Instantly, the bolts shot out and sailed up to arc over the railing of the ship, black nylon rope trailing behind with a zipping noise.

Each grapnel bolt landed and was rapidly hauled back until secured. Once the operator was sure of the hold, he cranked the climbing rope into position.

The youngest member of the Spetsnaz, a man known as Gregory to his follow mercenaries, sprang into action. A former Moscow police officer, Gregory was a lithe, wiry man whose specialized climbing skills earned him premier salaries on reconnaissance missions and high-assault operations.

With the muscled grace of a chimpanzee Gregory scrambled up the climbing rope, a silenced AK-104 folding-stock carbine slung across his back. Attached to his web gear was a lightweight cord secured to the first rung of a rope ladder to be used by the rest of maritime assault force.

Sliding over the top, the Russian cleared his weapon and secured his position. Behind him the radio attached to the dead sentry broke squelch. The voice sounded frustrated by the lack of response.

The window had just narrowed.

Gregory had come aboard just underneath a wrought-iron staircase running up the side of the VLCC main superstructure. At the top would be the bridge and navigation rooms. At this stage in the assault the defenders still had the advantage of elevation over the attackers.

Gregory turned to the edge of the railing and quickly grabbed hold of the grapnel's tether line. Working fast, he hauled up the rope ladder and clipped it into place on the safety railing by looping the thick hemp cables back over on themselves and securing them with D-ring carabiners.

He looked down into the waiting boat, met Fedorova's eyes and nodded.

The team leader returned the nod and then sent the first men up the ladder.

Somalia

THE RAMP CAME DOWN and the Phoenix Force warriors took a long first step.

The five-man team exited rapidly, one after the other out the ramp and into the night at thirty thousand feet. Below them the Horn of Africa lay out like a game board.

With expert precision Phoenix timed their drop into a line

of sequential openings that jerked the free-fall troopers into a seeming standstill as their parachutes blossomed.

Instantly, T. J. Hawkins reached up, grabbed hold of his riser attachments and hauled. He spiraled tightly and cut his altitude sharply. In rapid succession his teammates followed his example.

All members of Phoenix Force were experts at airborne operations. Hawkins, however, had spent most of his military career, first as a Ranger, then later as a member of Delta Force, executing a prodigious focus on airborne operational paradrops.

In acknowledgment of his expertise, the assignment of duties most often relating to jumpmaster and airborne navigational tasks was given to him. Often it seemed to the team that the Texan craved the adrenaline rushes of high-altitude drops the way a junkie craved heroin.

Night winds tore at him as Hawkins used a wrist-mounted compass, GPS and altimeter to guide Phoenix Force into the drop zone.

At twenty-one thousand feet the team caught the equatorial thermal that Kurtzman's meteorological programs had identified. Hawkins expertly guided the team into the stream of warm air, and dozens of miles slid by below them as they pushed away from the Somalia coast and out into the desert landscape.

Soon enough the GPS unit blinked a staccato flash of warning as the airborne team approached the designated coordinates.

"Phoenix," he said into his throat mike. "Approaching DZ, approaching DZ."

"Copy," each man replied in turn.

Once again Hawkins reached up and hauled on his risers, dampening his horizontal travel to concentrate on vertical drop. Below them ground began to take on more vivid detail.

The stretch of flat hardpan lay just east of a sharp line of hills beyond which lay the target village. Satellite imagery had narrowed down likely target sites, but the position had been chosen after running a cross index of the coordinates with JSOC Pathfinder archives.

Nine months before, a Special Forces team had landed in the same area on a long-range patrol operation. Their classified firsthand account of the landing zone as highly suitable had pushed the spot into number-one consideration during the mission-prep stage of Phoenix Force's operation.

Hawkins landed perfectly, rolling smoothly as the hard desert floor came up to meet him. Feet, knees, thighs, shoulder, tight roll and then he was up and disengaging the harness of his parachute as his teammates landed around him.

Easy part over, he thought.

Indian Ocean

GREGORY HELD POINT as the rest of the Russian team boarded the VLCC.

He held up his AK-104, covering the afterdeck directly behind the bridge from below. Two figures, one armed with an M-16 A-2 and the other with a Remington 870 pump action shotgun, just exited from the upper decks.

A third man, taller than the other two, emerged from the bulkhead talking into a radio and armed only with a pistol. The drone of the big diesel engines drowned out his words but the Russian infiltrator knew the dead sentry had officially been missed now.

Suracova, the unit's designated marksman, settled into position and lifted his SVD, sighting in on the man through the tangle of ironwork making up stairs, railings and gunwales. He would provide overwatch as the team moved toward the bridge.

The holds of the VLCC were filled with materials and goods well in excess of several million dollars, but the only thing Klegg's mercenaries were interested in lay in the safe of the ship's captain.

Fedorova came up and tapped Gregory on the shoulder, jerking his chin toward the stairs.

Immediately, Gregory lifted his Kalashnikov and made his approach onto the scaffolding staircase leading up to the gangways above. Behind him the other men of the team fell into place, Fedorova coming last and Suracova remaining in position with his SVD.

Behind them members of the Somalia band came over the side and began fanning out across the ship to silence any other possible opposition. Consisting mostly of merchant mariners the crew would be victims of a wholesale slaughter.

Up above them the private security contractor holding the two-way radio barked an order and gestured toward his men. The two Americans put their weapons at port arms and began to double time down the stairs.

Straight into the guns of the Russians.

Suracova pulled the trigger on his sniper rifle. The weapon kicked and the suppressor on the muzzle rose with the recoil. Above them on the afterdeck the contractor spun like a child's top, twirling blood behind him in the air, and fell hard to the steel grating.

Gregory raced up the stairs, weapon up and ready. The lead American, wielding the Remington 870, shouted in anger and lowered his shotgun. The Russian had the advantage of surprise, however, and that made all the difference.

The AK-104 ripped a tight blast and the security contractor took a triburst in his face. From behind and below Gregory a volley of weapons fired as the rest of the Russian team took down the final survivor.

The American's M-16 A-2 tumbled out of limp fingers and clattered to the stairs.

"Go!" Fedorova snarled. "Secure the bridge!"

On board the yacht Klegg swallowed an icy gulp of vodka. The entire scene unfolded like an IMAX movie on the monitor.

"Now that the trap is sprung, have the UAV go lower," the American lawyer instructed.

Milosevic grunted in response then gave the order into his com-unit.

Immediately the remote pilot complied. On the screen the picture clarified so sharply it was possible to see the pores in the Russian mercenary's skin. The blood was a vivid scarlet on the screen, so copious it seemed surreal, like that in a horror movie.

Klegg smirked around his vodka. "That's better."

Somalia

INSERTION COMPLETE, Phoenix Force worked quickly.

Rafael Encizo, armed with an M-249 Squad Automatic Weapon, walked the perimeter while the rest of Phoenix Force prepped for the overland infiltration to target.

With practiced precision they removed the HULC units from their rucksacks and assembled them. With the addition of the weight-bearing exoskeletons each man's combat load had risen to more than two hundred pounds, despite the long trek over broken ground that waited for them.

McCarter, lower body encased in the HULC, nodded toward Encizo. "We're good, bro. Go ahead and suit up."

Encizo nodded and the team turned outward in a circle, weapons ready, while Encizo quickly shrugged into his gear.

Gary Manning carried an M-4/M-203 combination as his primary weapon. However, with the addition of his HULC and in preparation for his assault he carried the XM-312 .50-caliber heavy machine gun.

Hawkins, in his role as team point man, utilized the same M-249 SAW as Encizo, but his HULC gear allowed him to carry the XM-109 25 mm Objective Sniper Weapon—OSW— to be used in the assault on the village.

Encizo served as the team fire support specialist, and in

this role his HULC kit was weighed down with an M-252 81 mm mortar and rounds. James served as Encizo's assistant gunner, and along with his medic kit and M-4 Commando he carried several additional 81 mm mortar shells. His role for the assault was not limited to assisting Encizo, however. On the initial strike he, along with McCarter, would be a primary missile operator using the FGM-148 127 mm Javelin weapons systems.

McCarter carried the same M-4 as Manning, the M-203 giving each man the 40 mm grenade option. Additionally he served as primary communications specialist, and his HULC kit included a DARPA sat kit and the field base station for amplification of the team's headset com units.

Each member of Phoenix Force wore a Kel-Tec PLR-16 5.56 mm pistol in a thigh holster, augmented by an OTs-38 Stechkin silent revolver in a shoulder rig for closer work.

Along with various grenades, each Phoenix Force veteran carried an M-9 bayonet and a Gerber Mark II fighting knife.

They were the finest soldiers, outfitted with the finest gear and backed by the finest chain of command of any unit in the world. Standing between them and their operational tasking was a company-size element of al Qaeda's elite bodyguard troops. Each one of those jihadists pledged to give his life in protection of his warlord.

Phoenix Force had come to see they kept their promise.

Indian Ocean

ALL AROUND Fedorova were the sounds of death.

The noise was something he'd grown accustomed to over the years. The bark of rifles, screams, the laughter of killers. It was a symphony of sorts and he knew its nuances very well by now.

On the bridge of the VLCC he peered out through the windows of the superstructure. Rows upon rows of rail cars stood stacked and lashed to the massive transport deck. On the horizon, ridiculously close to the vessel, he saw his employer's UAV circling.

He turned slowly and eyed the scene on the bridge.

The captain, second officer and ship's navigator knelt on the floor, hands clasped behind their heads. He could see the fear on their faces. He didn't blame them; they had much to fear.

With the muzzle of his AK-104 he gestured toward the heavy safe built into the bulkhead.

"Open it," he said, his English serviceable but heavily accented.

The captain, a portly bearded man in his early sixties but with some courage, shook his head sharply. "I don't have the combination," he said. "Our principal put the cargo in the safe when we sailed out of Tel Aviv. When we reach Maryland the new principal will have the combination. I don't touch it."

Fedorova lifted a thick Slavic eyebrow. "Really?"

The captain nodded earnestly. "Truly."

Fedorova shrugged. "I guess we'd better give up, then. No sense sticking around. I guess we've been thwarted."

He turned casually at the waist and pulled the trigger on his Kalashnikov carbine.

The weapon report was deafening inside the steel bulkhead and thick safety glass. The muzzle of the weapon lit up as the muzzle-flash burst like a ball of flame. Three high-velocity ComBloc slugs ripped out of the barrel and across six feet to strike the kneeling navigator in his upturned face.

CHAPTER TWELVE

Instantly the rounds blew the man's features apart, split his skull like an ax blow and splashed blood and brain across the bridge windows in a chunky soup.

Everything was caught on the powerful cameras of the UAV and transmitted via digital signal to the enclosed bridge of the Kroeniger yacht.

"Yeah, baby!" Klegg chortled. "Now we're cooking with gas."

Milosevic watched the murder with the impersonal dispassion of a head surgeon witnessing a first-year resident excise an odious but not particularly malignant tumor from a patient.

"Did you want me to burn you a copy for your personal use?" the Russian asked, voice dry.

Klegg shot him a sharp look. Despite the ridiculous yacht captain getup the lawyer wore like a Halloween costume, he remained stone killer enough that the Russian criminal fixer recognized another predator.

"Why? You want some pictures of what I did to Svetlana? For your personal use? Maybe we can trade."

The silence on the bridge of the yacht was strained. Each man regarded the other with a cold, unwavering stare. Then Fedorova's voice, amplified by his throat mike, spoke up and by silent consent each man looked to the display monitor.

"Now," Fedorova grunted. "About that combination..."

"Jesus!" the captain wept.

"I was raised a communist," Fedorova replied. "Even after the socialists crumbled I noticed this Jesus Christ didn't turn up with the regularity the faithful seemed to hope for." He strolled over and thrust the hot barrel of his smoking weapon into the crying man's face. "Jesus isn't going to save you. Open the fucking safe."

The captain was not a weak man. He was not a coward. He was, however, an ordinary man in an extraordinary situation. He wore the blood of a murdered friend on his face. He wanted to live.

He wanted to live and he understood something; they had been betrayed.

The shipment of the material by placement in a commercial cargo vessel had been intended as the perfect smoke screen. It was wagered that by mixing it in with all the varied freight hauled by a VLCC such as this one, the safety measures for the volatile material would go unnoticed by the curious eyes of the world's various intelligence agencies.

The captain had transported more than one government courier and goods this way over the years. The only link had to have come from inside. It was hopeless.

"I'll do it," he said. "Don't shoot anyone else. I'll open it." His voice was dull and lifeless to his own ears.

The contractor security element on board was made up of ex-Marines, combat veterans to a man. If they'd been taken out, then what the hell did they expect from him?

He was a simple merchant mariner who did his country a service now and then. If they'd blown operational cover, how could they expect him to save the mission on his own?

With shaking hands he entered his ID into the keypad. The indicator light above the tumbler lock blinked from red to amber to green. His fingers were unsteady as he began to work the combination.

After a moment the series of dead bolts built into the lead-lined titanium safe snapped back and the heavy door swung open.

"There," the captain said. He rocked back on his heels to

remove himself from in front of the strongbox. "Just take it and go," he said. Shame burned his cheeks to the high glossy red of a cover model's lipstick.

Fedorova triggered a second 3-round burst.

The captain's brains splashed across the open safe door. The man slumped to the floor, where his spilling blood mingled with that of the murdered navigator.

The second officer cried out in anger and fear.

He was a big man with powerful shoulders and a brawler's lumpy nose. He rose off his knees like a linebacker exploding out of a three-point stance on the line of scrimmage.

Gregory gunned him down and spread him across the rubber matting of the floor.

Fedorova looked into the safe. He saw the titanium box, roughly the dimensions of a commercial DVD player, and knew that it, like the safe, was also lead lined.

According to Milosevic the thing weighed over three hundred pounds. It seemed impossible that something so narrow and thin could be that dense.

"Try and pick it up," he grunted.

Dutifully, Suracova and Gregory shouldered their weapons and stepped forward. Grunting like power lifters, they attempted to lift the container. Muscles straining, faces red with effort, they removed the box from the safe.

"Heavy," Fedorova admitted. He shrugged. "Put it down. We'll have the *chyornyi* carry it. It's what they're good for anyway." He paused. "Once they're through killing the crew, of course." He turned and gestured toward the fourth Russian, a cadaverous-looking ex-Spetsnaz with Mongolian blood. "You are ready, Bayarmaa?"

"The charges are ready." The man nodded.

"Good. Get down to the keel and let's sink this ship."

Somalia

HAWKINS CREPT forward.

Ahead of him the sentry overlooking the approach to the valley sat in a sandbag-fortified position. Moving easily, cat dancing, Hawkins inched forward. The man lit a hand rolled-cigarette and laughed, saying something to the man behind the RPK machine gun.

The smell of the harsh tobacco smoke cut across the distance between predator and prey. The sky was graying with the lifting of night as the sun threatened to rise on the horizon.

Hawkins, using a line of thorny bushes as cover, crept closer.

Behind him, down the hill, the rest of Phoenix Force watched tensely as he made his approach. Should something go wrong the men would have his back, but the element of surprise would be gone.

Since failure was not an option, that would mean an ad hoc, even reckless assault. Such a situation would raise the potential of friendly casualties—hostile casualties being a given—to an unacceptable level.

Everything was riding on the Texan's shoulders and he felt that old friend adrenaline come to his aid, running through his body, lacing his bloodstream. The grip of the OTs-38 Stechkin silenced pistol was a comfortable weight in his hand.

Walking toe-heel in a choreographed series of steps, he stalked closer to the unwary sentries. Isolation was the greatest protector the al Qaeda training camp had and several weeks ago a team of Green Berets had made an airborne insertion, conducted movement to target then executed a reconnaissance operation on the compound below.

That information had found its way into the hands of Phoenix Force and now was being acted upon.

Gravel crunched softly under the tread of Hawkins's boot as he crept forward.

He froze momentarily. According to U.S. Army training on sentry removal he did not stare directly at the men. Rather he relaxed his vision so that he took in the whole scene without letting the full weight of his stare remain fixed on his target.

The terrorist with the cigarette said something to the machine gunner in a language Hawkins didn't speak. Neither man seemed keyed up or suspicious of potential trouble. This little pocket of Nowhere, Africa, was far off the beaten path since the invasion by the Ethiopian army in 2006 had closed down the desert highway.

Easing forward, Hawkins let pent-up oxygen leak out of his nostrils, releasing stress. The pistol in his hand lowered from the forty-five-degree angle at which he'd held it. If he moved much closer he risked silhouetting his head above the ridge line, exposing him to the training compound below.

Two shots to the head from twenty-five yards.

The terrorist smoking plucked his cigarette butt free of his lips and casually flicked it away into the shale and scrub. It arced out like a flare and landed on the ground next to Hawkins's boot. It smoldered there for a second.

The man's eyes followed the cigarette with a bored observation. His expression melted into one of stunned fright as the figure of the American commando materialized out of the predawn dark.

Hawkins put a round into his forehead.

The man sagged and dropped, landing heavily across the legs of the man lounging against the RPK machine gun.

Hawkins moved fast, like a sprinter out of the blocks. He covered the distance even as the machine gunner squawked in surprise and terror. The Texan went down to one knee less than five yards away and the still smoking muzzle of the Russian silenced pistol found its target.

Unable to bring the machine gun around to bear in time, the man clawed for a Tokaeraev pistol in his belt. Hawkins had all the time in the world. He narrowed an eye as he took the pistol up in a two-handed grip.

The man's mouth worked soundlessly. His shoulders slumped in resignation as he realized he'd never make it in time.

Hawkins took up the slack on the handgun. It coughed in his grip, the modified muzzle climbing slightly as the weapon discharged.

The soft-nosed slug cracked the man's forehead like an egg.

Turning at the waist, Hawkins made eye contact with McCarter. The Texan nodded once and gave the thumbs-up sign.

Phoenix Force moved into position.

Washington, D.C.

It was after hours.

Hal Brognola looked out the tinted window of his office at the panoramic vision of the nation's capital.

Wonderland on the Potomac, he called it, and with good reason. Most days he spent here were like brutal chute slides right down the rabbit hole. On good days it was only mildly surrealistic.

He looked away from the window and back to the computer on his desk.

The email on the screen would have been cryptic to someone not in the know and thus was rich with what lawyers and politicians referred to as plausible deniability. What that meant, as interrogators at the CIA were learning the hard way, was that when you did your job and the political winds changed in such a way that you found yourself seated before a closed-door session of some senatorial subcommittee on oversight, then you could look very sincere as you disavowed any knowledge of possibly extralegal behaviors.

Brognola grunted around the well-chewed end of his unlit cigar. He was mission director for Stony Man.

When presented with problems, Stony Man solved those problems. Stony Man lived in a world where ends justified means. If they didn't, there never would have been a Stony Man in the first place. It was, literally, just that simple.

The layers of misconception, deep dark security clearances, hidden budgets and asymmetrical command structures allowed Stony Man Farm to operate in an environment of total secrecy.

Because of all this Brognola now found himself in a very strange position. A Hammond Carter, deputy director of the Government Accountability Office, had requested a look at the balance sheets for the Department of Justice's Special Operations Group.

Hal Brognola was the head of SOG. SOG didn't do audits.

And yet, when he'd just phoned Ron Hackett, the President's chief of staff, to request the accounting bloodhounds of the GAO be put back in the kennel, something very strange had happened.

At first the request and acceptance had been textbook. Such requests weren't unheard of. It was the job of the GAO to follow money trails down spook holes and count the beans.

Infrequently these GAO suits bumped into the edges of the cost expenditures for running the Farm. No big deal. The Oval Office made a quiet phone call and explained that these expenditures were above your pay grade and the matter went away.

And it had seemed at first that this is what would happen again.

"No problem, Hal," the chief of staff had said. "I'll quash it myself after I meet with the Man."

"I appreciate that, Ron," Brognola had replied. To him the conversation was almost forgotten at that point.

"Hey, can you give me the name of the authorizing investigator? It'll go quicker if I contact him instead of the accountant on the ground."

"Sure," Brognola had replied, looking it up. No alarm bells.

"It's from someone I've never run into before, guy named Carter. Ring any bells?"

His query was met with a pause, and on the edge of his awareness Brognola's alarm bells had begun to stir in his belfry. "Ron?"

"Carter?" Hackett repeated. "From the GAO? Hammond Carter?"

Brognola double-checked the paperwork. "Bingo. Hammond Carter."

Again the pause.

"Uh, Ron? You all right?"

When the chief of staff answered, his voice was brisk. Gone was the you-scratch-my-back-I-scratch-yours camaraderie. The tone alone caused such a ringing of alarms Brognola almost looked out his window to see if fire trucks were arriving.

"Hal, you know the President fully supports the GAO in its mission and objectives. At this time I must inform you to handle the situation through the auspices of your office. The Executive Branch is not a smoke screen for Justice."

Brognola was stunned. Was that fear he heard in the man's voice? What the hell?

"Listen, Ron," he began, "is there something I should know—?"

"We're done having this conversation. You are not to bring this subject up again, and under *no* circumstances are you to speak with the President about this. Do you understand me, Mr. Brognola?"

"What? 'Mr. Brognola'? What the hell is going on here?" he demanded.

"I'm hanging up now," Hackett informed him. There was a brief pause and then he seemed to speak in his normal voice. "Play this one very carefully," the man warned.

"Sure, Ron," Brognola replied. "Talk to you later."

"Not about this you won't."

The line went dead.

Carefully, Brognola set down his chewed-up cigar. He reached over next to his coffee cup and picked up his package of antacids. He ate three. Then he bypassed his office phone and picked up his secure cell phone.

He thumbed it open and hit the number one on his speed dial.

"Barb? This is Hal. I don't care what Carmen is working on—pull her and get her to look up anything she can find on a bureaucrat out of GAO named Hammond Carter. I need it ten minutes ago." He listened to her reply then grunted into the phone, "Trouble. He's trouble, that's who he is."

CHAPTER THIRTEEN

Somalia

Phoenix Force moved into position.

In a tactic so simple yet brutally efficient that it had been ancient when Sun Tzu wrote about it in his treatise on war, they kept the rising sun at their backs.

The red-orange sliver knifed up onto the broken wasteland from the east and illuminated their target in the shallow valley below. It was a tired cliché, but their business was killing. If it went right it would be as industrial as Henry Ford's assembly line, each gear and sprocket turning perfectly in predetermined precision.

McCarter scoped the compound below them.

The village had once been only a simple collection of huts belonging to a clan of goat herders. The hills Phoenix Force now hid among provided foliage for the animals while a working well made the village possible in the arid heat.

Then the Soviets had come and helped the Somalian central government build a road across the Ethiopian border, putting a customs office and small barracks in the village. Soon the hamlet was a small town as traffic increased and merchandising began.

Then the Berlin Wall fell and the Soviets were no longer Soviets but Russians instead, and like the next domino in a long line the Somalian central government had fallen in the face of drought, followed by famine, followed by a civil instability that turned the Horn of Africa nation into some grim parody of a postapocalyptic movie.

Now two new forces had breathed life into the village: Al Qaeda in Africa and arms smugglers.

McCarter handed his binoculars across to James.

"What do you make of it?"

James scoped the target. "Same as the preop brief. It's a barracks town and training facility." He pointed toward the west. "There's the motor pool. You can see the firing ranges, shoot house and obstacle course, just like in the satellite imagery. Hell, you could film a damn terrorist commercial here. 'Come to sunny Somalia. Learn to kill the women and children of the infidel while enjoying local cuisine of goat, goat's milk and goat cakes.' The ad copy writes itself."

Two hundred yards downslope from them the shadows of buildings and the mud-brick wall that surrounded the encampment all stretched out like compass needles pointing west. Several dark-skinned men in tribal garb of loose robes and headdress walked a lazy sentry route, Kalashnikovs slung over shoulders.

"All right." McCarter nodded. "Let's finish setup."

Gary Manning washed down the last bite of his protein bar with warm Gatorade in a plastic canteen. He burped loudly and smiled. "Time to use my BFG?"

"Yes," McCarter agreed. "Time to use your big fucking gun."

"That's good." Manning nodded. "But I sure could go for a piece of Wethers's chocolate cake."

"One thing at a time, mate," McCarter told him. "One thing at a time."

The team unfolded into action, each man knowing exactly the part he was to play.

Their target was surrounded by an elite bodyguard of diehard jihadists, those in turn being only one element in an armed camp of criminal mercenaries and arms smugglers.

Phoenix Force was going to kill or scatter every gun-wielding combatant around the warlord, then subdue, kidnap and inter-rogate him.

Having already detached themselves from the HULC exo-skeletons, the Phoenix Force veterans began prepping the heavy weaponry to be used on the assault.

Despite the use of the HULCs their fatigues were stained with sweat and each man buzzed with the light euphoria athletes find in intense physical exertion. Near now to the killing, the old drug adrenaline began to course through their systems.

McCarter broke radio silence for the first time since inser-tion and contacted the Farm. According to the time on his wristwatch, he was exactly on schedule. Kurtzman answered immediately.

"Go for Stony Man," Kurtzman replied.

"Phoenix in place and ready to initiate contact," McCarter informed him.

To his right Hawkins had settled into position behind his bipod-mounted 25 mm XM-109 rifle. Ten yards down from him, Encizo finished adjusting the elevation on his M-252 81 mm mortar.

"Good copy. We have eyes on," Kurtzman acknowledged.

"Phoenix in play."

Miles overhead, in near-Earth orbit, the Stony Man Keyhole satellite rotated. The KH-13 orbiting camera contained the des-ignation USA193 when launched. Now it served the imagery intelligence needs of the Farm.

In geosynchronous orbit over the Horn of Africa, it gave Price and her team up-to-the-second real-time intelligence.

Next to Encizo, a line of 81 mm mortar shells stood in the shale and dust. Calvin James was sighting down on the terrorist compound through the optics of his FGM-148 Javelin weapons system.

Holding flank-anchor to McCarter's left, Gary Manning's square jaw worked incessantly as he chewed on a wad of caffeine-laced gum. The big Canadian nestled in behind the Jurassic-size bullpup design of the tripod-mounted .50-caliber XM-312.

"Hey, Gary," Hawkins called in his soft Texas drawl. He cradled the buttstock of his massive 25 mm sniper rifle.

"What you need, Hawk?"

"You do realize mine's bigger than yours."

"That's not what your mama said."

The team chuckled. McCarter peered through the optics of his shoulder-mounted missile launcher.

"That's the spirit, boys," he murmured.

His finger found the ignition trigger on the Javelin.

Indian Ocean

THE BOSTON WHALERS tore across the ocean at maximum speed.

Fedorova flared his nostrils, sniffing in the brine stink of the ocean. He looked at the waves skimming by beneath the boat. The keel of the Boston whaler seemed to split back the water into white foam peels as it sliced forward.

Out over the ocean to his right the sun was coming up and in the distance its reflection turned the water bloody. He twisted his head around on a thick, muscular neck and regarded the second Boston whaler filled with hired Somalian pirates and assorted thugs.

They'd returned from slaughtering the merchant marine crew of the VLCC with bloody machetes and ghastly grins. They'd performed their job in stopping an organized counterattack against the bridge team admirably.

Hard men doing a hard job. Fedorova could relate.

Behind them the side of the VLCC exploded outward as the Semtex charges detonated. A brilliant ball of fire punched through the hull like a flaming fist and rolled out across the ocean. A second explosion tripped hard on the first, ripping another hole, this one below the waterline.

Concussive force shoved huge air bubbles up, and Fedorova felt the shiver of the blast through the bottom of his speeding boat even from this distance. Almost immediately the gigantic vessel began to sink. It would be below the surface in a matter of minutes.

Fedorova felt a certain grim satisfaction at the act. Destroying something that big gave him such a feeling of... accomplishment.

He turned and regarded the speeding whaler just off his port. The Somalis were crowded in there sprocket-to-plug, laughing at the sight of the massive freighter as it slipped beneath the waves.

His eyes shifted toward the unnaturally heavy box at the bottom of his Boston whaler. He wasn't a physicist but it didn't take a Ph.D. in material sciences to realize an object that size shouldn't weigh so much.

He looked up and met Suracova's eyes.

The ex-Spetsnaz had a cigarette burning in the corner of his mouth. He arched an eyebrow at the team leader, his brown eyes questioning. Fedorova nodded once and took out his cell phone.

At Fedorova's signal Suracova leaned into the tiller of his twin outboards and the light whaler suddenly veered off sharply to starboard. In a handful of heartbeats the distance between the two raider craft was over fifty yards.

Gregory, who hadn't been informed about this part of the operation, looked up, surprised.

"What's the matter, Suri?" he asked, laughing, in Russian. "Couldn't stand the smell of the monkey meat anymore?"

Suracova grinned back around his smoldering cigarette and thrust his chin toward Fedorova, who was sitting with his cell phone in hand. "Burned monkey meat," the man said.

"What?"

Gregory turned to look at Fedorova. Fedorova smiled at him with pale blue eyes. He tapped the last number into his cell phone with the grimy nail of one thick thumb.

"Better cut," he told the younger mercenary. "Milosevic's orders."

The Somalis had noticed the sudden gap between the boats and were shouting questions as the African running the out-boards tried to close the distance.

Fedorova held his phone up so the confused Somalis could see it. The Somali in the bow, a skinny teenager, misunderstood the gesture and held his own hand up in acknowledgment, big white teeth flashing an uncertain grin.

"Fuck you," Fedorova called cheerfully.

His thumb came down and hit the send button on his phone. The signal left, bounced off the satellite and returned to Earth, reaching the sister phone encased in watertight wrapping amid a dinner-plate-size hunk of Semtex secured to the bottom of the pirates' Boston whaler.

The boat went up like a speeding car suddenly hitting a concrete barrier.

It flipped into the air, breaking apart and sending bodies and parts of bodies spinning out as a ball of fire and black smoke rolled into the air.

"Circle around!" Fedorova yelled at Suracova.

He lifted his rifle and snapped back the bolt, seating a round.

His men didn't need any further instructions about what came next. They were professionals. Ruthlessly they directed a steady stream of autofire at the bodies bobbing in the water.

Somalia

THE SUN was a bloody fist in the sky.

Hawkins moved up the notch of the bluff, the highest point

over the shallow valley, and nestled into position behind the bipod mount of his sniper rifle.

The walled village and terror training compound appeared in his optic like a slide plate under a microscope.

"In position," he said into his throat mike.

"Copy," McCarter said. "You on primary structure?"

Hawkins carefully dialed in his sniper optic.

His field of vision narrowed to a two-story building sitting in a dominant position over the rest of the town to the front of it and the training grounds to the rear.

He saw a sentry armed with a Soviet SVD sniper rifle slung over one shoulder. He checked out the man's scope and recognized it as a stock-issue 4x power.

"I'm on primary."

The operation plan, like all successful ones, was simple.

Most of the heavy weaponry deployed by Phoenix Force would be directed toward the collections of vehicles and the long, low, L-shaped structure identified as the barracks. The plan called for attrition of the target's primary weapon systems, vehicles and the warlord's bodyguard.

Once that was down to a manageable level, and using Hawkins as an overwatch platform on the high terrain, the four-man fire team of Phoenix Force shooters would proceed into the target area and close on the warlord.

Civilians would be allowed to funnel themselves outward or huddle in place. The only use of the indirect or area-effect weapons would be on known hard targets. Hawkins would provide suppressive fire in a surgical manner, allowing him to initiate cover for the team as it moved.

For the purposes of this operation the village had been designated a free-fire zone under secret executive directive. Any male of fighting age, and obviously armed or not, was a legal target.

Hawkins settled his crosshairs on the rooftop sentry.

The big bang of the 25 mm Barrett would initiate the attack, drawing the housed enemy combatants out in a flurry of activity, making them easier to target.

His body melted into place around his weapon as he slowly released his breath in an even stream. His finger took up the slack on the smooth metal curve of his trigger. He squeezed gently.

His trigger pull was so smooth that when the rifle discharged it came as almost a surprise.

He rode out the recoil of the massive sniper rifle. Inside the crystal ball of his scope the sentry disappeared. In his place the terrorist left behind a cloud of red mist and pink meat confetti.

"It's on, mates!" McCarter barked.

For long, long moments there was an unnatural stillness. The echo of the 25 mm gunshot echoed down the shallow desert valley until it evaporated in the distance.

Then, abruptly, there was an explosion of movement and the terrorist center took on the aspect of an anthill on full alert. Men burst from doorways, each armed, each frantically looking around to identify the unseen enemy.

Hawkins killed a second man standing dumbfounded in his doorway. He pulled the shot a hair to the right when he squeezed off the round and only winged the man in the shoulder.

The 25 mm round was so massive the shoulder joint simply disintegrated, taking the arm and a good section of the man's torso with him. The terrorist's body was tossed back inside his house.

Encizo dropped an 81 mm HE round into his mortar tube. It burped back out and sailed up over the valley before coming down hard just beyond the edge of the L-shaped barracks. It hit like a lightning bolt, destroying a battered old white Nissan pickup.

"Drop ten meters!" James yelled, looking through the enhanced optics of his Javelin weapons system.

Over on the .50-caliber machine gun Gary Manning began

knocking rounds down into the village, sweeping them through vehicles and buildings in precise patterns that left ruin and destruction in their wake.

The men in the village were well enough trained. It took them only moments to identify the source of the attack and respond. Men tried to make it to rooftops, groups attempted to set up stations using RPK machine guns and Russian-built 60 mm mortars and return fire.

The defensive plan was a sound one, but Phoenix Force had maximized their own advantages.

Hawkins put first one round then a second into the tanks of the fuel depot next to the training compound's motor pool. A ball of greasy fire lit up the sky, climbing out of a column of rich black smoke.

Encizo dropped a few clicks off the elevation on his big mortar and lobbed another round. This time his 81 mm bomb landed dead center of the barracks roof. The mortar round blasted through the ceiling and exploded with enough power to blow doors off hinges.

Men raced from the now burning barracks only to emerge directly into the heavy machine gun fire of Gary Manning.

The .50-caliber rounds punched through racing men and killed those behind them. Grazing rounds ripped limbs off, leaving men to die in agony, their panicked hearts pumping their lifeblood out into the indifferent dirt.

"Back-blast area clear!" James warned.

"Clear!" the men around him echoed.

His fingers depressed the firing stud and the 127 mm rocket jumped from the disposable firing tube. Moving slow enough for the naked eye to follow, the fire-and-forget antitank weapon raced toward its target, completely self-guided.

The rocket spiraled toward the sentry post set up to control the approach to the training center from the east. Two sentries, wildly firing Kalashnikovs toward the hills, had time to comprehend what was racing toward them and ran for it.

The rocket slammed into the sandbag position with a force originally designed to stop a main battle tank in its tracks. A flash of blinding light raised a swirling cloud of dust, and the sharp crack of detonation followed immediately.

Out of the roiling cloud a body spun straight up, rotating like a Frisbee. It landed hard twenty yards away and bounced, legs, arms and head all twisted at improbable angles.

CHAPTER FOURTEEN

As the dust settled the other sentry could be seen, missing a leg and crawling toward the dubious safety of the compound's mud-brick wall.

In a casual manner Gary Manning swiveled the XM-312 on its tripod and cut him in two.

Up above the team, Hawkins had reduced his field of fire to the big house containing the warlord. When bodyguards tried to make for the roof, he killed them. When he observed reinforcements darting through alleys to reach the command structure, he killed them. When the heads of defenders appeared in the windows, he killed them.

Suddenly, from a big garage, a self-propelled Chinese Type 95 SPAAA antiaircraft gun emerged.

It rolled out on six tracked wheels, the driver hatch buttoned down tight. The four-gun turret shifted as it rolled, putting the 25 mm autocannons into orientation toward Phoenix Force's high ground position.

"Jesus Christ!" James shouted in warning. "Armor!"

Both Hawkins and Manning shifted their aim toward the new threat, but before they could bring effective fire to bear, the Type 87 cannons opened up.

A storm of 25 mm projectiles whistled across the distance and started slamming into the dirt of the hillside just below their dug-in positions. Getting a face full of grit and rock shards, Encizo was forced to throw himself backward as James somersaulted off to one side and behind the defilade of the ridge line.

The big rounds slammed into the earth, chewing through rock and gravel like massive buzz saws. Below them the track moved forward, gaining speed as it narrowed the distance.

Manning was forced to tumble to the side as one of the 25 mm rounds struck the rucksack lying next to him and blew it apart. His .50 caliber fire died abruptly. On the upper knob Hawkins fired his last slug and dropped the 5-round magazine from the well before snatching up a replacement and moving to shove it home.

The Type 87 cannons vomited monstrous slugs that burned through the air around him, forcing the Texan, despite himself, to also duck for cover.

In the eye of the storm David McCarter remained motionless, crouched in a tight position right out in the open. The al Qaeda gunner working the antiaircraft gun rotated his turret, attempting to triangulate his blasts to fall on the lone silhouette kneeling on the ridge line above him.

"Back-blast area clear!" McCarter yelled.

A barrage of 25 mm rounds hammered into the ground only yards from his position as his 147 mm rocket leaped from its tube like a greyhound race dog from the gate. As soon as the weapon was clear McCarter threw the tube to the side and leaped for the cover of the nearest contour line.

Dirt slapped his face as rounds hammered into the earth just below him. The concussive force of the huge caliber rounds was terrifying in its power.

He flipped in the air, landed hard on his left shoulder and rolled over, flinging himself down the hillside. He struck the earth along his back and skidded down the loose scree.

Hawkins lifted his head from cover and brought his XM-109 to his shoulder. He quickly orientated the muzzle of the rifle and brought the SPAAA up into the crosshairs of his optics.

Below the team the Javelin rocket slammed into the self-propelled antiaircraft gun and flames spread like splashing water over the vehicle structure. The gun system rocked up on its tracks as metal was peeled back and a gaping hole split the top of the combat chassis.

Half a second later the ammunition hold went up in a string of explosions.

"Back on target!" McCarter ordered.

Phoenix Force scrambled back into position behind their weapons.

Above them Hawkins fired again and again, dropped his 5-round magazine and reloaded. Below them Phoenix Force's unwillingness to fire blindly into dwellings and possibly endanger civilians was giving the enemy a method by which to coordinate their defense.

Encizo dropped another three 81 mm rounds down on the barracks in rapid succession, helped by the presence of James, who fed him mortar shells.

Manning began directing his own fire away from the smoldering barracks and into the vehicles parked near the fiercely burning fuel storage tanks.

The attack priorities had been carefully crafted during the planning stages of the assault and every effort was being made to nullify the al Qaeda cadre's ability to make a motorized escape.

The big Canadian pounded out long ragged bursts, stripping the trucks and SUVs down to component parts, shredding rubber tires, ruining engine blocks and setting more than a few of the vehicles on fire.

Most of the compound's heavier weapons, crew-served machine guns, antiaircraft weapons and even their mortars, were vehicle mounted and to deploy them against their attackers the terrorists first drove them into position.

Commanding the high ground to such an extent left the compound and the movement of its defenders as open as a game board to Phoenix Force.

Each time a weapon-mounted "technical" made a break for position, Hawkins or Manning would methodically disable it then turn their attention to the weapon itself, leaving the mop-up of the fighters themselves to McCarter with his M-4.

Soon individual snipers, well ensconced inside the compound buildings, were attempting to return precision fire, but within minutes Hawkins's ability to shoot *through* walls had stilled even that.

McCarter put a series of 3-round bursts directly in front of a running man as Encizo dropped the last of his mortar rounds into the M-81 tube. The terrorist sprinted into the 5.56 mm Teflon-coated rounds and dropped instantly.

The final two mortar rounds hit a moment later, tripping hard one right after the other and completely collapsing the barracks.

"Prepare for assault!" McCarter ordered.

Instantly, each man unfolded in a choreographed series of motions.

Manning and Encizo manhandled their weapons into a shallow depression already containing the HULC exoskeletons, while James, an ex-Navy SEAL, prepared a short daisy chain of AN-M14 incendiary grenades.

Each canister held eight hundred grams of thermate. The chemical reaction of powdered aluminum metal and iron oxide would combust when ignited to produce a stream of molten iron and aluminum oxide. This reaction produced tremendous heat, burning at 2200 degrees Celsius.

The burning devices would reduce anything beneath them to a molten slag. Nothing would be left behind to provide irrefutable proof or useable equipment that could fall into the wrong hands.

McCarter took up a coil of climbing rope and heaved it down the side of the steep hill. It trailed out, carried by its own weight, and he latched in so that he faced the decline face-first, or Australian style, and clipped the rope into a D-ring on his harness.

Around him the other three members did the same.

Above them Hawkins fired round after round.

"I'm only getting resistance from the warlord's hacienda now," the Texan drawled into his throat mike. "Assuming no tunnels, they can get out the back door but won't be able to cross the alley without my see—"

His running update was interrupted as the 25 mm Barrett boomed.

"Seeing them," he finished. "Boys, you feel free to run on down and play now."

"Copy, mate," McCarter agreed, then called, "Online!" He looked around and saw the team were on their ropes. He lifted his weapon up then gave the command, "Forward!"

The four-man assault squad ran forward over the edge and down the steep decline grade. The ropes were not for a vertical rappel, but served only as tension guides to allow them to traverse the tricky grade more rapidly.

They pounded down the hillside, running full-out over the sliding gravel and broken ground. At the bottom they took their weapons up in both hands and simply ran off the ends of their ropes.

Behind them the thermite grenades sent up a noxious cloud of smoke as the metal and plastic of their gear and weapons melted into a useless pile of slag. Hawkins dropped an empty magazine and seated another.

Ahead of them small-arms fire broke out from the burning compound.

Stony Man Farm

PRICE STOOD riveted.

Above her the attack in Africa played out on her screen courtesy of the Keyhole satellite. The clarity was startling as the violence unfolded. Via the sat com booster in McCarter's rucksack she, the mission controller, was plugged directly into the tactical team's communication transmissions.

Beside her Aaron Kurtzman sat in his heavily modified wheelchair, multitasking with the precision of a tech-savvy professional.

Across the room Wethers and Tokaido worked at their stations while monitoring the progress of Phoenix Force on the screen. It was utterly compelling viewing.

"I just got a situation report on the A-Space network." Kurtzman spoke up. "About Africa—" he frowned "—well, almost Africa. But our mission profile said the compound was tied into pirate activity, right?"

Price nodded. "Sure. Manpower and the deployment of security through that region for ransom payments."

"A VLCC in the Indian Ocean just went off the grid."

Price frowned, eyes still on the screen. "Off the grid? They got taken?"

"Communication ended. Then the GPS signal went dead," Kurtzman explained. "The request is for imagery intelligence assets in the area to be diverted. The DOE is frantic."

Price turned from the screen, alarm bells going off in her head. "The DOE? Why does the DOE have their panties in a bunch over a VLCC in another hemisphere?"

"Clandestine transport op?" Kurtzman offered.

Price tapped her lip. Unless the Navy had reconnaissance planes out from the Diego Garcia station the most likely candidate for imagery intelligence asset was Stony Man's Keyhole satellite now in geosynch orbit over the Horn of Africa.

"Once Phoenix completes this takedown we need the uplink to run the interrogation for the translator."

"The plan is for them to wipe out everyone who's a threat," Kurtzman pointed out. "We don't have to reorbit. We just have to reorientate the camera."

"Sure, it's just like playing Xbox," she replied, voice dry.

Kurtzman shrugged his power lifter's shoulders. "Couple lines of code and the camera rotates out to the coordinates where the vessel was last seen. Kind of weird anyway," he added. "We're working a DOE case in Canada and suddenly they show up in trouble on the Indian Ocean."

"I don't like coincidences," Price admitted.

She eyed the screen. The truth was, the optics of the assault were a luxury as long as communication links remained open. There was nothing she could do to help Phoenix Force by watching the battle vicariously.

The real need was after the raid when the language guy from the DIA went online.

She tapped her finger against her lip then put her hands on her hips.

"Do it," she ordered.

CHAPTER FIFTEEN

Toronto

Inside the safehouse, Able Team worked methodically.

Rosario Blancanales cleaned and treated their superficial wounds, including sewing up his own elbow gash, while Hermann Schwarz worked with patient diligence on the electronics taken from Tsai's apartment.

They needed the next link in the trail they were building toward their final target.

Pacing relentlessly, Carl Lyons walked out of the kitchen eating a sandwich and past Schwarz. The electronics genius looked up from where he was working.

"What do you call cheese that's not yours?"

Lyons ignored him.

"Nacho cheese," Schwarz answered. Chuckling to himself, he bent his head and went back to work muttering, "*Not* 'cho cheese."

The electronics expert continued working diligently. Utilizing a Linux box, Schwarz initiated a Red Hat program. These devices had been taken off NSA models of the civilian versions and then further upgraded by Kurtzman.

"I am so *L*-three-three-*T*," he muttered.

Lyons looked over toward Blancanales and mouthed the question, "L33t?"

Blancanales went on cleaning the team weapons, scrubbing carbon from barrels, rubbing a light covering of oil on receivers and refilling spent magazines. "It's phonetic geek speak. *L*-three-three-*T* equals 'elite.'"

"Whatever."

At loose ends Lyons put his feet up on a dining-room chair, supported the weight of his body on his thumb and fingertips and began pumping out push-ups.

The tendons in his hand stood out like cables under tension. A body-hardening technique from his karate training, the exercise allowed him to strike with stiffened fingers made as dense as wooden blocks.

Working with a certain graceless rhythm, Schwarz pulled up a program designed to mimic, on a much more advanced level, the Mac OSX install directives.

Opening up the screen on his own SME PED where it was slaved to Tsai's PowerBook, he tabbed the Insert Disk penumbra program, clicked on the install icon, but didn't install. Instead, he followed the succession of opening windows until he got to the regular install screen, clicked utilities and selected Reset Password.

Schwarz started chuckling to himself.

The laughter had a slightly disturbing element to it, as if his genius were, if not mad, then certainly slightly off-kilter.

After the set of push-ups on his fingers Lyons began another, this time forming his hands into fists and resting his elevated body weight on his knuckles.

The stress here helped form dense calluses over his knuckles, simultaneously serving to protect the bones of his hands when he punched and also working to make the impact of those jabs and hooks more unyielding and devastating.

Over the years the exercise had built the ex-cop's hands to the point that it was as if he walked around with brass knuckles on at all times.

"Tsai was scared," Blancanales said, thinking out loud, connecting dots. "He's a criminal mercenary, not an ideologue.

There's only way you maintain that sort of discipline," he declared flatly. "Through terror."

Lyons climbed to his feet. "True enough. Only the most violent of rodents gets to be the king rat. But Tsai was also a loser at the bottom of the food chain. He was doing cutout, expendable scut work."

"True. But the fact that a street kingpin like Tsai was only a minor-league player for this Seven says something about them."

Lyons made a fist and the knuckles of his hand popped like a string of firecrackers under the pressure of his grip.

"He was taking orders," he agreed. "Him pulling a surveillance op on a DOE contractor? Doesn't jive. That boy was a fucking puppet and someone was pulling his strings."

"Who's a genius?" Schwarz interrupted.

Lyons looked over and the U.S. Army veteran was grinning like a used-car salesman. Lyons looked away, sighing, and spoke to Blancanales. "I hate this part. It's like working with an idiot savant."

"Who's a genius?" Schwarz repeated.

"I get it, I get it!" Lyons snarled. "You broke in, you got the info. Can we just have the high points?"

"Who's a genius?" Schwarz demanded.

"Tell him," Lyons conceded.

"You, Gadgets," Blancanales said, voice mild. "You're a genius."

"Yes, I am," the hacker cheerfully agreed. "I'm going to download this to my SME PED, send it on to Wethers at the Farm and let him run it through the Cray," he explained, referencing one of the two supercomputers located at Stony Man. "I've got Tsai's emails, his browsing history and all the numbers he dialed on his cell phone in the last month." He paused, looked up. "Thing is," he continued, "his encryption and security was damn good. Much better than commercial grade, even the high-end stuff."

"Like Puzzle Palace good?" Blancanales asked, referring to the nickname for the National Security Agency.

Schwarz shook his head. "No. Not that good. I wouldn't have been able to crack it here if it'd been first-tier-intelligence good. We'd have had to ship it straight back to the Farm. But it's as good as a China or say an Iran gives their guys."

"If this asshole was cannon fodder," Lyons pointed out, "and he's got that kind of tech to run street jobs in Toronto, for God's sake, then what can we expect when we climb up the ladder?"

Schwarz shrugged. "Probably the best available," he admitted. He smiled again. "But don't get your panties in a bunch, Ironman. These ass clowns don't have me."

"Yeah. Lucky us."

Somalia

UNDER THE GUN of T. J. Hawkins, Phoenix Force entered the town.

Each man had the route to the warlord's compound memorized and they moved quickly through the devastation, killing wounded terrorists as they proceeded.

Rafael Encizo led the way, his SAW up and ready, scanning ahead of him as he pushed deeper into the buildup of mud-brick buildings and worn, hard-packed dirt alleys.

McCarter followed ten yards to the rear, his M-4/M-203 covering rooftops and doorways from their seven-o'clock position to an overlap with Encizo's eleven-o'clock anchor point.

Right behind him came Calvin James, his own M-4/M-203 combo tracking the opposite side of the clock. Behind the team Gary Manning walked the rear security position in a sideway shuffle that allowed him to cover the four-to-seven-o'clock positions.

From elevation Hawkins watched over the team like some

murderous Old Testament angel wielding the power of thunder and lightning.

Encizo was sweating freely in the heat of the African morning, his breath coming rapid and shallow as he moved with purpose through the labyrinthine village.

A terrorist hung out of a window, complete only from the waist down. The rest of the man was pooled in a gooey mess around a busted AKM assault rifle on the street.

A burst of Manning's .50-caliber fire had liquefied him into two sloppy parts.

McCarter sensed movement above him. His carbine, already at his shoulder, snapped onto target. He saw a black-turbaned warrior in khaki fatigues crest a roofline, folding-stock AKS-74 in hand. The ex-SAS trooper's finger applied pressure to his trigger.

Before he could fire, the terrorist exploded. The sound of Hawkins's 25 mm Barrett rolled down the valley. Blood and bits of body rained down around Phoenix Force like a monsoon shower.

"Christ," McCarter rumbled. "That crazy bloke is having too much fun with that freakin' cannon."

Behind them a terrorist stepped out of a narrow pig-run of an alley. The man bounced off a wall like a stumbling drunk, blood trailing behind him from a massive cavity where his left arm had once been attached to his body at the shoulder.

Staggering from blood loss, he dragged his Kalashnikov behind him in his remaining hand. His face was white and slack with shock. An artery in his torso squirted blood like a lawn sprinkler from the ragged place where his arm had been.

Manning fired a tight burst into his chest, dropping him.

Encizo increased his pace, moving faster the closer they drew to the warlord.

He came to the edge of a warren-run alley and darted his head around the corner of the building to reconnoiter the open street. A burning vehicle rested up against a building. Two terrorist bodies lay sprawled out on the dirt road.

A burst of machine gun fire erupted out of an open doorway, and 7.62 mm ComBloc rounds ate into the mud brick next to Encizo's head like buzz saws. The Cuban combat diver jerked back behind cover.

His finger went to his headset. "You got an angle on the machine gunner?" he asked into his throat mike.

"Negative," Hawkins replied. "The building you're up against provides a defilade I can't see over. Plus you must have a structure or vehicle fire as the smoke is bad over that area."

"Copy," Encizo acknowledged. He looked at McCarter.

The Briton nodded. "By the numbers, mates," he said.

Encizo leveraged his SAW around the corner of the building and began burning through his 200-round drum in a sustained burst designed to make the enemy duck and cover.

McCarter looked at James. James nodded back.

Both men shuffled forward in hunched crouches. They peeked around the edge of the building as Encizo fired, one man leaning against the wall and looking high while the other crouched in a three-point stance and snatched a peek from closer to the ground.

"Got it," James said, pulling back.

"Good," McCarter replied. "Three, two, go!"

The men swung around like a car door popping open.

Each had his weapon up and firing before simultaneously ducking back as a wall of lead hammered toward them. Green tracer fire, eerily bright in the red light of the early morning sun, burned through the air.

Their weapons made the distinctive *bloop* sound as the 40 mm HE rounds popped out of the underslung tubes and sailed across the forty yards. The blunt-nosed bombs arced into the building like deadly footballs snapped from the hand of a prime-time NFL quarterback.

The accuracy was appalling.

The rounds slammed in through the open door and detonated in twin hammer falls. Yellow flame and dirty brown smoke gushed outward. The machine-gun fire ceased.

Encizo seized the initiative and came fully around the corner, taking the time to carefully aim his Squad Automatic Weapon. He put fifteen rounds straight through the wrecked opening at knee height and watched as his red tracer rounds bounced off something hard and skipped into the darkness.

"Let's go!" McCarter ordered.

As if moving under one mind, the men rose from their crouches and sprinted across the street. The desiccated African air seemed to be getting hotter by the moment as the sun climbed over the horizon.

Suddenly a knot of desperate terrorists charged from the gate of a courtyard. Small-arms fire erupted in a hailstorm.

Manning shuffled backward, firing his weapon.

Spent shells kicked up and out of the hot breech in a tight golden arch. The bolt locked in the open position as the last round in his magazine fired.

Smoothly, the Canadian grasped the spent drum, disengaged it from the magazine well and then yanked his backup out and slid it home.

He pulled his finger out of the trigger guard and reached up to tap the bolt release.

The bolt slid forward and chambered a round. Manning spun and fired into a pair of leaping terrorists. The rounds slapped into them and they crumpled, their forward momentum sending them into face-first slides.

An RPG round zipped out of the open window of a nearby house, and the four men split in a desperate attempt to avoid the explosion.

The warhead detonated. Shrapnel forced the diving men to hug the ground tighter. As the smoke cleared Encizo rose and saw James. Then he saw the terrorists.

"Go! Go!" he shouted.

James turned and looked for a clear path.

Terrorists were coming through the rubble all around them. Behind him an empty one-story structure stood like a tombstone alone on an empty prairie. It was nondescript and formed from a featureless concrete mold, and old blasts had stripped it of any vestiges of identification.

Behind him Encizo fired madly. He could hear his partner's bursts growing longer and more ragged as the terrorist grouping pushed on, heedless of their fallen comrades. James was hit with a sudden burst of inspiration.

He couldn't see McCarter or Manning.

He darted through the open door into the building.

"Encizo!" he yelled. "This way!"

Encizo risked a quick look over his shoulder, frowned.

He turned back around and cut loose with a long burst, sweeping his muzzle in a figure-eight pattern. He spun and sprinted through the door. Behind him the terrorists shrieked, leaping over the torn corpses of their brothers to give chase.

The weapons fired wildly as excitement and bloodlust spoiled their aim.

Encizo looked around, taking in the single room as he dropped the magazine from his weapon and inserted another.

The little building was a hollowed-out shell. The walls were scorched and the single room filled with dust and debris but nothing else. The window and door to the front were blown-out cavities along with two windows in the back wall.

It appeared a mortar round had scorched the building clean.

Encizo shot the first terrorists to come through the door. He turned and shot another climbing through the window.

Jesus, how many are there? He looked over at James just as the ex-SEAL pulled a grenade from his kit. Automatically, Encizo ran down the specs in his head.

MK3 A2 offensive hand grenade. Size 136 mm cylindrical. Weight 15.6 oz. Blast radius 22.9 mm. Encizo didn't consciously call the facts up; they popped unbidden into his mind, a product of conditioning.

He looked up as James yanked the pin and released the safety lever. He met the man's gaze with a huge grin. James dropped the grenade where he stood and spun toward the rear of the structure. Behind them terrorists poured through the door or dived through the empty window frame, mindless in their killing frenzy.

The two commandos sprinted toward the open window.

The room was thick with shrieking, firing killers. James leaped up and grabbed hold of the windowsill. Coming up behind him, Encizo unceremoniously shoved him up and out.

Behind him the room was a mob scene.

He caught movement out of his peripheral vision and twisted at the waist. The jihadists loomed above him, snarling as tried to swing his buttstock like a club.

James smashed the butt of his weapon into the combatant's mouth with a riposte maneuver and drove it back into the others.

Encizo turned and threw his weapon through the window before jumping up and diving after it.

In the hollow building the grenade went off and even through the chaos Encizo winced at the explosion. Shrapnel cut into the already perforated and scorched metal skin of a nearby pickup.

The building made a tremendous crash as it collapsed.

The Cuban combat diver came up, thinking, James!

In the next instant the black man emerged from the smoke and dust, grinning like a kid at Christmas.

"Phoenix!" McCarter yelled. Manning towered like an oak tree next to him.

The ex-SAS trooper jerked his hand toward the warlord's compound, sending Encizo forward in his point man role as James fell back into position.

Encizo crossed the street and ran up to the doorway of

another building. He charged a closed door and lifted up a big boot. Letting his momentum carry him forward, he launched a snap kick into the wooden frame.

The door exploded off its hinges and Encizo drove through the opening, his SAW held ready at waist level. James and McCarter were half a step behind him as they entered the mud-brick building.

CHAPTER SIXTEEN

A figure appeared in an interior doorway. Encizo's eyes flashed to the man's hands, his own finger tight on his trigger. He saw a weapon in the rushing figure's grasp.

The SAW ripped open and eight hardball rounds, green-tipped and Teflon-coated, struck the armed combatant center mass.

Coming in behind him, James leveled his own weapon. He moved through the space left empty by Encizo as the point man cleared deeper into the building. He came even with a hallway and saw motion.

His eyes went to the hands, M-4 poised.

He saw no weapon. He allowed himself to see the entire picture a heartbeat later. A woman in traditional grab had covered up three silent, huge-eyed children with her own body, terror naked in her own eyes.

"Civilians," James warned in a loud voice. "Three children and a female."

"Understood," McCarter answered. "Cover while we transition."

Manning moved through the front door, weapon held ready.

Ahead of them, Encizo pushed on through the structure to the final room and peered out the back door. Across the broad, hard-worn avenue, the wall of the warlord's personal residence rose up from the street.

Another pickup sat burning in the street and at the other end a pile of bodies lay scattered around a heavy-machine-gun position. On the roof of the two-story building dead men lay strewn with limbs hanging over the edge.

One of Encizo's mortar rounds had knocked a hole in the wall, revealing a brick courtyard just to the front of the house. There was a flash of motion and an armed man ran past the opening, weapon up.

From inside the smaller house McCarter eyed his target. His gaze hunted the upper-story windows of the warlord's big house. He could hear men calling out in a dialect he didn't speak, one bull voice shouting orders.

"You got eyes on the mansion, Hawk?" he said into his throat mike.

"Yeah, the boys inside are hanging low," Hawkins replied in his smooth Texas drawl. "Nobody's sticking their head out the windows or going up on the roof anymore. I can't place any shots between the front wall and the main house, though, not from very many angles anyway."

"Understood," McCarter replied. "I'm going to proceed with smoke, then. Go ahead and hunt for targets of opportunity."

"Copy," Hawkins replied.

McCarter looked to Encizo. The Cuban showed him two pale green cylinders, AN smoke grenades. "You going to drop one over the wall with the 203?"

McCarter nodded. "I'm thinking of using CS."

"That'd work." James spoke up. He still covered the silent family. "I bet the bodyguard unit is packed in there like sardines. We'll have to go in there masked up, though."

McCarter considered for a moment then nodded. "Let's do it."

Encizo pulled the pins on his smoke grenades and tossed them easily out through the cracked-open back door of the house. They bounced into the middle of the dirt street and began spewing gray smoke into billowing clouds.

Manning covered security while both McCarter and James

put on their protective masks. Once they were finished, Manning and Encizo followed suit.

Under cover of the hanging smoke clouds McCarter and James then loaded up their grenade launchers with CS rounds and crept carefully forward.

Swirling smoke obscured them while leaving the basic outlined framework of the structure they were assaulting readily apparent.

Each man put the collapsible stock of his M-4 carbine to his shoulder, fingers on the triggers of their grenade launchers.

Thunk! Thunk!

The rounds hammered out.

McCarter's projectiles arced high and short over the wall to land in the courtyard while James put his own 40 mm grenade on a flatter trajectory that tracked through an upstairs window.

"Move!" McCarter ordered.

Encizo rushed forward, leading with the SAW as Manning stepped out and lobbed a CS hand grenade of his own over the wall and into the warlord's courtyard.

Moving quickly, McCarter and James folded back into line.

Sprinting in Ranger file formation, Phoenix Force breached the wall and entered the compound.

New York City

MORNING TRAFFIC was already a fierce gridlock as the taxicab pulled up on Second Avenue. Carmen Delahunt tipped the driver, a Rastafarian with pictures of his five children taped to his dashboard, and got out.

She glanced at the slim Lady Executive Belarus watch on her wrist.

She was early, which was fine. The morning air was unseasonably warm and after the congestion of the avenue the sidewalk was surprisingly thinly populated.

Moving at a brisk pace, Delahunt crossed over to the door under the white numerals 837 of the street address and walked through the narrow entrance of the Palm Too restaurant.

She blinked the sun glare out of her eyes and acquainted herself with the cool gloom inside the building.

Ahead of her the back bar mirror showed her own redheaded reflection.

Chairs were up on the tables. Sawdust was scattered on the floor of the narrow room. A few patrons sat drinking despite the early hour, and the bartender nodded toward her as there didn't seem to be a maître d' on duty this early in the day.

"Help you, miss?" the man asked, his accent gently Bronx.

"I'm meeting someone," she informed him. She walked forward and took a seat at the bar. "Coffee for now."

There was a Yankees bumper stinker on the cash register, and Old Blue Eyes was singing softly about doing it his way over the sound system. The place was crammed with ambience.

"Coming right up to *youse*." The man smiled.

She noticed how he'd played up his accent and realized he must have pegged her as an out-of-towner. She smiled.

Compared to the Big Apple she guessed D.C. seemed provincial, though it was plenty big enough for her.

David King entered four minutes later, looking harried and tired. He was a heavy-set man with dark hair and sixteen years of service in the FBI.

"Carm," he said, and smiled by way of introduction.

Delahunt turned at his voice and was ready to reply when she saw the exhausted look in his eyes.

"Hey, David," she said. "Everything okay?"

"Let's sit," he said, indicating a booth. He turned to the bartender. "Another coffee."

The bartender nodded once; there was no mistaking King

for an out-of-towner. He was as New York as Palm Too was. As he sat he automatically reached for a pack of cigarettes, then remembered he couldn't smoke inside the building and frowned in a distracted manner.

"Dave?" Delahunt reached out and grasped his hand lightly.

He sighed and visibly relaxed, looking at the ex-FBI agent with tired eyes.

They'd known each for quite a while, had worked the bank-robbery division years ago. King remained one of Delahunt's best remaining eyes-and-ears inside the bureau.

Years ago she'd put two 9 mm rounds into a robbery suspect with a pump-action shotgun who'd already shot King once. He remembered and honored that.

"Dave?" she repeated.

"You know," he said casually as the bartender brought his coffee over, "I've never asked you where it was you moved on to."

Delahunt avoided his eyes, stirring sugar into her coffee. It was better than Kurtzman's. "I *did* tell you," she said. "I still work for the Department of Justice, just outside of FBI proper." This was true enough.

"I understand you work for Hal Brognola," King said.

"What if I did?" Delahunt countered, voice even.

Brognola's name wasn't a state secret. He was the man who'd ended the bloody rampage of the most infamous vigilante in American history, Mack Bolan, aka the Executioner, after all. It had made him a legend.

King shrugged. "Just saying. After that big day in Central Park when he brought down Mack 'the Bastard' Bolan, they say he went spook."

"Dave, I don't understand," Delahunt interrupted. "Are you fishing for something? I can promise you Brognola doesn't work for the Agency. I can promise you I don't work for the Agency." She set her coffee cup down. "Christ, Dave, Brognola's got an office right in the damn Justice building! You're making it sound like he exists on a supersecret compound in the woods. What's this all about?"

King leaned forward. "I know I owe you. And really, I know you, Carm. I don't mind helping you." He leaned back and looked around. "It's just that I don't want to get caught up in any interagency firefights."

Delahunt looked at him. "What did you find out?"

"That's just it," he snapped with sudden energy. "I found out nothing...or almost nothing. I got a visit from a goddamn GAO accountant asking to look into my expense account for my last sixteen operations and to see any receipts I had for the trip my wife and I took to Hawaii for our twentieth anniversary!"

"Wow," Delahunt said, impressed despite herself. "How many phone calls had you made before that happened?"

"Just a couple, and a database search—just fishing, you know? I think I made a mistake when I went to a buddy I thought might have worked with this guy."

"Yeah?"

"Guy I went to the academy with," King explained. "He went into white-collar crimes. He's worked with GAO investigators looking into misspent funds to contractors over in Iraq. I thought he might have had some insight poop."

"Did he?"

"None. Or none he was willing to share. And bang, five hours after I pay him a visit I've got GAO bean counters crawling all over my expense accounts. I don't need that kind of mess, Carm." He looked away, too embarrassed to meet her eyes. "I got two years left and I retire. Melissa and I got an eye on a condo down in Boca Raton. I'm going to do a little fishing." He lifted his hands up. "I just can't afford the heat."

"You can tell me something, anything?" Delahunt pushed.

She felt bad doing it, but here was the truth; if David King couldn't afford the heat, then an outfit like Stony Man certainly couldn't afford scrutiny.

Careers would end in flames, field operators could end up in Leavenworth prison if the details of some of Stony Man's ops ever made the front page of the *New York Times*.

"All I'm going to say is Hammond Carter is running the GAO the way J. Edgar Hoover ran the FBI. Except he stays below the radar in the number-three position where changing political administrations can't ever touch him."

"He's using blackmail to acquire power?"

"He may not know where all the bodies are buried, but he knows where all the money went missing, and that's just as bad. No one is going to stand up to him. No one."

King got up, picked up his coat. He put a hand on Delahunt's shoulder. "If you can cover your tracks, you might be able to dig up some information to give you a better picture.

"I suspect most mainline data servers in the government have some kind of tripwire program so that he finds out pretty damn quick who's investigating him. What you've got to figure out before anything else is, if he suddenly wants to start looking into you, then there's a reason.

"Try to figure out how and why he's turned his eyes in your direction," King told her. "Do that and maybe you can reverse engineer an escape hatch. But I don't know."

Delahunt looked up and smiled. "Thanks, David. It was good seeing you again. Give my love to Melissa."

"I will," King promised. "Hug those kids of yours for me, and for them, be careful on this one."

"Take care."

"Bye."

She watched him shrug on his coat on and leave the restaurant. As he walked out the door the bartender held up the coffeepot, asking if she needed a refill. Absentmindedly, she put her hand over the top of the cup and shook her head no.

With her other hand she pulled out her SME PED phone and used her thumb to plug in the speed-dial option. She tossed her head and flipped her red hair behind the ear she pressed the phone up against.

At Stony Man, Barbara Price answered on the first ring.

"Barb? Carmen. I'm on my way home."

Somalia

RUNNING HARD, Phoenix Force covered the distance.

Heated air from the burning vehicles created an eddy in the swirling smoke and CS gas that formed a pocket. Above the running commandos a terrorist appeared in an upper-story window.

He saw the sprinting assault force and leveled his AKM.

Suddenly he was gone.

The report of Hawkins's 25 mm round echoed across the shallow valley.

As Encizo plunged through the breach in the outer wall and entered the courtyard, the 25 mm sniper rifle boomed again. McCarter, James and Manning stormed the area behind the Cuban. Adrenaline charged through their system in greasy cold shots.

Their actions were precise, instantaneous, aggressive and lethally professional.

Where they aimed, bullets went. Where bullets struck, men died. The courtyard was a target-rich environment.

Several squads of the warlord's bodyguard contingent milled around in the blinding, choking CS gas. Men wailed as tears poured from burning eyes; they hacked and coughed and vomited, made nearly helpless by the harsh chemical agent.

McCarter swiveled from the hip as he moved through the toxic fog, the M-4/M-203 coming up as he sighted a knot of milling terrorists. The 40 mm grenade launcher *blooped* and a fléchette-stuffed antipersonnel round shredded the throng.

Men went down, flesh scythed from bone.

James triggered his own AP round and knocked more of

them to the ground in geysers of blood. Encizo opened up with his SAW from the front as Manning fired a third AP round.

Encizo's 5.56 mm slugs churned out with relentless intensity, the high-velocity rounds knifing into bodies, skipping off bones and chewing their way clear of bodies, leaving horrific wounds.

Encizo pulled the trigger back on the SAW and didn't release it until the rest of his 200-round drum burned empty.

When the bolt on his weapon locked to the rear he threw the smoking, red-hot weapon to one side and drew his Kel-Tec PLR-16 model 5.56 mm pistol from an open-sided thigh holster. The machine pistol held a 30-round magazine.

He was at the edge of the front door leading into the main house. Behind him the other three Phoenix Force members went to one knee simultaneously in a loose crescent formation.

Each man burned off a succession of 3-round bursts.

Wearing the protective masks forced the Phoenix Force marksmen to hold their weapons canted at extreme angles to compensate for their inability to achieve a seamless cheek-to-stock weld.

Despite this their aim was uncannily accurate in the kill chute of the courtyard.

In desperation the choking, blinded terrorists began firing wildly, their bullets striking each other. Men were screaming, crying out in anguish as Phoenix Force became their executioners.

Encizo rushed toward the door, Kel-Tec up and ready as he freed what appeared to be a commercial caulking gun from the side of his web belt. Working one-handed, he shoved the nozzle into the jamb where the handle was and pressed the leverlike trigger.

White foam spewed from the barrel, quickly setting and hardening in the air. He ran a line down the door from five feet up to the ground.

Slapping the metal eye built into the pistol grip back onto

the D-Ring carabiner suspended from his web belt, Encizo produced a timing pencil from his fatigue jacket pocket.

A burst of machine-gun fire tore through the door.

Heavy 7.62 mm ComBloc rounds punched through the wood and knifed through Encizo.

One struck the ceramic plate in his ballistic vest, shattering it and knocking him backward. His left bicep was mangled by a round, his right shoulder creased. A fourth bullet tore a gouge of meat off his trapezius muscle next to his neck, inches from his jugular.

The Cuban combat diver was slammed to the ground.

The kinetic shock left him feeling stunned. He blinked and the pain hit him like a tsunami and he gasped.

More machine-gun rounds ate through the door. In a dream-like moment he saw a green tracer burn past his face like a lightning bug on amphetamines.

He couldn't catch his breath; the protective mask was suffocating him. He seemed to be doing something with his left hand despite the wound to his arm. He fought back the pain, tried to figure out what the hell he was doing.

The timer.

He had armed the pencil timer on autopilot despite the shock of his wounds. He struggled to sit up and his neck felt as if the muscles had been torn in two, shredded like paper.

He screamed and almost blacked out.

More bullets struck the door, most not punching through. He did a half sit-up, rolling up, and shoved the end of the timer into the plastic-explosive foam-shaped charge.

He had fifteen seconds. He turned and tried to crawl clear.

He blacked out.

CHAPTER SEVENTEEN

Stony Man Farm

Barbara Price hung up her phone. Turning, she watched the satellite feed, her eyes narrowed.

"Give me the coordinates once more," Kurtzman instructed. "I've got to type the commands in down to the degree or we'll be off by miles."

From his position at the workstation Akira Tokaido slowly read off the coordinates as Kurtzman typed in the commands. On the monitor the geography of eastern Africa and the Indian Ocean shifted smoothly, scrolling across the screen, showing an extreme high-altitude view.

Barbara Price, by far the most experienced of the Farm personnel at imagery intelligence, from her years at the NSA, watched the feed with scrutinizing eyes.

In the upper corner of the image, numbers indicating latitude and longitude blinked as they counted down toward the target coordinates. As the satellite came to a stop, the coordinate numbers turned green, flashed twice, then locked.

"What's taking so long, Bear?" Tokaido asked. "You typing the instructions in using HTML? Maybe binary? You know our programs have automated plug-ins now, right? What are you going to do later, make a fire by rubbing two sticks together?"

"Screw you, son," Kurtzman replied, voice cheerful.

"There!" Price broke in.

"What?" Kurtzman demanded. "I'm dead on site. I don't see anything, let alone a goddamn VLCC ship."

"That disturbance on the lens."

"Clouds?"

"No." Price shook her head firmly. "That's smoke, people. We go to the coordinates given us and we find no vessel but only open water and a dissipating smoke cloud."

"How are you going to sink a VLCC *that* fast?" Kurtzman growled.

"With prior planning," Price replied. She paused, cocked her head to one side. "And a whole bunch of explosives," she added. "Pull out slowly, broaden our picture. As soon as we see any other ships we'll scope back in, get the info, pull back out and continue searching."

"We looking for anything in particular?" Kurtzman asked. His fingers hammered his keyboard.

"Sure," Price answered. "Someone who looks like they're running away." At that moment Hunt Wethers entered the Communications Room. "What do you have for me, Hunt?" Price asked, immediately multitasking.

"Short version? I've got what Able needs to chase down the next piece of the Toronto puzzle. Long version will go into my report. But I've got a name. There's a small snag."

"Always," Kurtzman agreed. He struck Enter on his keyboard and the image of an expensive yacht racing on the open ocean froze as the image was translated, copied and downloaded. "Always a snag. But Lyons usually handles complicated Gordian Knots of red tape in the same fashion as Alexander the Great."

"Yes," Wethers admitted. "He cuts right through it."

From his chair Kurtzman shrugged his massive shoulders. "Cuts it, throws it down, stomps on it, sets it on fire then pisses on it."

"Well," Wethers said, "if we consider diplomatic immunity

to be a sufficient knot, then indeed Lyons and company are the men for the task at hand."

"How many images does that make, Bear?" Price asked. She turned to Wethers, "Diplomatic immunity?"

"Six so far," Kurtzman answered. "We're starting to get toward the outer limits of probability given speed traveled and distance covered."

"A courier for Saudi Arabia's minister of foreign affairs, diplomatic service division," Wethers answered. "Name of Adel al Jubeir. Or I should say, *Prince* Adel al Jubeir."

"Let's push the limits of possible with the nearby vessels, just to be safe," Price directed Kurtzman. "Hunt, I need a full bio package done on his royal highness. Before I turn Able loose on him, I'll need Hal to inform the Man."

Her phone rang. She picked it up. "What do you have for me, Carmen?"

Washington, D.C.

IN THE SECURE reading room of the National Archives, Hal Brognola sat at a plain table in a nondescript chair. He read with studious intensity. A pile of manila file folders, computer printouts and reports from various agencies written out in longhand were placed on the desk in front of him.

The room was constructed like an industrial vault.

There were no windows to the outside, only a single door and no true concessions to comfort. This was a place much like a public bathroom, he thought with sardonic irony; you were expected to conduct your business and get the hell out.

In the corner a security camera in a blackout glass ball hung from the ceiling.

He finished reading, turned the page over and reached for a third file folder. He hadn't been reading long but he'd already grown to respect Hammond Carter.

The man had a long history as a career public servant:

wealthy family, Ivy League school, an ROTC program ending with a commission in Air Force intelligence. Two years as a major in the Defense Intelligence Agency.

Then an odd shift.

He'd taken a job as a research clerk in the Office of Management and Budget. Ten years spent there while rising to the rank of assistant deputy director to the Office of Federal Financial Management, just below the presidential-appointed director position.

Such a position gave his career, and thus his influence, built-in protection from politics and changing administrations in the Executive Office. From this niche Carter seemed to have acquired bureaucratic power on an unprecedented scale.

"The proof is right here," Brognola murmured to himself.

The man known as the big Fed had been in Washington, D.C., and the Justice Department for a long, long time. He knew the players and the movers on the game board, most especially in the intelligence and law-enforcement communities.

Every agent or officer who had opened an investigation or started an inquiry about Hammond Carter had gone exactly… nowhere. When people asked questions about him, Carter squashed the investigation, then he squashed the men.

Behind Brognola the room's door opened.

He looked up, surprised, as this kind of an interruption wasn't protocol. He turned in his chair, regarding the newcomer over the rims of his reading glasses.

He frowned.

The man was tall. Lean enough in his expensive suit to be considered lithe. The suit was off-the-rack Brooks Brothers, but tastefully tailored. The watch nice, but not too expensive, just like the shoes.

The man's features were sharp with a nose like a hatchet blade under a smooth brow and deep-set, intelligent eyes.

Gray colored the man's temples, but the rest of his hair, buzzed into a quarter-inch flattop, was the shoe-leather brown of his eyes. He had a mouth that had forgotten how to smile a long time ago.

"Hammond Carter, I presume," Brognola said, voice dry.

Somalia

JAMES BACKPEDALED hard, dragging Encizo clear of the doorway.

More rounds tore into the door and the members of Phoenix Force peeled back from the entrance to clear the field of fire.

"Move!" McCarter shouted. "Charges set!"

He and Manning poured return fire into the entrance as James hauled the unconscious Encizo clear.

Behind them, dead bodies were piled like cordwood on a cabin porch and pools of blood formed lakes of mud in the African dust.

James manhandled Encizo around a corner of the house and both McCarter and Manning stepped into cover. The bang of the breaching charge cracked like a thunder strike and the already abused door shattered like glass.

Encizo's wounds had slowed the team's momentum and an auxiliary entrance plan had to be conducted. What would have been two two-man teams would now have to be executed by only a pair of soldiers.

Adapt. Improvise. Overcome.

James pulled a knife free and began exposing Encizo's wounds after establishing that the man was breathing. From cargo pockets on the legs of his pants he began hurriedly removing pressure dressings.

Drawing their PLR-16 Kel-Tec pistols, McCarter and Manning prepped for their entrance. Each man looped the ring on the pin to a stinger stun grenade over the thumb of the hand used to hold the pistol grips of their machine pistols.

"Get it done, mate," McCarter growled.

"Yeah, I'm starting to feel peckish," Manning replied.

The men twisted the pins from the moorings and tossed the shock grenades underhand through the shattered door. The canisters bounced once just inside the door and angled deeper into the building.

The grenades exploded with loud bangs and blinding flashes of light as dozens of hard rubber pellets erupted outward like traditional bomb shrapnel, stinging the terrorist defenders inside.

McCarter was on the move half a second before the first explosion to maximize the seconds bought by the flash-bang grenade. He sprinted forward as the stun bombs exploded, Manning right behind him like a racing locomotive.

The commandos hit the doorway in rapid succession, Kel-Tecs up.

McCarter tried to button-hook to the left but discovered he'd breached into a narrow hallway. He saw a form stumble by past him and gambled the primary target wouldn't be this close to the action.

He fired a 3-round burst from the hip and put the figure down.

He lunged forward in a combat crouch, following his weapon into danger. His feet slapped off tile as he moved deeper into the kill zone. Over his shoulder Manning fired at something he couldn't see. Two more steps and he was clear of the residual smoke from the breaching charge.

The entrance corridor ended in a huge receiving chamber taking up almost a full half of the first floor.

He cut right around the corner as Manning moved forward. A two-man machine-gun team lay beside an overturned RPK on a bipod. One terrorist held his ears in pain while the other cursed into his hands where his face had taken several of the hard rubber pellets.

The Briton shot them both.

Manning reached out a hand as big as a dinner plate and snatched his team leader back by the collar. Surprised,

McCarter squawked as he came back. Manning, grizzly-bear strong, caught him with his free arm and drew both of them back into the narrow entrance hall.

From their three-o'clock position a hail of submachine gun rounds knifed through the air where McCarter had been standing. Moving free of Manning's grip, McCarter dropped to one knee and leveraged his muzzle around the edge of the corner.

He burned off his 30-round magazine as Manning, back to the interior wall, freed another stinger stun grenade. His bolt locked open as the last 5.56 mm burned out, McCarter pulled back and dropped the empty magazine to the ground.

Manning let the pin to the grenade drop as McCarter seated a fresh magazine in the well. The big Canadian tossed a riot-control canister in an effortlessly sharp lateral pass, like a power forward juking for position on the court.

McCarter tapped the catch release on his machine pistol and the receiver shot forward, seating the first round in the chamber. More gunfire burned across the room from the enemy position.

Once more a Phoenix Force grenade detonated inside the house of the warlord.

Staying tight, McCarter peeked low around the corner as Manning risked a fast look at high-man position.

A pair of turbaned gunmen, part of the bodyguard team, lay crumpled and moaning. Each man was disorientated, and their Skorpion v82 machine pistols lay on the floor beside them.

McCarter's and Manning's weapons blazed at the same time. The figures convulsed as the rounds slammed into them, then shivered and fell still.

The Phoenix Force commandos came around the corner, weapons up, and jogged for the staircase. They slowed as they approached the stairwell, cutting angles to afford them maximum visibility to the upper floor.

Slowly the two men turned so that their backs were to each

other, their weapon muzzles tracking through the smoke and uncertain light.

Smoke choked their lungs and stung their eyes. They saw the inert shape of several bodies cast about the room among the splinters of concussion-shattered furniture. One body lay sprawled on the smoldering staircase, hands outflung and a stream of blood pouring down the steps like water cascading over rocks.

McCarter moved slowly through the burning wreckage, approaching twisted bodies and searching the bruised and bloody faces for traces of recognition.

Around them the heat grew more intense and the smoke billowed thicker. Gary Manning moved with the same quick, methodical efficiency, checking the bodies as they vectored in toward the stairs.

McCarter sensed more than saw the motion from the top of the smoldering staircase. He barked a warning even as he pivoted at the hips and fired from the waist. His M-4 lit up in his hands and his bullets streamed across the room in violent storms of lead.

McCarter's 5.56 mm rounds chewed into the staircase and snapped railings into splinters as he sprayed the second landing.

One of his rounds struck the gunman high in the abdomen, just under the xiphoid process. The Teflon-coated high-velocity round speared up through the smooth muscles of his diaphragm, sliced open the bottom of the lungs and cored out the left atrium of the gunman's pounding heart.

Bright scarlet blood squirted like water from a faucet as the target staggered backward.

The figure, indistinct in the smoke, triggered a burst that hammered into the steps before pitching forward and striking the staircase. The faceless gunman tumbled forward, limbs loose, and his head made a distinct thumping sound as it bounced off each individual step on the way down, leaving black smears of blood on the woodgrain as it passed.

McCarter sprang forward, heading fast for the stairs.

Gary Manning spun in a tight circle to cover their six o'clock as he edged out to follow McCarter. He saw silhouettes outside through the blown-out frames of the patio doors and he let loose with a wall of lead in a figure-eight pattern.

One shadow fell sprawling across the concrete divider, and the rest of the silhouettes scattered in response to Manning's fusillade. He danced sideways, found the bottom of the stairs and started to back up.

Above him he heard McCarter curse and then the Briton's weapon blazed.

To Manning's left, a figure reeled back from a window. Another came to take its place, the star-pattern burst illuminating a manically hate-twisted face. The Phoenix Force commando put a 3-round burst into the screaming mask from across the burning room and the man fell away.

"Let's go!" McCarter shouted.

CHAPTER EIGHTEEN

The Briton let loose with a long burst of harassing fire aimed at the line of interior doors facing out to the rear of the building as Gary Manning spun on his heel and pounded up the steps past McCarter.

Outside, behind the cover of a bullet-riddled hulk of a VW automobile, an enemy combatant popped up from his crouch, the distinctive outline of an RPG-7 perched on his shoulder.

Down on one knee, McCarter fired an instinctive burst, but the shoulder-mounted tube spit flame in a plume from the rear of the weapon and the rocket shot out and into the already devastated house.

McCarter turned and dived up the stairs as the rocket crossed the big room below him and struck the staircase.

The warhead detonated on impact and McCarter shuddered under the force and heat. Luckily the angle of the RPG had been off and the construction of the staircase itself channeled most of the blast force downward and away from where McCarter lay sprawled.

Enough force surged upward to send McCarter reeling even as he huddled against the blast. He tucked into a protective ball and absorbed the blunt waves.

He lifted his head and saw Manning standing above him, feet wide spread for support and firing in short bursts of savage, accurate fire.

McCarter lifted his machine pistol as he pushed himself up and turned over as Manning began to engage more targets.

Twisting, he saw something move from the hallway just past the open landing behind his fellow Stony Man operator.

McCarter extended his arm with sharp reflexes and stroked the trigger on the Kel-Tec autopistol. A 3-round 5.56 mm burst struck the creeping enemy in a tight triangle grouping high in the chest, just below the throat.

The terrorist's breastbone cracked under the pressure, and the neck muscles were sheared loose from the collarbones. The back of the target's neck burst outward in a spray of crimson and pink as the rifle rounds burrowed their way clear.

"Go!" Manning shouted.

The tall Phoenix Force commando swept his weapon back and forth in covering fire as McCarter scrambled past him to claim the high ground.

The British commando pushed himself off the stairs and onto the second floor. Stepping over the bloody corpse of his target, he turned and began to aim and fire the machine pistol in tight bursts.

Under his covering fire Gary Manning wheeled on his heel and bounded up the stairs past McCarter. At the top of the landing he threw himself down and took aim through the staircase railing to engage targets below him in the open great room.

Nothing moved. Then from behind them a burst of fire burped out, driving them partway back down the stairs.

"James," McCarter said into his throat mike, "how you doing?"

"Rafe's taken some good shots, but he's breathing and I've stabilized his bleeding. You've got some time, but let's not dick around."

"Copy," McCarter agreed. He transmitted again. "Hawk, how's our top floor look?"

"Like some handsome badass with a high-powered cannon cleared them for you," the Texan drawled.

"Excellent."

Manning, moving in a light-footed shuffle, performed a

flanking maneuver known as "slicing the pie" to clear all visible lanes of fire on the stairs where they opened out onto the second floor.

"Grenade?" McCarter asked him, an eyebrow arched in question.

"Never hurts."

McCarter unclipped a flash-bang from his combat harness while Manning covered the staircase.

The second floor was just visible over the rise of stairs. A figure darted past the opening, and Manning, unsure if it was the primary target or not, put a warning burst into a wall as harassing fire.

McCarter jogged forward two steps and underhanded the grenade up the top half of the staircase and over the top step into the second floor proper. To encourage any defenders at the top to keep their heads down, both men fired more quick, suppressive bursts after the explosive.

The grenade banged out above their heads.

They raced up the steps again, heard men cursing in surprise as the hard rubber pellets cut painful vectors outward from the grenade. Three quarters of the way up, McCarter, in the lead, threw himself flat so that only his head and weapon cleared the top of the stairs.

He twisted left then right in rapid succession, clearing angles as Manning crouched behind him.

The second-story hallway bisected the structure, revealing doorways along one side toward the rear of the property while the wall on the other side of the corridor was broken only by windows, a sign of status in the desert community.

The windows were now only shattered teeth of glass.

In the middle of the hall a single disorientated terrorist pushed himself off the floor, reaching for an AKM assault rifle with a brown canvas sling. The man's face under a light-colored cloth turban was peppered red with impact wounds from the stun grenade's rubber pellets, and one of his eyes was swollen shut like a prizefighter's.

McCarter took aim, lining up his front sights with the peephole aperture in the rear. His field of vision filled with the terrorist's head and at a range of fifteen yards it was a point-blank shot for the rifle-caliber pistol.

This was killing up close and personal.

The ex-SAS trooper's finger squeezed his trigger without remorse.

The machine pistol cycled smoothly, the rounds tearing off with flat cracks as the spent shell casings leaped from his breech and bounced like shinning metal dice down the steps behind him.

The 5.56 mm NATO high-velocity rounds struck the confused terrorist in the side of his head and only his tightly wrapped turban kept his brains from spraying outward. The man jerked like a fish on the end of a line and slumped back down.

"Clear!" McCarter barked. "Clear!"

Manning came up the final steps like a charging bull. He cleared McCarter, stepped onto the floor of the hallway and sprinted forward several steps before putting his back to the outside wall and taking up a defensive position.

McCarter was in motion even as the big Canadian crouched.

Pushing himself up, he lunged up the final stairs and rushed just past Manning's position before taking a knee. Poised for instantaneous reaction, the fox-faced Briton squatted. His finger went to his earjack.

"Hawk, be advised," he subvocalized, "Me and the big man are on the second floor and moving toward the master suite."

"Copy," Hawkins answered immediately. "All clear in the village. Nothing moving but some stray dogs and curious buzzards. Stay put for a second and I'll recon by fire."

"Understood," McCarter acknowledged. "Four shots then we begin approach."

"I'm on," Hawkins finished.

There was a long moment while the two Phoenix Force members crouched, waiting. The silence stretched into tense seconds so uncomfortable they almost jumped when Hawkins began his final-phase objectives.

The outside wall at the end of the hallway exploded inward.

Baseball-size chunks of building material sprayed out in a wave as a 25 mm sniper round slammed through the mud-brick-and-rebar frame. The round, still lethal, crossed the hallway and knocked an interior door off its hinges.

"First shot!" McCarter snapped into his microphone. "First shot!"

"Too cool for school, boss," Hawkins purred into the com system. "The next three are going straight down the pipe."

Outside the villa the big Barrett banged three more times in smooth succession, each round passing through the breach hole formed by the initial shot and then tearing through into the room across the hall.

First the door was shredded, creating a ready access point for McCarter and Manning, then the psychological effects of 25 mm rounds served as a shock-and-awe vanguard for the two-man assault force.

"Gun down!" Hawkins warned as he fired the last bullet in his 5-round magazine.

"Moving!" McCarter replied.

He and Manning rose, two parts of the same organism, each moving in sync with the other as they crossed the hall even as the echo of Hawkins's last round rocked out across the desert village.

Nearing the doorway, McCarter dived forward and rolled expertly over one shoulder, clearing the room entrance and coming to his feet on the other side. Manning dropped down, squatting to rest on a ballistic armor knee pad as he shouldered up to the wall on the far side.

Inside, a man screamed in agony.

The drill was too well established at this point to need verbalizing. Each man armed and tossed a stun grenade through the entrance of the shattered door.

They couldn't hear the primed explosives land over the gurgled cries coming from inside the room, but the twin flash-and-bang detonations came hard moments later.

McCarter lunged forward, Kel-Tec primed as he passed through the door. Right behind him Manning barreled in like a halfback breaking through the offensive line to sack a quarterback.

A headless terrorist lay sprawled in a pool of his own blood.

Behind him another man, too tall, too thin, with too short a beard to be the primary target, wailed as he ran back and forth like a panicked chicken. Blood squirted from the lower left elbow where his forearm and hand had once been, before Hawkins had removed it from a distance of well over one thousand yards.

Manning shot him.

McCarter snapped his weapon around. Stopped, spun and cleared another section. He identified two dead bodyguards.

Beyond the corpses was a sitting area with a traditional rug and a low-legged table in a shallow alcove. A large, low bed dominated a far corner.

Like a prop in a French Foreign Legion movie from the 1930s a hookah sat on the ground under a scimitar hung by hooks on the wall next to a bright tapestry.

Next to the hook, lying flat on his back, was the primary target.

Manning growled like a Rottweiller on a leash. Moving forward, he snarled, "Knock-knock, asshole."

Indian Ocean

THE CAPTAIN'S QUARTERS on board the superyacht were appropriately luxurious.

Every amenity was handcrafted from teak. The stainless-steel surfaces gleamed like floodlights and semiprecious stones formed highlights and accents: obsidian-black, lapis lazuli–blue, topaz-green and burnished copper.

Against one berth, secondary navigational and communications equipment formed a sort of second bridge in the suite.

Klegg sipped his drink.

Milosevic was drinking now, as well. The excitement was nearly impossible to contain. The two criminal fixers watched as the Russian ex-special operations soldiers manhandled the narrow, impossibly heavy case into the room.

"Table," Milosevic commanded in Russian.

Fedorova, in his role as sergeant major, grunted instructions at his men. Suracova and Gregory, both men sweating freely, manhandled the burden onto the sturdy table in the center of the captain's suite.

"Leave us," Klegg ordered.

He moved forward, eyes shiny, almost wet with greed. The Russians glowered at being dismissed so casually, but at a nod from Milosevic they retreated from the cabin, leaving the two men alone.

"Do you want to open it?" Milosevic asked.

"No, go ahead." Klegg waved his vodka at him.

"Afraid the radiation will melt you?" Milosevic taunted.

Klegg drew his mouth in a tight line and shook his head in the negative just once. He refused to meet the other man's eyes.

Laughing, Milosevic set his own drink down and moved to the case. He looked at the case in bemusement.

"I still find it surprising that something so valuable was so lightly guarded."

"My government has a belief system for couriers that runs along the lines that 'invisible' is better than 'heavily guarded.'"

"In Russia we assume treason and carry twice as many guns."

"There is a certain poetry there," Klegg conceded. "Perhaps after this the U.S. Department of Energy will rethink some of its security policies."

Milosevic lifted the lid on the case, revealing its contents. What he saw struck him as anticlimatic.

"It's a rock."

"A meteorite," Klegg corrected.

"A space rock?"

"Yes. It was found on Ross Island, Antarctica, during the 1901 expedition."

"I realize meteorites are rare and all that, but Seven has gone to a terrible amount of time and expense. Hell, for that matter, why does the U.S. Department of Energy give a damn, as well?"

"Because six months ago a young Israeli geologist at the University of Tel Aviv got the bright idea to run a unique spectrum analysis on a quaint little souvenir in the college museum."

"Discovering?"

"Discovering that the origin of the meteorite was not just extraterrestrial, but also extragalactic."

"What?"

"This hunk of space rock comes from another galaxy. There has not been a find like it before in all the history of the world."

"Okay. It's rare. I still don't—"

"Due to its makeup it is ascertained that it comes from the Sirius system."

Milosevic scowled at the American. "I'm sure this is all very amusing for you, but I'm getting tired of stroking your ego while we play goddamn twenty questions. Just tell me what we have."

"In a word?"

"Preferably."

"Ascension."

Milosevic paused. He seemed to be running the word around inside his head. He looked sharply at Klegg, his deep-set eyes burning. "Seven's end game? Ascension?"

"Yes," Klegg confirmed. "It's a glorious time for us, my friend."

"Leave nothing out."

"Sirius is a binary system—that is, it has two suns. Because of this, gravitational forces there far exceed anything mankind has experienced in our own solar system. The material of life, the atomic and subatomic building blocks of such an environment, are considerably, almost incalculably, denser."

"The atoms are denser in this rock? This is why it is so heavy?"

"Yes. Now think. What is nuclear power but the splitting of atoms? That is the sum of atomic energy, the power generated by the splitting of atoms. A spoonful of dust from that rock could generate enough nuclear power to fuel any country on earth for decades, centuries to come.

"It would generate so much raw fissile energy it would make any nation on earth energy independent almost immediately—removing outside geopolitical pressures completely." Klegg downed the last of his vodka, then swirled the ice cubes around in his tumbler. "And weaponized? Forget about it."

Milosevic looked down at the dull gray rock. It looked… unspectacular.

His eyes noticed the smooth gunmetal sheen of it, worn slick under layers of ice over the course of untold millennia.

"Weaponized?" Klegg repeated, grinning like a jackal, a drunken jackal. "Well, weaponized it could turn the smallest Caribbean island into a world superpower." The American snapped his fingers for emphasis. "Just like *that*."

"And Seven just happens to own a Caribbean island," the Russian said without looking up from the rock.

"Probably." Klegg shrugged. "But what they don't own outright they control or influence from behind the scenes. After all this time the final gambit is unfolding. We will reveal ourselves before the world and ascend."

"Israel just gave this up?" the Russian asked, his voice sounded doubtful. "Even to America?"

"The trigger calculations for splitting an atom of this density are irregular. At the moment they are only theoretical. A mere handful of nuclear scientists alive have done any research into this area. All of them currently work for a private technological contractor in Toronto, Canada, under the direct control of the United States DOE. Israeli offered a deal. Parts of the rock in exchange for the technology. The Americans took it."

"It is insane that it was so lightly guarded," Milosevic repeated in wonder.

"Not so insane. Hiding it in plain sight would have worked just fine if Seven didn't exist. But it does."

"What now?" Milosevic demanded.

"Now you go tell your team of mercenaries they're going to Canada."

CHAPTER NINETEEN

Toronto

Charlie Mott kept the chopper deep in the cloud cover and navigated by his instruments.

Beside him in the long-range helicopter Hermann Schwarz methodically checked and rechecked his equipment.

As always in a helicopter he had the odd sensation of his center of gravity being above him instead of below him as it was on the ground, or even on an airplane.

After his flight from the Farm, out over the sprawl of Toronto right before it became the gray waters of Lake Ontario along the southern border with the United States, they conducted a refueling operation with an Air Force plane specially designated for the task by the officer in charge of the northern command at the personal request of Hal Brognola.

Once that was done, Charlie Mott put the nose of the endurance bird on a northwestern azimuth and ran it hard. He kept his speed at just under 280 miles per hour and avoided designated air traffic flight zones and military radar from half a dozen national agencies both U.S. and Canadian before picking up Schwarz at the rendezvous point.

Now the night was cobalt-black as he made his final approach. He reached over and put a hand on Schwarz's shoulder to alert the man before keying his headset.

"We're on the approach," Mott said. "Look out, you'll see the regional highway. The island of lights in the hills south of that road is Prince al Jubeir's mansion. Keep the road north and the property south and you should land right on target."

Schwarz nodded. "At five hundred feet there's not a lot of time to screw it up."

"Not enough for you to recover if you did, anyway." Mott grinned back. "You tell me when you're ready and I'll drop down."

Schwarz went through his prejump drill, securing his harness and double-checking his equipment and primary weapon.

He turned to Mott and gave the man a thumbs-up before removing the flight helmet. The Stony Man pilot nodded his understanding and Schwarz felt the helicopter begin to change elevation.

The chopper floated downward, dropping out of the clouds, and the checkerboard landscape beneath began to sharpen into focus.

Schwarz looked out of his window and quickly orientated himself using the landmarks delineated by Mott.

The highway was a curving black line through dark, forest-covered hills, connected by bridges where it crossed fast-moving rivers and deep but narrow canyons choked by heavy green brush.

North and east of the drop zone the lights of Toronto, Canada's most populated city, were prominently displayed, but just to the south of the highway the Phoenix Force commando could easily pick out the set of buildings belonging to the prince.

Mott looked over at him and pointed at the altimeter before giving Schwarz another thumbs-up.

"You're getting ready to jump into the toilet!" Mott shouted. "Be careful!"

"Toilet?" Schwarz repeated. "You know why Piglet looked in the toilet, don't you?"

"Please no," Mott begged.

"To find Pooh!" Schwarz cackled.

Beneath his feet, the Able Team electronics genius felt the

helicopter slide into a gentle precision hover as the Stony Man pilot settled in at five hundred feet above the ground.

He looked out the window and saw the clearing in the terrain they had picked out as a drop zone from the satellite imagery of the surrounding area.

Schwarz cracked open the copilot door and felt the rush of wind enter the cockpit.

He turned in his seat and backed out, stepping down onto the helicopter's landing skid. He felt the pull of the rushing air tugging at his clothes and felt the sensation of the earth falling away beneath his feet.

He grabbed the handle and slammed the cockpit door shut. Isolated, he looked through the window at Mott and the other man nodded at him again.

Schwarz took a step backward into space and the hovering helicopter veered sharply away from him.

Gravity snatched at him and he began to plummet, gaining speed rapidly. Immediately, his hand went to the ripcord and he deployed his parachute.

There was no backup. At five hundred feet he'd be on the ground too quickly to ever deploy one in the event of a mishap with his primary canopy.

THE LEXUS SUV cut along the highway running twenty miles per hour over the speed limit. Behind the wheel Carl Lyons leaned back in the leather seat and eyed the glowing numerals of the dashboard clock.

"Time?" he asked Blancanales.

Blancanales, sitting shotgun, held up his cell phone, using his finger on the touch-activated screen to scroll through tasking programs.

"We're good," he said. "The GPS readout on Mott's chopper has them running right up the back of the mansion now."

Lyons finished off a bottle of beer and dropped it at his feet. It clinked as it rattled against the other empties in the well. The smell of beer on his breath and the empties would reinforce his apparent intoxication.

Up ahead in the windshield the gated compound of the Saudi prince's property suddenly appeared. A guard shack stood beside an automated wrought-iron gate, which formed the only egress point in the ten-foot-high brick wall surrounding the estate.

"Seat belt?" Lyons asked, voice casual.

"Good to go, Ironman."

Lyons swerved across the middle lane and hit the smooth black tarmac of the prince's driveway while still accelerating.

In the flash of the headlights the guards' faces were clearly illuminated. The men's faces showed shock as the massive SUV crashed straight into the gate.

THERE WAS THE RUSTLE of silk in the wind. Already the air was warmer as Schwarz drew closer to the ground.

The parachute, an old-style T-50 colored black and designed to get him to the ground as quickly as possible, fluttered up and out behind him as he fell. Schwarz had time to wonder if he was screwed and then the chute flared and caught, jerking him hard in his heavy nylon body harness.

The fall immediately became more controlled, and he floated to the ground as he saw the black earth rising up to meet his boots.

Beneath him the rough topography of the ground expanded under his feet. He saw the strip of road he had picked out from Wethers's UAV imagery for his drop zone. The forest was a green-black smear.

Schwarz scanned the ground and road below him for any sign of security.

As he vectored in toward the road, rain lashed at him and, as he made his final approach, he picked out a spot with an invitingly wide section of road. He began expertly guiding his parachute in toward it.

As a gust of wind pushed him beyond his drop site he felt cold but familiar squirts of oily adrenaline splash his stomach. He knew he was going to miss the road and be thrown into the dense copse of evergreen trees beyond it.

He reached down and unsnapped the emergency release at his waist, letting his rucksack fall away below him. The effect was immediately noticeable and his speed tempered though he still rushed down into the trees at a deadly pace.

He reached up with both hands and clawed at the guides of his parachute.

Bending himself almost double, he hauled on his lines, trying to twist his direction of fall away from the trees and back onto the road. For one wild second he thought he was going to make it and his body swung in a compact 180-degree turn.

Then his boots struck tree tops and his parachute collapsed. Schwarz crashed through the canopy of pine trees like a camouflaged Icarus.

As he fell thick branches flipped him back and forth with brutal caprice, battering his back and limbs.

He struck a thick bole with his shoulder and spun off it. Leaves and branches slapped his face with stinging blows.

Still spinning, Schwarz hit another branch with his chest and bounced backward. The hard ground rushed up toward him.

This is it, he thought.

CHAPTER TWENTY

The impact crumpled the front of the SUV.

The iron fence sagged but held. Inside the cab both Lyons and Blancanales were thrown forward against their safety harnesses. Airbags exploded outward from the steering wheel and front dash.

"Loco caca cabasa," Blancanales muttered in exasperation.

"Yeah," Lyons groaned, "that was a bitch-mother."

"You were going faster than Schwarz's recommendation based on the impact math," the Puerto Rican commando accused.

"It's gotta look real, brother."

Outside the demolished vehicle three guards in uniforms ran forward, shouting in surprise and outrage.

"Showtime," Blancanales said.

Lyons belched loudly as his airbag deflated. He reached down to his door handle and jerked it open. The frame had bent slightly, making the door stick. He grunted and slammed his shoulder against the door.

Metal screeched in loud protest, then the door gave way in a sudden jolt. Rolling with the momentum, playing up his supposed intoxication, Lyons fell out onto the ground at the startled estate guard's feet.

A half dozen empty beer bottles tumbled out with him, one smashing on the jet-black tarmac of Prince Jubeir's private drive. On the other side of the car Blancanales shoved open his own door and muscled his way out.

Lyons pushed himself to his feet and staggered slightly as the private guards approached him. Blancanales opened his cell phone and tapped in 9-1-1.

After giving his name and the street address he launched right into his theatrical histrionics. "Yes, we've just had a car wreck! We need police and ambulance! Send the jaws of life, send an air ambulance. Oh, God. Oh, God, send everyone and hurry!"

Lyons turned as the first guard reached him.

"Fuck you, Johnny," he said. His voice was conversational.

The guard stopped, taken by surprise, and his jaw dropped. Lyons closed it with a right uppercut that snapped his mandible tight up against the maxilla hard enough to shatter a tooth.

The guard went down with a moan. The second guard backed away in horror as Lyons reached down and picked up one of the beer bottles with some liquid left inside.

He guzzled it, burped, then smiled. "Fuck you, Johnny," he repeated. He was really starting to enjoy this acting stuff.

The gate guard began calling for backup into his walkie-talkie.

SCHWARZ WAS JERKED short with a brutal snap.

He gasped as his parachute harness cinched up tight into his groin and his spine arched backward painfully. His head snapped to the side from the whiplash force, and a blinding flash of light filled his eyes though they were squeezed tight shut.

With a moan he opened his eyes.

He looked up and followed his lines to where they disappeared into the pine-needled branches above him. Reaching out, he tentatively explored the guides to see how secure his perch was.

They hung taut where they carried his body weight against the point where the canopy hung up in the interwoven branches of the pine trees.

Schwarz wrapped his fingers around the lines in an exploratory grip. There was a ripping sound and the bottom fell out from under Schwarz. He dropped straight down another ten feet before being jerked to a stop as the canopy hung up again.

Schwarz snarled a curse, part anger, part apprehension and mostly amazement that he was still alive and conscious after a jump like the one he had just made.

He looked down between his dangling boots and saw the forest floor still fifteen feet below him. He turned his head and looked at the lattice of branches around him. He was stuck out into space about eight feet from the nearest tree trunk.

Schwarz put his hand up to his mouth and bit into the leather tip of his glove, pulling his hand free. He spit the glove out and let it fall. Moving as quickly as he dared, he reached down to the cargo pocket of his black fatigues.

"This better be worth it," he muttered.

He came out of the pocket with a nylon cord secured to a D-ring carabiner. He played out the rappel cord from his pocket like a stage magician coaxing an unending series of silk scarves from his sleeve.

Eyeballing a likely branch, he flipped the carabiner over it then snapped the cord through the gate before running a double loop through each of the two D rings attached to his parachute harness suspenders.

He played a little cord out and then secured it with a fist he dug into the back of his hip, just under the curve of his buttock. He reached across his chest with his free hand and grasped the handle of a sheath knife hanging inverted from the suspender of his load-bearing equipment web gear.

Holding himself secure with his rappel cord, Schwarz reached up and sliced the guidelines to the entangled chute.

The blade of his fighting knife was a highly tempered, non-reflective metal alloy and boasted a blood groove. His bodyweight dropped as the last line was cut and the nylon rappel cord stretched to take his weight. Free of the hung-up parachute, Schwarz sheathed the knife.

Holding himself steady, Schwarz unbuckled his jump helmet and let it fall.

He cocked his head, straining to listen for any sound. A light freezing rain had begun to fall and drowned out everything in its monotonous rhythm.

His first priority was to find and secure his rucksack. Even inside the tangle of tree branches the rain was bitter cold and stinging.

Schwarz lifted his fist straight out to his side from its anchor at his hip and let the nylon cord play through his gloved hand. The friction was instantaneous but the drop was short and Schwarz completed his rappel quickly.

He sagged at the knees as he landed to absorb the slight impact and quickly disengaged from his parachute harness and rappel cord.

He put his feet together and kept a springy bend built into his legs. He hit the ground and went instantly with the force of his fall, rolling along his leg and the side of his body to absorb the shock.

He grunted with pain as a hidden rock slammed into his side. Then he was past it and coming up into a sitting position. His parachute hung like a shroud in the dark, the soft, billowing folds hanging limp.

He was on the ground and the clock was running.

Moving fast, Hermann Schwarz cut through heavily wooded hills. Prepped for a silent infiltration and reconnaissance mission, he was well equipped. His combat harness contained piano wire garrotes and several slim-bladed stilettos.

In addition to a silenced H&K MP-5 SD-3 submachine gun, he carried a silenced Glock 19 9 mm pistol in a shoulder holster and an M-1911 A-1 handgun with an extended magazine on his left hip.

His only acknowledgment to firepower was a pair of stun

grenades secured to his harness in case things went south in a bad way and he had to make a more overt escape.

He maintained a tactical map in the cargo pocket of his black fatigue pants, but he had committed the layout of the mansion grounds to memory.

Like many of the family Saud, the prince had spent his oil money lavishly. The man lived in a fashion that made other ambassadors look like paupers.

Hunt Wethers had lived up to his academic reputation on the cybernetics team, managing to locate the architecture company out of Dubai City, Dubai, responsible for the construction contract. Wethers hacked their records to provide the raw data necessary for an in-depth infiltration plan.

A dense wall of concrete block three yards high by one yard thick surrounded the entire estate, which covered an area roughly equivalent to fifty-three football fields.

According to the architectural plans, and confirmed by spy satellite imagery, only two openings pierced the thick stone wall: the well-guarded gate on the main drive and an insignificant culvert that channeled a small, swift stream out of the estate and into the surrounding hills.

If all was going according to plan, then Blancanales and Lyons were handling the front gate.

The prince was a rich man and he had built his estate with an eye to security, but it was neither a medieval fortress nor an armed camp.

The pampered diplomat was apparently using his money to run in some very dangerous circles, even though he seemed to always leave the dirty work to others.

A thick row of evergreen trees lined the concrete security wall on the inside, effectively obstructing the view of anyone beyond the boundary of the property.

Schwarz skidded down a slight scree-littered slope and headed toward the babbling stream at the bottom of the gully.

He stopped and surveyed the wild brambles encroaching the estate. The blueprints and plans had outlined the security systems in place, giving an overview of the multilayered defenses the Dubai business had put into place.

The mansion's security system consisted of three main elements: indicators, alarms and video cameras.

The indicators registered an event with the computer software housed in the mansion, such as the opening of a door, cutting of the wire running along the top of the block wall or the breaking of a window.

According to the commercially obtainable software templates, the prince's computer did not issue an alarm automatically, but instead registered the potential breach to the centralized computer screen manned by an observer.

The same center also housed the CCTV monitors for the several cameras positioned around the villa estate.

Piece of cake, Schwarz thought wryly.

Moving in close to the wall, Schwarz quickly surveyed the stretch for cameras. The sensor wire was running along the top, but he could see no security camera pod as he broke from the cover of the bushes and headed for the depression in the block wall that housed the culvert grating.

Behind him the obscured moon glinted off the black waters of Lake Ontario. There was the slight stinging scent of pine needles thick in the air. It reminded Schwarz of gin and tonics. Thankfully, the frigid rain tapered off.

He ducked under the lip of the culvert, shrugging off his pack as he did so. He crouched in the cool water of the stream, feeling it soak through the leather and canvas of his boots as took the Semtex from the pouches on his harness.

He scrambled overland to the wall and began placing precise amounts of the explosive compound along the wrought-iron structure at the points where it was secured through the aluminum body of the culvert and into the concrete block.

By applying the charges in an exact manner he could reduce

the sound of the explosions to very soft bangs, like muted pistol shots, too quiet to be heard across the distance to the main villa.

The charges themselves had been expertly constructed by the Stony Man armorer. Kissinger had exactly calculated the breaching demolitions to loosen the reinforced rebar from its moorings to such a degree that Schwarz could remove it by hand, thus further reducing the noise signature.

Shape charges in place, Schwarz scooted to the edge of the culvert and stepped around the edge.

The initiator timing pencil popped and the det cord followed suit, igniting in a rapid series of firecracker pops. Brief match heads of yellow flame flared with sizzling sounds, followed by small plumes of gray smoke that rolled out of the tunnel formed by the culvert.

Schwarz swung back around and checked his work. He smiled grimly after inspecting the metal bars and seeing the erosion.

He sucked in a lungful of air to gather his strength and shot both of his hands outward. The heels of his palms struck the metal grate in the center and easily snapped it clear of its moorings.

The metal grid fell into the gurgling stream with a small splash and he immediately hustled through.

He paused at the mouth of the culvert as it opened up onto the prince's compound. Slowly he peeked his head around the corner and looked out. Almost immediately he saw the security camera mounted on a metal bracket to the concrete wall, its black lens pointed directly at the culvert mouth.

Schwarz ducked back around the corner and out of sight. If the personnel at the CCTV monitor were on top of their job, he had already been seen. Chances were, however, that only prolonged exposure to the camera would be noticed.

Hopefully, Lyons was keeping the security detail very busy.

He gritted his teeth and burst out of the culvert. He took

two hard steps and somersaulted over a shoulder and passed under the camera to come up on his feet outside of the camera's range.

He paused and took a look around, orientating himself. He could see the lights of the main villa just about two hundred yards away. Beside the main house there was a four-door garage with a drive leading up from the main lane past the villa. The driveway continued past the garage and tied into an asphalt road that meandered through the property.

As Schwarz watched, one of the garage doors opened and headlights pierced the dark opening to the building. A Toyota Land Cruiser pulled out of the garage, turned west on the property road and began approaching Schwarz's position, gaining speed as it came.

CHAPTER TWENTY-ONE

Somalia

McCarter watched, weapon ready, while Gary Manning placed the Somali warlord in plastic riot cuffs and hauled him roughly to his feet.

The man kept his face impassive and he stood with a defiant jut to his chin, refusing to meet the eyes of his captors. McCarter wasn't impressed. Their captive would break soon enough. He turned back toward the front of the room and began directing the closing stages of the operation as Manning draped a black cloth hood over the warlord's head.

"James," he asked. "How's security? How's Rafe?"

"Tough bastard, he'll be fine if we can unass the AO here. You boys done playing?"

"Package in hand, mate," McCarter assured him. "Hawk? Status, over."

"I'm sitting pretty," Hawkins responded. "No movement in the village."

"Copy," McCarter acknowledged. "Jack, you ready to bring it in?"

"I'll be at the LZ in three mikes," Grimaldi assured him.

"Good to go," McCarter said. He paused, then broke squelch again. "Phoenix, we are leaving."

Gary Manning leaned in close and whispered in the warlord's ear.

"Wouldn't want to be in your baby-killing shoes right about now."

Toronto

SCHWARZ HUGGED the ground as the Land Cruiser slowly rolled past.

He kept his finger on the trigger of his H&K MP-5 and pressed down hard into the grass, willing himself to be a shadow among shadows.

The Toyota crept down the road where it bordered the stream and moved past the culvert and running stream without slowing. Keeping one eye shut to spare his night vision, Schwarz watched the vehicle-based sentries cruise past his position.

Through the open window he heard a babble of excited voices suddenly shout across the receiver.

Atta boy, Carl. Schwarz smiled.

The Toyota sped away down the road and headed toward the front gate. Schwarz was up and running. He crossed the drive and entered the bush on the other side. He tried to approach the house from cover, darting in and out of stands of trees and cultivated bushes, but the landscaping became sparse the closer he got to the house, and very quickly he found himself with nothing but open lawn.

Keeping one eye on the slowly patrolling Land Cruiser, he went for the garage next to the main house, running fast with his weapon up. He made the corner of the building without an alarm being raised and scrambled up onto the roof, breathing hard.

He hugged the top of the building and began to search the second-story windows.

The mansion was a sprawling building, a two-level rambling Tudor-style house. A pool took up the area directly behind the house and an elaborate flower garden surrounded the rear area. The front porch was a low brick platform covered by an extension of the roof supported by two brick pillars. A set of enormous Canadian oak doors comprised the main entrance.

Each of the doors was ostentatiously carved with a dramatic *J* monogram.

Schwarz stood and quickly took a second, more sustained survey.

Seeing no one, he quickly sprinted across the ground and leaped into the air. He jumped the distance between the roof of the garage and the redwood shakes of the house, landing lightly. He scrambled across the incline past an upstairs window and halted to see if any alarm was raised.

Satisfied, Schwarz approached a high faux retaining wall set between the garage structure annex and the main building of the residential complex. Scuttling silently, Schwarz approached the wall and casually scanned the area.

The wall was just over a foot thick and made of smoothed form concrete with a free-standing edge at the end of the wall nearest the garage.

Schwarz looked around once again, ensuring that he was unobserved.

Satisfied, he turned back toward the wall. Without hesitation he leaped onto the outer edge of the twelve-foot wall. His shimmy technique was a precise form of fieldcraft taught to urban assault climbers in the special operations community.

He grasped the edge of the wall farthest from him with his right hand cupped and facing back toward him. With his right leg he wrapped around the free edge of the wall and dug his heel in for support.

Suspended above the ground, Schwarz pushed the ball of his left foot into the wall and pressed down, creating a fulcrum of pressure with his right foot and hand grips. Using his left hand, he pushed down against the edge closest to him, palm pointed away from him and toward the ground.

Moving faster now, he began sliding out along the ledge.

LYONS LUMBERED TOWARD the second gate guard, beer bottle still in hand.

Behind him, Blancanales strolled around the wrecked

vehicle, casually directing the EMS and police crews to the site of the crash.

The guard popped out of his crouch and reached for the gun he wore on his hip. His eyes went wide as he saw Lyons suddenly hurtling toward him.

The big ex-cop raced in close, leaping into the air at the last moment as the gate guard abandoned his gun and attempted to fall back into a defensive martial-arts stance.

Lyons drove his knee straight into the man's side, forcing the wind from his lungs and throwing the smaller man back against the fence's crumpled gate.

"I'll sue!" Blancanales shouted.

The guard stumbled back and Lyons moved in, relentless as a jackhammer.

He clasped the shorter man with both his hands around the back of his head, using his body weight to push the man's face down. Like trip-hammers, Lyons's knees fired up, cracking hard into the line of the man's jaw near the point of his chin.

"Bastards made me wreck my car!" he shouted. "You rich sons of bitches think you can get away with anything!"

"Nice," Blancanales muttered. "That's great acting, Carl, really."

In the distance he could hear the staccato wailing of approaching police and ambulance.

Over by the gate it was finished in three moves and Lyons dropped the unconscious guard, leaving him in a heap on the ground. Behind him the third officer in the gatehouse hung up a landline and ran outside.

Not missing a beat, Lyons sprang forward and caught the third security officer as he tried to back up his partner. Lyons jerked him down off his feet and hurled him to the unforgiving pavement. The man gasped for air and moaned before Lyons's foot pummeled him into darkness.

"You going to let the police Taser you?" Blancanales asked. "That would really be something to see."

"Taser? I heard Canadian cops use maple syrup in their mace—that's what I wanna see."

The sound of sirens became deafening as two police cars slid into the driveway. Their headlights pinned Lyons in their beams as he bent to pick up one of the beer bottles.

The cops threw open their doors, weapons out. Lyons grinned and raised his hands in surrender, before taking a long drink.

"Freeze!" one police officer screamed.

"Put the bottle down!" his partner yelled.

"Yeah, good luck on getting syrup," Blancanales muttered, raising his own hands. "Schwarz just better bail us out."

AS HE HUNG from the wall the stress on Schwarz's body was prodigious.

His wrists ached and the muscles of his arms and shoulders clenched tightly against the strain.

Displaying great acrobatic strength, he began inching his way up the wall edge. He exhaled and inhaled in short, sharp bursts as he struggled to ascend the wall. He slowly, monkey-like, climbed eight feet of the wall this way.

Once within reach of the top, Schwarz slid his right hand over the edge and then clung there while he brought his left up to join it. Once secure, he pulled himself over the edge and scrambled onto the narrow summit of the wall. From there he quickly centered his gravity and rose into a crouch.

He shuffled forward, moving across the narrow space with catlike agility until he reached the anchor point where the retaining wall connected with the second story of the prince's building.

At the junction Schwarz stretched up to the limits of his height and slid his fingers into a shallow bevel line traversing a second ornate facade on the building's rear wall.

Roughly twenty feet up, Schwarz swung out into space, carrying the weight of his body and kit onto the strength of his grip. Slowly, he inched his way along the bevel line.

The muscles across his back bunched like straining animals under his clothes and his brow furrowed with the intensity of his concentration.

Five yards down Schwarz reached an ornate windowsill.

He stretched out and wrapped his already straining fingers around the lip. It was flat and smooth, offering him no purchase. The only thing that would hold Schwarz from the inevitable fall would be the downward force he was able to concentrate through his fingertips to counterbalance the weight of his body.

Now keeping his momentum to a tight minimum, Schwarz eased himself out underneath the windowsill. He moved his other hand quickly into position and pulled himself up so he could rest his elbows on the sill.

Schwarz reached out with an underhand grip and slid his fingers around the bottom edge of the window. He pulled himself up until his knees rested on the sill's ledge. Once there he rotated around until his buttocks were secure on the edge. He exhaled through his nose and shoved the window the rest of the way open.

Cat burglary 101, he thought.

As soon as there was space Schwarz swung his legs through the opening and slithered inside the building. He landed in a crouch and quickly slid over to the side to avoid silhouetting himself against the window. He paused for a moment, holding his breath.

He was in.

"EASY, OFFICER!" Lyons called. "You got to the wrong guy! Arrest these assholes!"

He lowered his hand and waved it at the moaning guards lying on the ground.

Behind him, a security vehicle with floodlights pulled up, brakes squealing, and a fourth security officer jumped out. He stopped, looked at the ruined gate, looked at Lyons. He turned and looked at his pummeled coworkers, then looked back at Lyons.

Lyons smiled in a friendly manner and winked. "Fuck you, Johnny." He turned back toward the police officers who were coming out from behind their car doors. "Arrest 'em! They tricked me into wrecking my car!"

"On your knees!" a sergeant screamed, shuffling forward.

INSIDE THE VILLA Schwarz slid a pair of night-vision goggles into place. He began his careful infiltration. He was a bogeyman, he hunted at night, he could see in the dark, he had claws.

Moving on silent feet, Schwarz navigated staircases and doorways. He glided through dark rooms. Below him toward the front of the house he could hear doors slamming and people shouting.

Even this far from the front of the driveway the sirens were clearly audible. Everyone was entirely focused on the drama playing out at the Saudi Arabian ambassador's front gate.

Like some technologically advanced version of Johnny Appleseed, Schwarz began carefully placing his listening devices.

"I'M THE ONE who called 9-1-1!" Blancanales protested.

"Save it for the judge," the Canadian cop told him.

The handcuffs went on with a conversation-ending click that was audible even over Lyons's histrionics.

A sleek black Jaguar XJ12 rolled to a stop beside the security SUV on the far side of the ruined gate. Blancanales saw a slight man of Middle Eastern descent and wearing silk pajamas step out of the car.

"What is the meaning of this!" Prince al Jubeir demanded in outrage.

Blancanales closed his eyes. He turned and spoke softly to the police officer covering him, "Here it comes."

"Fuck you, Johnny!" Lyons yelled.

The remaining officers converged on the Able Team leader.

THE AMBASSADOR'S elegant boudoir was a suite of remodeled rooms on the top floor of the mansion.

The chamber was filled with opulence to the point of ostentatious self-indulgence, a trait that Schwarz had found to be common among the rich and corrupt. The rooms he passed through were covered in thick pile carpeting, and expensive objects of decor littered the mansion like the forgotten toys of a messy child.

Schwarz moved through the connecting rooms like a tiger stalking its prey in a jungle. He moved carefully, weapon down, his night-vision goggles illuminating his path deeper into the villa's uppermost level.

He bugged a phone. Planted a booster under the lip of a sixteenth-century French coffee table. Farther on he secured more listening devices. He was wiring al Jubeir's house for sound.

He heard a door open from farther inside the suite of rooms.

In response he shuffled silently up to a single door and pressed his back against the wall, pistol raised by the side of his head.

From the next room Schwarz heard a woman's voice croaking instructions in Arabic. Another female voice of indeterminate age murmured a reply Schwarz didn't catch.

The door beside Schwarz swung inward as it opened and he tensed. A switch was thrown and the lights came on, illuminating the room as the person walked forward. He lifted the NVGs to the top of his head and extended the silenced H&K.

The machine pistol was steady in his fist.

A Middle Eastern woman in a servant's uniform walked fully into the antechamber.

The woman halted.

The blunt muzzle of Schwarz's silencer was less than six inches from the back of the woman's head. Schwarz's finger automatically tightened on the trigger.

Slowly he eased up, let the trigger go slack. The weapon was poised, ready to fire, but he remained undetected. The servant released a heavy sigh and then strode forward purposefully. Crossing the room, she opened the door Schwarz had just entered and walked out, pulling it closed behind her.

Schwarz stepped forward, lowering the machine pistol. He turned and regarded the open door he had hidden behind.

It was time to get the hell out of Dodge.

CHAPTER TWENTY-TWO

Washington, D.C.

Carter regarded Brognola with a small smile.

"Find anything interesting?" he asked. He waved a hand at the pile of folders sitting in front of the veteran Fed.

Brognola stared at the man for a moment, taking his measure, then slowly shook his head.

"No, I did not," he answered. "Which in itself is interesting, all things being even." He waved his hand at the folders. "I notice a lot of stalled careers here. A lot of government attorneys and agents who never seemed to move up the ranks."

"Perhaps there is something to be learned from that?"

"Only that I won't find what I'm looking for in these files." Brognola grunted. "Also that the legendary discretion of the clerks here at the National Archives seems to be somewhat lacking where Hammond Carter is concerned."

"Shall I tell you what I know about you?" Carter asked.

"Only if you have the code-word clearance to do so," Brognola shot back. "Because if you don't, I'll arrest you myself."

Above clearance level, top secret intelligence was broken down into code-word paroles specific to projects, investigations, departments and personnel. Having a certain level of clearance was not a carte blanche license to look into any covert operation at will.

Specific personnel were given specific code-word clearances on a need-to-know basis. Knowledge of intelligence or classified information that a person was not specifically vetted for knowing was a federal crime.

This part of the government security system had driven more than one highly placed political appointee mad with frustration.

Carter's cheeks flushed red and the lanky man's lips went white with sudden pressure. Brognola's point had struck home.

Score one for me, the Stony Man director thought.

"When it pertains to the ethical and legal spending of government funds by institutions of said government," Carter answered stiffly, "then I think even the man who brought Mack Bolan to ground would be impressed with my level of access."

Refusing to be bluffed, Brognola kept his voice cool when he replied. "In that case," he said, "you wouldn't have any problem giving me the appropriate code parole, then, would you?"

Like torches burning in caves, Carter's eyes were lit with anger.

Brognola realized he had gained valuable insight into his adversary. Despite decades as a behind-the-scenes mover and shaker in the Wonderland that was D.C., Hammond Carter was still capable of being driven by hubris, and as such, he could be manipulated.

"Let me tell you a little something I most certainly *am* cleared for," Carter intoned.

"Do tell."

"USA 193."

"I'm lost." Behind an innocent, blank look, Brognola could feel his pulse quicken.

"USA 193," Carter repeated. "Also referred to as NRO Launch 21."

"I'm not affiliated with National Reconnaissance Office," Brognola said somewhat truthfully.

Carter continued as if Brognola hadn't spoken. "Also referred to as KH-13. This designation, Keyhole Satellite 13, is not for the imagery intelligence program but for the apparatus, the hardware itself. A very expensive piece of government hardware, I might add."

Brognola caught himself reaching for a cigar and stopped.

"Tracking those expenditures is exactly my job," Carter continued. "Strange thing about this particular Keyhole—and this is common knowledge, made the news and everything, you can do a Google search on it—is that after launch all contact was lost with the satellite less than month after it went up.

"On February 21, 2008, the Navy supposedly destroyed the rogue Keyhole with a sea-launched missile." Carter smiled. "This was a fabrication."

Brognola already knew it was a fabrication. That KH-13 was currently under guidance by Stony Man Farm's Cray supercomputer.

"With all due respect, Mr. Carter—" Brognola stood "—I have no idea what you're talking about. And, frankly, if I did, I wouldn't be at liberty to tell you."

Carter magnanimously moved to open the door to the reading room for the big Fed. The bean-counter smiled like a vampire.

"You'll be receiving subpoenas to provide information for my audit shortly, Mr. Brognola. The taxpayers of this great nation deserve to know how their money is being spent. And I assure you, sir—" Carter's smile was gone now "—I most assuredly do have clearance to follow the money."

Brognola walked out of the room and slammed the door in the man's face.

Somalia

THE WAREHOUSE was an anonymous structure in the middle of an empty field.

It sat right under the reinforced air traffic control tower serving Djibouti International Airport and military patrols passed it several times a day, making it an unassuming location for a U.S. black-site prison.

In the days of Soviet influence it had served as a morgue. As such the gloomy structure had a concrete floor equipped with drains, examination tables, coolers and a dedicated sewage and water system.

A rolling door led into a bay where ambulances and hearses had dropped off their cargo of human bodies.

Calvin James held open a concertina-wired gate and McCarter drove past him. He hit the garage door opener on his visor and the bay door rolled open as James jogged across the weed-choked lot after him.

After stabilizing Encizo and turning him over to Navy flight nurses for transportation to a hospital ship in the Persian Gulf, James had prepared himself for the warlord's interrogation.

The rest of Phoenix Force was waiting with Jack Grimaldi at the airport.

Once they were both inside the converted morgue, McCarter hit the button again and the door rolled shut behind them. Once it closed, James hit the lights, illuminating the cavernous room.

The furnishings were industrial, spare and austere. There was nothing inviting or comfortable about the chamber. The lights overhead were naked fluorescent and glowed with a stark brightness.

McCarter walked around to the back of the vehicle as Calvin James went to the wall and pulled an ambulance gurney over to him, passing a metal table piled with twenty-pound bags of lye. McCarter popped open the trunk on the vehicle and looked down at Sheikh Omar Mahmud Abdullah.

The gurney clacked and clanked as its hard rubber wheels rolled across the uneven floor. McCarter reached into the trunk and pulled the warlord Abdullah into a sitting position.

Without preamble he snatched the black cloth hood from the man's head and threw it on the ground.

Abdullah's eyes remained tightly shut. His lips moved in frantic recitation as he quoted passages of the Koran in prayer. His hair was crumpled and messy, lying flat against one side of his head in some areas and sticking straight out in others.

McCarter reached out and slapped him hard across the face. The sound popped like a gunshot. Abdullah's cheek flushed red and he sputtered to a stop in his praying, his eyes springing open.

McCarter said, "You don't have time for prayers, mate. Got it?"

McCarter pulled his A.G. Russell Sting A1 boot knife out, showed the frightened man the carbonized-steel blade. He leaned close and growled into the warlord's face. "I've read your file, big man," McCarter snarled. "Kidnapping journalists and recording yourself sawing their heads off with a machete doesn't impress me. You understand?"

The man nodded, his eyes closed. McCarter slapped him again. "Answer me!"

"I understand," Abdullah stammered.

"Good, get out of the trunk."

McCarter steadied the shaking Seven captain as he unfolded from the trunk. The man moaned when he saw the straps and tie-downs on the gurney beside Calvin James.

His knees buckled in fear and it took both Stony Man operators to force him onto the gurney.

Despite his terror Abdullah kicked and struggled as they secured him to the hospital gurney. They forced the warlord's wrists and ankles into padded straps and secured them to the gurney frame. Then Calvin James buckled a strap across the man's chest and his forehead, locking his twisting head into place.

McCarter walked over to a spigot leading up to a shower head set in the wall above a floor drain. In the past it had been used to rinse the remains of autopsies clear. A mop and bucket on wheels were resting near the wall next to the shower spigot. The mop was stained pink.

McCarter took a pair of pliers off an examination table and used them to open the spigot's shower head all the way.

Behind him the Somali warlord tried to follow the American's movements with his eyes. Once the shower head was open McCarter returned the pliers to the table and hit the record button on a blood-smeared video recorder.

McCarter pointed the camera toward the wall so that the instrument would record nothing but audio from the session.

Calvin James reached over and gently tapped Abdullah between the man's wide-spread eyes. Abdullah looked back toward the ex-SEAL, took in the bushy, wild beard and deep black skin. James smiled and his teeth were very white.

"First, Abdullah," Calvin James said, "I want to assure you this isn't the first time I've had to do this. The last time was in Baghdad. I didn't like it then and I don't like it now."

The warlord stared up at James as the man spoke. All the color had drained from his face. White cobwebs of spittle had gathered at the corners of his mouth. His eyes set into hard slits.

"Fuck you, American."

James smiled. "That's great. I'm not going to lie. I was hoping you'd be a hard-ass, I really was. But that brings up a point. Lying. I will not lie to you. I will not," James said, his sincerity obvious. "Everything I say to you while you are strapped down and under my care will be the truth."

"Fuck your truth, I am ready for your torture. Allah gives me strength and I will tell you nothing."

"That brings us to another point." James nodded earnestly. "I'm not going to torture you. Nor will I give you drugs. Don't get me wrong—this won't be pleasant if you choose not to cooperate, but it isn't torture. And it sure as hell isn't torture compared to what you boys do to any infidels you happen to capture."

Abdullah opened his mouth to speak, his face twisted with rage.

James put one long finger against the man's lips. His eyes met Abdullah's and the warlord looked away and fell silent.

"No talking," James whispered. "No talking. I've no interest in your ninety-nine-virgins-martyr bullshit. I've got no interest in your tough-guy bullshit. None. If you don't have anything to say about Seven, then you don't have anything to say."

James removed his finger and pulled his face away from Abdullah's. He crossed his arms over his wide, powerful chest. His body seemed like a spring, pregnant with potential energy.

At the mention of Seven, Abdullah had paled. The color leeched out of his face with a horror so undistilled it was almost transcendental.

"That's right, mate." McCarter spoke up. "This isn't about you playing jihadists with al Qaeda in Africa. This is about Seven." The Briton leaned in close. "Think about it…we *know*."

"Do you have anything to say about Seven?" James asked.

Abdullah shook his head.

"Fine, now you listen. 'Cause remember when I told you I wouldn't lie? Well, now I'm going to tell you how you can get out of this without talking. So listen close, you baby-killing motherfucker, I've got the keys to the kingdom."

Calvin James wrapped his hands around the metal rails of the gurney and began to slowly push the gurney over to where McCarter stood beside the shower spigot.

McCarter was coolly attaching lengths of heavy-duty, OD-green masking tape to a white cleaning rag.

"I've given this exact same speech before," James informed the man. "But the last guy didn't listen to me. I don't expect any better out of you. There's been a lot of talk in the media about water boarding lately," James said. His voice was conversational and Abdullah had to strain to hear him over the squeaking of the gurney wheels.

The lights overhead flashed in the terrorist's eyes, hurting them with their brightness so that he squinted.

"Calling it torture and so on," James continued, "getting it wrong a lot of the time. It sure isn't two Nazi SS goons dunking someone's head in a barrel." James stopped walking, looked down. "Wait, I apologize. I shouldn't use the SS in that context with you, should I? Hitler's pretty all right with you, isn't he? I mean, that's what you guys who are affiliated with Egyptian Islamic Brotherhood all think? Right? Denying the Holocaust and all that? Never mind, not important.

"The point, Abdullah, is that I will not really be drowning you. In fact, here's a secret—you'll be able to breathe the whole goddamn time, isn't that a kicker? In fact, since your lungs will be higher than your nose and mouth at all times it is a physical impossibility for you to drown. Try to remember that, all right, Abdullah? Like I said, I told the same thing to the last guy, almost verbatim, but he didn't listen."

James halted the gurney and walked around to the side and kicked the support legs positioned directly underneath Abdullah's head. The hinge joint on the legs collapsed and the front half of the gurney folded down. Abdullah moaned at the sudden lurch and he came to rest with his feet up in the air.

"You will not drown," James continued. "You *cannot* drown. Remember that and I'll never break you because I will not hurt you, I promise."

Abdullah's face turned bright red as the blood in his body, driven by gravity and his wildly pounding heart, rushed into his head.

He began to struggle as he saw McCarter lean over, his frame blocking the harsh light as he placed the cleaning rag across Abdullah's face. The head strap on the gurney kept the warlord locked in place and McCarter was able to secure the cloth with the strips of tape he had peeled off while James had rolled the warlord over to the shower.

Calvin James knelt beside the inverted Somali warlord and

agent of the enigmatic Seven. His voice was a gentle purr in the terrified man's ears, his lips so close to the man's face that his breath tickled him with repulsive intimacy.

"It's all an illusion, Abdullah," James whispered. "The water can't hurt you. But it will feel like you can't breathe. It will feel like you are drowning even though you'll be screaming the whole time and you can't scream if you can't draw breath into your lungs. Your brain is fooled into thinking you're drowning and it creates feelings of anxiety, of panic in you, but it is an illusion, Abdullah, you can breathe!"

James stood and nodded at McCarter, who turned on the water.

Abdullah jumped at the sound of the water rushing out and splashing on the floor. He flinched as it struck his face with a light spray.

"Be a man, Mr. Warlord. Khalid Sheikh Mohammed lasted almost three minutes. I went five when the Survival Evasions Resistance and Escape school instructors did it to me!" James yelled. "I haven't even used cellophane!"

McCarter turned up the pressure, and the stream of water, hardly above a drizzle, splashed onto Abdullah's upturned face. Immediately the terrorist's gag reflex kicked in and he began to squirm and writhe on the gurney.

McCarter kept the flow of water straight down on the now sobbing man's face.

"Fight it, Abdullah!" James screamed. "The panic is a lie! You can breathe! Breathe, goddammit!"

Abdullah's muscles stood out in vivid relief along his arms and neck as he fought to break the bounds that held him. He was moaning through clenched teeth, and suddenly a spreading stain of yellow leaked across his crotch as his bladder let go.

"Uugghh!" He moaned. Then he choked and gasped, sputtered. Then screamed.

Forty-five seconds later he begged them to release him.

CHAPTER TWENTY-THREE

Calvin James reached down with one big, long-fingered hand and yanked the soaked rag off Abdullah's face. The man was crying, tears streaming down his face as he gasped again and again for air.

James grabbed the rail of the gurney and yanked the inverted Abdullah's head back to level. Then he kicked out the legs at the rear of the gurney so that the terrorist warlord was lying almost vertical with his head higher than his feet.

The man coughed rudely and sucked in huge lungfuls of air.

Calvin James watched him, his face a flat affect. McCarter stood just behind the coughing, bound man like a shadow. When Abdullah had recaptured his equilibrium James spoke.

"Now we come to another part of the session that has seen much debate in the news around the world." James launched easily into his memorized speech. "You said you're ready to talk. Okay. People say you'd tell me any lie, anything I want to hear to just get me to stop. God knows that wasn't any fun for you, was it? And I'm inclined to agree with that viewpoint, as far as it goes."

James stepped in close and put his face forward so that he was cheek-to-cheek with Abdullah. "If I were torturing you to get you to admit something you'd already done I wouldn't much believe your confession. Not a little bit. A man will admit to anything to get the interrogation to stop. Ergo, they say, rough tactics, even torture, doesn't work.

"But here's the thing, Abdullah. I don't want you to admit

to a thing. I'm not doing this to punish you or for fun. I don't want to convict you of some crime you've already done. I could care less right now.

"I want some information. I want some names. I want some locations. You'll give 'em to me because you don't want to take another shower. But what happens after that, my brother? What if you give me the wrong information? What if you do, indeed, *lie* to me?" James finished in a sudden scream, spittle flying from his mouth and landing in flecks on the helpless Abdullah.

The man sobbed and tried to shake his head against the restraints. "I won't lie. I swear, I won't lie."

"I know you won't, good friend," James whispered. "'Cause your ass is gonna be in a cell right here, Abdullah. If you lie, then I'll know. Then I'll come back here and we'll take another shower and the whole time I'm gone you're gonna be sitting there knowing that when I get back I'm gonna be pissed and that you're going into the water again—and the fear of a thing can be just as bad as the thing itself, right? That's why terrorism works, right? 'Cause of the fear? Right? Right, Abdullah?" James shouted.

Abdullah began to sob and shake, his eyes welling over with tears of terror and helpless rage. James laid a gentle hand on the shaking man's shoulder. He gripped him hard, reassuring the warlord.

"You aren't going to lie to me, are you, my brother?"

"No," Abdullah said, all the fight gone from him.

"Good. Then start talking. Speak loudly so the recorder can hear you and don't leave anything out. I'm feeling greedy today. I want to hear *everything* about Seven."

Stony Man Farm

"COME ON," Price said.

The SME PED she held rang again. Finally, Hal Brognola picked up.

"Go ahead, Barb," he said.

"We're on fire like gangbusters," Price said without preamble. "I have convergent threads."

"I'm listening," Brognola said.

"Schwarz planted the devices, got out of the prince's mansion and managed to bail out Lyons and Blancanales from the drunk tank."

"Was Akira able to purge their fingerprints from the system?"

"Like they were never there," Price told him. "The electronic surveillance paid off almost immediately. I've rescrambled Able."

"What's happening?"

"First let me tell you about what James and Phoenix got from the Somali."

"Okay."

"The Somali is another low-level cutout. We'll have plenty of time to get the nitty-gritty details out of him later. For now he confirmed something big for us."

"What's that?"

"The VLCC that went down was attacked for its cargo. The warlord supplied men as an auxiliary force for the assault. The Somalis were rented by another now-confirmed member of Seven, a Russian fixer by the name of Milosevic. Milosevic has been on our radar for a while. Bad guy. Well connected."

"And now we know he's with Seven."

"Right, only it gets better. Milosevic is CFO of a Bulgarian holding company that just happens to own a yacht. A yacht we caught satellite footage of leaving the scene of the VLCC assault. A VLCC that was carrying a very important item for the Department of Energy."

"Toronto," Brognola said immediately.

"Exactly. And guess who just called the good prince?"

"Our new best friend Milosevic."

"Exactly," Price confirmed. "Only we may be too late. By

the time we followed up on Milosevic we know he'd already sent a team of Russian commandos to Canada with an American lawyer named Klegg."

"Is Klegg important?"

"We're not certain yet," she told him. "He's obviously Seven, but we don't know how high up. What I need you to do is to get a hold of someone at the DOE and use your influence to figure out exactly what it is someone in their Toronto project is cooking up that Seven is willing to use Russian mercs to perform a strong-arm robbery so they can get their hands on it."

"What about Phoenix?"

"James is escorting Encizo back to the U.S. after his surgery, and McCarter, Manning and Hawkins have flown into Kiev to tie up the Milosevic loose end."

"Able?"

"They're on standby, monitoring the prince until we can figure out where the DOE ambush is going to take place."

"I'll see what I can do," Brognola promised.

Toronto

THE HELICOPTER OVERSHOT the park on the outskirts of Toronto.

"Keep going!" Fedorova shouted without using his intercom mike.

He pointed out through the bubble of the Little Bird windshield at a three-vehicle convoy speeding down a winding approach toward the scenic park. The vehicles were all jet-black Lincoln Navigators with reflective windows.

He didn't know what kind of global deal his boss Milosevic was putting together with such rapid back-to-back assaults, but he did know he was getting paid very, very well.

The Little Bird covered the ground in a straight line, burning up the distance in the whirlwind revolutions of its rotor wash.

The vehicles loomed larger as the Russian pilot flew knap of the earth.

"Bring it around and I'll wave 'em off!" Fedorova instructed.

The pilot nodded once beneath his flight helmet and swung the Little Bird into play. There was nothing left at this point but to do it, no matter how risky.

Fedorova could not take the chance of firing on innocents and not obtaining the package. The fast, deadly, egg-shaped chopper cut past the lead vehicle in the convoy, appearing out of the night like a mechanized thunderbolt.

Having alerted the convoy to his presence the pilot looped out wide and cut back in again, turning so that Fedorova was now exposed to the short line of expensive SUVs. The Russian kept his weapon down as he leaned out of the Little Bird passenger door, one foot on the skid.

He held out his black-gloved hand and waved the driver down.

Nothing happened and the convoy continued to speed in the direction of the hovering helicopter. The pilot gently toyed with the helicopter stick and let it drift just off to the side. The blacked-out window on the passenger side of the lead Navigator powered down.

A square face covered by impersonal black glasses appeared on a stout neck encircled by a crisp white dress shirt. The stony-faced security agent wore a tightly groomed circle beard and his hair was as neat and slick as a cable news weatherman.

The muzzle of the P-90 submachine gun was instantly recognizable to Fedorova as it emerged from over the lip of the car window in the man's thick fists.

The American snarled from behind his mustache.

"Go!" Fedorova yelled.

The pilot cut the helicopter hard to the side and lifted up, clawing for altitude. Fedorova saw the star-patterned muzzle-flash splash outward from the DOE vehicle.

The night cloaked the burning rounds, and none of them whistled close enough to perceive as the pilot performed his evasive maneuvers.

"Quit playing around!" he yelled.

"Easy, friend," Fedorova replied. "Bring it in tight behind the tail vehicle."

The pilot had already anticipated Fedorova's instructions, and the Little Bird moved in a comma pattern, coming up behind the tail gunner vehicle.

Without hesitation Fedorova swept his MP-5 up and began placing precise bursts on the luxury vehicle.

To his surprise and gratification the vehicle didn't appear to be armored. The Russian commando's exploratory burst flew wide and knocked sparks of the road.

He recentered his weapon and triggered another blast.

The little H&K submachine gun recoiled comfortably into his shoulder. A triple cascade of gleaming brass emptied out of the ejection port and was snatched away by the streaming wind just outside the helicopter door.

He saw the window of the rear hatch door spiderweb then shatter. A second later the snout of a weapon muzzle appeared in the hole. From the rear driver-side door a man clambered out the window and tried to bring a P-90 submachine to bear across the roof of the SUV. Both weapons began to fire simultaneously.

"No, no, no." Fedorova laughed. "Bet you wish you hadn't kept this little project so secret from your good friends the Canadians."

The pilot stood the Little Bird on its nose, then darted out to the left to dodge the attack while still providing Fedorova with lines of engagement.

The Russian pressed his trigger down. The weapon stuttered in his gasp as he cycled it through a series of 3-round bursts.

His bullets riddled the metal of the Lincoln Navigator's roof and knocked paint off the rear doors. More of his rounds skidded off the road in showers of sparks. Both he and the pilot heard stray rounds from the Americans pepper of the metal superstructure of the Little Bird helicopter.

Instantly the pilot cut back in behind the vehicle and Fedorova put a 3-round burst directly through the shattered window on the rear hatch door. He caught a flash of a figure tumbling away and then the pilot jerked them out of the second gunman's line of fire and up into the air.

"Jesus!" the pilot shouted.

Fedorova was almost thrown out of the helicopter as the pilot was forced to suddenly slip around a row of telephone poles and power lines. The mercenary pilot cut it close, just inching his skids above the danger, but once he was clear of the surprise obstacle he brought the Little Bird back around for the attack.

Next to him Fedorova settled in and began firing his weapon in earnest. The bullets found their mark, climbing up the side of the vehicle in visible dimples until the submachine gunner hanging out the window was riddled.

The man dropped his weapon from limp fingers and it fell away toward the ground. It bounced off the road as the gunner followed his weapon, dropping out of the Navigator.

He slipped over the edge of the car door and dangled for a moment before being sucked under the tires.

The vehicle lurched to the side as it bumped over the body, and the chasing helicopter swung immediately into action with an impeccably timed movement. The Little Bird cut between the second and third vehicles right in front of the tail car.

Fedorova ignored the man now firing at him from the front passenger window just as the pilot forced himself to ignore the danger coming from rear-facing shooters in the middle vehicle.

The Russian commando coolly sprayed down the engine compartment of the last Navigator. He pumped burst after burst into the vehicle. The hood was transformed into a sieve and after a moment both steam and smoke began to billow from under the hood.

After a wild moment the clasp on the front of the hood was sheared off by a subsonic 9 mm round and it snapped open. The wind stream instantly flipped the hood open, obscuring the driver's view.

The Lincoln Navigator suddenly shot off the road and out of control as the helicopter pilot pulled the Little Bird out of the way of renewed streams of fire coming from the second vehicle.

Bullets punched holes into the shatterproof and reinforced windshield of the agile helicopter. The pilot popped up to an altitude of several hundred feet and drifted out of range of the small arms firing from the convoy.

Breathing heavily, Fedorova watched the last vehicle as it careened out of control across the grass and smashed into a park bench under a streetlight. The lead vehicle was reaching the end of the access road for touring the park where it joined a major thoroughfare.

"All right," the pilot said. "We know the package wasn't in the tail vehicle!"

"Either that or the U.S. needs to hire more dedicated body-guards," Fedorova allowed.

From his elevated vantage point the Russian could see that the upcoming road was empty of traffic in the very early morning hour.

It was time to close in for the kill.

CHAPTER TWENTY-FOUR

Kiev, Ukraine

The Pravda Central Complex occupied the heart of downtown Kiev.

Twin fifty-six-story high-rise residential towers rose out of a huge complex of office buildings, entertainment galleries and civil amenities structures.

The complex was the iconic soul of the modern Ukrainian regional city, all sleek steel, gleaming glass and streamlined design. It said Kiev, while not Moscow, was ready for the twenty-first century.

On the fifty-third level of the west tower Milosevic had purchased an entire floor for his personal use. The level was made up of posh business offices close to the elevator bank and a succession of grand suites growing progressively more ostentatious the farther down the hallway from the floor lobby.

Klegg had been given use of a VIP luxury suite halfway down the avenue-wide hallway. Hip-hop music blasted from the most advanced stereo that money could buy, the American gangsta rappers talking about the perils of the hood, guns, drugs and the police along with how hard it was to run ho's, earn your money and shoot your friends in the back.

For himself, Klegg found a lot of what Karl Marx would have called proletariat wisdom among the profane lyrics.

Three dozen people wandered around the luxurious apartment drinking from champagne flutes and snorting high-grade cocaine from hospitality bowls set around the suite.

On a Louis XVI table of oak, two blondes he thought were international runway models writhed in a tangle of anorexic limbs, sweating and naked.

Nothing he saw in their blonde, thin, hypersexualized features recalled Svetlana to his mind. To him, it was as if she had never existed.

Klegg sat in a plush Gustavian divan sofa, his head spinning from the champagne. Two Russian sisters, ages fifteen and thirteen, their eyes glassy and red, sat on either side of him.

Milosevic, feeling magnanimous after their successful operation, had promised him that the girls had to be experienced to be believed. The Kiev-based oligarch had gone into great length describing the combined sensation of their oral talents, leaving Klegg nonplussed inside his new Italian leisure suit.

He'd see for himself.

Now he set aside his champagne flute and plucked up the platinum spoon on the chain around his neck. He leaned forward and dipped the utensil into the crumbling, flakey pile of cocaine set on the glass-topped table in front of the twenty-thousand-dollar divan sofa.

He put the spoon to his nostril and snorted hard, leaning back into the couch as his head spun in a swirl of euphoric pleasure. This is why I went to law school, he thought.

The teenage sisters began rubbing their hands across his chest and thighs in mechanical motions, their young eyes never leaving the pile of drugs on the table.

Vision swimming, face numb, with music blaring in his ears, the American looked across the table to his host, Russian kingpin Milosevic.

The man held a Diamond Crypto Smartphone to his ear, the Russian cellular device costing well in excess of one hundred thousand American dollars. Klegg decided right there he would need to get one for himself.

In his other hand he held a blunt the size of a Cuban cigar, the marijuana pungent and strong as it smoldered. Over his shoulder the runway models switched positions and Klegg realized he was quickly becoming jaded.

He wished he'd brought his *nunchaku* with him.

Milosevic pulled his cell phone from his ear and handed it to the woman on his left, a former EU beauty queen with an eighteen-inch waist and gigantic breast implants. She held the drug dealer's phone without comment, white powder in a sticky residue on her left nostril. Rhinoplasty had crafted her nose into perfectly symmetrical proportions. She had spoken as enthusiastically of the teenage girls' sexual talents as Milosevic had.

"My friend," Milosevic hollered across the table at the American. "Fedorova checked in with my control. He has delivered the Israeli item to the prince and they have begun the Canadian exercise." The cold-faced man grinned. "I will pass the information on to my six plus one shortly. You should do the same."

"I will once I'm sure Fedorova has the new package," Klegg replied. His six plus one was not a man to be informed prematurely. "I've learned never to assume success."

"It would be ironic, don't you think—" Milosevic leaned forward "—if it turned out your six plus one and mine were one in the same?"

Klegg felt a thrill of apprehension shoot through him. He didn't like to risk talking about Seven, even to a fellow member. But knowledge was power in any conspiracy.

"Then why pay you?" Klegg pointed out. "If we operated out of the same fiefdom, it shouldn't have been necessary."

Milosevic shrugged. "Who knows how they think at that level? Maybe they just wanted the money laundered. Still, how many of that rank can there possibly be?"

"True," Klegg conceded. "But I guess it'll be a long time before we know…if ever."

The Russian kingpin lifted a hand and snapped his manicured fingers.

Klegg saw the bulky frame of the Romaine Jerome watch, crafted out of steel salvaged from the hull of the *Titanic*.

Instantly a steroid-enhanced gorilla with a military-issue Glock 18 machine pistol in a shoulder holster stepped from his post by the wet bar and crossed to Milosevic. Klegg recognized Suracova from the assault on the VLCC.

The former KGB officer pointed at Klegg and nodded before settling back in his seat and taking a gigantic pull off his blunt. The woman next to him whispered something in his ear and he grinned, eyes glued to the deep valley of her improbable cleavage.

"What's this?" Klegg asked.

As Suracova handed the American a padded manila envelope, Milosevic looked over. "I received instructions from my direct superior," he said. "I give that to you. You take it back to your control."

Klegg leaned forward and took the envelope from the bodyguard. "I guess that means they're not the same person," he said.

Milosevic shook his head in disagreement. "I already had that, from a separate project. It comes from me. You could just be the courier."

Klegg put his glass down and opened the bubble wrap–padded envelope. Inside he saw a portable flash drive.

"That gives your control what you need," Milosevic said.

Klegg slid the envelope away. Hammond Carter would be pleased.

He intended to inform his superior just as soon as he finished with the girls and was certain the Russian commando, Fedorova, had delivered the U.S. DOE experimental trigger into the Saudi prince's hands.

"We will get you the contact," Klegg assured him.

Around him the apartment erupted into frantic cheers as the runway models unveiled their sex toys. Klegg snorted more cocaine and thought about his control, playing both him and Milosevic like pawns on a chessboard.

FIFTY STORIES BELOW the partying sociopaths Gary Manning grasped his sat-connected cell phone. As he spoke into the NSA-provided device his words were transferred to text, encoded and transmitted through priority route relay directly to the Farm.

"I repeat, I need the schematics for the east, not the west tower of the building."

Barb Price's voice answered with cool proficiency over the earjack pickup. "Carmen's running it down right now. Using the IBM Bladerunner I think we can simply give you security and engineering overrides to the whole building. There's no way anything less than the hardware we're running is going to crack those firewalls anyway."

"Fine," Manning acknowledged. "What do I need to do to shut down the alarms and commandeer the elevators, then?"

"Bear is telling me that if you can manage to crack into the building through a local access port he can slave the commands to your SME PED. We did it before for Able on an operation in South America. Should work perfectly."

"Fine. That's not a problem," Manning replied. "Walk in the park. All I need is a computer inside the building and its AV in/out port."

"We're good to roll, then," Price said. "Stand by for transmission of west tower blueprints and electrical schematics."

"Copy. Phoenix out," Manning said.

Toronto

"KNOCK HIM OFF the road before they make it to more populated areas," Fedorova ordered the pilot.

The man was already pushing the helicopter down toward the

fleeing automobiles. The major road ran downhill through thick forest carefully cultivated back from the two-lane highway.

The racing SUVs straddled the center lane to command more maneuverability on the road.

The muzzles of guns bristled from the windows of the vehicles as the security detail prepared for another play by the Little Bird.

Fedorova realized time was of the essence. If he was going to take the package down, he needed to do so ten minutes ago.

"Let's take the first vehicle," he said. "Maybe force the second to stall."

"Copy," the pilot answered through gritted teeth as he fought the Little Bird into position.

Fedorova leaned out the window as they flew out past the convoy, then doubled quickly back to race head-on at them. He leaned out of the bubble cockpit of the Little Bird and leaned forward.

Using his sling like a second hand, he jammed the folding stock of his MP-5 into his shoulder and steadied the weapon by the pistol grip. With his left hand he steadied himself.

From below, weapons fire began to converge on the charging helicopter.

Fedorova eased his breath out through his nostrils and pinched the H&K's trigger back. The weapon bucked. He ceased fire and reorientated his weapon, then depressed the trigger again. He repeated the process a third time as the pilot descended upon the speeding SUVs.

Bullets streaked past the helicopter on both sides. The windshield took several more hits and the undercarriage of the helicopter whined in protest at ricochets and small-caliber rounds being deflected.

Fedorova ignored the extraneous stimulus. With cool detachment and a sniper's deadly skill, he worked his black magic on his enemies.

His rounds punched into the deeply tinted windshield of

the leading Lincoln Navigator. They clawed through the safety glass and bored out softball-size craters. He put his next burst just next to the first and the entire windshield collapsed in an avalanche of flying glass, most of which was swept back into the vehicle by wind sheer.

The driver had an iron nerve. He fought to control the speeding behemoth of a vehicle even as he tried to shield his face with one arm.

His efforts proved futile as Fedorova put bullets in his sternum, Adam's apple and right nostril. The man was pinned back against the white leather of his seat, both hands flying from the wheel.

At seventy miles per hour the vehicle began to drift immediately without a driver's hand to steady it. The man sitting in the passenger seat lunged for the wheel as Fedorova's pilot flew the helicopter directly toward them just feet above the road, using the lead vehicle's own bulk to shield them from fire originating in the second SUV.

He neatly placed another 3-round burst into the diving passenger just as the man's frantic fingers found the wheel. His bullets struck the bodyguard under his stretched-out arm, caving in ribs and shredding heart and lungs for an instant kill.

The man's desperate reach turned into frantic claws that pulled the speeding vehicle's steering wheel in the opposite direction of its headlong drift.

The vehicle began to overcorrect as the pilot pulled up at the last minute, throwing Fedorova back into his seat. The front skids of the Little Bird cleared the turning SUV by inches as it showed its belly to the second vehicle.

Immediately, bullets pinged and whined off the helicopter as the submachine gunners in the main vehicle opened fire. Bullets punched through the Little Bird's floor and were soaked up by the Kevlar flooring placed there.

Each round made a sound like a solid punch connecting on a heavy bag.

A stray bullet cracked into the windshield, opening a coin-size hole in the reinforced safety glass. Then the Little Bird streaked past them and the mercenary pilot guided them momentarily out of danger.

Beneath them the out-of-control vehicle overcorrected and suddenly popped up on two wheels, skidding along the road before flipping over and beginning to roll down the road. As the helicopter spun around, Fedorova twisted his neck against the centrifugal force to witness the events below.

The second vehicle rushed headlong into the already tumbling SUV, T-boning it with a crash so brutally hard Fedorova could hear it clearly up in the helicopter.

The gas tank secured on the vehicle's undercarriage split open under the impact like a piece of wet paper and even with only the intermittent light of streetlamps Fedorova could see the volatile fluid gushing out across the road in a dark stain.

The turning SUV went into a slide and the friction between asphalt and metal caused pinwheels of sparks. The spilled gasoline lit immediately and a wall of flame erupted around the overturned vehicle.

The driver of the final operable SUV was forced to jam on the brakes as a sheet of flame briefly engulfed the front of his vehicle. The Navigator stood on its nose as he brought the vehicle up short.

Fedorova knew that action had to be throwing all the occupants inside violently forward and bouncing them around the inside of the cab. The vehicle abruptly stalled out at the brutal action.

"Now! Now!" Fedorova screamed.

The pilot swung the Little Bird alongside the Navigator and the Russian assassin brought his guns to bear.

As the pilot brought the helicopter down even with the stalled SUV, Fedorova let the H&K submachine gun dangle from its sling off his torso. With the smooth ease of an Old West gunfighter his right hand found the butt of a PH-45 Artic warfare pistol, his .45 ACP automatic.

He drew the hand cannon and leveled it as they zipped past the stalled vehicle. Through powered-down windows Fedorova could see the hapless passengers bouncing off the seats in front of them as they were thrown around by the suddenly braking vehicle.

The .45 boomed three times.

The first 185-grain rimfire slug shattered the driver-side window from less than ten feet away. The bullet struck the driver hard in the side of the head and Fedorova caught a Kodak moment of blood and brain spraying out to saturate the American bodyguard sitting in the passenger seat.

The next two rounds chewed through the Lincoln Navigator's V-8 engine block, instantly rendering the vehicle inoperable just as the helicopter pilot climbed sharply up and spun the Little Bird on its nose to make another pass.

CHAPTER TWENTY-FIVE

Kiev, Ukraine

While Klegg and Milosevic partied, Phoenix Force arrived.

Security proved to be little help as the American commandos entered by the back door.

Manning entered the building after Hawkins, then McCarter stepped forward and followed. So far the Briton could detect neither an audible building alarm or the sounds of approaching police response sirens.

Inside the building the team entered a network of office cubicles, computer workstations, copy centers and partitioned walls of the IT suites. Each member of Phoenix Force reached up and pulled night-vision goggles into place, transforming the office space into a surrealistic nighttime theater of muted greens and grays.

"Up ahead, on the left," Hawkins said.

The ex-Delta Force shooter jogged forward, turned a corner, ran down three steps on a memorized route, then turned a right-hand corner. He lifted his MP-5 up and fired on the move as he ran forward.

The single 9 mm round struck the glass of the interior door and shattered it.

He ran up to the breach and used the silencer on his submachine gun to knock loose glass to the carpet. Following behind him, Manning ran through the opening and entered the blade farm housing the massive building's IT station.

"I'll secure the access door," McCarter said, and peeled off.

He ran down a plastic transparent wall separating the building's CPU and blade server farm from the IT workstations. Inside the vault were several hard drives locked in transparent plastic cases and carefully stacked atop plasti-alloy filing cabinets.

On the other side was a small rectangular box of polished Brazilian walnut. The containment unit was surrounded by a cluster of sophisticated electronics: climate-control sensors, humidity readouts, seismograph, gas analyzer, barometer and temperature gauge.

On the other side of the glass Gary Manning used a sliver of thermite to burn out a security door lock as McCarter raced for one of the doors in the office complex that opened up onto the nonpublic access parts of the massive Ukrainian skyscraper.

"That was it, boys," Carmen Delahunt said into their earjacks. "We have the call. I'm moving to insert cross-channel traffic to slow down the communications, but the clock is ticking."

"Understood," McCarter said.

While Hawkins pulled security in the other direction, McCarter cracked the door and looked out on the service hallway and toward the private elevator bank situated there. He looked back to see Hawkins covering the primary entrance to the IT offices.

Gary Manning, speaking in a calm voice, broke squelch over the com link earjacks. "I'm linked up to the system, Stony Man."

"Copy that," Delahunt replied. "I'm initiating our Trojan program now."

A burst of angry Russian came from the front of the office, and McCarter had to stifle his instinct to turn and spray the potential danger.

They may have been trying to create the illusion that they were a criminal cartel hit team, but they had no intention of murdering innocent civilians to perpetrate the charade.

Three security officers in brown uniforms rushed through the doorway. Each man had a radio on his belt with a handset attached to the epaulet on his shoulder.

In their hands they carried side-handled batons and cans of pepper spray.

Hawkins stepped out of the shadows, lowered his MP-5 and fired off three short bursts. The 9 mm slugs tore the red exit fire sign above the door into twisted pieces of metal and a shower of sparks.

The second bursts punched holes in the Sheetrock on either side of the security officers as they crowded through the door.

"Jump back, get back!" Hawkins yelled in flawless Russian, and the frightened men stumbled over themselves to make their escape.

"Phoenix, listen, I have a sit-rep from the professor," Carmen broke in, using Wethers's nickname. "He's lifted an internal email from the Kiev metropolitan police saying they're scrambling a squad of *militsiya*. It doesn't say why or to where, but it's suspicious."

"The interior ministry's thug unit?" Hawkins asked. "The timing's not good for us, but it could be something else."

"No such thing as a coincidence," McCarter cut in.

"Sometimes I think you've lost your innocence, David," Hawkins said.

"Of course I've lost my innocence," McCarter snapped. "I was fifteen, she was a lovely widow twice my age from Bristol."

"Done!" Manning interrupted. "I have taken control of the building. Do not attempt to modify your vertical. Do not attempt to modify your horizontal. Let's get to the elevators."

A second later the building went black.

Four minutes after that Phoenix Force rode in the elevator up the west tower.

With command of the building completely under Manning's

control he had shut everything down except for the rear service elevator they had commandeered.

"You want me to hit the sprinklers and fire alarms now?" Manning asked. "Get everyone in the building running out just as the police and fire emergency show up?"

"Wait till we hit the floor," McCarter said.

"Not a problem," Manning replied.

The team stood there in silence as the elevator smoothly rose up toward the top of the building. Manning began to eat a candy bar as time seemed to drag out to improbable lengths as the floor numbers grew steadily larger.

Hawkins began to whistle a soft, distracted tune.

McCarter sighed and looked at his watch. Seeing the action, Hawkins leaned over and inspected the timepiece.

"That's nice. New?"

"Yeah, got it last week. Cracked the face on my other one when I took the hard landing on our training jump," McCarter replied.

"I got a new boat," Hawkins offered, looking at his own watch.

"Really?" Manning asked.

"Yep, little Bayliner," Hawkins said. "I got twin engines, though."

"That should be cool."

"Oh, yeah, I'll have you out on it. That extra outboard makes all the difference."

"Good enough weather we've been having," McCarter offered. "Back home I mean—for boating. Or flying." He suddenly recalled his last plane flight, the one to Martha's Vineyard, and winced.

"Oh, sure, super," Hawkins agreed, not catching on to McCarter's odd discomfort.

The elevator slowed beneath their feet and slid to a stop at their floor. The doors parted with a pneumatic hiss, revealing a small, bone-white service area.

Phoenix Force stepped out, Manning using commands from his NSA-upgraded SME PED device to keep the elevator locked firmly in place.

Inside the service area there was an empty bucket with a mop and a metal room-service cart with an empty champagne bottle on it. The American commandos freed their submachine guns from beneath their jackets.

"Will that elevator hold even against a firefighter override key?" McCarter asked.

"We're in so deep to this building's control system that that elevator will hold until I say even if they cut the goddamn cables." Manning laughed.

"They have room service?" Hawkins asked. He pointed at the fancy wheeled cart with the empty green glass bottle. The room smelled vaguely of disinfectant, and the fluorescent lights were stark and industrial, casting everything in a bright, harsh light that Hawkins associated with hospitals.

"The building has a concierge service," Manning told him. "It's only available to the top five floors."

"Fine," McCarter said. "Go ahead and hit the fire alarms now. When the authorities get here, I want thousands of people streaming out. I want us to disappear in a real mob scene."

Hawkins reached out and pulled open the door to the service lobby as McCarter stepped forward, lifting his H&K MP-5. Behind them Manning, grinning like a mischievous child, quickly typed a command into his SME PED.

The encrypted signal bounced along its traverse to the IBM Bladerunner under the Annex at Stony Man Farm, which interpreted the command and fed it into the building's network.

As they stepped out into the hallway all hell broke loose.

Toronto

AS THE HELICOPTER TURNED around, the Americans spilled from the now useless vehicle and began scrambling toward the tree line.

Fedorova blinked in surprise when he saw a tall and very thin female being helped by two shorter, stockier men holding FN P-90 submachine guns in their free hands. Beside those three, only one other man emerged from the stalled vehicle.

The prime courier was a female.

The Russian shrugged mentally, leveled the .45 and squeezed the trigger as the man turned and opened fire with his submachine gun.

Fedorova's shot struck him center mass and carved a gouge as big as a cereal bowl out of his side. The man was knocked to the ground where a creeping finger of burning gasoline immediately set his hair on fire.

"Here we go!" the pilot shouted in excitement.

The running men realized they would never reach the dubious sanctuary of the woods in time. Like the Praetorian guard the remaining bodyguards turned in defense of their boss.

One motivated bodyguard threw the tall woman with the briefcase down to the ground and hunched over her as he lifted his submachine gun.

The second paramilitary operator turned in the road and threw the stock of his weapon up to his shoulder.

Fedorova could see this was the man who had been splashed so liberally with his teammate's blood. His suit was stained with the sticky residue of the driver's death. Both men fired their weapons as they swept down on them in the helicopter.

The range was frighteningly close. More bullets opened jagged holes in the windshield of the Little Bird helicopter. Fedorova shot the face of the first man with his .45 ACP.

The player was knocked to the hard ground with merciless force. Fedorova shifted his aim and coolly eased back on the trigger of the .45 once more. In a splash of crimson the last bodyguard lost his right arm at the elbow and fell to the ground in shock.

The pilot was a pro. He saw the situation and reacted immediately.

He flared the Little Bird into a hard hover and dropped it straight down toward the ground. At eight feet Fedorova simply leaped clear of the hovering aircraft and onto the road. He dropped like a stone, landing on widespread feet and bending sharply at the knees to compensate for the impact.

He winced in pain, but his hand was steady on his gun as he saw the female courier lunge toward the shell-shocked bodyguard's weapon.

The automatic roared in Fedorova's fist.

The .45 ACP round struck the submachine gun and shattered the receiver and forestock into a dozen pieces. The pieces of the wrecked weapon were knocked across the road like billiard balls on a hard break. The DOE courier snatched her hand back from the ruined weapon and shoved bruised fingers into her mouth like a petulant child.

Fedorova shifted his aim to cover the wounded bodyguard in time to see the man slump fully into the ground. Blood gushed so quickly from the horrid wound the light in the man's eyes was shuttered with appalling quickness.

The man laid his head on the warm pavement and went to sleep forever.

Fedorova turned and looked at the huddled courier. Behind him the pilot settled the agile Little Bird onto the road. Off to his side the wreck of the Lincoln SUV blazed like a bonfire, casting wild, weird shadows across the scene.

In the flickering light Fedorova stepped forward and he could see in the cowering man's face that he must look like a demon. He loomed large over the courier.

The barrel of the .45 automatic was cavernous. Gray smoke trailed out of its depths as if from the pit of hell. The smell of cordite was on the Russian like the stink of sulfur on the devil.

The mercenary's voice was gravel on a tombstone as he spoke.

"You have something I want."

The woman blanched in fear.

Something caught the Russian's eye then and he looked up. It was flying so high above his situation that it was very nearly invisible, but Fedorova recognized it at once—a UAV.

They're watching, as always, he thought. Then he dismissed it from his mind.

CHAPTER TWENTY-SIX

The big-block V-8 engine roared like an angry grizzly.

Leaning forward against the steering wheel Carl Lyons rammed the big machine into fifth gear. Behind him in the SUV, Blancanales prepped his pistol for action. Riding shotgun, Schwarz did the same.

From their earjacks Hunt Wethers spoke with an urgent voice.

"Able, I have eyes on," the former college professor informed them. "We're too late."

"Goddammit!" Lyons slammed his palm against the steering wheel in frustration.

"I'm keeping eyes on the helicopter and I'm transmitting my location to the synchronous GPS unit in Schwarz's SME PED. I'll follow them and guide you in." The man paused. "I should be able to track them as long as I keep altitude, but hurry."

Lyons slammed the gas pedal on the SUV all the way down. "That won't be a problem," he promised.

Kiev, Ukraine

AN ELECTRONIC KLAXON began to screech.

The lights on the top half of the Kiev tower went out just as the ones lower to the ground floor had. Red glowing emergency lights clicked on low to the floor.

Overhead the sprinkler systems opened up and began to flood the area. An audio system of extensive power that had been blaring hip-hop music from behind one of the many hall doors suddenly cut out.

Phoenix Force moved down the center of the hallway, ignoring the chaos they had caused.

They were in a luxurious hall of marble tile, titanium-gold fixtures and black walnut woodwork. Four burly Russians in expensive suits came away from a teak desk and comfortable office chairs set in the middle of the hallway near the residential elevator doors decorated in gold filigree and Italian cut crystal.

Hawkins, the muzzle of his H&K submachine gun pointed down, walked forward, lifting his left hand up, palm out. "Good evening, my friends," he said in Russian. "We have a fire in the kitchen of the restaurant on the top floor. Everyone must evacuate using the stairs because of the gas leak."

A 9 mm Ingram M-11 submachine gun appeared from beneath the desk. "Why are you armed?" one of the men demanded, his face adorned with a thick Viking goatee. "Who are you? Where are your uniforms?"

Water from the spewing sprinklers began to pool on the desktop and run over the edges.

Doors began opening up along the hallway, drunken party-goers stumbling out in confusion, men cursing and more than a few females screaming in fear. The blinking red emergency lights illuminated the scene with a surrealistic quality.

McCarter stepped from around behind Hawkins even as Manning floated out even farther to the left. The Stony Man fire team revealed their silenced weapons and the criminal soldiers understood the situation instantly.

There was a triple echo of harsh, sound-suppressed coughs as the German weapons fired. The three commandos began moving forward, heel-toe in a synchronized line.

Phoenix Force's bullets tore down the wide hall in a pattern designed to avoid the clusters of intoxicated partygoers stumbling out of the rooms.

Bullets stitched into the bewildered bodyguards and the pooled water from the sprinklers turned a diluted crimson.

The dead men flopped to the ground as confused partygoers flooded the hallways. The fresh, leaking corpses were trampled on by a dozen different men and women in expensive nightclub clothes and cocaine-induced tunnel vision.

McCarter lowered his submachine gun to make it less obvious and stepped in front of Hawkins and Manning. He turned a big shoulder into the press of hysterical humanity and began to rudely push his way through, searching faces as he made for the door to the main suite.

Behind him Hawkins and Manning threw punches to knock the mafia hangers-on away from them and clear of the path. Twice, stoned street soldiers produced pistols in a threatening manner and were executed, their bodies dropping to the cold water-slicked tile like sacks of loose meat.

A topless woman tripped over one such corpse and sat up screaming, her face and hands painted red. Reflexively, Manning stopped and grabbed her under one arm to help. She shrieked and raked his exposed face with her nails, clawing for his eyes.

The Canadian jerked his face back and shoved the screeching drug whore away, barking out in pain and surprise as three red stripes were gouged into his face.

The hissing woman stumbled backward, eyes rolling wildly. The heel of her designer pump broke as she forced herself to her feet—then the crowd surged around her in the dark hallway and she was gone.

"What the *hell*," Manning swore, amazed.

"Hey, I wanted a building's worth of people clogging the halls and spilling out into the street when the *militsiya* showed up," McCarter said. "But these guys are like a zombie movie nightmare."

"Cocaine and Johnnie Walker Black Label will do that to you," Hawkins replied.

The team shouldered its way to the door, the thick crowd thinning out steadily as they approached the far end of the hallway.

The door to the master suite foyer hung open and Phoenix Force approached the entrance with caution, weapons held low but ready.

From inside, even over the scream of the fire alarm and the rushing howl of the sprinkler system, they could hear a man shouting angrily in Russian. McCarter stepped through the door and moved left, coming up against a table.

Behind him Manning followed him through and peeled off to the right. Hawkins anchored the door just to the right of the opening.

Inside the room a man they recognized from their briefings as the Russian oligarch Milosevic was snarling into an expensive cell phone.

Standing close by, a group of bodyguards watched him, hair plastered against their heads by the sprinkler system. As if controlled by a hive mentality, the squad of gunmen turned to face the intruders, hands darting beneath jackets to dig for the grips of pistols.

McCarter stepped forward and lifted his H&K MP-5 as one of the bodyguards pulled a Skorpion vz 83 machine pistol from inside a sky-blue suit jacket. The German-made submachine gun shook in the big American's hands and the 9 mm Parabellum unzipped the street soldier from belly to sternum.

The ex-Spetsnaz Bayarmaa died as he lived—quickly and violently.

Blood splashed the front of the man's shirt as his stomach was opened up and he stumbled backward. Manning knocked down the Russian gunman standing next to McCarter's target with a 3-round burst to the head. The sniper Suracova died that fast.

The young Russian mercenary known as Gregory began fighting for his life. From the doorway Hawkins hammered a third kill down with his own weapon as the other two swiveled to deal with the remaining bodyguards.

Gregory was dead.

The room flashed with light and cracked with the detonation of heavy-caliber ammo as unsuppressed weapons returned fire.

The German submachine gun shook in McCarter's hand, sending vibrations up his arms as shells came spinning out of his ejection port. All nine 9 mm rounds hit the Russian crime lord center mass, shredding his sky-blue silk shirt.

Milosevic folded inward under the impact of the pistol rounds, his shoulders slumping, his knees buckling. His face, frozen in a visage of disbelief, snapped forward as his head fell forward on a loose neck.

The man dropped straight on his ass, pistol flying to the floor, then flopped over onto his back.

In an incongruous moment it registered with the Briton that the man's pants were unbuckled and open at the waist, revealing a flash of silk boxer shorts the same sky blue as the man's shirt.

Operating on instinct and adrenaline, Manning's own failsafe blast carved the Russian's jaw off and shattered the man's spine just below his skull. The former Special Forces commando spun toward his partner, finger easing off the trigger to lie along the guard.

"Hawk!"

Hawkins was on one knee, his face twisted into a grimace and his left hand clutching his chest. With an exercise of sheer willpower the ex-Ranger rose, bringing his weapon into play.

"I'm fine," he gasped. "Let's go!"

McCarter was already moving forward. He caught a flash of movement and spun, dropping the smoking barrel of his MP-5, his finger finding the smooth metal curve of the trigger.

In the manner of all trained hostage-rescue experts the former SAS trooper's eyes went to the rushing figure's hands.

The rule was a simple dichotomy: weapon equals shoot. No weapon equals no shoot.

His finger slacked off the trigger of his SMG just before he almost fired a tight burst.

He saw empty, slim brown hands tipped by long, bloodred nails. He blinked out of his operational tunnel vision and saw the complete picture. The woman was nude, a sheer G-string revealing a bikini wax and silicon bags blowing her bare breasts up to an almost comical size.

In an adrenaline-stretched moment McCarter saw a glittering diamond necklace above the swaying, bouncing breasts and beautiful face twisted in terror, brown eyes tinged red as she screamed past perfect pearl-white teeth. He saw her eyes find the bloody, mutilated corpses of Milosevic and his bodyguards and he saw something snap in her mind.

She screamed again and darted for the door.

Toronto

ABLE TEAM RACED through the woods.

Overhead, the UAV circled, relaying the real-time information back to Stony Man Farm.

"They took the woman into one building and the package into another," Wethers informed the men on the ground.

The three members of Able Team crouched next to the same culvert Hermann Schwarz had utilized on his solo infiltration.

"No choice," Lyons said. "We split up from here."

"Gadgets has to get to the trigger," Blancanales pointed out. "That's where the bulk of the forces will be."

"Fine," Lyons agreed. "You and egghead go for the trigger. I'll get the woman."

FOR THE DEPARTMENT OF Energy Special Agent Sheila Links, her world had turned into a horror movie.

She had been transported with her head inside a pillowcase after the brutal ambush. She had no way of knowing that she was inside the isolated mansion of a Saudi Arabian prince and diplomat.

She thought she was in hell.

A hard, masculine hand grabbed her breast and pinched it cruelly through her blouse as she was manhandled into the room. Two hard-faced men in plain clothes stood sentry in front of the door as she was issued through.

They'll have to kill me, she thought, still in shock. He'll have no choice. I have no chance. Then a hand was up between her legs and she thought, bastard, as she tried to twist away.

She was thrown into a chair and her head yanked back by the hair when she tried to rise.

She looked toward the man who was holding her and saw a pistol inches from her face. Instinctively, she froze and she felt handcuffs slide around her wrists, locking her hands into place behind her back.

She saw one of the men come into the room, hauling her personal attaché case, not the trigger carriage. She was stung by a slap that snapped her head around. She felt blood in her mouth. Again the cruel fingers twisted into her hair and snatched her head back.

This time she found herself looking into black, laughing eyes, and she felt fear.

"What is the code to the case?" Fedorova demanded.

"It's in my case," she lied, gathering herself.

She had to stall. Had to command their attention until help arrived. She would tell them any lie just to eat up time. She looked away and spit blood out of her mouth onto the carpet.

The trigger had a tracking device implanted. No one at the DOE had expected trouble in Canada for God's sake, of course, but it was protocol.

Fedorova laughed. "Just in case you're wondering…" He

leaned in close and grimaced. "We've got the tracking signal blocked." He paused. "No one is coming to rescue you."

Agent Links forced a neutral look on her face. She could still feel the sting of the slap and knew her lips were puffing up.

"What do you want to know?" she asked.

She had no way of knowing who these men were, who they thought she was. They wore civilian clothes, but that meant nothing. She was in a room, but she didn't know where that room was.

She assumed these were foreign intelligence operators; it didn't seem possible mere terrorists could have gotten the inside information needed to snatch the trigger.

Despite this supposition their behavior and manner had not been coolly professional, but rather thuggish.

The backhand blow struck her across the cheek and snapped her head to the side. For the second time she tasted her own blood.

"Case codes!" Fedorova demanded.

He pulled a stainless-steel Ronson lighter from a pocket and began to absently play with it as he regarded her. His lips were thin but with a curdled quality that made Links think of slugs.

He snapped the lighter open. Sparked a flame. Snapped the lighter closed. Repeated. His eyes, the color of mud, watched her with predatory interest. Behind him his men stood in a loose, silent phalanx. Guns were visible now. One man, the tallest of them, leered at her.

She frowned. The man asking the questions was obviously Russian, but the others looked Middle Eastern.

Fedorova said something over his shoulder in a machine-gun cadence, sharp and dissonant to her ears. The others in the room chuckled in response. It was not a pleasant sound.

"Well, since you refuse to cooperate, I'm afraid we'll have

to take things up a notch." The man's voice was laconic. He snapped the lighter again.

"What?" Agent Links nearly screamed. "You haven't asked me anything yet!" Despite herself she was nearly frantic as she began to consider the implications of that flickering lighter flame.

"Oh?" The man feigned surprise. "You want to answer questions?"

"Sure." She nodded, just killing time. Give him time, she told herself.

"What is the code to the case?"

"I don't know." Her voice was frightened, even to her own ears.

"What is the goddamn code!"

"I don't know! They put the trigger in the case when I left. The principals at the other office would have taken it out when I got into New York! I never needed to know."

She hung her head as if in shame, now clearly exhausted and hopeless.

Fedorova the interrogator was on her in a flash.

He straddled her legs and pushed his weight down onto her lap, pinning her to the seat. He snatched her face up by the chin and jammed the muzzle of his pistol into her breast. He twisted it cruelly.

"Lies." His voice was metallically cold.

He leaned in very close, his lips bare centimeters from Agent Links's own bruised and swollen mouth. His breath was hot against her skin. She wanted to throw up.

"No," he continued. "That does not match the protocols clearly stated in Department of Energy's operations manual." His eyes narrowed. The gun muzzle was a rigid and deadly promise in the soft swell of her breast.

Links blinked in horror. The bastard was right. But how could he know so much about classified material?

"To get my message across," he whispered, eyes now bright.

"I'm going to have to do things to you. My men are going to have to do things to you. Things I did with great effect in Chechnya. Then we'll dump you and when they find you they'll know never—"

There was an angry shout in the hall, then an unmistakable thud of something heavy and organic falling against the door.

CHAPTER TWENTY-SEVEN

Kiev, Ukraine

The woman sprinted, shrieking with terror.

McCarter stepped forward and thrust the heel of his left palm into her sternum and knocked her backward, tossing her anorexic frame onto a Louis Baptiste divan.

She gasped at the impact and flew backward before bouncing into the cushions. He lowered the smoking MP-5 and trained it on her face.

She looked up, eyes white in terror, her lipstick smeared across her face. He leaned in close, menacing and huge, eyes angry slits. He spoke in perfect Russian, his voice an angry bark.

"Where's the American?" he snarled. "I want Klegg!"

"In there," she sobbed. A skinny arm thrust out and one of those scarlet-nail-tipped fingers pointed toward a double set of ebony wood doors across the room. "I swear to God, he's in there with the girls."

"Go," Manning ordered. He jerked his weapon muzzle toward the door, indicating the path. "Get the fuck out of here."

The woman sobbed in relief and sprang up off the couch. She sidestepped in a skittish dance past the bloody corpses of her former lover and his men, then raced out of the room.

Hawkins, still recovering from the impacts to his body armor, covered her until she left the room then took a knee again to provide rear security.

"Get ready," McCarter told Manning, voice low.

Manning nodded and took a flash-bang from under his coat. McCarter moved forward toward the door. "Come out, Klegg!"

From inside the room a pistol boomed five times.

The three members of Phoenix Force ducked as bullets slammed through the door, spraying splintered wood. The bullets cut through the room in wild, desperate patterns, none striking close to the Americans.

"Hard way. Always the goddamn hard way," Manning swore.

McCarter carefully lifted and aimed his MP-5.

He triggered a 3-round blast. The 9 mm Parabellum rounds struck the handle of the interior doors, shattering the lock housing. Instantly, two feminine voices screamed in terror from inside the room.

Manning and McCarter ran forward, each taking up a position by the door. Behind them they heard Hawkins's weapon cycle as he fired the suppressed submachine gun at targets outside the room.

Manning let the spoon fly off his flash-bang as he primed the grenade.

McCarter leaned forward, reaching across the door, and snagged the twisted metal handle connected to the shattered lock housing. He yanked his arm back and jerked the door open.

A pistol fired three times from inside the room. Manning tossed the stun grenade through the opening and both men turned away.

The metal canister landed on thick carpet and rolled to a stop. The voices of the Russian girls screamed again and a man cursed in fear. There was a brilliant flash and a sharp, deafening bang as the grenade detonated.

The occupants of the room cried out in pain and fear as dozens of hard rubber balls exploded like shrapnel, cutting through the room and raising welts on naked flesh. There was the distinct sound of shattered glass and Manning turned and charged through the bedroom door, his MP-5 up and ready. He darted inside and cut left as McCarter popped up out of his crouch and swung around the open door to enter the room and cut right.

Schwarz danced left in a sidestep like an NBA guard trying to cut off the center's drive to the basket. His own submachine gun up, McCarter sprinted right, the muzzle snapping through vectors as he cleared his assigned spaces.

The room was dark, but floor-to-ceiling balcony doors revealed a million-dollar view of the wintry Kiev skyline and provided light from the buildings around them.

Cold air rushed in through the shattered windows and sheer drapes fluttered like flags.

Manning saw a bed in the shape of a heart, the covers and blankets tangled into piles, a dozen pillows scattered around. To the left of the big bed, on his side of the room, he saw two skinny but eerily beautiful teenage girls, one dressed in jet-black lingerie and stockings, the other in gleaming white.

He felt a queasy sense of disgust as his adrenaline-sharpened eyes recognized the girls as looking so alike they could only be sisters.

The two young girls huddled in the corner of the bed. "Stay down," he ordered in Russian, and put a burst into the bed, slicing the sheets and kicking up stuffing. "Clear!" he snapped in English.

McCarter charged forward on his side of the room, clearing his vectors. He saw a tall, thin man in a pair of European-style fire-engine-red briefs. The deeply tanned and black-haired man was laid out on his stomach. A 9 mm pistol lay on the floor several yards away.

Klegg moaned, still blinded and deafened by the stun grenade, and attempted to push himself up on shaking arms.

McCarter ran forward and kicked him in the gut. The man gagged, almost puking at the impact, and sagged back down.

The Phoenix Force leader spun around and stomped the fingers of the American's right hand, breaking three of them, then hopped forward and kicked the pistol across the room toward the shattered glass window.

Manning stepped closer, keeping his muzzle pointed in the general direction of the teenage girls, but watching the downed American criminal fixer with a reflexive, mechanical suspicion.

McCarter moved closer to the man as he gasped for breath and let his submachine gun hang from its strap. He dropped down, driving his knee into the man's unprotected kidney.

Klegg shouted at the pain and spasmed like a fish yanked into the bottom of a boat.

McCarter snatched the man's arms while he was too hurt to resist and slapped on a pair of handcuffs. Once the bracelets were secure he popped back up and dragged the lawyer to his feet.

He reached down and squeezed the criminal agent's fingers together, grinding the broken fingers in a viselike grip.

Klegg screamed.

McCarter leaned in close, maintaining pressure, and whispered in Russian, "You are fucking coming with us. If you give me a moment of problem I'll break your arm at the elbow. If you try to run I'll machine-gun your kneecaps. Do you believe me?"

Klegg didn't answer, panting from the pain. McCarter snarled and crushed his hands harder. "Do you believe me?" he repeated.

"Yes, yes—I believe you." Klegg nodded.

"Good. Let's go."

McCarter shoved the injured American forward, driving him out of the room despite the man being dressed in nothing but underwear.

Kept up on his toes by the painful hold the ex-SAS trooper

kept him in, the bewildered and overwrought Klegg meekly complied.

Manning danced backward toward the door, searching the room for further possible intelligence or dangers.

He saw the American's clothes in a pile at the foot of the bed and he stooped to rifle the pockets quickly. He took the man's wallet, cell phone and a manila envelope containing a portable flash drive. As he secured the finds he looked over at the girls. They had stopped crying and watched him with huge, dark eyes.

"Don't be afraid, ladies," he told them as he backed out of the room. "You may now return to your regularly scheduled programming, okay?"

The girls hugged each other until they were sure the killers were gone. Then they went out into the gore-painted suite to steal money and drugs from the dead men.

HAWKINS LED THE WAY down the dark hallway. He moved quickly, stepping past the occasional corpse of a Milosevic bodyguard and ignoring the spraying sprinklers.

The water was two inches deep on the floor and Phoenix Force splashed as they hurried down the hallway toward the elevator.

McCarter initiated his throat mike. "Stony, we have the package. We're making our exit now."

"Copy," Price replied immediately. "Everyone okay?"

"Hawk took a few rounds to the vest but he's mobile," McCarter acknowledged. "We'll be clear in minutes. Tell Jack to warm the plane up."

Toronto

IN THE STRETCH of lawn between the prince's main house and the massive multicar garage, Able Team split up.

Working under direction from their own personal eye-in-the-sky, Huntington Wethers, the three-man death squad peeled off on their missions. Moving between a fleet of parked cars, the three men approached their entry points with weapons up and ready.

Carl Lyons had just entered the main house to try to rescue the captured DOE courier when Blancanales and Schwarz were ambushed.

From a window in the massive garage a stun grenade flew out, exploding in the air like a sonic boom.

Blancanales, closer to the detonation, went flying and lay limply on the ground.

His Glock 17 came up in Schwarz's fist as he rode out the shock wave.

He thrust the weapon forward and stroked the trigger, sending half a dozen rounds through the window as he skipped backward.

Glass shattered under the impact of his 9 mm rounds. A burst of automatic gunfire erupted in answer from inside of the garage.

A brilliant flame of unsuppressed muzzle-flash splashed behind a hanging window blind.

The weapon fired at such close range that the expensive bamboo covering caught fire.

Bullets ripped through the air around Schwarz and sailed out across the yard. Schwarz went to one knee and fired a tight trio of bullets into the burning blind.

He heard the audible smacks as his rounds found a target and then the flaming blind was ripped aside as a falling body crashed through and rebounded off the broken glass of the windowsill.

He shifted to the left, putting himself at an angle to both the window and the garage door. From his vantage Schwarz had a good view of a large segment of the open bay. Figures moved inside its confines and he shifted his posture into the familiar Weaver stance as he searched for some sort of substantial cover.

There was nothing. There was no cover for him to get behind, nor any he could outrace a fusillade of bullets to get to. He was caught in the open by opponents who wielded superior firepower.

His only hope for protection would be to retreat toward some of the prince's automobiles parked behind him. To do that he would have to leave the immobile Blancanales where he lay.

That wasn't going to happen under any circumstances.

In the shattered window, flames licked up as the burning curtain ignited other flammable materials inside the room.

From behind the growing flames two men rushed forward, Russian Bison-19 submachine guns held up at the ready.

Schwarz threw himself flat-out on the asphalt. He brought up his Glock 17 and sighted from the prone position.

He squeezed his trigger coolly and an untidy third eye opened up on the forehead of one of the gunmen. A red mist appeared behind the man's head and he crumpled forward, his submachine gun tumbling from slack fingers. The falling man's corpse fell halfway out through the shattered window.

The second gunmen flinched as his comrade's sticky hot blood and brain matter splattered across his face. The body-guard's triggered burst sailed wild as he jerked in surprise at the gore splatter.

Schwarz shifted his pistol's aim to center mass and pulled the trigger on the Glock 17 twice.

The man staggered back like a punch-drunk fighter, arms flailing wide. Schwarz brought the muzzle of the Glock down, sighted and put a final round through the man's throat and he was driven down by the kinetic force of the 9 mm round.

Unsure of how many others might be in the garage, Schwarz threw himself up and rushed forward. Inside the building the fire spread rapidly. A nylon dust cover on an antique automobile caught and then burst into flame.

Thick black smoke began quickly filling the structure.

Schwarz shuffled forward, weapon up as he moved. He heard shouts coming from around him, a woman screamed and doors were opened and then slammed shut again.

The inside of the garage was fully engulfed in flames now and, cursing, Schwarz began moving away from the room and toward where Blancanales lay.

Black smoke poured out through the shattered window and billowed up into the sky. Flames licked at the edges of the window, completely unaffected by the slight rainfall.

Schwarz turned sideways away from the building, still watching it, and began to move at a faster pace toward the unmoving Blancanales.

No matter what, he was going to have to go into that garage. There was no other choice.

Just as he reached Blancanales, the man stirred, eyes blinking in confusion.

A gunman came through the window screaming. His Bison-19 submachine gun fired wildly as he leaped over the sill.

Schwarz again threw himself flat across the confused Blancanales as a wild, ragged spray of rounds slapped out in his direction. He hit the asphalt hard and grunted.

Schwarz thrust his arm out straight and rolled onto his side as he tried to target the charging man. Still firing, the man shuffled toward the nominal protection of a dented Aston Martin.

He went to one knee behind the bumper of the dark blue car and brought his weapon to his shoulder.

Schwarz didn't hesitate. He rolled onto his stomach and took his Glock 17 in both hands. He released air out through his nose in a steady stream and used both hands to home in on the automobile.

His first shot hit wide of the gas hatch. His second punctured it. A jet of gasoline shot out of the hole in an arc and splashed onto the asphalt.

Schwarz squeezed his trigger twice and put two more bullets through the bleeding gas tank. The second bullet ignited the flammable gases trapped inside the tank and it went up with a whoosh. A ball of flame erupted and was followed hard by a wave of concussive force.

The gunman was knocked clear of the car by the force of the explosion. His hair ignited and he rose screaming, dropping his submachine gun and slapping at the flames licking around his head. Schwarz dropped him with a precise 9 mm slug to the head.

Bullets ricocheted off the pavement a yard in front of where Schwarz lay prone on the asphalt.

He pivoted his head back toward the garage and saw a gunman standing in the doorway of the smoldering, smoking structure. The man had been sighting in on Schwarz when the vehicle had gone up. His burst was knocked wide in his surprise at the sudden force of the exploding automobile. He cringed back from the rolling heat, one arm thrown up protectively over his face.

Schwarz twisted, rolling up onto his left shoulder and bringing his pistol to bear on the target. Schwarz pulled the trigger once and the man's frame shuddered. Blood spurted from a hole in the man's upper thigh and he sagged farther back against the door frame. The man swept up his weapon as Schwarz sighted in again.

His weapon erupted. Pistol rounds slammed into Schwarz where he covered Blancanales with his own body.

Schwarz fired again and hit the man in his stomach and then put a second 9 mm bullet into his sternum. The man's clothes billowed out under the twin impacts and he dropped down, collapsing.

Blood began pumping out rapidly in a growing pool around his body. His weapon clattered against the asphalt. His eyes fixed open, staring, and from where Schwarz lay they showed a glassy reflection of the flames burning around him.

Schwarz tried to stand, but found he couldn't.

Blood pooled in his lap, and he couldn't feel his legs.

"Easy, Gadgets," Blancanales said.

Schwarz grabbed his partner by his arm.

"Go," he insisted. "I can't walk. You have to stop them. Go!"

CHAPTER TWENTY-EIGHT

Inside the main house Fedorova was rising off Agent Links's lap, twisting with the pistol toward the sound of the gunshots just as she lunged.

Her mouth found the side of his head and her teeth found the lobe of his ear. Her jaw snapped shut like a trap and blood squirted into her mouth, salty and hot. The Russian screamed in surprise even as his men were turning toward the door.

Bullets burned through the door, shattering the lock mechanism. A moment later the door snapped open, splintering along its length in the process with a sound like a gunshot.

A sentry in plain clothes standing next to the door swiveled and swept a lethal-looking submachine gun out from under his suit jacket.

A dark and mangled shape came hurtling into the room. Gunfire erupted. She had a brief flash-image of a huge blond man charging forward, a dead body in his arms as a shield like a football tackling dummy.

The corpse's head looked odd, like a deflated balloon. She could see the blue-gray scrambled-egg pieces of the dead man's brain sticking to his hair.

Agent Links jerked her head hard to the side and ripped off Fedorova's ear. He screamed out loud and threw himself backward. Blood splashed her face as his weight lifted off her.

He rose and punched the bound woman hard in the face, knocking her over backward in the chair. She bounced off the table behind her and fell to the floor.

She grunted with the impact and twisted to look up.

The Russian loomed above her. Blood soaked the side of his face and clothes. The pistol was in his hands. He lifted it and sighted down the barrel at her. His thin lips were pulled back over square teeth stained with his own blood. His muddy eyes were wild.

The shot sounded loud from so close but it also merged in with the panoply of gunfire echoing savagely in the room. There was a muzzle-flash half a second after the man jerked to the side.

A 9 mm round burned into the wall next to Links's head, tossing splinters into the air. The Russian spun around and dropped forward, gun falling from his slack hands. An exit wound had blown out his left eye and temple, turning it into a saucer-size cavity.

The man's weight tumbled forward and flopped across Links, crushing her bound hands cruelly against the thin carpet of the floor. The chair she had been secured to snapped under the pressure along its back and legs.

Agent Links grunted as the wind was driven from her under the impact. She struggled to rise. The table blocked her view. Her own ragged breathing confused the sounds. She heard sharp curses and anguished cries.

She heard living bodies striking inanimate objects. From all around her the sharp, pungent miasma of cordite sliced into her nose, burning it.

She struggled to lift the dead body off her by pushing up, but with her hands still bound behind her back it was nearly impossible. She scissor-kicked her legs and fought to rise.

More of the man's blood spilled across her.

She got her head up and saw a Middle Eastern man in plain clothes stumble backward, arms flung out wide, red geysers blossoming in his white dress shirt.

She fought to rise, pulling her legs underneath her and shoving at the body. Her head cleared the edge of the chair and she saw bodies splayed across the room like forgotten toys. The walls were splashed with blood. The television screen had been shattered. A picture on the wall held the evidence of dual bullet impacts.

A corpse, glassy-eyed and gory, lay sprawled belly-down on the bed.

She twisted her head and saw the blond man locked in a deadly dance with the final survivor of the room's squad.

The bodyguard fought with the blond man over possession of an automatic pistol, but she didn't quite comprehend what she was seeing until suddenly the blond man bent at the waist, dropping his center of gravity, then rose again while twisting at the hips. He held the other man hard by the wrists and when he uncoiled his body the man tumbled over his own arms and was planted headfirst into the ground.

Still holding on to the man's captured wrists, the blond man bent the barrel of his weapon down and it fired three times in rapid succession. Links could hear the wet, flat impacts of the rounds as they burrowed into flesh from brutally close range.

Carl Lyons lifted his head.

He met the American woman's eyes as she rose. The moment ended in a heartbeat and Lyons crossed the room and quickly worked to unlock her cuffs with the key he took from the dead interrogator's pocket.

"Thank you—" she began.

She wasn't gushing, just grateful and controlled, though her heart was beating in her chest. She could still remember the feel of the men's hands roaming her body at will, insulting her sense of self, her dignity.

Lyons cut her off, stress evident in his voice.

"We've got to get moving. I have someone trying to get to the trigger but we have to get you."

Links threw the handcuffs down and quickly buttoned her shirt as she listened to the man's instructions. As he talked she reached down and took a pistol from a still-warm corpse, jacked the slide and slid it home behind her back.

"How are you doing?" he asked.

"I'm ready," Links said, voice firm.

Lyons touched her face, noted the marks there, the swelling and the bruising. He smiled, half to himself, at her courage. She was a lioness.

"Good," he said.

He turned to go and Links followed close behind him. He crossed the room, stepping over carpets and dancing around spreading pools of red. The enclosed space still reeked of cordite but a sweeter, more biological smell had already started to creep in.

A fan turned overhead. She heard the hum of the air conditioner.

Lyons reached the door, hands on his pistol. He quickly looked around the corner, then ducked his head back. He stuck his head out again and took a fuller look. He turned back toward the DOE courier.

"It's clear. We've got to get to the service elevators. If there's a problem, shoot anyone armed. You've got to get out."

The two stepped out into the hallway.

She saw the crumpled heaps of the sentries she had seen on her way into the torture chamber. Both men lay like discarded dolls with slack mouths and glassy eyes. Their spilling blood was very bright against the subdued hues of the hall carpet.

She reached out and grabbed the blond man's arm as he scanned the hall. "I don't even know who you are. Are you American? With DOE?"

"No time for that." Lyons shook his head. "I'm here to get you out. Now let's get."

"Fair enough," she said. From somewhere on the property they heard gunfire break out.

Then they ran.

BLANCANALES CROSSED the blood-splattered driveway and headed for the heavy door leading to the levels below the burning garage.

"Boss, you on?" he queried.

"Go ahead," Lyons replied instantly. He sounded out of breath.

"Our boy is down on the driveway. He's conscious and able to defend himself, but he can't walk."

"Understood," Lyons said. "I'm rolling to that twenty now."

"I'll see you on the flip side," Blancanales said, and signed off.

He ignored the pouring smoke and creeping flames as he pushed his way through a door leading under the garage. He went down a short flight of concrete stairs and came up to another door.

He readied a Beretta automatic pistol in his fist and took up the door handle. He turned it quickly and smoothly before gently pushing the door open a crack and looking out.

He saw a long hallway, windowless, poorly lit and grimy.

From the direction he was looking it ran for about thirty yards before ending in a solid door. A nervous-looking guard stood with slung P-90 submachine gun, smoking a cigarette and knocking the ashes straight onto the linoleum.

Blancanales eased the door closed and frowned, pensive.

He had no idea what was in the opposite direction of that part of the hallway he had observed. How many men might be posted there or with what weapons. He had to secure the DOE trigger; everything, the whole world, rested on that fact. The rock stolen from the cargo ship was less important than the trigger; they could recover the rock later. But the trigger was mission critical.

He wiped a hand across his sweating forehead and his sleeve came away damp. It was uncomfortably warm, stifling almost.

Blancanales burst through the door in one fluid motion. He

lifted the silenced Beretta 92-F up in both hands and squeezed the trigger. The pistol coughed twice and 9 mm Parabellum rounds slapped into the startled sentry.

The man went down, his rifle sliding off his shoulder and his burning cigarette tumbling from limp fingers.

Blancanales stepped fully into the hall, spinning to cover the opposite end of the hall axis. He saw more hallway, broken by doors and ending in a wall set with a corkboard. He saw no other targets and he rose from his crouch, keyed-up and tense.

There were three other doors in the short hallway besides the one he had just emerged from. He quickly tried the handles. One was a broom closet, long disused with faucet and mop bucket, both covered in cobwebs and built-up grime.

The other two led into rooms that at one time could have been used as personal offices but were empty. He found no clue as to where the trigger was being held.

He stopped at the still leaking corpse of the sentry and pulled the man's subgun free of the body. He looped the sling cross body from his shoulder so that the pistol grip was snug up against his right hip in easy reach. Maintaining his grip on the silenced Beretta, he reached out for the knob of the door the man had been standing in front of.

He eased the door open a crack and stepped over the cooling body. He heard the rumbling white noise of industrial blowers and running generators, and hot, dry air washed over his face, irritating his narrowed eyes.

The room was thirty feet wide by twenty feet long. A series of large potted plants had been set up and the lights had been kept low. Directly across from him, Blancanales saw another door.

He stepped into the room, realizing that the underground building he was in had to be very large indeed. He had no promise that his escape would be either easy or quick.

It appeared that the Saudi diplomat's Canadian estate was

a more significant base for Seven than the Farm had first realized.

He crossed the room wondering at the reason for the plants as he made his way through them. He heard a clink of metal on tile suddenly from his left and turned in that direction, pistol ready.

The panther screamed and lunged toward him, yellow eyes bright.

He saw fiendishly long incisors and copious amounts of foaming spit on the thing's jaws as he threw himself backward. The cat lunged forward, big paws spread wide, razor-sharp claws unleashed.

Suddenly it was jerked up short by the chain fastened around its neck and Blancanales found he could breathe again. The cat screamed at him again, and Blancanales scooted back farther out of the beast's range, his pistol still up.

"What the hell," he muttered as he came to his feet.

Nothing about this made sense. The cat was enraged. Its eyes were red and wild, and it dripped saliva from its jaws in an overabundance of foamy spittle. Blancanales kept his gun trained on the cat as he backed away from it. Its aggression seemed unnatural, demonic even.

He could see the chain running from the wall fixture and could gauge that it was unable to reach either door. He wondered if the wild beast was the prince's idea of a pet or ornament.

Keeping a watch on the strange presence of the creature, Blancanales moved to the door. He opened it, pistol ready and looked out.

He saw a forty-foot hallway with four doors set on either side and a single door set at the end of the hall opposite him. He frowned. He had awoken in some labyrinth of endless doors, strange rooms and twisting halls.

He felt obligated to check each option he came across so that he didn't inadvertently miss the trigger or leave hostile forces at his back.

Should the prince attempt to escape, Blancanales was assured that Wethers wouldn't hesitate to use the missiles on his UAV. No one on the estate would be calling for law enforcement, either.

Of course it would have amused Blancanales highly to see the looks on the faces of the cops when they showed up and found the "drunk drivers" from the other night out on bail and starting World War III.

He moved forward to the closest set of doors on either side of the hall. The doors were heavy industrial constructs without windows or discernable cracks beneath them. He tensed, then tried first one door, then the next.

They were both empty.

Each one was a basic ten-foot cube containing a bed, toilet and sink. There were no windows, no pictures on the wall or rugs on the ground; they were cells. The doorknob would not turn from the inside.

Blancanales's sense of unease continued to grow, but he moved forward to the next set of doors.

He opened the one on the left-hand side first.

He swung into the room pistol up, his senses keyed to react. What he saw shocked and sickened him.

The Asian man sat on the floor, slumped against the low edge of his bed. His lap was a pool of blood that had spread out across the floor beneath him in a wide puddle.

Blancanales squinted in the weak light from the single bulb burning overhead. The man's wrists had been torn open, and the wounds there were ragged and gaping. Blancanales saw with sickening understanding that the man's mouth was ringed with dripping red. There was also a copious amount of saliva around his lips, just like the panther.

He had stumbled into a circus of horrors, a medieval dungeon.

He stepped back and closed the door. His sense of urgency in finding the trigger tripled in that instant. Whoever Seven was, they seemed utterly capable of using the technology they'd stolen for evil.

He tried the door directly across from the suicide victim and found it empty, as he did the first of the pair of doors beyond that.

The next door opened up on the now familiar cell. Blancanales tensed as he saw the figure lying on the bed.

"What's your name?" he demanded, lifting the Beretta.

The figure on the bed gave no answer.

CHAPTER TWENTY-NINE

Blancanales stepped forward into the room, careful not to let the door shut behind him. The figure on the bed was a Caucasian female in her late twenties with a full figure on a small frame and long auburn hair.

Her eyes were wide-open and staring at the ceiling. Blancanales could see her chest rising and falling as she breathed. Thick ropes of foamy saliva drooled out of the corners of her lips and soaked the mattress beneath her head.

He caught a whiff of something foul and realized the woman had soiled herself. He stuck his knife in the jamb of the door to keep it open and moved closer. He reached out and shook the woman.

"Hello?" he said.

He got no response, and he saw that though her eyes were open their blue irises were filmed gray and that her breathing was very shallow. He passed his hands in front of her face, but she didn't blink.

"Hey, wake up," he said again, louder. Out of desperation he used the knuckles of his left hand to rub her sternum, a last-ditch effort to elicit a pain response from the woman.

He still got no response.

He backed slowly away and retrieved his knife from the doorjamb. He felt anger rising in him. The woman was beyond his help, though she still breathed. Her coma seemed more than a simple fugue. She was catatonic and her breath so fetid Blancanales gave her hours to live and not days.

Someone needed to pay for treating human beings in such

a fashion. Blancanales adjusted his grip on the handle of his pistol and stepped out of the cell, letting the door close behind him.

After finding more empty rooms, he finally discovered a living victim.

Blancanales opened the door to find a teenage male crouched on his bed. Blancanales stepped forward, keeping the door ajar with one hand and lowering the muzzle of the Beretta.

"Easy," he said. "I'm hear to help you, son."

The shivering boy turned his back toward Blancanales and remained on the bed. Blancanales took a step away from the door, toward the crouched figure on the bed.

"Do you understand me?" Blancanales repeated.

The boy continued to cower on the bed, his back to the newcomer. Blancanales frowned to himself, then took another step into the cramped room, his left arm stretched out and holding on to the door behind him.

"Come on, kid," he said. "Let's get out of here."

Blancanales was no fool. He knew the potential of what he faced in trying to help the boy. It was still the right thing to do.

Because he wanted to believe, he was a moment too slow when the boy sprang.

Screaming like the panther, the boy whirled suddenly and leaped toward Blancanales. The teenager had the same wild red eyes and dripping, foamy drool as the others and his hands had formed into clutching, ragged-nailed claws.

Blancanales stumbled back to avoid losing control of the open door. He jerked the hand holding the pistol back, snatching it out of the way of the insane, leaping boy.

The slight teenager crashed into Blancanales, staggering him, but far from knocking him over. Blancanales stepped back as the boy clawed at him. He let the open door bounce off his shoulder as he twisted out of the boy's way.

The mad youth's hands tore at him, scratching skin and

tearing at his clothes. In that moment the boy's searching hands found the hilt of Blancanales's straight blade and snatched it free.

Misunderstanding the wild boy's intentions, Blancanales snapped the butt of his pistol down and struck him on his shoulder.

The teenager howled in pain and rolled away, giving Blancanales a chance to collect himself. Too late, Blancanales realized the boy's intentions in stealing his knife. The kid looked up at him from across the room, eyes wild, and howled in triumph.

Blancanales sprang forward into the hall, his jaw dropping in surprise as he shouted an emphatic, "No!"

He was too late by a country mile.

The boy used a skinny arm to lift the knife up. The fighting blade looked almost comically large in the teen's slender hand. The boy jerked his arm back without hesitation and drew the sharp edge of the weapon across his own throat.

Blancanales sagged beside the youth in the hall, cradling his fallen form.

Blood was everywhere and the knife tumbled from limp fingers as the child gurgled to death. Blancanales felt his stomach spasm in protest at the sight, but knew it was hopeless; nothing could save the child.

He gently laid the boy's head down on the hall floor. The spreading pool of blood soaked his pants at the knees where he knelt next to the cooling body of the child.

Confused, Blancanales snarled in outrage and took his knife back. He kept his gaze locked on the peaceful face of the boy as he wiped the knife blade clean and slid it back into its sheath. There would be hell to pay for this, he promised himself.

"Blancanales to Wethers," he said into his throat mike.

"Go ahead," Wethers answered.

"Let the bosses know our intel on the prince's property was too shallow. There is a major underground structure here and possible chemical weapons or narcotics experimentation. This place will have to be treated as a biohazard site."

"Understood," Wethers replied. "Do you want to come out?"

"Negative," he replied immediately. "I'm getting that trigger. There's no way I'm taking a chance on them slipping away out some back door."

"Understood."

Moving quickly, Blancanales rose to his feet and approached the hall door.

LYONS MOVED DOWN the hall at a brisk walk, Links close behind him.

His earpiece came to life and he listened while Blancanales gave Wethers the situation report.

"We have to hurry," he said, urging Links forward. The woman wasn't arguing.

They jogged up the last flight of stairs and yanked open the servants' entrance to the top floor of the mansion.

With Links close behind, Lyons began walking quickly down the corridor, his feet silent on the carpet. He shrugged his knapsack off his shoulder and began to rummage in it as he approached his target door. He stopped in front of the dark-grained wooden doorway and manipulated the door handle.

It moved easily under the weight of his hand. The door came open as Lyons used his free hand to secure his pistol.

The Beretta 92-F was smooth and well balanced in his grip.

The extra weight of the sound suppressor was negligible. His finger found the smooth curve of the trigger and took up the slack as he pushed open the door.

Silently, he warned Links back.

He followed tight in behind the swing of the door, taking up the Beretta pistol in both his hands and tracking the muzzle in shorts snaps, dividing the room into instantaneous vectors then clearing them.

He stutter-stepped into the bedroom and scanned for the targets of diplomatic security forces. He saw a man at his feet struggling to rise, a black pistol half pulled from a shoulder sling.

Lyons lowered the muzzle of the Beretta and it coughed once, the pistol recoiling smoothly in his grip, the barrel barely rising off target. Enough blood and brain to fill a soup bowl was splashed onto the carpet behind the man's head, and Lyons stepped across his corpse.

The ex-cop caught a flash of movement out of the corner of his eye and saw a snarling bodyguard in a cheap business suit sweeping up a submachine gun, swinging the muzzle around toward the intruder.

Lyons tossed twin bursts into his throat and chest, staining his clothes crimson and knocking the security agent back. Instantly, he pivoted at the waist even as he shuffled forward a few more steps into the room.

He saw a figure push itself up off the floor. His eyes narrowed into crosshairs and his finger tensed on the trigger.

There was a starburst of flame as the pistol in the uniformed security officer's hand came to life even as Lyons was throwing himself to the side. He squeezed the Beretta's trigger as he leaped, but the rounds went wide and punched holes out through the window behind the enemy gunmen.

Behind him he heard the wet smack of bullets hitting flesh and then Agent Links's scream.

He heard the pistol's angry bark as he landed on the floor next to the corpse of the second man he'd killed and bounced back up. Coming up, Lyons twisted his torso into position as two 9 mm rounds of enemy fire slapped into the wall.

The Able Team leader's shot was hasty and he only scored a gut wound. The bodyguard staggered, one hand flying to his leaking belly. Lyons shot again and put a burst in the man's shoulder, chest and throat.

Blood sprayed out and seemed to hang in the air for a moment as the man sagged. The soldier went down and his own blood rained down on him. Lyons twisted around to cover the front of the room in case there was another member of the security entourage in the room.

Lyons stepped into the hallway.

Links looked up at him, pain twisting her features. She tried to smile but all the blood had drained out of her face. Suddenly her eyes rolled back up in her head and she passed out.

"Jesus!" Lyons snarled in frustration.

He tossed a look over his shoulder and saw more uniformed estate security standing at the end of the hall. Without thinking he bent and scooped up the unconscious Links into a fireman's carry.

Instantly, he was soaked with her blood.

The security force held Shipka Bulgarian submachine guns.

The Shipka, probably chambered in the 9x18 mm Makarov configuration, was of a boxy, straightforward design, using simple blowback operation and firing from open bolt. The lower receiver along with pistol grip and trigger guard were made from polymer, while the upper receiver was made from steel. The simple buttstock was made from steel wire and folded to the left side of gun.

It was an easily concealed compact weapon perfectly designed for urban operations and capable of firing 700 rounds per minute. Exactly the kind of firepower Lyons wanted to avoid in such a congested environment.

He did the only thing he could do.

He ran.

A line of slugs chewed into the wall just over Lyons's shoulder and the acoustic chamber of the hallway carried the gunfire reports painfully to his ears like claps of thunder.

Oh, they're pissed, he thought.

He ran forward and hit the fire door with his shoulder, knocking it open, then lunged forward, throwing the door closed behind him to slow pursuit.

Please don't die, please don't die, Lyons silently told the bleeding agent over his shoulder as he raced forward. He suddenly realized that in the run-and-gun scramble he'd taken a wrong turn somewhere.

He didn't know exactly how to get out of the house.

Then he saw the handle turning on the door in front of him and realized someone was coming through from the other side.

DEEP IN THE SECRET labyrinth below the Saudi prince's estate Blancanales continued his desperate hunt for the trigger device.

He turned a lock at the end of the corridor and opened the door.

He found himself in a bare hallway running for sixty feet before taking a sharp turn to the right. It was a windowless structure with overhead track sodium lighting and linoleum floors. The walls were painted in two-tone industrial green, dark on the bottom and light on the top.

Blancanales began to navigate the hallway.

His uncertainty at how far underground he was, combined with the mazelike layout, left him feeling slightly claustrophobic and trapped. His eyes searched the ceilings for cameras and the walls for intercom stations but he found nothing.

The strange, almost surrealistic encounters with the panther and obviously drugged inmates had left even the battle-hardened Blancanales feeling slightly off balance. Despite this, he pushed back his fear and uncertainty with the resolution of a survivor.

He would find the trigger and make his way out of this chamber of horrors or he would die in the attempt; it was that straightforward, that simple. He turned the corner in the hall using a sliding shuffle into a modified Weaver stance.

It was more of the same.

Thirty feet long and identical to the first section in every way but one. At the end of the narrow passage there was a door set in the wall. Blancanales covered the distance in the hallway quickly, his weapon poised as he moved toward the danger area presented by the doorway.

Sooner or later he was going have a change in luck and meet armed sentries.

He paused at the door, hand resting on the knob. He decided on speed and aggression. He knew that behind him lay only a dead end where he would be run to ground.

Each door he moved through brought him closer to freedom, so attempting to sneak and peek was merely delaying the inevitable. Blancanales jerked open the door, pistol up, and moved through it.

He was instantly aware he was in a laboratory. The room was long and wide, running one hundred feet by forty feet under fluorescent lighting. Test stands, lab tables, equipment racks and computer stations were interspaced among a large chemical centrifuge, a refrigerator and monitoring devices.

Lights were dimmed in the room as if Blancanales had found the place during a down period or after hours. He recognized a closet door on his right by the narrow glass window set in the center. Against the left wall he saw interior windows behind which a light burned.

Directly in front of him across the room was a door beside a run of windows fronting a narrow hall, across which were what appeared to be office doors set next to dark interior windows similar to the ones in the laboratory.

Lights were dim in this hallway, as well, but with the wall of windows it left the formerly claustrophobic Blancanales suddenly feeling naked and exposed.

He turned in slow motion, covering the open area across tabletops with his Beretta poised.

On the table nearest him he saw a red leather binder with Arabic script. He moved around a stand of glass beakers to get a better look and as he did so the light behind the interior windows set in the right-hand wall came into view.

A thin, bald man wearing a white lab coat and round eye-glasses sat on the other side of the glass at a work desk covered with scattered papers, making notes with a Montblanc pen. The man had hazelnut skin that looked golden in the haloed light of the lamp next to him. He recognized the prince.

Blancanales saw bookcases, filing cabinets and a chalkboard next to a word processor and a corkboard filled with pushpins behind the man. The office was spacious with comfortable furniture and tasteful decorations.

Blancanales froze for a long moment.

Then the prince looked up from his paperwork and negated all of Blancanales's options.

His jaw dropped and his eyes grew wide behind the glasses. He leaped to his feet and began to scramble toward a desk-mounted phone bank set next to his PC station.

Blancanales's brain unreeled a string of mental images in hypertime.

There was the box holding the trigger on the table.

He leveled the silenced Beretta.

He stroked the trigger as the man fumbled with the phone re-ceiver. The 9 mm Parabellum round struck the interior window with the succinct force of a ball-peen hammer. The effect was instantaneous and the glass shattered and fell like a rushing stream spilling over the lip of a waterfall.

The glass cascaded down, showering on the floor and splash-ing out in shards and splinters across the laboratory and the surface of the man's desk. The effect on the prince was equally instantaneous. He dropped the phone, number undialed, and jerked open his desk drawer.

"Freeze!" Blancanales barked, moving forward.

The prince paid him no heed and his hand was shaking as he pulled a stainless-steel revolver from his desk.

Blancanales recognized the Colt Cobra .38 Special instantly. He didn't hesitate. His finger stroked the trigger of his silenced Beretta and red blossomed on the lab coat directly over the heart of the upper-echelon Seven member.

The prince sputtered and stumbled backward under the impact.

CHAPTER THIRTY

The Colt Cobra tumbled from the prince's hands and clattered to the floor. He buckled at the hips and slid backward, his left hand scratching for purchase at the surface of the desk. His searching hand met only broken glass and loose papers. He tumbled backward and dropped out of sight.

Blancanales cut across the laboratory and ran up to the shattered observation window separating the two rooms. He leaped through the opening and slid across the desk, knocking glass, paper and the phone to the floor.

He landed with smooth agility on the other side and came down with the Beretta up, ready to cover the man. The lab coat was stained scarlet, and the man's eyes stared up at the ceiling, pupils fixed and dilated.

Satisfied, Blancanales rose and looked around him. A door in the same wall led out into the hallway he could see through the interior windows of the laboratory.

The door itself had a top half comprised of a large viewing window of thick glass reinforced with wire mesh. The ex-Green Beret scrutinized the area at the head of the hallway.

His eyes were drawn toward a softly burning amber light. He hissed and drew back into the depths of the office, stepping over the leaking corpse of the lab-coated prince. The camera was a cheap commercial model sharing little in common with the more powerful and efficient models used at Stony Man, for example, but despite that they would do the job of alerting security forces if he should suddenly appear on a CCTV screen in a control room somewhere in the building.

He snatched the trigger, a device roughly the shape of a Coleman camp stove, and shoved it into its carry box.

He tried to make contact with Lyons or Wethers but found his communication gear wasn't working. He looked back at the security camera, case in hand.

The camera was not on a sweep-motor drive and was set up high on the corner wall. He realized he could predict the areas of coverage by triangulating the height of the pod, diameter of the camera lens and angle of orientation.

From the shadows of the office facing the long laboratory, he gambled that the security camera's coverage only extended about halfway down the twenty-foot-wide corridor.

He stepped closer to the glass-littered desk of the dead Saudi and looked across the equipment-cluttered laboratory out through the observation windows.

He could see the hallway opened up onto a larger space where he spotted a miniforklift, stacked pallets and a few clusters of oil drums. What he couldn't see was another camera stand.

If he was guesstimating correctly he should be at the very edge of the camera pod's radius if he left through the main lab door and immediately turned right toward the open storage area.

He also realized that much of his contemplation was pointless; he had to keep moving or die. He jerked an extra lab jacket off a hook on the wall and shrugged it on. He slid his subgun around on its sling so that the muzzle pointed toward the ground and the weapon was obscured by the coat.

He went back over the desk, through the shattered window and made his way through the equipment and computers toward the main door.

Move or die. Where were the prince's bodyguards? All responding to the alarms? All dead?

It didn't matter. His world had come down to that simple binary code. Move or die.

He opened the door to the lab and stepped into the hallway.

He immediately turned to his right and presented the bland picture of his lab-coated back to the security monitor. He held his Beretta by his side and lifted the clipboard in a rudimentary attempt at subterfuge.

He wouldn't be able to fool anyone upon closer inspection but he would take the advantage of seconds the ruse might offer him.

Leaving the hallway, he stepped into the loading bay. Once again he was amazed at the scope of the operation being conducted in Toronto.

The ceiling was higher in the bay than in the hall and the chamber took on the aspects of an empty warehouse. Besides the few pallet stacks and scattered clusters of oil drums the floor of the forty-yard-by-twenty-yard space was empty.

A prefabricated trailer like those used as offices at construction sites was set on the edge of the open bay.

There was a hallway identical in size and makeup immediately on Blancanales's right and another directly ahead of him on the far side of the storage area. A pair of metal double doors broke up the stretch of wall between the two halls.

In the hall directly in front of him Blancanales could see a second camera pod set up in a right-hand turn in the corridor.

He tried to simplify his options and gather momentum. He saw a bar of yellow light burning under the door of the office trailer and headed for that. He crossed the space head down and waited for a shout of recognition. None came and he crossed the wide-open floor without incident.

Approaching the trailer, he saw a single green metal door with a larger numeral 3 painted on it set in the wall opposite the prefabricated structure.

He jogged up a short flight of wooden steps and reached the door to the trailer, then walked up the last step, set down the trigger case and opened the door.

Finding it unlocked, he stepped through the entranceway,

retrieved the trigger case and pulled the door closed behind him. He found himself in a little office filled with cheap but sturdy furniture and a door set at a right angle to that just past the desk.

He moved forward and opened the far door.

He was afraid he had turned down a blind alley in his haste, but he was faced with a yet another short hallway ending in a door and broken up by a kitchenette space.

In the middle of the hall was a second door. Suddenly a toilet flushed from behind the closest door and Blancanales went into high alert.

He stepped forward as the door swung open, lifting up the Beretta and letting the lab coat fall open.

A heavyset man with messy hair stepped out of the trailer bathroom. He wore a neat pin-striped suit and carefully trimmed mustache.

He turned his face toward the sudden motion as he stepped from the doorway and froze in horror as Blancanales swept down on him like a hawk.

In the main house Lyons leaped forward and jerked the door open, seizing the initiative.

The door opened wide and Lyons found himself face-to-face with a Saudi security guard. The man had a pistol in a holster on his web belt and a long black nightstick was clutched in one fist. A second security guard shuffled forward behind the first man.

Lyons reached out with his right hand and grabbed hold of the nightstick, crushing down hard on the baton, locking it into place. He squatted, dropped off the moaning Links, then rose. His left hand fired out in a brawler's roundhouse, clipping the man in the ear with his pistol.

The man sagged against the doorjamb, dazed but still conscious. Lyons rotated his shoulder back and brought his next pistol-whip punch lower while the man attempted to cover his head from the second blow.

Lyons's strike drove into the man's side, bruising past his lower rib cage to pummel his liver. The man gasped in sudden pain and crumpled to the floor. As he sagged, Lyons snapped his knee up and caught the falling man on the point of his chin, knocking him senseless.

Lyons twirled the nightstick in smooth, tight revolutions and brought it down like a hand ax into the unprotected neck of the second guard, dropping him, as well. The man fell in a stupor across the crumpled heap of his partner.

Lyons tossed the baton aside and reached down to reshoulder the moaning Links. The woman cried out once in agony as he took her weight, then she blacked out.

From below them on the staircase Lyons heard doors slam as someone charged into the stairwell.

Time was running out.

He risked a look as he went through the next door.

He saw the ugly, angry faces of the prince's security detail, Shipka submachine guns in hand. One, perhaps a leader or NCO, looked up and the two men locked gazes.

The man screamed something in outrage and Lyons ducked back.

He knew he didn't have time to remove the unconscious heaps of the security guards even though they were like neon signs pointing the way to his escape route.

He hopped over the downed men and pushed open the door, stepping out into a hallway identical to the one he had just fled. He saw the door to a service area just off at a right angle and plunged through it.

He saw a long narrow room filled with extra service trays, and unattended vacuum cleaners.

The door to the service area burst open and a frantic security guard ducked his head inside, panting and casting wildly around. He saw Lyons and lunged forward, bringing up the Shipka subgun.

There was the *thwat* of the silencer as Lyons put a 9 mm round into his throat at ten feet then pulled his own door shut.

The next door opened up on a staircase leading up. He cursed in frustration. He felt like a kid chasing through a carnival funhouse at Halloween. Nothing made sense about the mansion's blueprint.

He raced through the door leading to the staircase. Looking down, he saw nothing, but the sound of feet hammering on the steps was undeniable. He saw another door, this marked with a metal plaque covered in red writing. He tried the door handle just to double-check but found it locked.

He looked over his shoulder back down the staircase, then turned, shot the lock in the knob and pulled open the roof-access door, his finger going to his earpiece. He broke his radio silence.

"I'm making entry to roof now. How copy?"

Wethers, having obviously been waiting for this signal, answered immediately. "Good copy. I'm getting worried about the smoke from the garage fire—there may be emergency vehicles called soon."

"I'm sitting tight in the driveway," Schwarz noted. "I've stopped the bleeding, but I still can't walk. I haven't made contact with any further opposition yet."

"I understand," Lyons replied to both of them. "I'm coming out now. I have the American agent but she's wounded, as well."

"This op has gone to hell," Schwarz said, exasperated. "I can't raise Pol on the com, either."

"Understood. Stay tight."

Lyons signed off and rushed through the door.

He heard footsteps coming up the stairwell on the floor below them and he slammed his door shut.

He turned, saw a single-run stair running up to a scaffolding, forming a 7-shaped structure. A final, metal fire door was set at the end of the scaffolding accessing the mansion roof. Lyons ran up the stairs and out onto the roof. He was met with a strange industrial landscape filled with conduit housing, exposed pipes, maintenance shacks and HVAC units. The space was so cluttered that it formed an obstacle course, and running across the roof would be like a sprinter racing over hurdles.

Behind him the door to the access stairs was pushed open, but Lyons was waiting. He triggered his pistol and put two bursts into the structure. The metal scarred with divots under the 9 mm impacts and sparks flew. The door swung shut again.

Lyons turned and ran.

He twisted and leaped, darting over and around obstacles. He winced every time Links's body shifted on his shoulder, imagining the damage being done to the wounded girl.

He went to one knee beside the lip of the roof and turned to face the way he had come, bringing up his pistol. Dark columns of smoke twisted into the air from the nearby garage fire.

A security guard darted around an industrial blower housing the size of an automobile, Shipka up and ready in his hands.

Lyons fired.

His burst caught the man in the stomach and folded him over. His second burst tore the top of his head off and cast brain matter across the roof. The downed bodyguard's comrades appeared behind them and opened fire with their own Shipka submachine guns.

Lyons glanced over the edge of the roof. Below was a lower roof. Lyons tucked his pistol into his shoulder holster, then caught the outside cage of a maintenance ladder and scrambled down it using only one hand, holding Links steady with his other. She woke partway down and screamed before blacking out again.

He came to the end of the short ladder. Looking up, Lyons saw forms at the building edge, now commanding the high ground. He shot one across the distance in a feat of exceptional marksmanship, and the man tumbled over the lip, his body curved into a comma shape and trailing blood until he landed and lay still.

The final two members of the security detail rushed to the lip of the building and went to one knee, bringing up their submachine guns.

Lyons ran.

CHAPTER THIRTY-ONE

Inside the maze of subterranean buildings on the mansion grounds, Blancanales pistol-whipped the startled Saudi along the neck with the butt of his handgun, putting the man down instantly.

Blancanales straddled the stunned man and put a knee in his back as he pressed the still warm muzzle of the silencer against the man's ear. He used his left hand to snatch the man's head up by his messy hair and shake him roughly.

The man moaned and his eyes fluttered as he came back around.

Blancanales leaned down, driving his bodyweight through the pistol and into the end of the silencer, cruelly pinning the man's head to the thin carpet.

The man reacted with stunning agility.

He reached up and slapped the pistol away from his head, stunning Blancanales with his audacity and speed. The man rolled to his feet.

From down the hallway a door swung open and a screaming woman rushed into the short hall.

Her face was twisted with frenzied anger as her long, black hair streamed out behind her. She wore an oversize man's T-shirt as a nightgown and her legs were smooth and brown beneath the hem. In her tiny fists she wielded a Skorpion Vz 82 machine pistol.

Blancanales reacted on instinct.

He kicked the rising man with one big boot and sent him stumbling forward as he swept up his pistol. The man lurched forward, shoulder striking the paneling on the wall of the short, narrow hall.

The woman's wild eyes locked on to Blancanales and she pulled her trigger.

The little stutter gun burped to life with a burst of 9x18 mm rounds. The man stumbled into the path of the bullets, soaking up four in the face and chest.

Blancanales fired a precision shot of his own over the staggering man's shoulder and dropped the machine-pistol-wielding woman with a single round to the forehead.

The woman's eyes rolled up in her head as if trying to locate the wound. Her knees buckled and she dropped straight onto the floor on top of her dead paramour.

Blancanales wasted no time on emotion. He sprang forward lightly and cleared the cramped bedroom quarters. He found nothing but a messy bed and tiny closet.

He jumped lightly over the intertwined bodies of the lovers, giving them no thought.

People chose sides and causes in life that put them at opposition with others who had chosen different sides and different causes. Sometimes conflict between those same causes and sides was unfair. Sometimes they merely came down to questions of survival based on split-second decisions.

Based on what he'd seen of the hell house Seven was running in Toronto, Blancanales wasn't going to shed any tears over the dead couple.

In Stony Man's world the dichotomy was often reduced to the most brutal and simplest of archetypes: the quick and the dead.

He opened the door and scanned the open area, checking to see if the woman's short burst of gunfire had brought reinforcements.

He saw none. Wasting no time, he jogged down the steps, crossed the space and opened a single green metal door.

Inside he found a metal staircase running up to another door.

He put down the trigger case to shrug out of his white lab coat, then grabbed the case and ascended the stairs. He opened the door there and went through, stepping out onto the next level of the facility.

The doorknob turned under his hand and he jerked it open, rushing through the entranceway without preamble.

Again he found nothing but a short hallway with three doors off which sat a multitude of unidentifiable equipment, long disused. One room showed three low beds, all made but empty. Blancanales didn't waste time shaking them down. He moved back out onto the catwalk and finished his sweep of the sub-basement operation level.

Again he tried to make contact with his teammates or Wethers; again he failed.

The final door revealed a staircase leading upward and Blancanales took the stairs with bitter resignation.

He was growing frustrated and his frustration was growing hungry for violent expression. He had been separated from his allies and he feared for their safety at the hands of the men who were capable of the horrors he'd witnessed.

He moved up the staircase, the muzzle of his silenced Beretta in front of him and the pistol grip of his stolen submachine gun within easy reach.

He found a door at the top of the dark and narrow staircase. The door was made of heavy metal painted gray and green and had a small glass, wire-reinforced window set in the top.

Blancanales approached the opening carefully and peered through it.

He saw a hallway painted in the same industrial colors as the door. In the middle of the hall, about twenty yards down, were three men dressed in casual civilian clothes and armed with the ubiquitous P-90 machine pistol.

Blancanales ducked away from the window, cursing softly under his breath. There was no question that he would be forced to go through the three obstacles in his path.

He had no idea how many others were nearby, however, which forced him to rely on the silenced pistol instead of his subgun.

A pistol against three submachine guns was not an advantageous playing field.

Blancanales took several deep breaths then stopped second-guessing himself. He had no choice. He would act.

He would run the high wire because to do otherwise would only remove him from the competition. He was unwilling to accept defeat.

He jerked open the heavy door with a hiss of the hydraulic hinges.

The three gunmen turned in his direction. Time stretched like taffy around Blancanales as his adrenaline and anger speeded up his actions. He saw the faces of the gunmen, saw the sudden looks of fear and determination.

Smoking cigarettes were dropped and tumbled in showers of sparks as hands scrambled for the triggers of submachine guns.

Blancanales's first shot took the one on the left in the face.

The man's head jerked and a loop of blood splashed out and splattered the wall and floor.

The man crumpled inward, bouncing off the terrorist next to him. Blancanales knocked that man down with a round to the throat that blew the back of his neck out in a spray of wet flesh and crimson.

Blancanales continued shuffling forward.

The third man found his pistol grip and dropped into a crouch as he swept up his P-90 submachine gun. Blancanales hammered home a 9 mm nail through the gunner's forehead.

The man spun in a half circle and dropped to the ground.

Blancanales rose out of his crouch, smoking Beretta held in both hands. He forced pent-up breath out in a steady stream through pursed lips and willed himself to relax. His heart was beating hard against his ribs. He turned his head and spit the taste of cordite out of his mouth.

Blancanales moved forward quickly to the dead men, keeping one eye cocked toward the bend in the hallway ahead of him and on the door where the knot of men had been standing. He stripped the still warm corpses of their magazines before standing.

He heard the greasy click of a metal latch being manipulated and he turned his head toward the hallway door.

He saw the handle finish turning and the door begin to swing out. He rose as the door to the room opened. He brought up the Beretta.

The man was slight of build with a wispy beard on a narrow, pointed chin. As Blancanales leveled the Beretta, he saw the man's eyes grow wide in shock, saw the man's hands scramble for the pistol grip of the P-90 submachine gun slung crossbody.

How many of these bastards are there? he wondered in amazement even as he completed his scramble.

Blancanales let his finger constrict around the cool metal curve of his trigger. The muzzle of the Reflex-model silencer still trailed a lazy curl of cordite-rich smoke and was less than a yard from the gunman's startled face.

Blancanales finished squeezing the trigger.

The pistol jumped slightly in his hand and the slide racked back, dispensing an empty 9 mm shell in a casual arc. The man was kicked backward, his face disappearing in an explosion of blood. Blancanales was close enough to feel the hot, salty spray splatter unceremoniously across his own face.

He stepped forward and twisted at the hips, catching the closing door with his free hand while keeping the pistol up and ready. Seizing the initiative Blancanales charged forward through the open door. At his feet the dead man hit the ground and sprawled, head bouncing crudely off the concrete floor.

The room Blancanales rushed into was an office of some

sort, though what purpose it served the enigmatic Seven he had no way of telling.

There were calendars on the wall and several desks. A man in rolled-up shirtsleeves and wire-rimmed glasses rose from one of those desks.

Blancanales saw the man reach for the P-90 resting on the edge of the table and shot him, firing twice into his torso, pinning him back into his low-backed office chair.

The man shuddered under the twin impacts of the Parabellum rounds and toppled dead out of the chair. Blancanales turned in a smooth, tight circle, covering all angles of the cluttered room. He found no other targets.

Being ignorant of the building layout was beginning to make the Puerto Rican commando feel claustrophobic.

He was a veteran of riding adrenaline highs out of impossible situations, but the helplessness of not knowing what lay beyond the next corner was getting to him.

Combined with his sense of curiosity at how such a facility had come into play in Toronto, just several short miles from the U.S. border, combined with his sense of shrinking timeline for his mission objective, all served to pin Blancanales under a crushing sense of powerlessness.

Only his courage and self-discipline would see him out of this situation.

That and a fast gun hand.

ON THE LOWER LEVEL of the roof of the mansion, Lyons darted around an obstruction, skipping over some electrical conduits set only a few inches off the roof as he did.

The security detail behind him opened fire and bullets peppered the roof around him. He knew the range was extreme for accurate submachine gun or pistol fire but the sheer volume of rounds allowed for the possibility of lucky shots.

He ducked through the obstacle course on the roof, then came to an open area where the lights of the city lay on the horizon, offering a slightly surrealistic promise of safety and normalcy.

Toronto might as well have been on the moon.

Lyons ran across the danger zone. On the far side of the danger area the mansion roof rose like the parapet of a ship, and there was a maintenance ladder identical to the one he had scrambled down now leading upward. He tucked his pistol into his shoulder holster and started to climb.

He scrambled up quickly as a cacophony of explosions and gunfire from beyond the roof was suddenly punctuated by the sharper reports of weapons firing close by.

Bullets chattered into the wall below him. Lyons dug his foot onto the next rung, flexed the big muscles of his quadriceps, took up slack with his arms and heaved upward.

Bullets followed Lyons as he came over the top and rolled Links to safety behind the lip of the roof edge.

Automatically, Lyons's hand found the butt of his pistol as he spun and scanned the area. He heard the sharp staccato report of an Asian language he didn't recognize coming from scant yards away.

The voice was authoritarian and angry, and Lyons triangulated the approximate position of the speaker while still not seeing the man in the broken topography of the mansion rooftop.

He dived forward and finished his roll across his back, spinning like a kid on a top, flipping his legs toward the new threat as his pistol cleared holster leather.

He had the impression of a figure in dark clothing, saw the Kalashnikov in the man's hands and pulled his trigger. Two of his rounds struck the bolt housing on the assault rifle, and the third made the distinctive slapping sound of a bullet striking Kevlar.

Lyons lifted the muzzle of the Beretta, following the recoil, and blew off the man's face from less than two yards away.

He saw an a gunner dressed in black SWAT-style fatigues

tumble away, the AK-104 Kalashnikov carbine falling away. Something else struck the asphalt of the roof, as well.

A black box.

Lyons blinked, focused. He saw that the black box was a commercial model Detonics laser range finder.

His mind ran an analytic algorithm.

The effective range of an AK-104 precluded the need for the range finder. The range finder was for distance shooting.

Spotter, Lyons realized.

The dead man was part of a security sniper team deployed to the roof.

Lyons sat up, then ducked his head as submachine gun rounds from the trailing security detail poured over the lip of the building.

As he rose, Lyons spotted another street soldier in reflective sunglasses and black fatigues come scrambling up off a shooter's pad beside the edge of the building facing the front lawn.

A Soviet SVD sniper rifle was in his hands, and the man was trying desperately to bring the unwieldy long gun to bear. Lyons had a heartbeat to act. To act or to die.

He shot the man, putting two rounds into his head.

The man sagged, blood gushing from the exit wound in his skull. Lyons's slide locked open and he dropped his empty magazine. He reached up to his shoulder holster and pulled another free.

He slapped it home, dropped the catch on the bolt and chambered a round. Links moaned like an animal as she lay on the roof. Blood was everywhere on her, soaking her shirt.

Lyons slammed his Beretta back into its shoulder and snatched up the AK-104 from the first man in the sniper team he had killed. He quickly checked it, then rolled back across on his stomach and came up against the lip of the building.

Without looking he shoved the muzzle of the carbine over the edge and fired off a long burst of harassing fire. Keeping the trigger down, he did a crunch movement and snuck a peek over the lip.

He saw the security detail scrambling for cover, having crossed two-thirds of the way over the roof.

Lyons showed them no mercy.

He rose on one knee and used his superior firepower to finish the battle. The men spun and stumbled as the rounds slammed into them. They were pinned down on the roof and Lyons raked them with his carbine.

Satisfied, he flung the smoking weapon from him and turned toward the wounded DOE agent. He raced forward and hauled the woman to her feet.

Links looked up into Lyons's eyes, tried to smile, then her head sagged.

"No!" Lyons snarled.

Frantic, his fingers went to the woman's neck, feeling for a pulse.

There was one there. The woman had merely succumbed to shock and fatigue again. Lyons lifted her in his arms, cradling her like a baby.

He stood and began to race the last fifty yards to safety.

At the far edge of the building Lyons laid her down on the roof.

Working quickly, he shimmied out of his tactical rucksack.

He reached inside and drew out a rappel ribbon along with a commercial Swiss Seat harness. He worked quickly, sliding on the rappel harness and a welder's glove.

He clipped the rappel ribbon around the antenna for a communications satellite relay station, then ran it through the twin D-rings on his Swiss Seat. He dropped the coil of ribbon over the edge and moved to the immobile Links.

The woman's eyes fluttered under the lids but she didn't rouse. "I'll get you out," he promised. He bent and yanked the woman up once more before ducking down and draping her over his shoulder.

CHAPTER THIRTY-TWO

Blancanales looked around. He saw that one half of the cramped room served as an armory. Gun racks holding P-90 submachine guns and M-4 carbines in pristine condition filled one wall.

The desk next to the racks held several cell phones, an old model PRC-77 field radio and several night-vision goggles. He didn't know what operation Seven was planning to launch from this base, but they looked ready to start a major paramilitary campaign.

He tried his communications link once more, got no response and decided to keep on running.

He burst through the door into the hallway, cleared his sectors then began making his way toward what he hoped was the building exit. He stepped over the corpses of the men he had killed and moved away from the door leading further underground.

Just before he came to the bend in the hall he encountered a pair of doors. One opened onto a dirty bathroom with a constantly running toilet. The other accessed an office, this one stripped of desks and set up with military cots, again empty.

Once those rooms had been cleared Blancanales took the corner in the hall, moving around it in a low crouch, the Beretta up and tracking in front of him in a modified Weaver stance.

He came around the edge of the wall in a smooth, fluid motion, rising as he searched for threats.

He saw a curtain of black smoke and realized he'd reached the ground level of the garage. He felt like Alice emerging from Wonderland.

Blancanales eased the tension from his trigger and pivoted the smoking muzzle, tracking for any sentry. In between the gap of two doors he found his target hurriedly running out from between a stretch limousine and a much smaller Porsche, also black.

Blancanales breathed in the pungent smell of spent cordite as it mixed with the miasma of the burning around him.

Blancanales exhaled softly through his nostrils and caressed his trigger.

The man's head jerked oddly to the side and he crumpled to the ground.

Blancanales rose and moved quickly, the trigger case in his hand. He crossed the ground in an easy jog, his head up and scanning for trouble, the silenced muzzle of the deadly Beretta machine pistol tracking ahead of his every turn and move.

Free from observation he ran outside and away from the building at last.

ON THE EDGE of the roof Lyons prepared to make good his escape.

With good technique and a solid harness, rappelling could easily be conducted with only one hand.

For military application this allowed a weapon to be fired, and specific methods such as the face-first Australian style had been adapted to capitalize on that.

For Lyons it meant he could keep one arm around the unconscious DOE agent and control his descent from a single fist tucked behind his right hip.

He stepped over to the edge of the building and looked down. He saw some figures running across the lawns and gardens set between the mansion and the highway. They didn't look up and he remained unnoticed.

He stepped over the edge, balanced briefly, then lowered himself smoothly until his legs were parallel to the ground. He kicked out away from the wall and bounded down, tightly controlling his speed by squeezing his fist around the sliding ribbon.

As always physical prowess was a paycheck Lyons cashed time and again in his operations. He was a commando, and like a professional athlete he lived or died, excelled or failed by his state of fitness. His muscles and endurance were not meant for posing mirrors and sunny beaches; they existed to propel him through time and space in a violent, self-assured manner.

He dropped the fifteen stories in leapfrog movements, kicking away from the wall, falling, swinging in, kicking out again, dropping farther. The rope screamed as it slid through his grasp and the heat was building up across his palm, threatening to create a friction burn.

Links was a still, inert weight over his shoulder as he slid down the last two stories in a final jump and quickly unhooked the excess ribbon from the D-rings on his Swiss Seat harness.

"Schwarz!" he called out.

"Here!" Schwarz answered.

Lyons could easily hear the pain in his teammate's voice.

He saw two gunmen, one from the uniformed security detail and a thin one in civilian clothes emerge onto the driveway from the main house.

The skinny man whirled and his eyes widened when he saw Lyons standing next to the wall with an unconscious Links thrown unceremoniously over one shoulder.

The uniformed man plunged his hand into a brown canvas suitcase and reemerged with a cut-down Chinese shotgun.

Lyons pivoted, bringing up his pistol as the man tossed the suitcase away. Just over the shotgun-wielding assassin's shoulder Lyons saw three more gunmen in the same plain dark suits running toward them.

From off to the side Schwarz fired several times and one of the men went down.

Lyons saw submachine guns ready in their fists. He stroked the trigger on his Beretta from the hip.

The shotgun shooter sagged as a triburst hammered into his chest. Beside him the assassin in the security uniform was clawing for a pistol on his belt.

Lyons, still sprinting, shot him on the fly, striking him high on the shoulder in his haste.

As he adjusted his aim he realized he wasn't going to beat the men behind the initial pair to the trigger. He shot the first guy as he dived forward, letting Links hit the ground and go sprawling across the grass.

Schwarz fired again, then from out of nowhere Blancanales arrived on the flank, guns blazing.

The final security gunmen racing toward the battle lifted their weapons. Desperately, Lyons tried to bring his own pistol around to bear. He hit the ground and bounced, flinging his gun hand out straight and trying to take aim.

The pair of assassins suddenly began to twist and jerk like marionettes in the hands of a hyper child.

Jets of scarlet burst from them in arcs and craters were blown out of their shirts and flesh. An instant later Lyons heard the staccato hammering of an assault rifle.

He turned his head toward the river and saw Blancanales with a Kalashnikov carbine chattering in his hands.

"Come on!" he screamed.

Lyons jumped to his feet and began firing.

Suddenly, the last man fell and silence rolled over the battlefield.

"That was the last of the combatants I see moving," Wethers informed them. "I suggest you gentlemen make your exit now."

"Copy," Lyons said. "Able rolling out."

CHAPTER THIRTY-THREE

Washington, D.C.

Akira Tokaido popped his gum and pulled the earbud of his portable music device loose as he looked up at the massive building housing the Government Accountability Office. Behind him pedestrians pushed their way down crowded sidewalks, a mix of political aides, lobbyists, lawyers and bureaucrats all milling around in front of the steps.

The building itself was seven stories of square windows and gray concrete in a long rectangle adjacent to the National Building Museum. Boring, man, boring. Tokaido shook his head. He felt sleepy just looking at the nondescript monstrosity.

Tokaido wore his urban camouflage of navy power suit minus wide shoulder pads but maintaining the sharp cut and general stiffness of shape that seemed to speak volumes to the hive mind of the worker bees milling around the young cybergenius.

Beware, he warned them silently, I come to upset the honey making.

The Homeland Security checkpoint just inside the doors consisted of a metal detector and a conveyor belt for items to be run through an X-ray machine, the setup almost exactly like those used at federal courthouses or airports.

One security officer was a tall, bulky man with skin the color of basalt and a gaze that could bore holes in steel. The other was a petite Native American woman with long, almost shimmering hair worn down her back. Her gaze made the other officer's look mild.

Tokaido headed toward them, smiling like a frat boy on spring break.

"How you doing?" he asked. His eyes scanned the female agent's name tag. "Jennifer," he added.

"Please empty your pockets and place all bags on the rollers," Jennifer answered. "Step forward through the uprights and present your ID to Officer Scathers."

Tokaido dropped his voice an octave. "Well, all right, then." He turned toward the man-mountain and grinned. "Spunky."

"ID, please," the man growled.

Tokaido emptied his pockets of keys and change, then put his PowerBook through the X-ray machine. He handed his ID credentials to Scathers. The man scrutinized the identification with a bored competence. More people began falling in line behind Tokaido.

Satisfied, Scathers handed the ID badge back. "Please step forward, sir," he said.

Tokaido moved through the uprights of the metal detector without a blip and collected his items from the other side.

"I should be done in an hour or so," he called out to Jennifer. "In case you want to get a cup of coffee or something."

The agent remained fixated on the screen of her machine, not bothering to answer.

"Okay, maybe later," Tokaido called as he walked away, voice cheerful. Ten yards down the hall he spoke casually into his secure cell phone. "I'm in."

The West Wing

HAL BROGNOLA LOOKED DOWN the hall past the doors to the Roosevelt Room.

The President's chief of staff stood arguing with the press

secretary. Looking harried, the press secretary strode away as Brognola walked up and stood next to Ron Hackett.

"Hal," Hackett said.

"Ron," Brognola acknowledged.

The big Fed stood still for a moment, pretending to be lost in contemplation of an oil painting of Andrew Jackson. He reached into his suit jacket and pulled out a manila envelope.

Without taking his eyes off the painting, he silently handed it to the chief of staff, who took it in surprise.

"What's this?" Hackett asked.

"The end of an era," Brognola replied.

Hackett opened the envelope and shook its contents into his palm. A portable flash drive sat there like some high-tech version of Moses's stone tablets. He looked up at Brognola.

"That represents all the information contained in Hammond Carter's files at the GAO."

Hackett looked down. His brow furrowed. "I see." His voice trailed off.

"Yes," Brognola said simply.

"Yes?" Hackett echoed.

"Yes." Brognola nodded. "I've read it. I know what Carter was holding over the President. But that is the only remaining digitalized document trails remaining after we crashed the GAO computer system."

"That was you?"

"It'll be in my report."

"No, it won't," he shot back. "It won't be in any report any-where, ever."

"Either way, Carter's taint has been purged from the sys-tem."

"And Carter?"

"Gone ghost," Brognola admitted. "Seven has tentacles ev-erywhere. The influence is huge. The connections are incred-ible. But we'll get him."

"No matter how long it takes?" Hackett suggested.

"No matter how long," Brognola agreed.

"I'll let the President know that the Farm is now the keeper of his secrets," Hackett said.

Brognola turned. "You do that, Ron, you do that," he said over his shoulder as he walked away.

CHAPTER THIRTY-FOUR

Uzbekistan, six months later

T. J. Hawkins jumped from forty-five thousand feet, opened the canopy high and parasailed in from out over international waters.

He wore a thermal suit and used supplemental oxygen to help him withstand the rigors of the high altitude.

Over time the ex-Delta Force operative had come to excel in such airborne insertion operations. The nature of their deployment was such that stealth was an even higher priority than the lightning-quick speed of heliborne and fast-boat delivery methods. The preferred option was a HALO—High Altitude Low Opening—jump.

The Stony Man teams would leave the jump plane at up to thirty thousand feet, then free-fall down to a height of fifteen hundred to a thousand feet, waiting to the last possible second before deploying their parachutes to minimize exposure over the target.

In the HAHO—High Altitude High Opening—jumps, as in this instance, Hawkins's insertion relied on not only the extreme altitude of the plane, but also on the substantial topographical distance. The Stony Man commando entered northern Uzbekistan, invisible, death from above.

The country was an armed camp.

Uzbekistan contained a civilian population motivated and conditioned to a degree of loyalty only possible under the iron fist of a strongman ruler.

To help ensure the probability of remaining uncompromised by a chance encounter, Barbara Price had picked a landing zone in a remote section of very rugged terrain in the mountains above the objective.

After being outfitted at a Joint Special Operations Command forward operating base in Djibouti on the way in, Hawkins was now dressed in complete tree landing gear: padded suit, football-style helmet with full face mask, reinforced ankle guards. The Farm's planning called on him to make a tree landing in an isolated valley, rappel down from the tree canopy, then make his way down a steep crevice and into the Syr Darya River tributary.

He carried nearly two hundred pounds of mission-essential equipment, weaponry and survival gear for the operation.

The mission plan called for infiltration into the target site by means of the river, so he jumped with a scuba system. Given a choice, Hawkins would have preferred walking in, cutting through the border to the south by means of routes already secured and verified by other Special Forces teams assigned to counterterrorist operations in the region.

But as happened so often when Stony Man Farm was called into play, the operation depended on complete invisibility while at the same time remained hamstrung by the competing necessity of extreme expediency.

The train Hawkins intended to intercept was going to be on target and on time, for only a brief window of opportunity. Stony Man was determined to exploit that opportunity.

Hammond Carter and his masters in Seven had thought he'd disappeared.

They were wrong.

The Oval Office wanted a surgical strike with no collateral damage, so a missile attack was out. Thus Hawkins's complicated infiltration was the bastard offspring of the rushed marriage between the disparate and competing elements of speed and stealth.

For much the same reason it had been decided that a single-operator mission provided the best chance of success. Each man on both Able Team and Phoenix Force had volunteered to get payback on Carter.

Hawkins had won.

The land was arrayed below the plummeting commando in a checkerboard of blacks and grays. He flared his canopy hard at the last moment, attempting to curtail his momentum as the ground rushed up.

He heard then felt his rucksack crash into the copse of trees, then two heartbeats later his feet, tightly clamped together, broke through the mesh of interwoven branches at the top of the canopy. He kept his legs pressed seamlessly together as gravity yanked him down through limbs, branches and tree trunks.

He took several bone-jarring impacts before his parachute caught and his neck whiplashed hard into the special support collars, leaving him sore but unharmed.

Taking stock of his surroundings, he looked down and saw that he was about forty feet from the ground, caught halfway up a good-size evergreen. His chute seemed securely trapped above him, but he was too far out from the main trunk for the branches to have enough girth to support him.

Hitting his quick-release clip, Hawkins let his rucksack fall. Once that was done he pulled himself along the branches of the evergreen until he was on a more stable support. He disengaged the jump harness and secured his nylon ribbon of a rappel cord from a pocket in the lower leg of his padded suit.

He slipped the strong, flat cord through a D-ring carabiner positioned at his waist and kicked out from the tree, dropping to the ground in a smooth arc. On the forest floor he quickly removed his jumpsuit, helmet and supplemental oxygen, along with the rest of his rappel harness.

He made no effort to retrieve his chute and paid only cursory attention to camouflaging the gear he was leaving behind him.

If there was anyone close enough to stumble up on it in the dark then he was probably FUBAR in any case.

From his pack Hawkins secured first his primary weapon, a Chinese-model AKM with folding paratrooper stock, and a set of night-vision goggles.

Like a modern-day version of the childhood bogeyman, he hunted at night, could see in the dark and was armed with fearsome claws. Straining against the weight, he slipped into the shoulder straps of his rucksack, then took first a GPS reading before double-checking his position with a compass survey to verify his start point.

Satisfied, he set off down the steep, narrow valley toward the dull gleam of the wide river below.

In many ways his cross-country navigation down the steep gully was almost more dangerous than the HAHO airborne jump had been, or even more than the potential difficulties he faced in his coming swim.

Every model of night-vision device available offered depth-perception difficulties. The scree-covered terrain was rocky and steep, making his footing uncertain, and he was cutting down not an actual path but rather a natural gully.

With 150 pounds on his back, each step downhill sent a biting jar through his knees and lower back and threatened to turn his ankles constantly as his heels came down on loose gravel and powdered dirt. The topography was so steep and uncertain he spent half the descent sliding on his ass as opposed to up on his feet.

By the time he reached the floor of the wash, he was drenched in sweat and breathing hard. He squatted among the cover of some weeds behind a row of dense shrubs well back from the two-lane blacktop that ran parallel to the river. He had eaten a good meal before getting onto the plane, following a carbohydrate-loading diet like a marathon runner or triathlete for the seventy-two hours prior to his insertion to ensure that his optimal nutritional requirements were well maintained.

Hawkins rested in the bushes long enough for his heart rate to recover and his breathing to even out. He washed down a couple of the go pills the military gave their pilots on long flights with a full canteen of water.

He watched as an internal-security unit patrol traversed the road and passed by before opening his rucksack and breaking out the dive gear. By his watch he noted he was seven and half minutes ahead of schedule.

With such a strenuous overland hike and steep descent he had been unable to don his wet suit until just prior to submersion or risk heat fatigue and dangerous dehydration. He quickly stripped, then donned the neoprene wet suit. Once he was dressed he pulled on Uzbekistan army fatigues over the insulated swim gear and retied his combat boots.

He was stripped to the essentials for his swim now, and other than his primary weapon everything he needed was tightly packed inside an oversize butt pack or secured across his body in the numerous pockets of his fatigues or pouches on his H-harness web gear.

Working quickly, he fit the poncho-style vest of the Dräger rebreather system over his head and shrugged it across his shoulders before pulling the neoprene hood of his wetsuit into place. He fit the mouthpiece and tested the oxygen circuit.

Designed for short, shallow dives, the rebreather offered the user scuba capabilities while eliminating the telltale trail of bubbles of other commercial diving rigs.

Holding his face mask and swim fins in one hand, Hawkins cradled his primary weapon in the crook of his arms and high crawled out from his place of concealment and into the mouth of the metal culvert running under the Uzbekistan highway.

Coming out the other side, he slid into the cold, sluggish water of the Syr Darya River with all the deadly, fluid agility of a hunting crocodile. Once in the water he spit into his mask and rinsed the faceplate before putting it on and then tucking his swim fins into place around his boots.

Submerging into the frigid and inky black, he began kicking steadily out into the middle of the deep river where the current was strongest. Staying about six feet below the surface he used the luminous dials of his dive watch to judge the approximate distance he'd traveled.

Kicking steadily with the strong current, he stayed under for fifteen minutes before surfacing. Of all the tasks required for his infiltration, the sensory deprivation and bone-numbing cold of the gray rushing water came the closest to unnerving him.

He fought the almost overwhelming urge to surface several times and escape the claustrophobic weight of the winter water. It was a lesson he had learned a long time ago as a much younger man: there could be no courage without first conquering fear.

He stopped kicking and let the current carry him in among the heavy beams and stout pillars supporting a railroad bridge across the river. Working quickly, he stripped off his dive gear and let it float down into the cold gray water. Reaching up, he grabbed hold of a wide crossbeam and began to climb.

He pulled himself up, hand over hand, twisting around the crossbeams and climbing higher and higher above the surface of the river. Above him the horizontal beams supporting the tracks grew closer and closer and a wind picked up the nearer he drew to the lip of the canyon. He climbed with his Kalashnikov hung muzzle down across his back, and by the time he reached the top he had stopped dripping water behind him.

He double-checked his watch and crawled into position, fitting himself tightly into the trestle joist.

Intelligence had it that the protocol for all military rail transports leaving the Syr Darya River restricted military zone stopped on the other side of the bridge to allow for routine security inspections of transport documents.

There were schedules to be kept, protocols to be followed, routines to be honored. He would have the three-minute window it took for the brakeman to change the tracks to get out from under the bridge and on board the train without being seen by the armed sentries of the army of Uzbekistan.

Carter had managed to oversee an arms purchase from a criminal militia within the national forces. The traitorous American would be there to oversee the purchase.

Hawkins was going to kill two birds with one stone.

The stone in question was a large amount of Semtex plastic explosives.

The time frame itself was demanding but not impossible, though any delay along the way could have thrown the whole operation into jeopardy. Hawkins focused his mind wholly on the task in front of him and with the patience of a trapdoor spider he lay in wait as the Uzbekistan freight train first approached then skidded to a stop in a shower of sparks and the harsh squeal of steel on steel. Spotlights glared down the length of the track as the sentries at the military checkpoint on the far side of the bridge followed their established practice.

Hawkins scrambled up through the girders and pulled himself onto the train track. He looked down the serpentine length of the transport train toward the lead engine and saw two men in heavy military overcoats climbing up into the engineer's compartment. The searchlight mounted at the top of the checkpoint shack began to rotate and play along the length of the train.

Hawkins began moving fast.

He scrambled up next to the coupling housing between two boxcars and out of the path of the advancing searchlight. The powerful beam of illumination ran down the train, and Hawkins shrank back into the protective enclosure of the boxcar's shadow. Once it was past, he scrambled, climbing smoothly until he had reached the apex of the boxcar.

At the summit he slid over the end of the train and quickly scanned both directions. Five cars down there was a gap between the roofs of the olive-green boxcars, indicating a flatbed railcar. Beneath him the train began to sway as the brakes were kicked off and the engineer let go with a whistle blast to signal the imminent movement of the long train.

The industrial locomotive lurched to a start and began gathering speed, slowly at first but then with greater and greater momentum as the train began pushing forward. Hawkins hugged the roof as the train moved past the checkpoint and plunged into the sharply mountainous countryside beyond the river. He clung precariously for several minutes as the train continued gathering speed. Finally ready, Hawkins lifted off the roof of the boxcar and began to navigate his way down the line of cars.

CHAPTER THIRTY-FIVE

The missile components were housed in wooden crates, but there was no disguising them if you knew what to look for.

The main crates were thirty-two feet long, holding the medium-range intercontinental rockets, while additional storage boxes housed the powerful engines and the advanced computer guidance systems inside the conical tips.

Stony Man intelligence had them en route to Syria and from there to the PLO by freighter.

Hawkins had been deployed to send a message about the traffic of such advanced and powerful weapon systems, and he carried enough Semtex explosives in his kit to guarantee there would be no misunderstanding.

Killing Carter after all these months was a thrilling gift on top of the broader necessity of the mission.

From his position on the boxcar overlooking the flatbed where the pyramid stack of rockets had been secured, Hawkins was able to count four guards.

The train was traveling at full speed now and the mountain winds were bitter and harsh, driving the sentries into sheltered alcoves. Hawkins felt confident he could place his demolition charges unobserved.

He moved quickly, coming off the roof and sliding down the iron ladder built into the boxcar. He landed on the access platform just as a fifth soldier, with NCO markings on his uniform, came around the edge of the car on the signalman's catwalk.

The man was shorter than Hawkins by half a foot, stocky

with high, flat cheekbones and dark brown eyes that widened almost comically in surprise at the sudden apparition of a dark-clothed interloper. The man clawed for an old Tokarev TT30 9 mm pistol as Hawkins, hands empty, leaped forward.

The man managed a signal, a short bark of surprise, before Hawkins finished him.

Lunging forward, Hawkins lifted his left knee up to his chest and explosively kicked outward, driving the heel of his combat boot in the man's chest and driving him over the railing of the catwalk.

The soldier flipped backward and struck the basalt-and-gravel dike running next to the tracks in a spinning tumble before bouncing away. Then the racing train was gone and sparks flew as a burst of AKM fire slammed into the railcar next to Hawkins's head.

Spinning, Hawkins dropped to one knee even as he cleared his silenced pistol from its shoulder holster. From the walkway next to the rockets on the flatbed another soldier leveled an old Soviet AKM at him, aiming for a second burst.

Hawkins's pistol kicked in his hand and spent brass tumbled out of his breech and over the edge of the racing train.

The sentry jerked under the impact of the 3-round burst, his head snapping back and black blood splashing off to the side. He tumbled to the floor of the railcar and his partner suddenly appeared directly behind him in Hawkins's vision.

For a heartbeat the two men looked at each other, then Hawkins's rounds found the other man's chest and he pitched forward, victim of a lead coronary. The man struck the floor of the flatbed, then rolled off the side and was sucked away in a flash.

Hawkins leaped forward and grasped the cold metal railing in one hand and vaulted the barrier onto the railcar. The wind cutting across the exposed carriage was hard and cold, almost metallic in its intensity. He had to move quickly. The burst of weapons fire must have alerted the other pair of armed guards, but he could only hope that the noise of the train had deafened the reports for any reinforcements positioned inside the railcars.

Hawkins landed hard on his Vibram-soled boots, which absorbed some of the shock of his impact. He went down to one knee then bounced back up. His right hand tucked the smoking pistol away as his left reached around and swung the silenced Kalashnikov from behind his back on its sling. He took up the assault rifle just as a third soldier rounded the corner at the far end of the platform, his weapon up and hunting for a target.

Hawkins squeezed the Kalashnikov's trigger from his crouch and felt the recoil of the long rifle thump into his shoulder. The heavy-caliber rounds burned across the space between the two combatants and ripped the other man apart.

Then Hawkins caught a flash of motion out of the corner of his eye and instinctively pivoted to face the new threat.

The final guard had circled around and climbed over the secured crates housing the disconnected rockets. The muzzle of the man's weapon blazed a star pattern and the clatter seemed enormous, but green tracer fire poured harmlessly past Hawkins as he drew down and punched the man from his perch with a 5-round burst.

Hawkins did not hesitate. He ran forward and leaped across the body of the second man he'd killed and charged down the length of the flatbed. As he ran he let the silenced AKM drop to his side and he pulled his ready-prepped satchel charges from their web belt carriers and rushed to put them into position.

He scooted back and forth in a huddled crouch around the ends of the rockets, working with feverish efficiency.

The Semtex was such a powerful compound and he had packed so much into his satchels that the procedure was hardly difficult. Proximity with the engines was enough, and he slapped them down and primed their radio receivers for his signal.

He wasn't interrupted, though he knew that with so many of

the sentries missing it was only a matter of moments before he was discovered; the law of averages demanded it. He worked coolly, planting the satchel charges as efficiently as he could, then standing and sprinting for the next boxcar. Only one more flatbed to go and he would have ensured the destruction of the rocket housing, guidance systems and engines.

The PLO would just have to figure how to get along without them.

He turned and scrambled to the edge of the flatbed. The train swayed and rolled beneath his feet, and he carried his weapon up and at the ready as he circumvented the heavy chain tie-downs and sharp-edged corners of the crates housing the rocket components.

Looking back the way he had come, Hawkins turned and sprang lightly across the distance between the two railcars, letting his primary weapon dangle off its sling against his torso. He caught hold of the hard steel rungs of the ladder set into the freight car and quickly climbed upward.

As soon as his head cleared the edge of the carriage, wind tore into him. He scuttled over the side, came to his feet, caught his balance and began moving forward. He ran steadily, scanning ahead of him and hunting for the second flatbed containing the unmarked crates and their deadly payloads. The second hand on his watch continued cutting off segments of time with irrevocable consistency.

Finally he saw the break in the row of boxcars indicating the second flatbed. On one side of the train the mountainside, thick with evergreen trees and heavy bushes, soared upward like a retaining wall, while on the other side the drop away into the valley was sheer and unforgiving. His luck had held mainly due to the relaxed posture of an army long used to a subjugated population and one too technologically and financially challenged to provide its ground units with radio communications.

Hawkins stopped running and went to one knee, the AKM

up and in his hand. He cursed in a low sound under his breath. A curve in the track allowed him to see the boxcar directly in front of the second flatbed from more than just one angle for the first time and the news was not good.

The final railcar was a club carriage designed to carry passengers, and on a military train that could only mean more soldiers. To reach the second rocket storage area he was going to have to cross a railroad car filled with armed men tasked with the protection of his objective.

Just that quickly the factors working against his success had multiplied exponentially. Hawkins turned his head and spit, letting the wind snatch it away. His hands worked the pistol grip of his assault rifle as he shrugged his shoulders against the weight of the modified rucksack on his back.

He rose and approached the sleeper car.

The curve of the railroad track continued along an inward spiral against the side of the mountain, exposing the inside surface of the train to Hawkins from his position on the boxcar roof. He saw the dark face of the passenger car suddenly split open and a rectangle of yellow light spilled out. Hawkins froze then went flat on his belly as a dark figure stepped out onto the train platform.

Immediately, Hawkins noticed that the figure was dressed in civilian clothes with a leather overcoat draped across his fireplug frame. The man was talking animatedly into a cell phone and from less than twenty yards away Hawkins was immediately struck by how compact, and thus how new, the communication device was.

Cutting-edge cellular phones were not the province of the average Uzbek citizen, or even the average military officer. By default Hawkins realized he was seeing someone very important. In his other hand was a black leather briefcase Hawkins recognized as a laptop carrier.

His heart began to beat faster; the man looked Western European.

Perhaps serendipity was swinging in his favor.

Moving surreptitiously, Hawkins brought his NVD goggles up by the strap around his neck. He had taken the apparatus off before his swim and kept it secured while he moved along the train.

Now he moved carefully to bring them up over his eyes and then zero in with the zoom function.

The man on the cell phone jumped into abrupt focus. There was plenty of ambient light coming from the passenger car for the advanced-technology glasses to bring every stark line of detail into view. Hawkins played the image enhancement lens across the man's face.

Hammond Carter. At long last.

Hawkins pushed up off his stomach and brought his silenced AKM up to cover the man.

Catching the motion out of the corner of his eye, Carter turned in surprise. He gaped in shock as he saw the black-clad apparition loom above him.

He barked out a warning and dropped his cell phone. It clattered to his feet and bounced away to be pulled under the thundering wheels of the train. His hand clawed inside his overcoat as Hawkins danced lightly to the edge of the boxcar roof.

The traitorous American agent pulled his pistol free and tried to bring it around.

Hawkins triggered a 3-round burst to the man's face from under six yards and splashed his brains across the steel bulkhead of the railcar behind him.

The mercenary agent was thrown backward by the heavy-caliber rounds, and his laptop case fell from slack hands as he pitched forward and crumpled to his knees on the steel mesh of the boarding platform.

Hawkins sprang forward and leaped recklessly across the distance between the two cars.

He landed hard and folded up, but fought to keep his feet

in the sticky pool of Carter's spilling blood. The door opened and a uniformed soldier with an AKM in his hands appeared in the entranceway.

Hawkins didn't hesitate and knocked him back into the passenger car with a quick burst that clawed out his throat and blasted off the back of his head.

The man fell backward and Hawkins caught a glimpse of more soldiers rushing forward as the dead man tumbled into the car. Hawkins threw his weapon to his shoulder and poured a long, ragged burst into the tight kill zone of the passenger car hallway, chewing men apart with his bluntly scything rounds.

Still firing one-handed, he scooped up the fallen laptop case and sprang for the metal access ladder set into the side of the railcar superstructure.

CHAPTER THIRTY-SIX

Moving fast, Hawkins shoved the briefcase through a suspender on his H-harness web gear and let the silenced AKM hang from its cross-body sling. He pushed himself hard, felt the laptop start to slip and stopped to shove it back into place.

Below him a burst of gunfire tore through the open train door and bullets rattled and ricocheted off the boxcar behind Hawkins.

He heard a man screaming in anger and more than one in pain as he lunged over the top of the railcar and onto the roof. Below him another soldier rushed onto the grille of the landing and swung around, bringing his weapon to bear.

Hawkins flipped over onto his back in a smooth shoulder roll and snatched up the pistol grip of his weapon. He thrust the weapon forward against the brace of the sling and angled it downward.

He pulled the trigger and held it back, letting the assault rifle rock and roll through half a magazine before easing up and rolling to his feet. He took two steps and the laptop case fell. He dropped with it and caught it before it bounced away.

He used his left hand to unsnap the carbiner between his web gear belt and suspender. Quickly he hooked that through the handle of the case and reconnected it to his belt.

He was almost too late.

He saw the muzzle of the Chinese AKM thrust over the edge of the railcar roof and he dived forward. He tumbled haphazardly as the soldier on the ladder let loose with his weapon.

Hawkins's chin struck the metal roof and he bit his tongue, filling his mouth with the copper tang of his own blood.

Green tracers and 7.62 mm slugs tore past him as he slid toward the edge of the roof and the long, steep drop below.

He reached out with his left hand and grabbed hold of the metal lip running along the top of the passenger railcar, spreading his legs wide to slow his momentum. From just a few feet away he thrust the muzzle of his AKM forward and triggered a burst.

His rounds tore into the exposed weapon firing at him and ripped it from the soldier's hand as the hardball slugs tore through the stock and receiver, shattering it beyond use. The soldier's hand disappeared in an explosion of red mist and his scream was ripped away by the rushing wind.

Hawkins spun on the slick metal of the roof and came to his feet. He pushed himself up, fired a second burst of harassing fire and then turned and sprinted in the opposite direction. He ran with reckless speed across the top of the railcar toward the other end.

As he neared the edge of the car and the flatbed containing the second shipment of missile components came into view, he saw a soldier scrambling into position while trying to bring his own assault rifle into position.

Hawkins fired and knocked him spinning off the railcar.

The man screamed horrifically as he tumbled over the edge like a pinwheel, bounced off the basalt lip of the track and plunged down the mountainside below like a stone skipping across the surface of a lake.

Hawkins leaped into the air and landed on top of the flatbed car. He ducked and slid down over the side of the pile just as yet another soldier sidled around the end of the flatbed.

The soldier fired as Hawkins was freeing the last of his satchel charges filled with Semtex. Hawkins thrust his assault rifle forward by the pistol grip, using the sling like a second hand, and pulled the trigger.

The shots were hasty and he was off balance as he fired, but he hosed the area in a spray-and-pray maneuver designed to force the man backward. He rolled, feeling the hard edge of the wooden crate bite into his hip, and squeezed the trigger again, then broke off, recentered and fired once again.

The bullets caught the soldier center mass and the rifleman staggered under their impact, his weapon tumbling from useless hands as Hawkins let the muzzle recoil climb so that bullets chewed the man apart, unzipping him from sternum to skull in a staccato hail of slugs.

Hawkins turned and slid the last satchel into place, keying up the transponder to respond to his electronic signal.

Soldiers rushed to the edge of the roof of the boxcar next to him and started firing down at him. Wood splinters flew in the air as a fire team of soldiers shot at him. He ducked behind the end of the crates and threw his rifle to one side.

Green tracer fire burned past his position as he recentered the shoulder straps of his specially outfitted rucksack.

He pulled the transmitter out of his pocket as more and more rifle fire was drawn down on his position. Grabbing hold of the electronic device, he turned toward the edge of the train overlooking the open valley.

He sucked in two quick breaths and sprinted out from under cover. Three hard steps and he was on the edge, then he kicked off and threw himself into space. Behind him the withering fire petered off as the uniformed men on the train watched him fall, hypnotized into stunned amazement.

Hawkins felt the air rushing up into his face with surprising force. He saw the snakelike twisting of the Syr Darya River five hundred feet below him.

He turned and hit the button on his transponder. There was a pause half a heartbeat long, then the train was blown off the mountain at the two flatbed points containing the rocket bodies and engines.

A yellow ball of fire rolled out from the mountain and a wave of heat descended on Hawkins as he fell.

His fist came up to his left breast just beside the suspender of his H-harness web gear and jerked the D-ring handle. There was a pause that lasted for entirely too long in his racing thoughts as he plunged below three hundred feet and the dark water of the river came into sharper focus.

· Then the minichute, also called a stunt chute—of the kind used by BASE jumpers—rushed out and caught. Hawkins was jerked to a stop for a moment, then gravity reclaimed him and he began to fall toward the river again, his descent only modestly slowed.

At fifteen feet above the surface, when the dark water of the river filled his vision beyond his dangling feet, Hawkins hit the cutaway, dropped out of his harness and fell like a stone.

He struck the cold water for the second time that night and felt it rush in over his head. He let the current take him, still warm in his wetsuit, and his hand went to his waist where he shrugged out of his web gear and let it float away, keeping only the laptop carry case.

He kicked for the surface and deployed his final piece of gear, a life vest designed to keep him buoyant in the water.

Above his head the side of the mountain burned.

Working quickly, he kicked over to the side of the river and pushed the expensive carry case out of the water. Putting one knee down on the gravel against the current, Hawkins first opened the briefcase to make sure it had kept the water out and then resealed it.

Moving fast he used the airtight pouches that he had transported his satchel charges in to insulate the case, then, after securing the case to himself, he kicked back out into the fast-moving current.

Forty minutes later he activated his emergency beacon and let the river carry him out toward the Aral Sea, where Jack Grimaldi flew the seaplane in low under the radar and put the pontoons down on the chop out beyond the breakers fronting the rocky shoreline. There were naval units responding from both Uzbekistan and Kazakhstan as he pulled out of the situation, but aggressive electronic jamming operations by units of the U.S. Air Force based out of the Bahgram Air Base easily outclassed their counterparts in the Central Asia.

Six hours later Ron Hackett, the President's chief of staff, quietly informed the Man in the Oval Office that the situation had been brought to a resolution. Stony Man, yet again, had prevailed. Both Hammond Carter and the entire Seven organization had been neutralized, and the trigger device and the rock stolen from the cargo ship were back in the hands of Department of Energy authorities.